Critical Acclaim fo...
Gods Go ...

"Written in a style that is u...
phosphorescent desire and shade...
—*The Baltimore Sun*

"A terrific book: street-smart, savage, brutally funny but also
intelligent and compassionate."
—*San Jose Mercury News*

"A meditation on the Vietnam War and on race, desire, and urban
gang wars [that] equals the passion and originality of [Véa's] earlier
work . . . He is becoming one of California's best novelists."
—*Los Angeles Times*

"A tightly wrapped tale of mystery, desire, hopelessness, and
death . . . Véa composes his plot with great skill, leaving the
reader strongly convinced of his story's credibility."
—*Publishers Weekly*

"An ambitious, complex story tracing the efforts of
several men and women to put the horrors of
Vietnam behind them . . . gripping and intriguing."
—*Kirkus Reviews*

A practicing criminal defense attorney and the author of two previous novels, *La Maravilla* and *The Silver Cloud Café* (both available in Plume editions), Alfredo Véa was born in Arizona and
lived the life of a migrant worker before being sent to Vietnam.
After his discharge, he worked a series of jobs—from truck driver
to carnival mechanic—as he put himself through law school.
Winner of the 1999 Bay Area Book Reviewers' Award for Fiction,
Gods Go Begging was also named one of the Best Books of 1999 by
the *Los Angeles Times*. Véa lives in San Francisco.

ALSO BY ALFREDO VÉA

The Silver Cloud Café
La Maravilla

gods go begging

ALFREDO VÉA

A PLUME BOOK

PLUME
Published by the Penguin Group
Penguin Group (USA) Inc., 375 Hudson Street, New York, New York 10014, U.S.A.
Penguin Group (Canada), 90 Eglinton Avenue East, Suite 700, Toronto, Ontario, Canada
M4P 2Y3 (a division of Pearson Penguin Canada Inc.)
Penguin Books Ltd., 80 Strand, London WC2R 0RL, England
Penguin Ireland, 25 St. Stephen's Green, Dublin 2, Ireland (a division of Penguin Books Ltd.)
Penguin Group (Australia), 250 Camberwell Road, Camberwell, Victoria 3124, Australia
(a division of Pearson Australia Group Pty. Ltd.)
Penguin Books India Pvt. Ltd., 11 Community Centre, Panchsheel Park,
New Delhi – 110 017, India
Penguin Group (NZ), 67 Apollo Drive, Rosedale, North Shore 0632, New Zealand
(a division of Pearson New Zealand Ltd.)
Penguin Books (South Africa) (Pty.) Ltd., 24 Sturdee Avenue, Rosebank,
Johannesburg 2196, South Africa

Penguin Books Ltd., Registered Offices: 80 Strand, London WC2R 0RL, England

Published by Plume, a member of Penguin Group (USA) Inc.
Previously published in a Dutton edition.

First Plume Printing, September 2000
10 9 8 7 6

Lines from "The World's Wonders" from *The Selected Poems of Robinson Jeffers* by Robinson
Jeffers. Copyright © 1951 by Robinson Jeffers. Reprinted by permission of Vintage Books,
a division of Random House, Inc.

Ⓟ REGISTERED TRADEMARK—MARCA REGISTRADA

The Library of Congress has catalogued the Dutton edition as follows:
Véa, Alfredo.
  Gods go begging / Alfredo Véa.
    p. cm.
  ISBN 0-525-94513-X (hc)
        978-0-452-28115-8 (pbk)
  I. Title.
PS3572.E2G63   1999
813'.54—dc21   99-14338
                                                                             CIP

Printed in the United States of America

PUBLISHER'S NOTE
This is a work of fiction. Names, characters, places, and incidents are either the product of
the author's imagination or are used fictitiously, and any resemblance to actual persons,
living or dead, business establishments, events, or locales is entirely coincidental.

dedicated to all the boys on all the hills.

Thank you

Rosemary Ahern, Sandy Dijkstra, Hong Thuc Ha,
Shannon Raintree, Jeff Biggers, Carla Paciotto, Edmund K. Oasa.
Thanks to all the vets who shared their stories with me.
Above all, thanks to Carole Conn.

Contents

It is easy to know the beauty of inhuman things, sea,
        storm and mountain; it is their soul and their
        meaning.
Humanity has its lesser beauty, impure and painful; we
        have to harden our hearts to bear it.

I have hardened my heart only a little; I have learned
        that happiness is important, but pain *gives*
        importance.
The use of tragedy: Lear becomes as tall as the storm he
        crawls in; and a tortured Jew became God.

            —Robinson Jeffers, *The World's Wonders*

gods go
begging

1

the amazon luncheonette

For a time, they both held on to their lives, gasping softly, whispering feverishly, and bleeding profusely, their two minds far, far away from the cruel, burrowing bullets that had left them mere seconds away from death. Face to face, they spoke their last words in crimson-colored breaths. Theirs was a withering language, one for which there are no living speakers.

Then, like warriors abandoned on the field, they lay in unearthly calm as the things of life deserted them. They had seen the mad commotion boiling in the air above them. In bemused silence, they heard the alarms, the screams, and the growing wail of sirens.

Pronounced dead on a cold city sidewalk, they held on to each other as the gurney rolled from cement to asphalt and into a waiting ambulance for a long, anonymous ride. In the end it was clear to every onlooker that neither dying woman would ever let go of the other. Leaves of lemon grass had drifted to the ground from the dress pocket of one of the women, marking their trail to the ambulance. Some of the sprigs and blades were bloodstained, adding spice to the liquid life that had trickled away.

Now they lay nameless on a long metal tray, two cooling women, breastbone to breastbone. Struggling together in motionless travail, they had become wholly entwined—their arms, their fingers, their final breaths; even their histories had become entangled. The tags tied to their toes bore the same name.

From a growing distance the dead women watched in nonchalance and saw in the swelling dimness the chief coroner and his assistant doing their lonely work. Unashamed, they saw themselves stripped naked in an airless, comfortless room and they felt dispassionate probing and bloodless cutting as if it were being done to bodies far, far away. From that great distance they watched their own innards sliding out like roe.

Devoid of cushions and warmth, it was a room of numbing dimension, a room made of corners, certainly not a place meant for living things. It was an empty, airless space with walls that concealed gleaming, heartless edges carefully arrayed within rows of silent drawers. Its hidden compartments were lined with finely honed contrivances, sharpened saws, and suction pumps. That nature that so abhors a vacuum must detest a sterile straight razor even more.

It was a chamber of stainless steel and sanitized white tile backlit by banks of lifeless light. Even sounds were frightened to death in a room like this one; bold timbres and shy tenors alike were suffocated, haunted into silence by a legion of echoes. A hall of mirrors for the spoken word.

"My wife says that music happens whenever you take the time to look carefully at another human being. Well, no one on earth looks closer than I do," he said. He grunted as he shifted the large object beneath the cloth and rudely tugged the material to his right and away from the table. "And I have yet to hear a single solitary note, much less a melody."

The assistant medical examiner grabbed a stiffened brown shoulder with his right hand and an ivory-colored one with his left. To get a better grip, he pushed his hands between two brassieres and toward the two breastbones. As he pulled, his words reverberated from the walls around him. The sound of his own voice coming back at him again and again never failed to make him dolorous. It was a dolor that had tormented him for three years now. He had consistently mistaken it for a migraine headache. So many echoes, yet no voices ever overlapped in this room; no matter how many spoke at once, each voice always sounded alone.

"My wife keeps telling me that there really is a melody in the slow, shifting weight of a mature woman walking on the beach, the easy metronome of her breasts; that if you watch a child quietly playing alone, you can detect definite musical tones and the overtones of an imagination running wild. Personally"—he shrugged—"I think my wife is worried that I've handled too many women. Maybe she thinks it'll make her body less special to me."

"What is your wife anyway, some kind of poet?" asked the chief medical examiner, his voice a mixture of humor and disdain. His own wife was waiting at home, and the very thought of her evoked at least a dozen reasons to work late. He nodded his head, indicating his impatience with his assistant. It was a common gesture. The subordinate quickly stepped back, allowing the chief to attempt a solo separation of the women.

"Not really. She's a dancer and a painter hidden inside the body of an office manager. She's in a modern dance troupe here in town, but she needs to keep a day job." The assistant paused to let an image of her form in his mind. "She hates what I do for a living."

With all his might the chief medical examiner strained to pull the two shoulders apart. He set his legs farther apart on the tile floor, then tried again, holding his breath for strength.

"Give me a hand, will you?" he said, finally exhaling his fatigue and exertion into the room. His assistant moved forward and reached out with both hands, placing one palm in an armpit and the other on the top of a shoulder.

"If the truth be known, I've seen a lot more men than women while I've been here," said the assistant. "I guess it's the nature of this business."

"I've got half a dozen specimens of manhood laid out and cooling in back right now," answered the chief. As he spoke he nodded toward the darkened morgue. Behind the wall to his back there were five males lying stretched out on refrigerated metal racks. One poor soul had been a bystander at a botched drive-by shooting. Another one was the victim of a carjacking; his body had been found by a jogger in McLaren Park.

Two other bodies were those of homeless veterans who had expired of unknown causes during the night. The corpses had been found beneath the elevated freeway near Potrero Hill. Their dark skin had been hardened by exposure and their knuckles and knees had been indelibly discolored by dirt and grass stains. The fifth body was that of a young schoolboy who had been driven over the railing of the Golden Gate Bridge by years of unnatural affection from his own father. His brother before him had done the same thing.

"Did you hear about John Doe 39? He came in about three hours ago. He was working underneath his classic car when his wife and her boyfriend lowered the jack on him. We got a full name for him just about an hour ago. The guy still has a brake pad embedded in his skull."

The younger man secured the shoulder closest to himself and the two began pulling in opposite directions, each with one foot on a bar beneath the table for leverage. They had been straining for twenty or thirty seconds when one of them released his hold suddenly and without warning. The other almost fell to the floor, just catching himself by hanging on to the stiffened arm of the smaller woman. The two embracing bodies hung precariously over the edge. The long hair of the smaller woman was hanging down like a shimmering tent, enshrouding their frozen faces.

"Let's get them back onto the table," said the chief, out of breath and a bit embarrassed at the crudeness and clumsiness of their attempts. "My wife never lets me touch her anymore," said the chief. "I think she's projecting." He gasped. "I've noticed that sometimes she's repulsed by my hands. She pulls away from my touch." He examined the mutual death grip more closely. "I think we're going to have to cut them apart. Is there family listed, any claimants? Someone to object?"

"If we knew the answer to that question," said the assistant, who nodded toward the toe tags, "we wouldn't have to Jane Doe them." The assistant laughed uncomfortably. He had lost his mental balance for a moment. During his three years in this office the chief had never once mentioned his wife or his home life. He had never shared even a single personal opinion or feeling. The assistant knew that his glib remark had offended the chief medical examiner, so he added quickly, "Cut the fingers? Should a procedure like that be included on the protocols? What if the relatives do show up?"

After thinking about it for a moment, the chief shook his head. "We have to do what's necessary. Cosmetics are the least of our worries. I can see now that just one of them has her fingers completely interlocked. I think we only need to cut her at the tendons. Let's put that on the 36 protocol. After they're separated you can work on 37. Well, what do you think?"

"About what? Number 37?"

"No, damn it, about my wife!"

"She's afraid of you," said the assistant in a lowered, more respectful voice. "When she's alone she imagines what your eyes must see when you look at her. She may take her clothes off in front of you, but she knows you've seen women far more naked. You've seen women stripped of life."

The chief medical examiner did not respond. There was deep regret in his eyes for having said anything about it. He might have responded a decade ago, before death had become so completely empirical to him, so damned quantifiable. Lately his wife had stopped wearing makeup and she was letting the gray in her hair overrun the auburn. She had even stopped buying wrinkle cream.

"Fire them up!" he snapped.

His assistant nodded, then moved to the console near the back of the room. There he turned on the amplifier and tape recorder marked table 3. The first doctor tapped the microphone softly and watched the VU meters jump. Satisfied, he began to speak.

"Refer to crime scene investigation this date regarding original location of Jane Does 36 and 37, both pronounced dead at the scene. They are two women, one black and one Asian, both dressed, though number 36 has no panties and number 37 has no shoes. They are in a face-to-face position, each with her arms wrapped tightly around the other. Number 36, the larger woman, has her fingers interlocked in the small of the back of number 37. Number 37 has her arms around the neck and head of the other."

"Do you think they were lovers?" asked the assistant, who was testing his own microphone. The chief medical examiner shrugged and continued his examination. Then he slowly nodded his head, yes. He disliked looking beyond the bodies to the people who were once there, and now he was beginning to dislike the assistant.

"The police and the paramedics at the scene were not able to separate the two. No medical intervention was attempted." He slid open a drawer and withdrew his favorite scalpel. *"I shall do so now by cutting . . ."*

"Must be old age," said Persephone Flyer. "My fingers are simply aching." She flexed them and grinned. "Luckily there's never been any arthritis in my family." There was a frightened but hopeful intonation in her voice.

Her friend in the next room laughed. "You will never have arthritis. In my country an ache in the fingers means that you want something very badly; your hands are aching to touch something."

"Certainly not these tomatoes." Persephone laughed, tossing a large pile of tomato skins and seeds into a small garbage can beneath the sink. She cut the skinned pulpy flesh of thirty tomatoes into squares then tossed the pieces, dividing them evenly, into two eight-gallon pots. She walked to a second stove, where she used a wooden spatula to plow under a tall mound of steaming Italian sausages, rotating the cooked ones to the top and the uncooked to the bottom of an enormous black frying pan with a diameter that spanned two burners. The powerful fragrance of fennel and oil filled the room.

"How are the spices coming?" she called out, as she drew a sleeve across her sweating brow. Outside her makeshift kitchen the glorious scent of her handiwork had commingled with a breeze and was prying at her neighbors' windows, pushing in over the usual smells of Potrero Hill and the housing projects and overwhelming everything with the combined perfume of Palermo, Baton Rouge, and Saigon.

The sublime aroma broke up baseball games in the street. It silenced a heated game of dice and caused a substantial lull in the local drug traffic. In the projects, the street gangs stopped cleaning their weapons to inhale the scent. Like all armies, they marched on their stomachs, and the boys on the hill were always hungry. For a moment, the Up the Hill Gang, the Down the Hill Gang, the Wisconsin Street Posse, and the Prisoners of the Projects called an uneasy armistice in order to breathe in a few molecules of the sauce. For a moment no one on the south side of the hill looked warily over his shoulder, then checked his waistband for the comforting bulge of a gun.

The aroma even found its way into the nostrils of a drunken sot and momentarily kept him from hitting his cowering wife.

It wafted down afternoon sidewalks and into nearby warehouses where greasy auto mechanics and squinting printers stopped working to anxiously peek at the time clock. Women in nearby houses and apartments were soon busy washing Mason jars, soup kettles, and hermetic cauldrons in which to carry the source of the magical smell.

Children at the Potrero projects ran to tell their weary mothers that something was cooking at that lesbian place up on Missouri Street. Excited shouts were traded over back fences, and telephones were ringing everywhere on Potrero Hill, as the good news was passed from Texas Street to De Haro: "Miss Persephone and Miss Mai are cooking again! The Amazon women are at it again!"

"Is it that cellophane chicken? Never tasted nothin' on God's earth like that cellophane chicken!"

"Is it that beautiful jambalaya? Is it okra stew and dirty rice? Did you taste that corn pudding they made last week?"

"Could it be them chicken necks in coconut milk?"

"No, it's that spaghetti sauce again! Smells like heaven!"

Mai came from the back room, her small hands cradling a large wooden bowl of spices. She was always careful to prepare the spices out of public view, as the recipe was a valuable and closely guarded secret. All of their collected recipes were precious. Only she and Persephone knew what lay hidden beneath the piles of bay leaves, oregano, and thyme, that down under the sun-dried tomato flecks and the basil there were dark little chiles from the Louisiana bayou and West African peppers.

"The seeds for these angry little peppers were brought here three hundred years ago in the intestines of slaves," Persephone would explain. "It's how they kept warm in the holds of those ships."

Beneath these peppers were still other secrets: long, tender shreds of aromatic lemon grass and a pint and a half of pungent nuóc mám nhi, the ultimate Vietnamese fish sauce. Mai had mixed it and fermented it herself in a small wine barrel on the back porch. She would always smile as she mixed these spices. There was a little nook near the rear door of the house that smelled of her beloved homeland.

She shoved a small stepladder closer to the stove, stood precariously on the top rung, and using her delicate fingers, began to divide the wondrous spices between the two pots of simmering sauce. She put a small bouquet of lemon grass in her pocket for good luck. Using a huge wooden ladle, she stirred both pots, scraping the bottoms to keep the thick liquid from building up and burning. As she descended the ladder, she adjusted the flames beneath the pots.

"Won't be long now," she cooed in a raised voice filled with joy and anticipation. Her gaze fell onto the shiny new Sub-Zero refrigerator that had been delivered just two days ago. "*Không cólâu dâu.* Won't be long now." It had become one of her favorite English sentences, almost a prayer. "Tomorrow they'll deliver that beautiful eight-burner Wolf stove and that three-horsepower range hood and then we can really start cooking! No more of this part-time stuff."

Even as she said it she began once again to imagine how the little restaurant would soon look. Just last week the workmen had knocked down two walls to create a large comfortable front room. A single bay window had been installed to replace the three double-hung windows that had been facing the sidewalk. The solid front door had been replaced by one made of thick glass.

To the right of the door there would be a new Formica counter and a line of stools. The stools would be bolted to the floor and they would have soft, red cushions. They had to discuss everything about the business, but on the subject of stools, Persephone and Mai heartily agreed. To the left would be six, maybe seven tables, each with its own intimate lamp and starched tablecloth. Mai imagined the paintings of a local artist hanging on the walls.

"There will be flowers everywhere," she said aloud. Those words had been her mother's, too. In Vietnamese, Mai's name meant yellow cherry blossom. Mai smiled to herself. How Persephone loved flowers! Each spring the earth and air of her garden would be filled with them. Coaxed by the slightest breezes, the scents of jasmine, wisteria and fuchsia would mix and remix into an ever-changing display of novel, weightless perfumes.

The restaurant would be just about the same size as her dear father's noodle café at the corner of Công Lý and Lê Loi Streets in Saigon. As she took a moment to daydream, the scent of *bò viên*, beef ball smothered in chile-garlic paste, filled her nostrils and her stunned soul. On her tongue is the sweet taste of *cà phê sua*, the sweet Vietnamese iced coffee. In her ears is the ping-ping sound of smoky Lambretta scooters, the huffing of shirtless men peddling cyclo-cabs, and the buzz of tiny Vespa trucks overloaded with brown packages, brown children, and white ducks.

For a moment the street outside is much wider, a grand boulevard filled with the spinning wheels of hundreds of old bicycles. Beautiful women are window-shopping in colorful *aò daì* dresses of flying silk flowing beneath wide sun hats. The sidewalks are jammed with noisy vendors and with lines of schoolchildren in their bleached uniforms. Shelves are ablaze with fresh fruit, candles, and cloth. Across the street, a bright-orange queue of mute Buddhist monks is winding its way through stalls of betel nut and spices.

For a moment her dear father is alive again and darting attentively, happily between the cloth-covered tables. There is his gold-toothed smile, preserved perfectly in her memory. There were his large-knuckled hands, his fingers bent crooked by year after year of honest work in the kitchen. There they are, his old French-style pantaloons and Chinese military-surplus shoes. There, in the air about her face, is the pungent, painful odor of his infamous Câm Lê cigarettes. Mai's mother always hated those cigarettes, their bitter, black tobacco and brown paper. Now her daughter was in San Francisco, straining to recapture the scent.

His precious café had been called the Tu Do Café, the Liberty Café. It had been an open-air café in the old French style, with blue canvas awnings that hung down over the sidewalk. Beneath this awning, customers could linger for hours, sheltered from the sun or the monsoon rains. Mai's older brothers had labored there as waiters and cooks, but that was before they left to fight in the war. Hong and Kien were there in her memory, working happily side by side in the days just before they became mortal enemies.

"What do you think about naming it the Amazon Luncheonette?" It was Persephone, calling her tiny friend back from her reveries. The temporary business license tacked to the front door had a blank space where the name of the new establishment would eventually be officially entered. Some unknown, midnight scrivener had already written in "The Amazon Luncheonette." It had probably been meant as an insult, but Persephone liked the name. Since then, someone had spray-painted the name on the east wall of the building.

"You know it's what everyone up here calls our little unnamed restaurant-to-be. All the folks on the hill think we're lesbians." She laughed. "My God, Mai, if they only knew what it is that you and I have in common. The Amazon Luncheonette," she repeated with a laugh. She liked the name. "If they only knew."

Mai smiled at her tall friend while allowing her gaze to run the full length of her Creole body, from the glaring nail polish on her brown toes to her thick, curly black hair. Persephone had piercing green eyes, expressive, acrobatic lips, and a cinnamon-colored face filled with vital electric energy. There were brilliant sparks in her face in her moments of enthusiasm and there were bolts of lightning in her moments of anger. Mai smiled to herself. There was no one like Persephone Flyer in Vietnam. In the letters that Mai sent home to her youngest brother, her only surviving relative, she had tried in vain to describe her beloved friend. In her next letter she would send a photograph. Imagine, thought Mai, Persephone had three sisters. In this world there were three more women just like her!

Mai had been astonished to learn that both she and Persephone had taken classical ballet as young girls. Even more amazing, they had both rejected the extreme discipline of that dance and longed for some freer form of expression.

"Jane Doe 36 is an African-American woman in her mid- to late forties. The head is symmetrical and there appears to be evidence on the scalp of heavy trauma. The head hair is long and curling. The ears are intact and unremarkable. Using the scalpel, I am reflecting the scalp. Lifting the pericranium, I note contusion and bleeding above the left ear. Upon opening the skull, I expect to find a subarachnoid hematoma and possible contra-coup from a sharp blow to the head.

"As expected, there is diffuse bleeding present; therefore, the blow is definitely antemortem. As I noted previously, there is an entry wound four centimeters behind the left ear. It is a distant wound in that there is no visible stippling or powder burns. As there is no marginal abrasion apparent, the origin of this gunshot was directly from the left side at ear height. I note no exit wound."

"Before the sauce is done, I want to take a shower and shampoo my hair," said Persephone, as she left the front room and picked her way down the hallway toward the small, crowded apartment behind the cooking area. She lifted her blouse over her head as she walked. Her march to the bathroom was soon marked by a trail of clothing.

"I won't put curlers in, though, and I'll cut the facial down to twenty minutes. I won't wear that green mudpack out into the front room. We can't be scaring the customers away, now, can we?"

In the makeshift kitchen Mai heard the shower coming on, and beneath the floor of the Amazon Luncheonette the ancient plumbing began to chatter and complain as hot water was pumped through its brittle and clogged arteries.

"I'm shaving my legs now!" yelled Persephone from behind a curtain of plastic and steam, "dragging a blade against the grain." Her forceful voice could be heard half a block away. "Now, let's see, I'm shaving them because I'm not really a mammal and these follicles on my legs are biologically meaningless!" Between Persephone's sentences Mai could hear soft, nervous humming above the rush of the water.

"I'm shaving my armpits now, and the whole damn neighborhood should know it! These hairs were obviously placed here in a tight bunch so they could be forcibly removed en masse by an old, rusty single-edged razor. Oh yes, I am a natural woman! Oh my, did I forget the bikini line? Heaven forbid! How could I dream of serving spaghetti sauce without shaving my pubic hairs? Now I am using harsh detergents to rob my hair of every life-giving drop of natural oil."

The shower water stopped. There were two or three minutes of absolute silence as Persephone stood dripping beneath the showerhead, remembering the day the waters had run red. Years ago she had miscarried while bathing. For a decade she had only taken sponge baths, but recently she had returned to the shower, filling the air with words in the same way that a boy walking through a cemetery fills the air with whistling.

"Now guess what?" she announced. "I'm plucking my eyebrows, second-guessing my maker's plan for this lovely face!" There was a moment of silence as selected hairs were strategically uprooted.

"Next, a couple squeezes of the lash curler. And now for the foundation. I am applying some thick, colored putty to my skin so that my poor pores will have absolutely no way to breathe. And on top of that I will daub on a couple of slashes of rouge here and there to add some emphasis to the high, exotic cheekbones that I've never had! Now some eyeliner, a lip liner, and voilà, a completely organic woman! Here I am stepping naked from the half shell. And oh yes, the final touch, *un audace de bleu*, an audacity of blue!"

There was a second or two of silence as Persephone dabbed, then spread, an azure eye shadow just above her lashes, lining her upper eyelids.

"Did you know, Mai, that some anthropologists think that make-up and lipstick are just a visual echo of the erogenous zones? It seems that some female monkeys somewhere in the wilds of Tanzania have faces that look like their hind ends. Hell, some of our customers look exactly like that, but they're all men!"

Persephone's laughter filled the building. The door of the medicine cabinet slammed shut. Some final facial condiment had been applied, then returned to its shelf.

"What a ridiculous process! Why do we women keep putting ourselves through this?" Even as she said it she glanced at the front door and imagined her young husband standing at the threshold and taking in her beauty with his eyes.

"None of my three sisters used makeup until their thirties. Of course, they didn't need it until then. Mai, have I told you about how my three powerful sisters tried to keep their men from going off to war? They tried to use the one power that no man can resist: desire. My poor sisters. They didn't know that desire is the essence of war."

Persephone fell silent suddenly and Mai knew why. Once again, her friend's eyes had fallen on the photograph behind her. Its reflection was there in the bathroom mirror. It was one of only two photos in the entire house. It was in a silver frame just to the right of the bed, resting on a small vanity. They are both there on that light-sensitive paper. Persephone and A. B. Flyer are smiling and hugging near the dazzling, child-filled carousel at the entrance to the San Francisco Zoo.

Persephone raised her hand to touch the reflection of the photo in the mirror. In truth she was reaching beyond the paper, beyond the developer, the fixer, and the stop bath, and finally, beyond the image. With all her heart she yearned to reach past everything to touch that precious living instant. Her other hand settled on the flat plane of her abdomen, the place where no child would ever be.

It is Christmas 1967 and the Tết offensive is just a few weeks and ten thousand miles away. It is Christmas 1967 and Amos is so tall and handsome in his dress greens and class A shoes. His left breast is covered with badges, ribbons, and decorations. At the very top of these is a new Combat Infantryman's Badge, his proudest possession. The air is clear and cold. His breath is a white cloud frozen beneath his chin. In his dark eyes is the gleam of twisted desire.

The restaurant in San Francisco was A. B. Flyer's idea, his dream.

His parents had run a small café in a tiny town called Happy Jack way down in the Plaquemines Parish in Louisiana. It was his grandfather who had changed the family name from La Fleur to Flyer. A. B. Flyer and his new wife had begun saving all their money to buy a small house somewhere in the City. Just one more tour of duty and they'd have the money to pay for a complete kitchen and a food-service permit. The second-tour bonus, along with hazardous-duty pay, almost doubled a staff sergeant's paycheck.

Amos had considered locating the restaurant in Hunter's Point or in the Mission District. He would never have believed that a place on Potrero Hill would become available—a hilltop location with a view of the entire bay, from the Richmond Bridge to the San Mateo.

"You're so lucky, Mai," said Persephone in a soft, dreamy voice. "You've got no hair at all on your body." Persephone was hearing what the photograph could not portray: the beautiful, unearthly blare of the carousel's organ pipes playing "Over the Waves." "Not one hair," she continued. "None of these depilatories and tweezers for you. No chemical creams. Girl, I swear, your skin is like Italian marble. All you do is put on a little lipstick and comb your hair and you're done! You're ready to break some hearts. I tell you, there's no justice in this life. No justice at all. Even your feet are so petite and pretty. Just look at mine—so damn big, and my husband never did like my breasts. Too big or too saggy or something. You're a real heartbreaker, girl. If I was a lesbian, honey, I could do a lot worse than you!"

"Jane Doe 37 is a small Asian woman in her mid- to late forties. I can see no adipose tissue. Her breasts are soft but not pendulous. She is well muscled and unremarkable except for the fact that I can detect no remote scarring or injuries on the epidermis. She has beautiful skin. Delete last sentence from written text. There is significant bruising to all fingers, the palms, and the side of the hands opposite the thumb. There are small lacerations on the bottom of the feet and some evidence that she had recently run without shoes. These injuries are consistent with defensive wounds or with an attempt to escape some sort of captivity. See crime-scene report this date.

"There is a blurred tattoo noted on her left forearm. The tattoo is unusual, and judging from the diffusion of the ink, seems quite old. The words found there are barely legible but do not appear to be Asian script.

I can just make out the words 'San Francisco,' and the word 'Perse-phone.' It is clearly not a professional job. There is some discoloration around her waist and across her back that is the result of the pressure applied by the arms of Jane Doe 36.

"There is a single punctate wound of entry on the midline of the back in the upper quadrant. The larger wound of exit is noted in the throat area just below the chin. Examination of the wound path shows impact with the spinal column at the sixth cervical vertebra. The spinous process is shattered and the dura mater and spinal cord are insulted and severed. There is significant hemorrhaging at the vertebral artery.

"The wound path shows a slight deflection upward, penetrating the thyroid cartilage and exiting at the hyoid bone. The bullet was found at the scene by this examiner. It was spent and resting on the chest of Jane Doe 36, on her dress, between her breasts. The nose of the bullet is severely deformed."

There was a second picture frame hanging directly over the center of the headboard. It was a black-and-white photo surrounded by a handmade frame of lacquered bamboo and hammered brass. The last photograph ever taken of Trin Adrong was trapped there behind the glass. There is a brightness in his eyes, the beginnings of some strange desire. In the background is the Tu Do Café. Mai was smiling now. Two soldiers from opposite sides of a terrible war were now sharing space in the same bedroom in San Francisco. All of the old thoughts that were flooding back to Persephone had also caught Mai in their thrall. As it always happened, the deluge of thoughts was hers, too.

Mai cooking in the kitchen and Persephone dressing in the bedroom were soon loving at once, swaying softly at a heart's rhythm and pace to supple patterns, edgeless shadows, enchanted glimpses of times long past. Here, in this memory, is the click of a heel on pavement, the dissolving ghost of a warm breath against glass, the confident taste of a man's voice, now the sharp pinch of bamboo grass beneath her naked back, now the wistful shadow of an un-knowing last glimpse . . . graceful, graceless, awkward . . . suddenly over. There is a glimpse of Hong Kong and of the French Quarter. Here, in this memory, are the faces of four sisters: a bride and her bridesmaids. There, in that recollection, is a tattoo in the shape of a spider and violin. Candles flicker on pavement in this burst of memory. There is asphalt and heat and the blinding flash of a reflection from a passing windshield.

There is shapeless, weightless longing in their captured souls, the last enduring embers from the furious and desperate friction of moistened skins. The two standing women are sighing, sweating lovers now, stretched out in far-flung beds, caught in the thrash, pitch, and lurch of the single being with two bodies. They are surrendering simultaneously to the living, dying thing above them, beneath them, between them. In their ears are the voices of two recumbent males, two separate tongues whispering promised things into the cooling darkness of two bedrooms, worlds apart, and into two sets of symmetrical, unremarkable ears.

"When the war is over for me, we can open up the restaurant," said a deep baritone that resounded with the elongated drawl of the Louisiana river delta and the bayou. "This time my paychecks will be sent directly to you. That way I can't spend it all like I did on my last tour of duty. This time, when I leave the Nam, I'll rotate out at Fort Lewis and jet straight on down to you, Persephone. I ain't gonna re-up again, I promise. No more U.S. Army for me. I've had it. I'll even do the cooking every other day. You know my crab cakes are the best."

These joyous, chameleon words always made Persephone so sad. She had seen through his promises to the true color of his feelings. A. B. Flyer had seemed almost anxious to go back to Vietnam.

"When the war is over, I will march victoriously down Lê Loi Street with my comrades." It was a soft Thuong dialect from the Central Highlands, the voice of an excited, nearsighted young man about to leave for Hanoi. "I will return and reclaim my bride when the new order has come to power. And I will protect your family and the Tu Do Café, I promise."

The two women's spirits met as they strained to reconstruct that final glimpse. Was it on the gangway? Was that Amos smiling through that small window of the airplane that would take him so far to the west? Was it the front door of the Tu Do Café? Was it a hasty salute, or had it been a final wave of Trin's hand when the cadre leaders came at midnight to take him so far to the north?

Neither woman had ever seen or heard from her man again. There had been a few letters from Amos, but they had been strange and rambling. His last letter had gone on and on about bebop ballet

at the Pas de Calais. Try as she might, Persephone could not decipher the meaning of it.

They both knew in their minds, if not their hearts, that their men
were dead. Neither woman failed to fall asleep each night without
wondering how her husband had died. Neither knew when they
were killed or under what circumstances. Sergeant A. B. Flyer was
listed as missing in action somewhere near the Free Fire Zone where
Laos, Cambodia, and Vietnam converged.

Twenty years after his disappearance, the army moved him from
the missing-in-action category to the missing-and-presumed-dead.
Persephone had received some of his personal effects, but aside from
that final letter, nothing from his last days, and nothing truly personal to him. The things that came in the mail were from his hooch
in Dong Ha. There were letters and books, things that Persephone
had sent to him. There had never been a grave site to visit; there was
nowhere to place a bouquet of flowers.

Along with most of his company, Trin Adrong had never been
found. His entire battalion had been annihilated somewhere in the
highlands. A small, unmarked package of his belongings had been
left at Mai's home in Saigon just before it fell. There was no information in the package, just a few small personal items that were charred
black and smelled of cordite and damp earth.

There had been a pair of melted Russian-made wire-rimmed
spectacles, a melted Chinese watch, and a small Catholic Bible
whose cover had been removed and replaced with a cover from a
book of Chairman Mao's bad poetry. Communist or not, Trin would
always be a Catholic. Trin and Mai had been married by a priest. Inside the package, Mai had also discovered a single bloodstained scrap
of paper with some strange incomprehensible writing hastily scribbled on it. The yellowed paper had been wrapped around a small,
smooth sliver of dark-green jade.

Though she could not read the printing, Mai felt that it was something of great significance. At first she had attempted to memorize
the strange writing, but its intricacies eluded her. She had even
placed Trin's piece of jade on her tongue, but even then, the scrib-
blings would not reveal their secrets. When the writing and the
paper began to decompose, in desperation she had located a sewing
needle and some black ink and she had tattooed the markings into
her own forearm. A year later the captain of a company of Vietcong

would demand to know what the letters and numbers meant. Wasn't it written in English? Wasn't she a spy? Three years later a Thai captain in a squalid refugee camp in central Thailand would place a gun to her head and demand a translation . . . among other things. Wasn't it proof that she had been a whore for the Americans?

While Persephone and Mai grew a day older with each rising of the sun, their two lovers were still trapped in that time before the Têt offensive, green and adamant and sheltered by a callow shield of youthful immortality. They had become men steeped in strategies, clandestine movements, radio call signs, azimuths and quadrants. They were men who kept secrets that inevitably leaked out, made meticulous plans that always fell to pieces, played hunches that invariably ended in misery. They were romantic men who had pushed their women away to go groping for a weapon.

Both Persephone and Mai hated that moment in their memories, that moment when young men left to prove themselves, to prove something. As a result of this hatred, neither woman could bear to watch most American movies. "Soft rape," Persephone would call them, countless movies about postpubescent men winning sexual license by rescuing the once unattainable, now helpless girl-woman, by using daring and violence to skirt around acts of intimacy, words of communication and commitment.

"Kill enough people and you qualify for a waiver of the courtship requirement. Don't take her to dinner and talk to her," Persephone would scoff. "Heaven forbid! Just use kung fu on all of her sweaty assailants! Save her from all those scowling bad guys in sunglasses and Italian suits, then walk in all bloodied and bruised and sweep her off her feet! It's funny, isn't it? Here Amos went off to shoot at your husband so he could get some kind of macho sexual license, and before he left, Amos hadn't touched me twice in two years." Persephone would fall silent, then whisper to her friend, "The men never go home, Mai. They never go home."

Suddenly a vision of Persephone's father rushed into her mind. The old man is sitting in the center of the kitchen back in the family home in Louisiana. His four daughters are busily preening and primping him—making him look years younger so that the old fool widower could go off and seduce a child bride.

"Men never stay home," she spat out. "They just ride off into the sunset. And there ain't no damn responsibility in the sunset."

Persephone sighed her wonted sigh. Mai, in the kitchen, spoke toward the photograph of Trin as though the image could hear.

"I have made love to no one," she said. Her voice was calm and reassuring. "I have made love to no one."

Amos and Trin were young men who couldn't have known that the time would come when they would trade it all—their rank, their male tribes, their war, everything they had—for a taste of Mai and Persephone's magical spaghetti. Mai's and Persephone's memories always came together at this particular place: at an unimaginable death in a lonely and unmarked place.

Together, they pored over maps of Vietnam and longed to know where and how their lovers had perished. Was it a painful death? Did they think of their wives? It was the single most important mystery in their lives. Had it happened west of Pleiku? Did it happen south of Khe Sanh? Had their two lovers passed each other in the jungle? Both longed to be there at the end, lending comfort, giving companionship into the next world.

"I'd walk into hell to get him back," said Persephone. "As God is my witness, I'd walk into hell."

"I would go there with you," murmured Mai.

On the front porch of the Amazon Luncheonette was a small wooden table that, once a year, served as an altar. On the night of the full moon in the lunar month that corresponds with July, the tall white candles and the long rods of incense were lit. The table was covered with fresh fruit and pastries, newly baked moon cakes, and a bowl brimming with Creole pralines. Each year, Mai or Persephone would go downtown and buy a Monopoly game, remove the play money, and ceremoniously burn it on the front porch. Both women now observed Lê Cúng Cô Hôn, the traditional offering to the lonely dead and to deceased soldiers.

"Ma'am, can I buy a pot of sauce?"

"Beg pardon, Miss Persephone, is the Amazon Luncheonette open for business?"

When Mai looked up from her doorway in Saigon, and Persephone glanced sideways from her gate at Travis Air Force Base, they were startled to see a long line of hungry, expectant people, pots and jars in hand, waiting patiently at the door of their restaurant-to-be. The two lovers shook their heads clear of memories, smiled at each other, and went to work.

"The wound path through the brain of Jane Doe 36 shows no deflection. It penetrates the skull and it travels without change of direction through the dura, the arachnoid, and the pia mater. Now I am cutting and sectioning into the brain itself, I find the path to be consistent through the midbrain and into the opposite lentiform nucleus. The bullet is visible now, resting against the skull behind the right ear. There is little deformation of this round."

When the two huge pots were empty, Mai shut the front door and leaned wearily against the glass. A thin layer of sweat matted some of her hair to her forehead. Behind her the last customer was trudging off toward home with two warm jars of sauce in his arms. Persephone busied herself by scraping the pots before washing them. As usual, a single jar of sauce had been set aside for the local homeless man. Mai placed the jar, along with some French bread, on a wooden bench in the back-yard garden. After setting the hot food down, she cupped her tiny hands to form a megaphone and shouted the man's name twice in two languages into the night sky.

"Mr. Homeless, Ông Không Nhà! Mr. Homeless!"

As always, the jar would be empty in the morning. It would be washed, rinsed, and upended on the bench to drain. Neither woman had ever caught more than a fleeting glimpse of Ông Không Nhà, but his presence was unmistakable. To pay for the food, he would weed and cultivate Persephone's flower garden, repair the clothesline, mend the fence, and wash the windows, among many other chores.

Mai had once noticed an odd behavior in the man as she strained to see him in the dark. He seemed to be dodging and squatting as he moved about the garden. Only months later did she realize that this man was trying so hard not to damage the fragile, silken spiderwebs that adorned the entire garden.

Sometimes they heard a strange, indecipherable mumbling—a singsong buzzing coming from the back yard—and knew that it had to be Ông Không Nhà. He was a man who always worked in the dark, and though Mai found his presence a bit unsettling, it somehow comforted her. The living shadow in her yard felt like a fond memory.

"We sold over sixty quarts of sauce," said Mai with a tired smile. "Not bad, but we could've served almost two hundred dinners with that much sauce. With a green salad, pasta, and a drink, that would be a lot more money." She sighed as she placed the night's proceeds into a cigar box near the bed. "We'll need to get a deep freezer so we can serve dessert. Scoops of *cà rem dâu*." She laughed to herself at the word *cà rem*. It was obviously the French word *crème* that had been Vietnamized. "Strawberry ice cream. Won't be long. All we need to do now is hire a dishwasher, some nice boy from up on the hill."

As she spoke, two young men appeared at the front door. One was slightly taller and very lean, while the other was shorter, with a rounded face. They were both from the projects up on the hill. The taller one smiled, then began to rap loudly at the door. He then placed both palms on the glass door and playfully began to push, insisting that he be let in. The smaller boy had a pot in one hand and a lid in the other. He smiled shyly.

Mai smiled broadly when she saw him. She recognized the shorter young man and decided then and there to offer him the dishwashing job. On two or three occasions she had caught this same young man stealing the Vietnamese pastries that she had put out for Mr. Homeless. Over time she had developed a warm feeling for this young thief.

"*Duá bé giao bánh bích quy,*" she said with a laugh, but she hesitated in opening the door, because the boy he was with gave her an odd, uncomfortable feeling. His smile seemed false. She had never seen the boy before, but somehow she knew who he was. He was leering through the glass like one of those spirit faces on the Miriamman Hindu temple. As a child, she would take the long route to Ben Thanh market to avoid seeing those strange, eerie faces. Now one of them was staring down at her and pleading to enter her restaurant.

"There are two more people at the door, Persephone." There was an odd quaver in Mai's voice. "Should I let them in?"

That night on Potrero Hill all manner of pasta was cooking on fifty stoves and hotplates. Dancing and diving in pots filled with water, olive oil, and salt were white squares of ravioli, tangled strings of spaghetti, and curling waves of fusilli. There were gnocchi and cappellini, even shells, wagon wheels, and bowties, shimmering above the flame. Some pasta was undercooked; some was cooked far too long. Some was thrown against the wall beside the stove, where some of it stuck.

Eventually all of it was drained and put on plates and smothered with the wonderful Amazonian sauce. The scent that once had its epicenter at Twentieth and Missouri now emanated from scores of homes, tiny rented rooms, and crowded efficiency apartments.

It was while this small world was eating that the spell was broken. It was while they were tasting their sumptuous meals that the chilling screams pierced the night air. Most who heard the screams rose to lock their doors, then returned to their delicious food. But some people, either out of curiosity or out of fear, walked to their windows and looked out into the street. These people saw a crying woman running furiously up Twentieth Street from Missouri, her arms and her dress flying. Some noticed that her panties were down around her right ankle and that they flew off as she ran. Her eyes were wide with fear. Only one witness, a homeless man, could see the invisible war that raged at her back as she ran.

The witnesses watched as she went directly to the pay phone on the north side of the street. All of those who stayed at their windows saw him as he ran up behind her. He was running and hopping on one leg as he attempted to put on a white athletic shoe with his left hand. In his right hand there was a large black gun.

Two witnesses said that they recognized the woman as the lady from the Amazon Luncheonette, though neither could recall her name. They related that she seemed utterly terrified. Three tearful witnesses said that she spoke breathlessly into the telephone, while another said that she spoke a few words directly to the young black man with the gun. All the percipient witnesses related that they saw her drop the phone, then step back until her shoulder blades were pressed against the wall.

All of them looked on helplessly, transfixed by horror as the young man slowly raised the ugly weapon to eye level, aimed at the pretty woman's face, then fired a single shot into her head. One sobbing witness said that the killer had pulled a nylon stocking over his face, but she was sure that she saw him smile as the victim dropped to one knee, then onto her back.

For a few moments the gunshot stopped every meal within earshot. Mothers in the Potrero projects ran to their babies' rooms to make sure they were still breathing. Winos on the sidewalk felt the perimeters of their own benumbed bodies for a wound. Though dozens saw what happened after the first gunshot, only seven would eventually come forward.

All of them were doubly shocked when they saw the small Asian woman come running at full speed, screaming as she appeared from the southwest corner of the block. She was barefoot and her long black hair was trailing behind her like a flag. None of the petrified witnesses could decipher her screams, but all heard two distinct words shouted over and over again at the top of her lungs.

"I think it was something like 'tan lens,' " said one shivering witness. "Tan lens. Foreign words, probably gook words."

"No, it was more like 'ten lands,' " said another who dabbed her eyes with a small towel.

They told the officers that she had headed in a straight line, directly toward the woman who was bleeding to death beneath the telephone. Those who gave statements said that she seemed to ignore the man with the gun, that she must have seen him aiming it right at her head as she ran. He was standing no more than ten feet from the body.

"She run past him like he wasn't there. I ain't never seen the like," said a man who lived above the nature-food store. "She run up to where the other lady was and she threw herself right on top of her. She didn't care spit about that man and his bullets."

Four stunned witnesses reported that the dying woman had slowly lifted her arms from the sidewalk and thrown them around the Asian woman. Two of the four stated that the dying woman had been moving her mouth as though she was saying something to her friend. All of the seven who came forward to give statements said that the gunman had walked up even closer to the women, taken careful aim, and fired into the back of the smaller woman. The flash from the muzzle had lit up the dark street. Some said that it had lit up the low clouds overhead, turning the world a ghastly yellow. Both victims had jerked for a few moments, then gone still.

"Never seen nothin' so cold as that," said a sad widow who lived in a third-floor studio. "Nothin' cold as that."

The young gunman had then run into the middle of the street and brazenly pointed his gun at all the faces that were framed by window shades and curtains and were backlit by lights that had once presided over a peaceful dinner. The eyewitnesses had ducked or receded into their homes. Some had turned off their lights and returned to their windows, while some had gone back to their darkened, cooling meals. Others who had seen the horrible acts of savagery in their street would not eat for days.

All the witnesses would agree on one thing: that someone had screamed a single name into the night air: "Calvin!" Those who had returned to their vantage points saw another young man step from the blackness of shadows, thirty or forty feet away from the phone booth. Loud words had been passed between the gunman and his accomplice, then the second boy had taken the gun, held it in front of himself for a moment, and run off toward the hill that rose up behind the Amazon Luncheonette. The shooter had followed at a slower pace, his frigid eyes turned toward the two women lying on the sidewalk. One witness swore that the one called Calvin had pulled the trigger. This same witness swore that someone had called out the word "forever."

Two of the witnesses recognized the shorter boy. One witness knew his mother. He had certainly been an accomplice, nothing less. A single witness stated that she had seen a third man kneeling near the bodies in the time between the killers' escape and the arrival of the police. He had been an older man, not a boy. When pressed for a description of this man, she could give none, and she soon began to doubt in public that she had seen him at all. In truth, she knew exactly who he was.

Few people on Potrero Hill would finish their dinner while the street outside was glutted with idling ambulances and police cars. For long hours on end, the night air on the hill would be stunned senseless by the rude noise of radios and the intrusive glare of spinning and flashing lights. The unnatural, ghastly white of flashbulbs would push the night away for instant after time-freezing instant. Chalk marks would circle bodies and expended casings. A perimeter would be created, using yards of yellow plastic tape. A little boy would point excitedly toward Persephone's panties beneath a car.

The street would fill with spectators who would crowd together for comfort, to gasp and gossip at the ghastly amount of blood at the scene, and at the police department's clumsy attempts to separate the embracing women. Some of the wiser spectators would smile discreetly and nod knowingly between themselves that the inseparable women were lesbians. Didn't their last mortal acts on earth prove it?

"Stone lesbians."

"Loin-lickin' lezbins."

Children would climb to the nearby roofs to watch as the chief medical examiner and his assistant finally arrived to survey the scene and to remove the bodies. They too would struggle with the bodies for a while, then give up and place them both on a single gurney. A trail of lemon grass and blood would lead to the ambulance.

Gloved fingers would sift and comb rudely through the Amazon Luncheonette for shards and scraps of physical evidence. Wooden boxes of yellow onions and African peppers would be shoved aside. Bottles of spices would be knocked over and spilled. A barrel full of nuóc mám would be upended. The sweet, pungent scent would fill the neighborhood for weeks. A young police officer would drop the photographs of two soldiers into an evidence bag. The glass that had once protected the photos would be swept into a corner. The night's proceeds from the sale of sauce would follow the photos into the bag. A Catholic Bible written in Vietnamese would be placed in a manila envelope.

There were other strange items on the floor that had probably been pulled down from the wall or swept from the top of the vanity: a melted Chinese watch, some melted glasses, and a purple heart, among many other things. Rather than ask which items might be of importance, the young cop dumped it all into the evidence bag. From the new glass front door of the Amazon Luncheonette, the fingerprint technician would lift two perfect sets of prints, palms and all. On the sidewalk in front of the luncheonette was an empty pot and a lid with even more usable latents. The light of morning would see a wide band of yellow tape drawn across the front door like a banner across a wreath.

No one on the hill would ever admit it, but in their heart of hearts they deeply resented the terrible death of the Amazon women. Random killings and drive-by shootings over in the housing projects were one thing. They usually involved stupefied drug addicts and rough squads of remorseless, fatherless children—tiny mercenaries who had accepted the risk. They were acceptable losses. But these two women were valiant warriors who had armed themselves against gossips, braced themselves against liars, and girded their loins to do battle with a male world. They had carefully surrounded themselves with ambitious plans and used their shared female strength to fight off every mean stare and unkind remark. The pathway to their door had been mined with aspirations.

In their most secret hearts, some people on the hill began to resent the women themselves. They whispered among themselves that Persephone Flyer and Mai Adrong had reached too high. They had overreached. The women had erected an amazing fortification to fend off attacks of loneliness, pessimism, and failure.

"You can't tempt God like that," they said. "You can't raise a temple that high."

"Fire from heaven will strike you down," said an old retired minister. "His fire will strike you down."

Theirs had been a castle. All the local serfs could build their homes next to it, find comfort in its presence. Yet this grand, imposing fortress had been so easily breached. The people on the hill would shiver for months at the very thought of the two lovely women, torn and sundered by a mysterious God. They would avert their eyes whenever they passed by the Amazon Luncheonette. They would shoo away the memory the way they shooed away a house cat that has brought home a suffering bird.

"Rock breaks scissors," the dumbfounded would say. "Stupid kills beautiful."

"You see"—a mother would wave a finger at her two young daughters—"you can't go getting above your raising. You can't go being what you ain't."

No one on the hill would admit it, but what they resented was the death of hope.

"*There is evidence of trauma about the vaginal opening of Jane Doe 36. I note some tearing and a small laceration just above the perineum. There is marked swelling and redness of both the labia majora and minora. I see no evidence of semen or any other fluid; however, I am swabbing the vault now for testing.*"

After a few minutes of labeling plastic bags, the chief examiner returned to his microphone to sum up.

"*Evidence of sexual assault is present. Cause of death: penetrating gunshot wound to the head. Conclusion: homicide by criminal agency.*"

The chief examiner turned off the overhead light and the microphone and mechanically removed his gloves and mask. He used his lab coat to wipe his brow. This had not been a good day. He had shared a secret with someone whom he had never even bothered to know, and the fact embarrassed him. On days like this, his days in the military seemed idyllic. As captain of the graves detail in Da Nang, he had gone for whole months at a time without speaking with a subordinate.

He reached into a cabinet and pulled out a large tube of Super Glue that his assistant would use to close all the openings and replace all the reflected body parts on both cadavers. The mortician would do the rest, unless, of course, there was to be a cremation.

"There is no evidence of sexual assault in or about the vaginal vault of Jane Doe 37."

The assistant turned off the microphone at his station. After he had weighed the brain and entered its weight on his protocol, a thought had suddenly occurred to him. "You know," he said in a strange tone, "consciousness is a weird thing. People who are blind, deaf, and dumb are most certainly conscious. There is self-awareness even when physical sensation ceases. Even dreamers with no external stimuli are aware of themselves as an embodied being."

It was a continuation of an ongoing conversation he'd been having with the chief examiner. It was always a very one-sided conversation. The chief medical examiner wasn't much for small talk.

"I've read somewhere that the basic level of self-awareness might be sustained by as few as five neurons firing in harmony within the cortex or the corticothalamic net." He looked closely at the folds of the brain as he spoke.

"Out of billions, just five neurons are enough to keep the pilot light on! Is that what conscious life is, just five harmonizing sparks? Is it possible they could be listening? Could they be watching us cut them up?"

The assistant looked around for a response, but the chief medical examiner had already discarded his gloves and left the room. He was on his way to the parking lot and dreading the drive home. His wife would be sitting in the front room, waiting up for him. He had heard the assistant's question, but he had long ago given up considering such foolish things.

"Hell, ten synchronous neurons could be an entire dream, a whole universe! She could be dreaming right now," the assistant said to no one. "Their spirits could be searching for each other, maybe even linking up." He heard his own voice coming back to him again and again as he looked down at Jane Doe number 37 and her lover. Before leaving the room he made his final entry:

"The heart weighs two hundred eighty-three grams."

Even as he wrote, he realized with a sudden rush of terror that this career would stalk him; it would take careful aim at his native curiosity, his romanticism, his passion. For the first time in his life, he felt the full weight of his own heart. In time even his wife's lovely ears would become unremarkable.

"They both could be dreaming right now."

2

the house of toast

Down deep in the restricted bowels of the Hall of Justice a small windowless cafeteria rang with sharp laughter. It was not the blithe, easygoing talcum and Rolex mirth of manicured civil lawyers that was swirled over heaps of greasy chow mein and between heated steam tables filled with glistening fried rice and orange-tinged meatloaf. Nor was it the modest giggle, the discreet holy titter and righteous snickering of newly ordained assistant district attorneys that caused the overhead lamps and the menu board to shiver.

It was icy gallows humor, foxhole laughter soaked with dolor and with the great relief that remains when hours and days of mental trauma are now only harmless memories, though still very painful ones. It was the numbed laughter of wary men and women who know that a recurring danger has passed . . . for the moment. This kind of solemn mirth did not occur very often. It was a periodic ritual with a liturgy that included obsessive declarations of worry, grief, and panic and an occasional word of joy. This rite of laughter was a rhythmic purging, a monthly concurrence evolved over time to match the phases of the moon, much as when the menstrual periods of a group of close female friends have slowly become synchronized.

More often than not, defense lawyers met in this cafeteria to grumble about pro-prosecution judges, to wait nervously for jury verdicts, or to swig down cups of acrid caffeine and to bounce questions off the mind of a peer.

"What will the jury think about these facts? My client is one of five Mexican guys arrested in a 1954 Nash Rambler parked behind the Sheraton Palace Hotel at three in the morning."

"There's probable cause to arrest right there," interjected a voice.

"Suppose each one of the suspects had a flashlight, a pair of pliers, and a screwdriver in his pocket. Further suppose that one of the windows at the loading dock had been broken but nothing was taken. No prints were lifted from the glass or the sill. It's all circumstantial, right?"

But periodically, something more was called for. An organic imperative demanded ceremony: a formal gathering of warriors and a holy, saturnalian festival of sardonic humor. It was a profound act of ritual purification, an act of mending. It was incantatory, a precious rite of common healing. These war stories always began with the defense attorney's preamble: "I once had this guy."

"I once had this guy, a fifty-year-old child molester who woke up one morning believing that a ghost was trying to rape him. This guy was so terrified of being sodomized by this ghost that he came to court with his left hand down the back of his pants and his thumb jammed right up into his asshole. I can still see him now," said the laughing lawyer, "bouncing around the courtroom like a paranoid jumping bean, making sure his back was never turned toward the spirit world." The speaker shook his head at the memory. "He was all right until some smartass bailiff told him that a pervert ghost could poke him right through the wall. When my boy heard that, his tiny mind just snapped in two. Within twenty-four hours he was on the bus to Atascadero State Hospital. Can you imagine that bus ride? Three hundred miles, two cheeseburgers, a Coke, and hour after hour of invisible sodomy."

"That's nothing," said Newton Lam, with a tone of mock disdain. The Chinese lawyer laughed as he wiped dribbles of coffee from his chin. "I once had this guy who decided to break into a house up on Pacific Heights." The laughter around him subsided as another story began to unfold. "One of those huge, thirty-room mansions near upper Broadway. Anyway, this guy had five prior residential burglary convictions, all hot prowls—you know, the husband and wife asleep in the next room. So here he was, a five-time loser on the second-floor landing of a mansion, breaking the antique latch on a set of imported French windows. If he gets caught this time, it's a mandatory life sentence.

"Now, when I first saw the initial police report, I thought that the owner of the mansion was a real tightwad, because he had neglected to install burglar alarms on the second floor; all of the sensors and magnetic switches were down on street level. The alarm company he hired hadn't installed motion detectors. I decided at the time that he had figured no one was going to bother with climbing up to the second floor. I guess he'd never heard of a second-story man.

"So my boy is feeling real good about this job. He's cased the place thoroughly and he knows the alarm system is only on the ground floor and he knows that there's no guard dog on the premises. He's checked out that, too. He looks around for a dog run and he lifts the lids on the garbage cans. There were no sacks of dog food anywhere, just a big pile of bloody butcher paper near the service entrance. This time no one is going to catch him. He could get in and get out in ten minutes, go sell the stuff to a fence, buy some heroin, and still have enough time to see his parole officer in the morning for his monthly urine test."

Cigarettes were snuffed out and coffee spoons were stilled as bodies leaned forward to listen closer.

"So he cracks open the window and steps inside. Now my boy is smiling from ear to ear, because the place is pitch black and quiet as a church. There are no lasers, no pressure sensors. This job is gonna be a cakewalk. But when he turns his flashlight on, what do you think he sees?"

No one responded—not even a shrug was ventured. There was anticipation in every lawyer's face, but no attempt to hazard a guess. Over time, each of them had learned better. Irony is delicious and distasteful, soft and savage. Irony is not to be trifled with. Its very essence was that it could never be predicted.

"There on the Persian rug in front of my man is the biggest cat he's ever seen . . . and that was just the cub! He lifts his flashlight a little higher, and behind the cub is a huge pair of crimson eyes, as big as the taillights on a Harley. The owner of those eyes is a four-hundred-pound Bengal tiger!"

A groan of believing disbelief went up around him as he continued. On noticing that the cooks in the kitchen were smoking, Newton lit a cigarette for himself.

"So here's my homeboy staring at this enormous cat! She's sitting on the rug with a whole bloody sheep's leg in her mouth. Now he knows why there's all that butcher paper in the back! By now, he's so fucking scared that all of his tattoos are sliding off his body. There are ink stains on the carpet. His stomach lining is turning into menudo, and he is so petrified that he doesn't even hear the cub crying. It seems my boy had his right foot planted right on the cub's tail."

"Oh my God!" someone moaned.

"The supplemental report said that the cops located my client in a Dumpster across the street by following a clear trail of feces and urine, not to mention blood. The mother cat had torn off most of his right leg . . . and the all-important middle finger of his right hand. Seven cops and a paramedic couldn't pull him out of that Dumpster. They had to send one cop over to a rest home near Park Merced. They dragged my boy's dear, sweet mother away from her bingo game and drove her to the scene of the crime. It took her twenty minutes to talk him out of that garbage can. *'Antonio, mijo, el tigre, ya se fue.'*"

The table was quaking with sardonic giggles, tragic guffaws, sympathetic wails.

"Out of ten fingers, the tiger eats that one. His primary means of self-expression had been chewed off and swallowed. It would be like one of us losing our voice. When I went to see him at the hospital, he only had two things to say: 'Hey man, you a lawyer, tell me, ain't tigers illegal? Ain't they against the law?' After I recovered from my disbelief, my client begged me to ask the owner of the tiger to look around the house for his high school ring."

Another burst of laughter filled the House of Toast, as this particular eating establishment was unofficially named. Like all such places in government buildings, the contract to serve sumptuous and appetizing food had gone to the lowest bidder. The lowest bidder—a petulant, brooding group of smoking Vietnamese cooks—did not look up from their tedious work. They had grown accustomed to the incomprehensible banter of these coffee-swilling lawyers. Though most of the cooks had learned to speak some English, the dialect these lawyers were speaking seemed totally alien.

Back home, in a South Vietnam that no longer existed, there were lots of police and lots of prosecutors, but no such thing as defense lawyers. One of the cooks wiped the sweat from his brow and sneered at the circle of men in suits and shirtsleeves. Back home any decent person would rather cross the street than walk on the same sidewalk with a lawyer.

"That was Antonio Ruiz, wasn't it?" said Matt Gonzalez, the Tejano lawyer. "I represented him over at San Quentin."

"Señor Antonio 'El Tigre' Ruiz to be exact," said Jesse Pasadoble, a Chicano lawyer who was a veteran of the Vietnam War and of almost two hundred felony trials. "He renamed himself after that case and became a minor celebrity in the jails. You should have seen him at his sentencing. There he was, on crutches, flipping the judge the bird with that phantom middle finger of his. The judge cited him for attempted contempt of court. Of course we argued both legal and factual impossibility, but the judge thought the intent to flip the bird was sufficient. Why were you representing him in custody?" Jesse asked, turning to Matt.

"He got caught burglarizing the cells of his fellow inmates! They caught him by using the state of the art in forensic science and crime-scene detection. It seems the cells at San Quentin are pretty dusty and the thief left a series of shoe prints—all of a left shoe."

"At least he's consistent," said one laughing voice. "How does he describe himself these days, as a cat burglar?"

"He told me," said Matt, "that he wasn't scared of getting caught burglarizing in the pen. After that damn tiger, those guys in the Aryan Brotherhood and the Mexican Mafia looked like a bunch of sissies. El Tigre is back on the streets, you know. Some Mexican lawyer got all of his priors stricken and worked out a great deal."

He winked at Jesse, who smiled back.

"I saw him not too long ago. You won't believe it! He went and bought himself a used prosthetic limb. Only problem is that it's another left leg! At first I thought something was wrong with my eyes. I was talking to him for a few minutes, and I kept trying to clear my head, before I realized he was wearing two left shoes! Poor bastard. If you tell him to move to the right, he's paralyzed!"

Matt laughed deeply at the memory, then gathered himself for his own contribution to the contest.

"But my dear, dear friends, I've got one even better than my man Antonio Ruiz," he announced with a look of perverse expectation and masochistic glee dancing in his eyes. His arms were upraised in ministerial dignity, and his fingers were spread to signify the importance of what he was about to reveal. He paused for a long moment to heighten the suspense. The Right Reverend Gonzalez was about to testify before his congregation of peers. Surely he was about to relate the defense lawyer's worst nightmare come true.

"I, Matt Gonzalez, was doin' a rape trial a couple of years ago in front of old Judge Garfield. Do you remember him?"

"Yeah," said a disapproving voice. "The old geezer with the inflatable doughnut pillow for his hemorrhoids and the stack of girlie magazines in the bottom drawer?"

"Yeah, I remember him, too," said Jesse with a scathing, sarcastic tone. "Did you know that his clerk had this electric switch hidden under her desk that she would flip on whenever an objection was being lodged?"

One or two at the table knew of the secret switch. The rest had looks on their faces that spanned the full range of human emotion.

"That switch activated a strong electric vibrator under His Honor's seat that would shake him awake, and he would jerk bolt upright and shout at the top of his lungs, 'The motion is denied with prejudice! The objection is overruled!'

"The last time I tried a case in his court, one of the jurors had a heart attack right there in the jury box. God, it was something! It was pandemonium. The bailiffs were screaming into their walkie-talkies and running into each other. A nurse who had been on the jury panel was performing CPR right below the witness stand. The court clerk was pushing that switch so hard that it was lifting her desk clear off the floor, and the judge was rubbing the sand from his eyes and screaming, 'Defense motion denied, defense motion denied!' "

"That's my man," said Matt, with a wide grin. "Last time he read the Evidence Code, it was written in cuneiform. Come to think of it, I think his girlie magazines were Sumerian. Good-looking women, those Sumerians. They all have such beautiful eyes. Anyway, here I'm doin' this rape trial and the victim is up on the stand. I'd just finished cross-examining her, and the prosecutor was up doing his paint-by-numbers redirect. Even after being prompted by the DA, the victim, bless her soul, had just admitted on cross that she could not really identify her assailant."

There was a gasp of disbelief at the table. Most victims simply identified as their assailant whoever was sitting next to counsel at the defense table. On several occasions victims have been known to choose the attorney as their attacker when the defendant happened to be dressed in a better suit than his lawyer's. An honest victim is as rare as an honest defendant.

"She had told my investigator the same thing months earlier. She had never seen her attacker's face. She had real courage, that lady. Well, I didn't really have any more questions for her beyond that. They had no fingerprints and no other eyewitnesses. After her identification fell apart, the prosecutor's case was purely circumstantial and with no direct connection to my boy. A few hours after the crime was committed, my client was arrested down in the Tenderloin, near Leavenworth and Hyde Streets, with some of her credit cards in his possession. He had tried to use an automatic teller machine."

"He found them," Newton intoned convincingly.

"He bought them from the perpetrator," said Chris Gauger, a new arrival at the table.

"Exactly," said Matt. "Even though I believed it was a thin, circumstantial case, I could still sense that the jury wanted to convict somebody. You know what I'm talking about."

Everyone knew what he was talking about.

"Anyway, the poor woman felt so filthy and violated after the rape that she douched and showered almost immediately afterward. Of course there was no semen to test. They just couldn't make my boy with the evidence they had. Even with all of that jury sentiment, he was as good as free. His black ass was already out the door.

"So after the witness failed to identify the perpetrator, the prosecutor was sweating bullets in front of the jury box and just dying on his redirect examination. The jury wasn't buying any of what he had to sell. But then, all of a sudden, my client started elbowing me and screaming at me, 'Ask her if he had a scar on his ass! Ask her if he had a scar on his ass!' "

There was a knowing groan around the table. Eyes closed in pain and arms were upraised in despair. Each two- and three-piece suit around the table was turning slowly to rags and sackcloth.

"I told him to sit down and shut up, but he persisted. The toothless sumbitch was screaming his demand directly into my right ear. I tried to quiet him up, but every person on the jury heard it. I swear his breath was so bad that I've had straight hair ever since." He raised his eyebrows as he looked up toward his own brown, once curly head of hair.

"He kept getting louder and louder, insisting that his stupid question be asked. Finally, in desperation, I stood up and moved for a recess. The clerk hit her secret switch; the judge jerked upright, blinked twice, denied my motion with prejudice, and promptly suggested that we take a recess. I sat my man down in the holding cell and tried to explain, but it was useless."

Every cup of coffee at the table was being allowed to go cold. Here, in all of its glory, was irony.

"I pleaded—I begged the damn fool to let me run my case. I even promised to show him my diploma from Georgetown School of Law. I think some three-time loser must have planted the crazy question in his head while they were together in the weight room. Despite my firm assurances about the state of the case, my client insisted that I ask that damned question."

"Jailhouse lawyers," Newton grunted. "It kills me that the biggest losers are always the ones handing out the most advice."

"So I made my record in chambers, and I moved for a directed verdict of acquittal based on a clear failure of the evidence, but the judge pointed out that all of the evidence had not been heard yet," continued Matt. "Old Judge Garfield woke up long enough to rule that the defendant had a right to have his question asked, even if it was against the advice of counsel. When I personally refused to ask the question, the judge sneered through his yellow dentures and informed my client that he himself could put the question to the witness."

"That was kind of him! Did you know that he had his dentures tinted to match his only remaining tooth? The DA must've been salivating," said Jesse.

"Not as much as the judge was," said Matt. "The old man actually stayed wide awake long enough to hear the question propounded and the answer given. He was up there on the bench grinning like the Cheshire cat, though I think I did detect some shallow breathing and rapid eye movement. So after the DA was through with the witness, my genius client Dewilliam Magpie—I swear to God that was his name—stood up, extended his arm, and pointed a stern and accusatory finger at the witness."

"The jury must have loved that," muttered Jesse.

Matt only shook his head dejectedly.

"Meanwhile, back at the defense table, here I am acting all nonchalant, but inside, you know my shit was going to pieces. After staring her in the eyes for a painful eternity or two, Dewilliam launched his brilliant question at her. I could see it! I swear I could see that idiotic question as it ran down from his shoulder, across his elbow, over his wrist, then leaped from his pointing, untrimmed fingernail! That question jumped from his inept brain like a madman leaping from the Golden Gate Bridge. 'Miss Victim, did the man who attacked you happen to have a scar on his ass?' "

The entire table moaned in the throes of agony.

"At first the poor woman looked a bit puzzled by the question, but after a moment her eyes began to grow huge and a look of tremendous excitement transformed her face. 'Yes, yes!' she cried. 'There was a scar on his buttocks! I remember it now! I saw it when he was done with me and getting dressed. It was jagged, like a bolt of lightning.' As she said it, her index finger drew the shape in the air above the witness box. I could see that all of the jurors were leaning forward in the box. There were tears in her eyes and flowing down her cheeks. 'It was on the right side.'

"Well," said Matt, "y'all know what happened next. The bailiff called for more backup, and right in front of the jury they dragged my fool client into the holding cell. Then they pulled down his pants and took a couple of Polaroid shots of his funky butt. Then they brought the defendant back into the courtroom and proceeded to give the pictures to the prosecutor. Both of those bailiffs were grinning like they'd just won the lottery, and when I saw that my heart fell through the floor. When the photographs were shown to the victim, she began sobbing at the top of her lungs. 'That's the scar! Oh, my God, that's the scar!' "

The lawyers were roaring now in aching, throbbing spasms of ironic laughter. Dewilliam Magpie and others of his ilk were legendary, archetypal clients, men whose stupidity was used first as a sharp sword when they committed their awful crimes, then later as a frail shield to protect them when they were caught. Their stupidity would shield them against logic, against the tide of evidence, against the advice of counsel, and finally against the verdict and even against the sentence that would follow. It would protect them from everything but their own foolishness. Even years later Dewilliam would not be able to comprehend how it was that the victim had come to identify him in that courtroom.

Decades later, safely ensconced in the maximum-security wing of Folsom Prison, he would pass interminable hours and days blaming it all on his lawyer. His dumptruck, shyster lawyer had fucked him. Surrounded by tattooed men who declared themselves to be daring bank robbers and worldly drug traffickers, but who were, in actuality, only lewd pedophiles and compulsive mailbox thieves, he would proclaim his eternal martyrdom: "Muthafuckin' lawyer fucked me."

"Stupidity is always its own best defense," said Jesse, his face caught somewhere between anger and pity. "I've had a hundred like Dewilliam Magpie. Five hundred."

"Just tell us your worst one," said Matt. "We of the defense, we of the single reasonable doubt, we of the long odds and the short end of every stick want only the finest draughts of sweet liqueur at this auspicious, albeit monthly gathering. Only the most sublime distillations of our craft are recounted here." He raised his arm in a sweeping, evangelical gesture as he spoke.

"Do you mean," said Jesse, smiling, "the dude who was accused of robbery and stood up in court and announced to the judge, 'Your honor, you have to dismiss this case. I can't identify this here victim. That ain't the guy I robbed!' "

Jesse looked around the table at his laughing friends. They reminded him of his fellow soldiers in Vietnam. They had to laugh now and then and it was good that they did. Criminal defense is the emergency room of the law, and the constant pressure had to be relieved somehow. Grunts of the law, he thought, field medics performing triage in the crowded jails and holding cells behind the staid courtrooms. We tend the wounded, he thought, those who were wounded by life, by testosterone, by poverty. In this business, everyone gets wounded. Every lawyer at the table had suffered for his or her clients.

Real trial lawyers were like weary foot soldiers or sweating defensive linemen in football—tireless, maverick, and cynical. Their true skill was measured by how far they strayed from the lawbooks and from the cant of sterilized language and practice. The prosecutors were offensive linemen—neat and efficient. They were an orderly phalanx, a disciplined picket line that always deployed in perfect five-meter spreads. In the stylized warfare of the courtroom, the defense lawyers were the guerrillas, the Vietcong.

But in all truth, this business of criminal justice was nothing like the infantry or football. Jesse shook his head without knowing it. He had been shaking his head in disgust for almost fifteen years.

Somehow the action comforted him, freed him in some small measure from the war that haunted him. In the morning, after a bout with his nightmares of Vietnam, he would rise from bed shaking his head in sorrow.

Here, in the House of Toast, after a morning in court, he would shake his head in disgust. In this business, even the third- and fourth-stringers played. They were everywhere, maneuvering themselves to get the prettiest law clerk or the next judicial appointment. They had become public defender supervisors without caseloads. They had battered their clients into plea bargains. They had evolved into pipe-smoking elder-statesmen attorneys merely by their presence in the hallways for a decade or so. The Mexicans called such lawyers *cagatintas*, ink shitters. In the Hall of Justice, there were *cagatintas* everywhere.

Jesse shook his head once more. This army was top-heavy with deskbound colonels jockeying for judgeships. In this business, it was easy to hide. Beads of sweat began to form on Jesse's brow as familiar feelings of anger rose up once again. His anger at the *cagatintas* was becoming muddled, confused with the horrid dreams that had wakened him so early this morning. He took a deep breath to calm himself. His internal heat began to subside only when he looked around the table and reminded himself that he was surrounded by grunts, people whose asses were still in the high grasses. There were no *cagatintas* here.

Jesse unclenched his fists and closed his eyes to help release the anger. The Veterans' Administration psychologists had taught him how to distract himself with unrelated thoughts whenever the pangs came.

"Or perhaps," said Jesse, as his thoughts returned to the circle of defense lawyers, "you want to hear about el Médico Largo, the famous Dr. Long? Remember him? He called himself 'El Pitón,' but his favorite alias was Felix Meterpalo."

Only the Spanish speakers laughed at his puns.

"He was the phony sex therapist who was charged with about thirty counts of rape a couple of years back? He treated sexual dysfunction in older women by administering his now infamous 'hot beef injections.' The DA's problem was that every one of those acts was completely consensual."

"I remember that one," said Matt excitedly. "He was a dapper little Mexican guy who wore a toupee and always dressed in a shabby white tuxedo. I was there for the preliminary hearing. I swear, it looked like a goddamn beauty shop in the courtroom with all of that blue hair and rouge, and it smelled like the perfume counter at a drugstore. I seem to recall that not one single victim testified against him."

"Not a soul," smiled Jesse. "They all steadfastly refused, and good Judge Moscone wasn't about to issue a contempt citation to witnesses who looked just like his own dear mother. None of the alleged victims wanted their money back either. El Médico Largo kept saying all along that no one would press charges. After his case was dismissed, Dr. Long left with two of the victims—two widows, twin sisters, I believe. They all climbed into a white Bentley limousine and disappeared toward Daly City. I think he was driving."

Jesse laughed at his own private joke. In Spanish the verb "to drive," *manejar,* can also mean "to screw."

"Why wasn't it a hot chorizo injection?" asked Newton.

Jesse grinned. "If he had been Chinese he would have called himself Dr. Oolong."

"Do you think those women loved him, Jesse? How else can you explain their refusal to prosecute him for fraud?"

"I don't know anything about love," answered Jesse quietly. "Maybe it was. I suppose it could have been something close to it, a mimic of love or an isotope. You're asking the wrong person."

Jesse looked away from his friends. All of them were married and most of them had children. All that Jesse had been able to manage had been a series of aimless affairs. He had been lucky in the war. He was ambulatory. His sight and hearing were intact. All that had been amputated was his ability to give or receive love.

"But the good Dr. Largo wasn't the most interesting of all of my cases," continued Jesse. "I can offer up the absurd tale of one Mohammed al-Farouk, formerly known as Willie B. Shipwright of the renowned Sunnydale Project Shipwrights. His street name was Keloid.

"Now, Keloid had four or five burglary priors and in his new case was charged with about fifteen counts of residential burglary. In other words, he was looking at forever in custody. They would be playing the Super Bowl on the moon by the time Keloid was released.

"Here was a real pro. Keloid literally left no stone unturned. If there was a stone, my man would turn it and leave a fingerprint. Fifteen burglaries and lo and behold, there are fifteen pristine sets of fingerprints. And all in the exact same location: the flush handle of the toilet. It seems Keloid had a thing about using the toilet in every house he burglarized. I guess the one at home didn't work.

"Amazingly enough," continued Jesse, "Keloid was out on bail. You know, these idiots never appreciate their dear, sweet little mothers. Mrs. Winnie B. Shipwright had to take out a second mortgage on the family home to get him back on the street. Well, on the day of the preliminary hearing, he waltzes in with his entire family in tow, and he's dressed up like an honest-to-goodness college boy. I swear he came in wearing corduroys, a plaid shirt, a leather belt, and a pair of suede Hush Puppies."

"Oo-wee," sang Matt, "my man was smokin'!"

"On his left wrist was a nice gold watch and he had on a pair of tinted sunglasses. *¡Ay, qué guapo!* It was truly a moment of sartorial splendor. I'll never forget how proud his dear mother looked that morning before the hearing. *Pobrecita*.

"Well, the district attorney came into court and offered ten years in state prison to settle the case."

"A gift," said Newton.

The others nodded their heads in agreement. Given his fingerprints and his possible exposure—six years for each current burglary charge and five years more for each prior—it was more than a gift, it was manna from heaven.

"Of course, no one dressed like that is going to take ten years. His mother was aghast, fanning herself and screaming. 'My dear little boy take ten years? You go tell that district attorney to forget them ten years! Lord Jesus, have mercy! Where is the justice? Where is the love?'

"I explained to Keloid that his exposure was immense—well over a century in prison—and that he could be out in five years if he accepted the latest offer, but he gracefully declined. 'Fuck them ten years,' he bellowed after making sure his sweet mother and his adoring family couldn't hear. As a precaution I asked him if he had any proceeds from any of the burglaries on his person. With a truly wounded look on his face, Keloid said, 'You think I done this, don't you? Mr. Lawyer, just whose side is you on?'

"Well, the first witness to take the stand was the fingerprint expert, who placed Keloid in every one of those bathrooms and his hands on every one of those flush handles. I remember that Keloid turned to me and said, 'It ain't against the law to take a piss. They ain't proved nothin'.'"

The lawyers around the table heaved a sigh of sad familiarity.

" 'It'll prove that you were there,' I explained, 'and each of the residents will say that you had no business being there.' The fingerprint expert added that he had never seen so many perfect sets of latent fingerprints. 'They lifted off that stainless steel like pancakes from a griddle.' When I asked him questions about the actual comparison, he laughed out loud and said that he could have compared them over the telephone. He stopped at twenty points of similarity on each one, then he pointed out a crescent scar on the right index finger that was present at every lift. The expert said that Keloid might as well have signed his name.

"When he heard this, Keloid leaned toward me and said excitedly, 'We got 'em now! We got 'em now! I can't write!' "

The evening's most formidable wave of laughter washed over the table. There was the froth and foam of empathy and embarrassment tipped with the jovial sadness of people who have slowly, over time, developed an immunity to the presence of the unbelievable. It all happened; everything happened in the courtroom, and defense lawyers had to be there to absorb the blows and to attempt to explain it all away.

"So after the fingerprint expert left the stand, the prosecutor put on the cops to explain where and how Keloid was arrested. Then came the residents."

Jesse Pasadoble breathed deeply. What happened next had appeared and reappeared in his minor nightmares. He leaned back in his chair and began again. Two other lawyers who had witnessed the actual events began giggling with expectation. Even those who had just heard passing references to the case over the years were filled with an unnatural anticipation. This case was some sort of weird landmark, a milestone of the absurd.

"The first witness testified as usual as to what property was missing or moved and that no one, including Keloid, had permission to enter the premises. When he was done testifying, he stepped down from the stand to sign the witness list, but suddenly turned toward the judge. In an awkward and halting voice he addressed the court: 'Your honor, may I please say something?' I objected, of course, there being no question before the witness, but the judge allowed the man to speak. 'Your honor,' he said meekly, 'that man has my shoes on.' "

The table shook with guffaws of sympathetic derision. Chairs rocked backward and table edges were pounded with closed fists. Spilled coffee rolled onto sleeves and sheaves of legal paper. The sound rolled from the dining room and out into the hallways, where it splashed onto the steel doors of four elevators and onto the swollen racks of the evidence room at the end of the hallway.

"So the bailiff seized the shoes from my client's feet and the witness pointed out the place inside his shoes where he had written his initials in laundry ink. When they took the shoes away, old Keloid started bawling, 'What's this mean, man? What's this mean?' The tears were streaming down his face. I think there was even some snot hanging from his upper lip. Right before my eyes old Keloid, the confident, self-assured collegiate, was rapidly reassuming his ancient courtroom persona as the helpless innocent, a poor cork bobbing on a swelling sea of unfairness.

"Anyway, the second witness took the witness stand, then, after the same litany of evidence, ended his testimony by saying, 'Your honor, the defendant is wearing my pants.' "

Those who had never heard the story before were unable to control themselves now. Their facial muscles were aching with laughter. What they were hearing was yet another incredible incarnation of the defense lawyers' worst fears.

"After the pants were removed from Keloid's body, the third witness recognized the plaid shirt as a special one his mother had sewn for him for his thirtieth birthday. I couldn't believe it! They were stripping my boy naked right there in the courtroom. His poor mother was fainting and grabbing at her huge heaving chest and screaming, 'Help me, Lord Jesus, help me!' Her makeup was streaming down her face and there was one false eyelash stuck in her cleavage. The other members of his family were leaving, one by one. Seminaked Keloid was anointing the counsel table with his salt tears and snot. But it wasn't over yet.

"The last witness closed his eyes and recited word for word the inscription on the back of the gold watch that the bailiff had taken from my client. It had been a graduation gift from his late father. So there is my once proud client, sitting there in his underwear and his tinted shades—his entire wardrobe placed into evidence and mucus covering his entire upper lip—sobbing. 'What's this mean? You supposed to be my lawyer. What does this mean?'

"You know," said Jesse, as he removed his glasses to wipe his eyes, "I still get hate mail from that man. Even his mother sends me hate mail. She says she knew all along that she should've hired a white lawyer. She still calls me on the phone to tell me that I railroaded her poor child. She says her son isn't a thief and that a real lawyer would have known that those clothes were stolen."

"Is this the legend of Keloid?" asked a woman's voice, barely heard above the laughter. It was Freya Horne, a veteran public defender and a longtime member of the circle. She walked slowly around the group, looking for an empty seat. There was a look of distress and fatigue in her dark eyes as she sat down.

"Sank heaven for leetle girls," she sang weakly, as she removed her tweed jacket. It was her parody of Maurice Chevalier and it could only mean one thing.

"You got another child molester?" moaned Matt Gonzalez.

Freya nodded slowly, sadly. "Jesus, I hate these cases. More than anything on earth, I hate these cases." She nodded her thanks as someone handed her a cup of coffee. "The mother allegedly caught Gramps molesting his own granddaughter! Well, there's one more family down the tubes. And to top it off, the little girl is two years old."

A groan of deep pain and frustration rose up around the table.

"And . . . there's forensic evidence," she added, her eyes glazed with moisture.

The table was silent now. There it was, the tearing of the labia, the redness, the immobile sperm heads. There it was, so measurable and demonstrable: the instant when the irreversible happened, the bud that would blossom into a lifetime of suffering. There it was, the end of a childhood, the end of a relationship between a father and his daughter. No matter how the case turned out, no memory would be left untainted, unsmeared by an old man's wayward fluids.

"Do you want to trade, Freya?" said a voice. "I'll take that case and you can have one that I can't stand." It was Chris Gauger, one of Jesse's favorite lawyers and a close friend. Jesse noticed that Chris had two of his fingers resting on the seam of his paper coffee cup. He had once been a minor-league pitcher; a junk-baller who had spent less than a week in the majors, two or three days with the Royals, and a cup of coffee with the Athletics.

"I have a leather murder," said Chris, "a real kinky sadomasochism homicide with lots of handcuffs and alligator clips. There's even some chicken wire in the evidence, an enema kit, and a jar of mayonnaise. I'm fairly sure it'll end up being a voluntary manslaughter."

"No thanks," said Freya, her face twisted into a mock expression of disgust. "I can do my own case. It'll just take a little while to get over the initial wave of revulsion Who knows?" She shrugged. "Maybe he didn't do it." The defense lawyer's reflex had begun to kick in and the others at the table breathed a sigh of relief.

"Maybe he didn't do it."

Freya sipped her coffee, her mind drifting with the steam that rose from her cup.

"So," said Freya as she simultaneously reached out to touch Jesse's shoulder, "I hear you got the Flyer-Adrong murder case." There was a look of sympathy in her eyes.

"Which one is that?" asked Newton.

"The Amazon Luncheonette case," replied Chris, "that double homicide up on Potrero Hill. That was so cold-blooded. You have that one, Jesse?"

Jesse nodded solemnly. He had just been to the medical examiner's office. The autopsies had been done a week ago, but the coroner's reports were still not ready. Jesse had the color blowups of the autopsies in his briefcase. His investigator had gotten them a few days before. As soon as he left the House of Toast this evening, he would be going up to meet the defendant for the first time.

He should have gone to see his new client the day he got the case, but something made him put it off. Had it been those photographs? Had it been the photographs or the photographer that had unnerved him? Somewhere in his nightmares there was always a photographer, someone who had squinted at death to find the aesthetic vision. At first he had only glanced at the photos. The two women had been so beautiful, even in death. Jesse had seen so much power and determination in their unmoving faces. On second viewing he had found himself staring into the photos for hours, trying to imagine the two women alive and smiling. He had found himself wishing—with every ounce of his being—that he had known them both.

Jesse hated death. He did not fear it, but he hated it with all of his heart and soul. A year and a half of incredible fear in the highlands of Vietnam had been transformed into an almost anguished love of the living, intact moment, the moment that can never be possessed. Like many men who have witnessed the best and worst in themselves, who have been given a glimpse of the end of their own lives at a very young age, he had lost the power to be lonely. That power had been replaced by something else: a soul sickness; a hunger for beauty, but only at a distance. Though he could not love his own life and the things within it, Jesse hated death.

"That horrible case," said Freya, "makes me happy that mine is only a puny molestation. The Good Lord knows a little child should not have to start out her life like that, but at least she has a chance to live out her allotted days without some trigger-happy, testosterone-ridden idiot putting a bullet through her head or her spine. There's just something so eerie and unsettling about that Flyer-Adrong case."

"It was an execution," said Chris. "The police described the placement of the bullets as efficient, almost professional. Were there juveniles involved? How old is the defendant?"

"Eighteen," answered Jesse. "Calvin Thibault is his name. The other suspect is still at large. My boy is a real sophisticate, I'm sure. The eyewitnesses are at odds over which of the two is the actual shooter. The homicide detectives all suspect that the other perpetrator is Little Reggie Harp, but Calvin won't cop to it."

"Not if he ever wants to see his family again," said Chris. "Word on the street is that Reggie Harp is one evil dude. Everyone on the south side of Potrero Hill is scared of him."

"One oddball witness says there was a third guy at the scene of the murder," continued Jesse, "some sort of daredevil bystander. But they all agree on one thing: Calvin Thibault was there when those women died. From what I've heard and read, everyone on Potrero Hill had an opinion about those two women. People either loved or respected them, no one disliked them. For whatever reason, their small cooking business was quickly becoming the true heart of that community. Their restaurant was due to open in less than three months. My investigator tells me that the little restaurant is beautiful."

The feeling of hatred flooded back once more. There would be so much hope lodged within the walls of the Amazon Luncheonette, unrequited, useless hope. The human hearts that created that hope, that held up those walls, were lumps of clay now—senseless, dumb and cold.

"I don't think the prosecutor will ask for the death penalty. Aside from stealing Twinkies and Kool-Aid from the corner store, the kid has absolutely no prior convictions. He's never been arrested. Jesus, he sure as hell started right at the top. A real child prodigy. Why the hell couldn't he have gone the traditional route? Start out by stealing tires and move up to an entire car? The DA might go for LWOP though," said Jesse, referring to a life sentence without any possibility of parole.

"I have to go up and visit Calvin tonight. I promised his mother. God"—he exhaled deeply—"I'm not really sure that I have the energy for another life makeover!"

Everyone at the table understood what Jesse meant by the phrase "life makeover." It referred to the agonizing, time-consuming process that he had developed over the years to prepare all his clients for the rigors of the courtroom and for the frightening possibility that a semiliterate, bookless, wordless, and thoughtless young man who was accused of premeditated murder would have to take the stand and explain himself to twelve people—twelve white people who would never deign to set foot in his world, who would clean their shoes if they ever did. Twelve people who would swear an oath to judge Calvin fairly, without preconceptions or prejudice, but who would also lock their car doors if they noticed him walking nearby.

"But that's not the worst part," he said. "I have to go visit the supreme being, too."

"Oh shit!" moaned Newton. "I was wondering who had that idiot's case. Oh Jesus, Jesse, you've got my sympathy! Make sure you bring up some Handi Wipes and a bottle of spray disinfectant! That dude is bad news."

"Not to mention breath mints," smiled Jesse. "It seems that the price of racial supremacy is a set of really bad teeth. I'm bringing up more than Handi Wipes. I'm bringing up alcohol swabs and a battery of IQ tests, graded, stamped and sealed by Dr. Wooden." Jesse looked at his watch. "In fact, I'm meeting the doctor and my investigator up on the seventh floor in just about ten minutes."

"The IQ tests again." Newton laughed.

"Yeah," answered Jesse. "Normally I have to pull this arrow from my quiver once every two or three years. Lately it seems like I've been doing it once a month. It's like I said before, stupidity is its own best defense."

"I'm surprised the supreme being would ever agree to it," said Matt, whose distaste for the man was obvious.

"I goaded him into it," said Jesse. "Actually, it was quite easy to do. Besides, this test was fun. My guess is that Dr. Wooden pulls the questions from one of those trivia games or from his history books. Who was Berengaria of Navarre? Name the sons of Eleanor of Aquitane. What was the Counter-Reformation? Now that I think of it, this is the second time this year I've had to do it. I swear, I almost died laughing when I got to the question that asked us to list the twelve tribes of Israel."

"Hell, I couldn't answer that question," exclaimed Freya Horne. "Could you?"

"Of course." Jesse laughed and winked at her. "Even the least-educated Mexican peasant can answer those questions! But you should've seen sweet mr. supreme when he got to that question. I thought he was going to explode in the interview room. The veins on his red neck were just about to burst and all of his tattoos were stretching. But the question after that one was even worse. 'Name three jazz musicians who rose to prominence during the Harlem Renaissance.' The supreme being almost shit in his Christian Identity pants. When we got to the questions about syncopated rhythms, Red Garland's right-hand technique and cigar-cutter saxophones, he smashed his pencil lead on the paper. It's taken some time, but I think I have my relationship with the supreme being all worked out."

"Let there be darkness," said Chris Gauger.

People were standing up now, grabbing their books, jackets, and briefcases. Some were gulping down the dregs of their coffee and swearing never to buy the dishwater brew again. Someone who had eaten the oily wonton soup was hurriedly looking for his bottle of Maalox. They were heading off to open law books and read advance sheets, to peer into another failed life, to view the uglier faces of desire, to examine a twisted moment of grief or cruelty, to take it on—to assume its weight for a client who could not or would not, for a client who should not.

"Why is it that you are taking IQ tests with one of your clients?" asked a departing voice.

"Because el señor supremo is a white supremacist," answered

Freya, who had been fired by the repugnant man in a previous case. She continued speaking as she walked toward the jail elevator. "He hates just about everyone: Japanese, Irish, Italians, Samoans, Jews, Mexicans, Africans. He hates the National Endowment for the Arts, the Boy Scouts, librarians . . . everybody. But here's the best part of all: he believes himself to be a great legal mind."

"Yeah," added Jesse with a large smile, "and the winner of this IQ test gets to be the lawyer."

The entire group walked to the elevators. Chris wadded up his paper cup, spread his fingers for a four-seam fastball, took careful aim at a trash can, then missed it by a mile. Behind them the cooks were mopping the floors and setting the chairs on top of the tables. As the elevator doors were closing, leaving behind an empty hallway, the voice of one defense lawyer could still be heard referring to the sadomasochistic murder case.

"What on earth do you think the mayonnaise was for? Listen, I once had this guy . . ."

At the same moment that the elevator filled with defense lawyers began rising up the hollow spine of the building, three women were leaving the coroner's office and climbing silently into a taxi that was headed for the San Francisco airport. The sisters of Persephone Flyer had just arranged to have the body of their loved one flown back home to Alexandria, Louisiana. When they learned that there were no claimants for Mai's body, they shipped her back to Alexandria to be buried next to their dear Persephone.

Once back home, they would shoo away that old mortician and spend a full night, from sunset to sunrise, with their dear sisters. None of them knew if the tradition, the deep need for this death watch, was French, Indian, or African, but they all knew it had to be done. It had always been done this way. The moment the three sisters had learned of the death, they had begun the process of carefully choosing the clothing in which Persephone would be buried. Now their hands would dress her, their eyes would remember her, and their lips would fill the air with stories of her life.

As the eldest sister held Persephone's heavy, sleeping head, the other sisters carefully bathed her with her favorite beauty soap, then moistened her with fragrant oils, removing as much evidence of the coroner's hand as they could. No one would mention the scalpel cuts on her fingers. One sister would quietly cover them with soft daubs of foundation makeup.

"My, my, but that scar she got when she shinnied up that telephone pole still hasn't gone away," said the youngest sister. "*C'est trop dommage.* These panties," she said softly as she pulled a pair of pink panties past the knees, "were the ones she wore on her wedding day. Damn if they don't still fit. Look here, her tummy's as tight as a schoolgirl's. *C'est incroyable!*"

The others would agree. There were no stretch marks on her tummy. No burgeoning fetus had spread her hips. How she had wanted those telltale marks. One sister would begin to cry. One would whisper that Persephone had miscarried out of loneliness. Two of them would lift her midsection. Another would pull up a pair of cinnamon pantyhose to cover the panties. Then one of the sisters would remove a limp, lacy bra from a brown bag and lovingly relate the tale of Persephone's adolescent fear that her breasts would never grow. Laughter would rise up from the mortuary at midnight as they recounted Persephone's subsequent, anguished prayers that her swelling breasts not grow any larger.

"*Mon Dieu,* she was so all-fired worried about her titties, about becoming as top-heavy as Mama! Remember back when I had my breast removed? Remember what she did?"

All three sisters laughed the only laughter of the night that was not pierced by poignancy.

"She read somewhere about some crazy doctor over in Baton Rouge who did a mastectomy on a lady and removed the wrong breast. Well, Persephone got so fired up about it that she ran into my hospital room that evening before my operation, pulled down my gown in front of God and company, and with a felt-tipped pen wrote a sentence on my good breast!"

"Leave this one alone!" screamed the three sisters in unison.

As the laughter diminished, the oldest sister opened a brown bag, then stood to let the cloth and thread in her hands fall down to its full length.

"She bought this dear dress when she found out she was pregnant. I had never seen her so happy."

Together, they lifted her arms and upper body and pulled the maternity dress down until the fit was perfect. A small pillow was then placed on her abdomen beneath the pantyhose. She would lie for eternity in her second trimester. One sister saw to the matching shoes and handbag while the other three worked on the makeup. She would have her favorite French perfume and her favorite lipstick and rouge. Her lips would be as red as pomegranate.

"I am applying thick, colored putty to her chin," the sister would tearfully chant, "so that her poor pores will have absolutely no way to breathe. I'm daubing on slashes of rouge here and here to add emphasis to the high cheekbones she never had."

Her precious earrings, bought by her husband while on leave in Thailand, would be hung from her lobes. One sister would lovingly brush dark mascara onto Persephone's lashes while another squeezed a lash curler over each closed, unmoving eye. A pair of small, pink toe shoes was placed in her hand to further hide the cuts. Persephone had broken her mother's heart by quitting ballet. As they washed and combed her hair, none of them would ever mention the dark bullet hole hidden beneath her locks.

When Persephone was ready, they would move on to Mai, a sister they had never met. The three had gone to the Amazon Luncheonette and collected Persephone's belongings. One of the sisters had found the beautiful red *aó dai* hanging in the closet along with silk slippers and panties. They would lift Mai's body and dress her in the *aó dai*.

"Have you ever seen such beautiful skin?"

"Have you ever seen such hair?"

"Do you think that she and Persephone . . . well, you know?" asked one sister sheepishly.

"I sure as hell hope they did," spat out another sister. "Men ain't nothing but grief and trouble."

In soft, dancing candlelight they would pass the earliest morning in tale after tale of childhood and youth and courtship. None would feel the chill or the dark or the orange warmth of a waking sun.

"Wasn't Persephone's husband so handsome! *Si beau!* That Creole boy had such a smile. Now, there was a real ladies' man. I didn't think she would ever trap that boy. Didn't they make such a beautiful couple?"

"He should have come back from Vietnam after that first tour, and stayed home with her, where he belonged. What on earth was it about that godforsaken war that made him keep going back? Why do men keep going off to fight?"

"It was that war that took them both. It was that war that took Mai and her man. As I live and breathe, it was that war."

Each sister would alternately giggle, then sob, then sigh. At daybreak the ancient mortician would shuffle quietly into his small office and hear the women talking outside his door as they left their sisters alone. He walked into the room they had just exited. The cold, hard room was ablaze with candlelight. The air about his face was filled with femininity and perfume. There was a warmth on the mortician's skin that he had never experienced in this old, drafty building.

The women lying there looked strangely contented, almost alive. He shook his head. His lifetime of professional experience could never match what the sisters had done. The world outside had delivered an unclaimed body and a dead, barren woman to his premises. In the morning he would bury a mother-to-be whose face was flushed with joy, and a beautiful Vietnamese bride. Somehow they had accomplished so much more than mere cosmetics ever could. Slowly, he walked to his office to call for the hearse and the limousine. The three women would be back for the burial in just a few hours. They had been very insistent. Everything had to be ready.

As the chorus of women left, they were a strange admixture of mirth and mourning—staunch, straight, powerful, but momentarily enfeebled women who were missing a precious part of themselves. In hours they would be back, renewed and imperious as ever and leading squads and troops of family. Wearing white gloves, veiled hats, somber dresses, their shoulders weighed down by epaulets of grief, they would shout orders here and make firm, incontrovertible suggestions there. They would direct the movements of flesh and blood as it embraced and relinquished its own.

Their eyes beneath their darkened brows would be surging with tears and memories. Their families—their silent, obedient husbands and polite children—would be following behind them, rolling in their wake like the leaves of fall.

3

the male recumbent

Jesse Pasadoble rode the elevator toward the top floor of the seven-story building. As usual, the walls of the lift were smeared with antipolice graffiti and the floor was littered with cigarette butts and newly discarded property envelopes. As with every ride in this machine, the sloppy, sideways movements of the car reminded him of the Huey helicopters he had once ridden. As he approached the felony cellblocks, he braced himself by grabbing a handrail as he began to experience the familiar yet still disconcerting sensation that his upper body was being pulled to the side and downward toward the floor.

Every ride up to the seventh floor was always the same; it was as though the force of gravity itself were contorted and twisted whenever the elevator rose past the sixth floor. In actuality it was not a gravitational effect at all but a temporal effect—a severe warpage of nearby space caused by the presence of so much time concentrated in such a restricted area.

The jail reminded Jesse of the famous Mystery Spot, a small roadside attraction in the mountains above Santa Cruz. All the tasteless billboards leading up to the attraction claimed that the physical laws did not apply within the confines of the weird little building. Metal balls dropped to the floor would roll mysteriously uphill. People who were standing erect seemed to be lying down. Feathers fell faster than rocks. All perspectives were skewed.

The seventh floor was a horizontal world where all of the inhabitants lived in a position that was at total odds with the rest of the world, perpetually perpendicular to the working men and women on the floors and streets beneath them. This was the supine floor. Except for stilted and shackled movement to and from the courts, prisoners seldom if ever stood up in these long, barred bays. They all clung to their thin bedding and small cots in the same dull way that stunted, unmetamorphosed caterpillars might cling to their ill-woven cocoons.

These recumbent males, unable to change their own botched lives, had somehow managed to partially transform their bunk beds and cots. Simple metal and spring frames with cloth coverings had evolved into complex, finely tuned machines capable of travel through time and space. Their beds were geared for long distances, for trips to Alpha Centauri and the Sombrero Galaxy. Everyone doing time knew you had to sleep the years away in a state of suspended animation in order to reach your destination alive. All you had to do was format the mattress computer, load in the linen software, and program it for two years, nine years concurrent, or two life terms back to back. Few, if any, of the prisoners would ever really learn to fly their four-cornered ships. Most were limited to clumsy flights backward into the past. It was the rare prisoner who could move forward.

For most prisoners the bed, powered by a decent pillow, would merely calculate your good time credits automatically and wake you up when your time in stir was done. Someday these stunned and immobile travelers would step blinking and yawning from their time capsules. As Einstein had predicted, their souls and their futures would be completely unchanged, while the world around them had evolved and gone on. Men who barely belonged in one era were doomed to be set loose in another, even stranger time.

Jesse Pasadoble knew that those men lying down up there were all stuck on cruise control, going from place to place without any discernible motion. They moved from county jail to state prison to federal prison and even to death row in the same insensible condition: half alive and asleep, moving only in the fourth dimension.

Jesse walked through the electric gate and toward the third interview room on the right. The door was open and he could just make out the voices of Dr. Wooden and Edmund Kazuso Oasa, Jesse's investigator. The psychologist was a tall black man with a wide smile. He had a beneficent face, large eyes, and a tiny set of metal-framed bifocals that were perched precariously on his nose. Jesse guessed that he wore the bifocals for his clients' sake. He needed them to compensate for his boyish, almost childish face.

Jesse laughed to himself. The effort to look more professional had been a total failure. But Jesse liked his face. It effectively draped a kind demeanor over a gentle soul. He shook the doctor's hand, then smiled at Eddy. "You ready for this?"

"I'm never ready for this," sighed Eddy, who nevertheless slid a chair out from beneath the table and sat down. Eddy was a Hawaiian man of Japanese descent. He wore a mustache and a short beard that was just beginning to gray. His hair was jet black and combed straight back in a long sweep that went down past his neck and rested on the collar of his brown leather jacket.

"Are you ready?" Jesse asked the doctor. Dr. Wooden only smiled patiently. Jesse inhaled deeply, then turned and walked down the hall toward the small office at the head of the mainline.

"Can I see mr. supreme?" Jesse asked the deputy sheriff at post eight. There was a full apology in his voice and in the droop of his shoulders.

The deputy sheriff was a huge, grimacing black man.

"Shit!" he grunted. "You want that crazy son of a bitch?" He cursed again under his breath, then lifted his walkie-talkie to his lips and shouted, "Post nine, this is post eight, send me up Sykes and Porter. . . . I don't give a shit what they're doing. We got to get the supreme being outta his cage for an attorney visit."

"Roger that," said a voice in the walkie-talkie. "Jesus, not again!"

"Well, Mr. Lawyer," said the sheriff, "I just now ordered up two of the biggest, blackest bloods in the house to manhandle that fool out here for his visit. Six hundred pounds of angry African flesh is gonna drag that idiot out here because you want to see him."

There was a look of disgust on his face as he accosted the lawyer with his index finger. "Do me a favor, man, the next time you want to see that damned fool, do it on a Tuesday or Wednesday. That's when I'm off work."

Down the long hallway the sound was beginning, just a tense murmur at first. There was a soft breeze of curious whispers that began to blow harder when a certain isolation cell was approached by the hulking forms of Sykes and Porter. Even from this distance Jesse could see that the two sheriffs were huge, their green uniforms stretched to the limit by too many bench presses and too many pork rib sandwiches.

The murmurs grew into a brisk wind of low utterances as the two sheriffs ducked simultaneously when something was thrown through the bars and at the tops of their heads. The supreme being's special diet had been splattered against the wall opposite his cell. Sliding down the wall were globules and smatterings of white rice, white gravy, white turkey breast, white potatoes, white milk, and mayonnaise. Behind Jesse, Eddy and Dr. Wooden were standing in the hall now, having left their seats as the tide of sound reached them.

"Can't you forget this interview?" asked the officer at post eight. There was desperation in his eyes. "If someone gets hurt on my shift, I'll be here filling out forms until midnight."

"I've got to see him sometime," said Jesse. "And it's never going to be any different. Besides, I canceled the interview last time. Don't you remember? I can't do that again."

Down the hallway the two behemoths had managed to unlock and open the cell door. From the darkness behind the bars a raspy and hate-filled voice was screaming the phrase "mud people" over and over again. Sykes and Porter ducked as more of the food flew through the doorway at them and crashed against the wall behind them. This was followed by a plastic spoon, a paper cup, and finally a roll of sheets and bedding. Around the cell the squall of utterances had transformed into a storm of catcalls and loud discord. From there the tempest of drowsy voices became a raging cacophony.

Suddenly the two officers raised their arms to protect their faces. Then, after counting to three, they disappeared in unison into the bowels of the cell. There was one final cry of "mud people" from within the cage, then deathly silence. A moment later the two officers emerged. There was a tall man hanging limp between them, his feet dragging on the linoleum. He was making no attempt to walk.

The tall man was Clorox white, chalk white—almost deathly white when contrasted with the two men who were at his sides. Even at this distance Jesse could make out blotches of facial color: the roseate, whiskey-induced stippling of dead capillaries covered the man's nose and cheeks. Now he could see that the skin of his entire body was mapped with lines of jade and black. He looked like a human who had been turned inside-out, so that his green veins were on the surface of his skin for everyone to see. His skin was covered with tattoos. His left eye was closed and bleeding.

"Mud people!"

The words spewed out once again from the man in the middle. From the cells that lined the long hallway, spoons, combs, and wads of trash were being thrown at mr. supreme as he moved down toward post eight. The cacophony had become a din, an assault of words in English, Spanish, and Vietnamese. Jesse could see that each of the two huge sheriffs had one arm jammed beneath the armpit of the prisoner and was using the other arm to control one of the prisoner's hands.

"If you spit on me again," yelled Sykes above the terrible noise of three hundred angry voices, "I'll bash your goddamn head against those bars. Do you understand me?"

The prisoner did not respond. He only strained against his human restraints, his green face red with exertion. As he got closer, Jesse could see the shape of familiar forearms and biceps emerging, the result of hundreds of hours in a prison weight room. He could just make out the chiseled, hardened face of his client. Actually, thought Jesse, it was not the face and arms that were familiar but the tattoos on that face and those arms. In truth, no one would ever attempt to describe mr. supreme. Except for the crimson and purple nose, the usual human landmarks were now practically invisible, obscured beneath a collection of acronyms and arcane symbols. Even police bulletins and prison records did little more than describe the writings upon his skin. The identity underneath had long ago been lost.

The Aryan Nation tattoo was the newest and it was located on the forehead, between the eyebrows. The tattoo was so fresh that the needle holes beneath his hairline were still bleeding. The insignia was little more than a muddle of scabs, blood, and ink. Somehow the supreme being had managed to tattoo himself using the broken refill from a contraband ballpoint pen as a needle, and the metal flush handle on the toilet as a mirror.

"From here that thing looks like a third eye," said Dr. Wooden.

"A third eye that's bloodshot," added Eddy.

"Given enough inbreeding . . ." mused Jesse aloud.

On his chest, covering his upper abdomen and pectorals, there was a huge American bald eagle with green wings that swept upward to touch each of the man's shoulders. The defiant head and beak of the creature reached up to his Adam's apple. On the man's arms were several swastikas, a topless hula dancer, and a list of arcane numbers that commemorated the dates when federal authorities had abused their powers by oppressing the only real human beings on earth. Interspersed among these were various badly rendered symbols of the White Aryan Resistance, the Silent Brotherhood, and even the Aryan Olympics.

"What the hell is an Aryan Olympics?" asked Eddy.

"They have events just like any other Olympics," answered Jesse, "only they're held in a trailer court somewhere up in Idaho. They have tobacco-spitting marathons, and I think they toss cans of Spam for distance. There's only one running event because they believe there's only one race."

The din on the mainline diminished and died away when the supreme being was taken through post eight and dragged into the interview room. Sykes pulled out a chair, and his partner roughly shoved mr. supreme into it. The huge black man bent down until his face almost touched that of his prisoner.

"Listen here, Mr. Skelley," growled Sykes, "my name is Norman Sykes, and my partner here is Norman Porter. Any more shit outta your so-called Anglo-Saxon ass and we're gonna have another Norman Conquest right here. Do you get my drift?" He turned to face the lawyer. "Do you want one of us to wait outside the door?"

"No, thank you, officer," answered Jesse, "I think Bernard will be fine."

"Fuck you!" screamed the tattooed man. "Don't ever call me Bernard."

Outside the interview room the huge officer lifted his walkie-talkie to his lips to answer an inquiry about their 10-20, their location.

"Roger, post nine, we're ten sixty-six at post eight, over." There was a huge smile on his face as he slapped his partner's open hand. All the sheriffs who heard it knew that 1066 was not a proper call sign. Most just shrugged and went about their business. Few if any of them remembered what had taken place in the British Isles in that distant year.

"Bernard Skelley," said Jesse, "that's your true name, isn't it? Your Christian name?"

"I don't want to talk to none of y'all muddy son of a bitches! I didn't ask for the last interview and I ain't askin' for this fuckin' interview! If y'all want to talk to me, you can address me correct, as a foot soldier of the New Aryan Army."

"Aryan Army?" asked Jesse incredulously. "Soldier?"

Dr. Wooden and Eddy glanced at each other warily. They had both seen the veins rising in Jesse's neck. They noticed that his fists were clenched and bloodless.

"What would you paintball, potbellied militia idiots know about being soldiers?"

Dr. Wooden placed a firm hand on Jesse's shoulder. The lawyer understood the gesture. Once again, a sudden slice of the nightmares that haunted his nights had lit up his mind like a flare. There had been this hill, a small hill near the Laotian border. He leaned back and closed his eyes for a moment to compose himself. The holographic image that had invaded his thoughts slowly dissipated.

"What you might want, Bernard," continued Jesse in a stern but controlled voice, "and what you ask for are irrelevant here. In fact, you are irrelevant. Do you understand that? It's not my job to help you or to care about your sorry ass. It's not my job to worry about what you want. I can't waste my time with menial garbage. My job is to try and beat this case. You've done your job, Bernard, and you've done it to the best of your very limited ability. You've succeeded in being arrested and charged with a hideous crime."

"Irrelevant!" screamed Bernard. "Irrelevant? Whatever in hell that goddamn word means! You must've learned that big word in some white university on one of them affirmative-action scholarships that I couldn't never get. You sure as hell didn't learn to talk like a white man at no spic university."

"Bernard, you couldn't get a scholarship to pet obedience school. You certainly must enjoy being wrong," said Jesse with a grin, "because you do it so often and so very well. As a matter of fact I went to a spic university. You've heard of Brown University, haven't you? Everybody there is brown-skinned, the whole student body and faculty are as brown as mocha java. Even the buildings are brown. The school is named after Osawatomie John Brown and James Brown, the godfather of soul, the famous Brown brothers."

Now Jesse sat nose to nose with the supreme being.

"After a couple of wonderful years at Brown," continued Jesse, "I went down to Rice University in Houston. It's a school dedicated to the rice-growing regions of Asia and the Southern United States. A lot of Chinese and Thai students go there. But you must've known that!"

"Gook school," muttered Bernard.

"Then I went to Morris Brown, a Jewish-Mexican school where I got a master's degree in shtik—humor from the Catskills, with a minor in Mexican cooking. Are you following all of this, Bernard? When I'm done you can fill me in on your progress toward a GED. For my law degree I went to Cisco College down in Texas. The Cisco Kid started that school after he and Pancho broke up the act and the television show went off the air. Duncan Reynaldo and Leo Carillo were two of my favorite professors."

"Ah, the Robin Hood of the Old West," announced Dr. Wooden with a childish grin. "I myself went to Auburn. It is a school of great traditions. Since time immemorial they have hung a brown paper bag in front of the admissions office, and if your skin was lighter than that bag, you just couldn't get in, no matter how good your grades were." Dr. Wooden closed his eyes to better remember the happiest days of his life. "Before I lost all of my hair, I had the most beautiful three-finger wave you ever done seen."

"Where did you go?" scowled Bernard as he turned to face Eddy, "a fucking Jap school?"

"As a matter of pertinent fact," said Eddy Kazuso Oasa without changing expression, "I attended college at picturesque Peru State up in Nebraska. As you might expect, the student body is mostly Peruvian, though there are a few Bolivians and an Ecuadorian or two. At Peru State llamas and alpacas are allowed free run of the campus and the dormitories. There is a full-scale replica of Macchu Picchu on the campus quad. Japanese students go to school there, then go down to Peru and get elected president. In fact, it will be my turn to be president of Peru in the year two thousand and four. I'm just working as an investigator for fun until I can get my hands on the keys to the presidential palace down in Lima. I can't wait."

Bernard stood up suddenly.

"I'm gettin' the fuck out of here," he announced. "I don't want to be around you fucking mud people and all your bullshit universities."

Jesse rose from his chair and stood in front of Bernard, blocking his pathway to the door.

"You're gonna hear me out, Bernard. If you move one more inch I'll send the doctor and Eddy outside and they'll close the door behind them. It'll be just you and me. Ten minutes from now, everybody—every black, brown, yellow, and red man on the mainline—will know that their favorite prisoner, mr. supreme, got his ass kicked, one on one, by his own lawyer. Believe me, Bernard, it will be my pleasure."

Bernard and his lawyer were face to face, their noses still almost touching. Bernard's face was glowing a beet red around a clenched set of tan, pitted teeth. His eye had swollen shut. Bernard felt the heat in his own face and was proud of the feverish, crimson blush. Blood in the face was the mark of a true white man. No one else could blush like this, not Hindus or Mexicans or Jews.

Bernard Skelley looked down into Jesse Pasadoble's face and despised it. It was so goddamn brown . . . so inhuman. But the son of a bitch didn't seem to be afraid. Bernard considered punching that face—a quick left jab, then a right. But something held him back, kept him from the risk. Why, Bernard wondered sadly to himself, did that traitor Max Schmelling have to go and lose to that black monkey Joe Louis? The whole American South had once gathered around their radios to pray for Max Schmelling. His father had wept with each telling of this tragic story. Every real human being had suffered so much from that defeat. Then there had been those other losers Henry Cooper, Ingemar Johansson, and Jerry Cooney.

"If you hear me out," continued Jesse in a calmer voice, "we'll be gone in ten minutes and you can go back to your cell with all of your personal bullshit intact."

Bernard slowly lowered his body back down to the chair behind him. Jesse nodded toward the doctor.

"Mr. Skelley," said the doctor in a professorial monotone, "on the test that I administered a few weeks ago, you got thirty-one correct answers out of a possible one hundred. Your lawyer got ninety-seven correct out of the same one hundred questions."

"I missed three?" exclaimed Jesse. "I demand a recount."

"It is my strong suggestion, therefore," continued the doctor, "that you let your lawyer handle your case. You have to fight with your best weapon, Mr. Skelley. You know his reputation. I'm sure that some of your friends in the jail have told you about Mr. Pasadoble. Think of it as your using him to get out of jail. Can you do that? Can you use him, Bernard?"

A small smile began to cross Bernard Skelley's lips. Even a clouded mind like his realized that this day could be salvaged. After all, he wasn't paying anything for the services of Jesse Pasadoble. The smile grew wider. He could easily think of his brown lawyer as a slave. This whole building was filled with niggers in black robes and judges with tits. His slave lawyer would know how to handle those kinds of people. He could use him.

"Defend me!" he said suddenly. "Y'all do what I say, now, y'hear? I order you to defend me."

Bernard turned his head toward the wall and spat. A huge wad of speckled spit stuck to the wall, defying gravity. Proud of his work, Bernard turned toward his lawyer and grinned a wide, broken-toothed grin of disdain.

"No doubt about it," said Jesse in a low voice, "the lower your IQ, the more you need to floss. Now, here is how we're going to work this. There will be no more of these useless interviews. I will write out my questions to you on a sheet of paper. I will put a signed court order on the outside of the envelope telling the sheriff's department that they are not to read the contents of the writings, though they may perform a cursory tactile search for contraband.

"You will read the questions and answer them as well as you can. If you have a problem with spelling, just sound out the words or try chewing on your tongue."

Bernard's broken capillaries were glowing with rage.

"If you want to avoid life in prison, answer the questions, no matter how much you may hate doing it. In other words, Bernard, if you ever want to run out to the outhouse again and flog your log to a crumpled picture of Betty and Veronica, answer the questions. If you ever want to drink cheap whiskey for courage and wear that dear white sheet again, answer the fucking questions. Eddy here will pick up each envelope and bring it to me. He and I will work on the case. I don't want any phone calls from you—"

"You sure don't have to worry about that," interrupted Bernard.

"I'm the one talking now," hissed Jesse through tightly clenched teeth. "You're charged with over a hundred counts of molesting one Minnie Skelley, your own niece. When asked who it was that was molesting her, she pointed to a photograph of you in a photo spread of eight people. You could get up to eight hundred years if you're found guilty."

Jesse pulled a photograph from his binder. It was a full frontal photo of the supreme being with his shirt removed. There was the eagle. With her tiny index finger, little Minnie had reached out and touched the right wing.

"At least it's not life," Eddy said. He laughed. Dr. Wooden smiled, then quickly reassumed his professional demeanor.

"Eddy will interview everyone in your family, including little Minnie. I don't want to hear from anyone you know unless it's about the case," continued Jesse. "I will not see you again until we are in a trial court picking a jury. Anything I have to say to you will be in those envelopes. Do you understand that?"

Bernard said nothing.

"Do you understand me?"

"I'm just using you," said Bernard as he jumped to his feet. "The white race doesn't need any of you." He leered at the three men. "Pretty soon we're gonna take our country back."

"I think there's a big Apache fellow down in cellblock C-3," said Jesse. "Why don't you go down there and tell it to him? And while you're at it, tell him your charges. All the boys down on the mainline would love to know that you're charged with having short eyes, with dancing that old ballet rose. Besides, you idiots need everybody. Other than inbreeding and rifle racks, no redneck has ever invented anything. Bernard, if someone like you ran the world," shouted Jesse, who had moved back to a position just in front of Mr. Supreme, "we would still be five hundred years away from inventing the wheel."

"From now on," sneered Bernard, "you will address me as Sergeant Skelley."

"I know about sergeants," said Jesse softly but with great intensity, "and you're no sergeant."

Bernard stepped angrily out into the hallway and walked silently toward post eight. The two huge deputies saw him and ran to intercept him.

"You don't have to go so soon, do you?" Jesse called out in a mocking voice. "You forgot to take a copy of your IQ test with you. You didn't do too badly, Bernard. The job-evaluation index says that you could get a good job as the personal valet to an out-of-work busboy." Jesse watched as his cursing client was escorted to the bars that separated post eight from the mainline. "Y'all come back now, y'hear?" he shouted to the departing figure of Bernard Skelley. Once again projectiles and curses filled the air between the bays. Back in the interview room, both Eddy and the doctor were sadly shaking their heads.

"You shouldn't let him get to you, Jesse. I always feel so disappointed when I allow myself to fall to his level," said the doctor as he packed his briefcase to leave. Eddy, who was still seated, nodded his agreement. Even he had succumbed to his own anger. He reached out to touch Jesse's arm.

"Carolina says you're not sleeping, that you're drinking again," said Eddy. There was a look of concern in his face. "She called last night and we talked for a while."

"What the hell does she know about me?" retorted Jesse angrily. "I haven't seen her in weeks. What I do is none of her business. It's over between us."

Jesse fell silent. He knew that these two men cared about him. He knew that Carolina cared even more.

"We rise above Bernard Skelley by working the case," said Jesse in a barely controlled voice. "We don't have to like him in order to work the case. There's no way I could ever like someone like that and I sure as hell won't pretend otherwise. I can't believe it, doc! Ten years ago you told me that I was going to explode if I didn't let my emotions out, and now you're saying that I'm too goddamn emotional. I wish you shrinks would make up your minds."

"Your pendulum," said the doctor with a sigh, "has got to swing to the middle, Jesse. Ten years ago you barely spoke to anyone. You never smiled. You were almost as hateful as Bernard. This is not Vietnam, Jesse. Life is not a war."

"It's not?" answered Jesse, a look of surprise on his face. "Don't we live in a free-fire zone? There are seventy-five wars going on in this world right now, and only one of them matches the homicide rate in this country. Didn't Skelley call himself a soldier? Listen, doc, I can't stand the bastard, but I will do something that he and his kind could never do. I will stand up for him in a court of law, and I will do my best. Besides, I think I deserve a little anger. It's certainly not like it used to be. I'm not like I used to be."

Jesse's voice dropped as he remembered how it had once been. There had been years of silence and rage. He had transformed every disagreement into a battle, every act of intimacy into an invasion. Then he thought of Carolina. She made him want to succeed, but once again he had failed. Healthy, genuine love had presented itself and Jesse had been paralyzed by it.

"You're not like you used to be," said the doctor, "but you're a long way from where you could be. You've gone from hurting people to helping people, but you still can't do anything for yourself."

"Now, I'm going to have the sheriff bring up Calvin Thibault." Jesse extended his hand to the doctor, who reached out with his own. "Thanks for coming, doc." He had heard the doctor's words but did not acknowledge them.

"That's that double killing up on Potrero Hill, isn't it?" said the doctor with a note of sadness. "What a shame that was. Such a terrible shame. My wife knew those two women. She used to bring home some of their famous spaghetti sauce. Best I've ever had. Such a shame. You've got a hard row to hoe on that one, Jesse. But call me if you need me. I can do a profile on the Biscuit Boy."

"The Biscuit Boy?"

"That's young Mr. Thibault's street name," said Dr. Wooden. "I don't know where it comes from but I first heard the name up at Juvenile Hall. He was always getting picked up for truancy."

When the doctor was gone, Jesse returned to the interview table with his investigator. The tape machine was already set up and ready to go. Next to it was young Calvin's confession on cassette tape. Jesse and Eddy sighed deeply in the calm interim between storms. Down the now darkened and silent hallway, Sykes and Porter had thrown Bernard back into his isolation cell and were now moving to C-block to secure their next prisoner.

"Thibault!" The jailer was rousing the young man from his sleep. "Goddamn it, Biscuit Boy, this ain't Juvenile Hall!" The deep voice reverberated down the hallway. "You can't cry in here! You're an adult now. You're in adult jail. You done killed two women who never did you no harm. Time for crying is long past. Now, get your little raggedy ass up and go see your lawyer."

Calvin struggled to stand on his feet but the warped space around his bed kept sucking him back in. Calvin stretched, trying to break his gravitational bonds. He moved his lips and tongue, smacking them in order to stun them back to life. They had been numbed into senseless clay by their very first taste of dead time. Finally, he was able to pull himself up by grabbing the bunk just above his own. The occupant of the upper bunk cursed fitfully, then rolled over. Calvin yawned and eventually stepped cautiously away from his mattress for an hour or so of extravehicular activity.

Jesse and Eddy waited in silence, the taint of Bernard's presence still hovering in the room. Then the lawyer opened a binder to a certain page, closed the binder, and leaned toward his investigator.

"The little girl Minnie Skelley said in her taped statement that the thing she remembers most about each episode of touching and of digital penetration was the eagle that flew above her head. She said that she saw that eagle every night for two years. It's strange that she would say in the same taped statement that she was only molested one night a week. She indicated in her second statement that the actual acts of rape did not begin until just a few months ago. Minnie could not see an eagle during the rapes but she says it was the same man who molested her. Why couldn't she see the eagle during the rapes?"

Jesse was silent and sat with his eyes closed as he thought about the seeming discrepancies. Had she seen her assailant every night? Had he left her in peace six nights of the week? Had there been only manual molestation on those six nights? Was the little girl having nightmares?

"What is a ballet rose?" asked Eddy, recalling the phrase from Jesse's outburst at the supreme being.

"It's a phrase I learned a long time ago, in Vietnam. Well, I didn't learn the exact same phrase, but its counterpart. A ballet rose means lewd acts with an underage girl. Some dance, huh? Some dance."

Eddy shook his head sadly. He was a man who loved children and cats.

"It doesn't look good, Eddy. I can see the prosecutor right now, demanding that Bernard Skelley stand up in front of the jury and unbutton his shirt. Unless things change, the jury is going to see that eagle tattoo and spend more time picking a foreman than deliberating. But I happened to notice in the discovery package that Bernard's brother Richard and his family moved to San Francisco about six months ago. That means that the rapes happened here but most of the molestations happened over in Oakland. I think you've got to go over there for a couple of days."

"Check out the old neighborhood?" asked Eddy.

"Yeah. Talk to the neighbors. People of color might have something to say about a family like this one. There's bound to be a lot of juicy gossip in the streets and over the back fences. They lived near the Acorn project, didn't they? In the midst of the enemy? It's pretty unusual for a white family to live in Ghost Town. I'm sure they rubbed a lot of people the wrong way. Talk to the little girl's friends. Talk to her schoolteachers and the school nurse. They'll have their suspicions. Who did Minnie confide in? Anything you can find."

"Workplace, acquaintances and habits, and a complete family tree," added Eddy without requiring a response.

"See if you can get into their old house. If they had to move in a hurry, they might have left their furniture and possessions with someone else. Get some pictures," added Jesse. He turned to the laboratory analysis and forensics page. Bernard was a secretor: his blood type could be found in his semen and his spit. The lab tests looked bad, but they had only done A-B-O and P-G-M testing. Bernard had not been excluded by either method. Both tests had included him. He wondered why they hadn't done DNA testing, then the image of the eagle reappeared in his mind's eye. Perhaps it was best that they hadn't. The defense would have to commission a DNA test to be done on the sly.

"When you get back here, start working Potrero Hill," said Jesse, turning to Calvin's case. "Maybe we can go over the ground together. I'll need everything." Jesse sighed, pleased with the fact that he would not have to tell Eddy how to do his job. Eddy was independent and inquisitive and would overlook nothing. "I need everybody's life story on Biscuit Boy's case, too, especially the victims'. Get me the 911 tapes and your synopsis of the evidence to date. Did you look at the autopsy photos when you picked them up?"

Eddy Oasa nodded his head in the affirmative. "There is no justice in this life," he muttered. The sight of the two women was still haunting him. It was the fervency of the embrace that had both enthralled and saddened him. In those color prints he had seen a double death grip that had spoken so much more eloquently about life . . . about their lives.

At that moment Calvin Thibault walked slowly, sleepily into the interview room. He was about to say hello when Jesse gestured with a hand to silence him, then signaled sternly for him to sit down. Confused, Calvin started to speak when he was shouted into silence and into a seat by an angry lawyer.

"Here are the rules for tonight, Mr. Thibault," said Jesse forcefully. "You will not say one single word tonight. Do you understand?"

Calvin was about to answer when Jesse lifted his hand once again. "No! Just nod your head if your answer is yes and shake it if your answer is no. Do you understand?"

Calvin nodded his head. There was fear and confusion in his young eyes. The residue of tears still clung to his cheeks.

"Eddy, play the tape for the Biscuit Boy."

The investigator placed the cassette tape into the recorder, then pushed the play button. The hard baritone voice of Inspector Normandie could be heard giving the date, time, and location and the identities of the parties present. Then the questions and answers began. After a few preliminary queries, Jesse sat up in his chair and told Calvin to pay close attention.

Q: You know the shooter, don't you? Don't shake your head. The tape machine can't see you shake your head.

A: I don't know who he be. He had on a mask. I swear, I don't know who he be.

Q: It was Little Reggie, wasn't it? It was Little Reggie Harp?

A: I don't know no Little Reggie.

Q: Funny, you were arrested with him less than a year ago. Don't lie to me, Calvin.

A: I was arrested with him? I been arrested with lots of guys. I never heard of him. I ain't never been convicted of nothin'.

Q: You went to the Amazon Luncheonette with somebody, didn't you?

A: Yeah, but I ain't never saw him before. I just met him on the hill. We was both going the same way. That's all.

Q: So you knew that person was goin' up the hill to see the women?

A: Yeah.

Q: And you knew he had a gun, didn't you?

A: When? What you mean? I don't know nothin' 'bout no gun.

Q: You didn't shoot the women, did you? We know you didn't
do that, Calvin, so don't worry about that. You don't have to
worry about us callin' you a shooter. You ain't the shooter.
You don't have to worry about that at all. You ain't the button man.

A: I ain't shot nobody. That's right. Nobody.

Q: That's right. That's right. But you did see somebody shoot
those women, didn't you?

A: Yeah.

Q: He did it with a gun, didn't he?

A: Yeah.

Q: So you knew he had a gun, didn't you?

A: Yeah, I guess so.

Q: You saw him aiming at those women, didn't you, Calvin?
And you knew that Little Reggie was crazy?

A: Yeah. He always be shootin' at shit, cats and dogs and passing
cars and stuff. But I ain't never saw Little Reggie or nobody
do nothing. The man had on a mask.

Q: So you knew he was gonna shoot them, didn't you? And
don't give me any shit about a mask. Fifteen witnesses saw
the shooter's face.

A: No. I ain't knowin' that!

Q: He was aiming at them, wasn't he?

A: Yeah.

Q: And he's always shootin' at shit. You said that yourself just a
second ago. When you aim a gun at something, you shoot it,
don't you? You don't aim a gun for nothing. So you knew he
was gonna shoot, didn't you?

A: Yeah, I guess . . .

Q: That makes you just like the shooter, doesn't it? You knew
what he was like and you knew he had a gun and you were
with him. That makes you just like the shooter, doesn't it?

A: I guess.

Q: In fact . . . in plain God's truth, you were the shooter, weren't
you, Calvin? You just want us to believe that Reggie's guilty,
don't you? You don't want us to believe that you did it. Isn't
that true?

A: I don't understand. I guess.

Q: You've seen that gun before, haven't you? In fact you knew
    just where to hide it.
A: (*Inaudible*)
Q: Is that a yes? Is that a yes?
A: Yeah.
Q: Now, I want you to sign this statement, Calvin. It just says
    what we just agreed to here. It says you ain't the shooter. By
    the way, that's good for you. That's real good for you. It says
    that you was with somebody that could be Little Reggie. It
    says that you knew this guy had the gun and that you knew he
    was gonna shoot them women. It says that you wanted us to
    believe that Reggie is that shooter and you aren't. It says you
    hid the gun after the fact. Now, sign right over here. No, not
    there! Right here by that X.

Jesse nodded toward his investigator, who reached over and turned
off the cassette player. There was anger in Jesse's eyes once again as
he reached into his binder for a sheet of paper and handed it to the
defendant.

"Is that your signature? Just nod. Did you bother to read it before
you signed it? I didn't think so. When is the last time you read a
book? One year ago? Two years? Just hold up one finger for each
year."

The boy shrugged his shoulders, then held up all ten fingers.

"Do you think your illiterate soul is worth saving, Calvin?"

The boy shook his head, no.

"You are going to do what I say, Biscuit Boy. Your puny little life,
for whatever it's worth, belongs to me now. Your ass belongs to me.
Do you understand? You ain't in the world no more. From this day
forward I am your family, your mother and father. I am your best
friend. Look around you. You are in the armpit of the world, the asshole of the world."

He was echoing the words of every drill sergeant from Fort Lewis
to Parris Island.

"Here's a book." Jesse reached into his briefcase, then threw a
paperback book at his client. It was *A Gathering of Old Men*, by
Ernest J. Gaines.

"Read it. Look carefully at the language. Read each word aloud.

Feel each word on your tongue. Once a week you will copy one paragraph from that book and mail it to me. My address is inside the front cover. I also want a paragraph from you explaining why you picked that particular paragraph. When you're done with that book, I'll give you another one.

"From this moment until the jury files back into the courtroom with a verdict, you will not say one cuss word. Not one 'shit,' 'fuck,' or 'damn.' Do you understand me? Not one cuss word to Eddy or to me or to any of those fools down on the mainline. I will give you three dollars a day for your commissary. Every cuss word will be one dollar less. The sheriffs will tell me if you've got a foul mouth. Do you understand?"

Calvin nodded without lifting his eyes. He was staring downward at the book. Just turning its pages would require all of his strength. It would take all of his energy to fight off the lethargy of eighteen years in the projects and the seductive, soporific gravity of his bed. His universe had been the Potrero Hill dwellings. His was a world without clocks, without books, without schedules, without a reason to wake up or a good reason to go home at night. It was a world without the need for specificity.

In his world, adverbs and similes had been allowed to wither and die and drop from the vine. Past tenses were all but extinct. Like the larger world around his projects, metaphor and symbol had already perished along with literary allusion.

"You have to learn about words. Your fate will be decided by words, Calvin," said Jesse pensively. He wondered how on earth an angry mute like himself had chosen a profession based on words.

"The prosecutor and I will reconstruct the murders of Persephone Flyer and Mai Adrong using only words and a few pieces of hard evidence. He will prosecute you with words and I will defend you with them. He and I will jump up and down in the courtroom objecting to the use of words and to the words given in response to questions. Your fate will be rendered in words. You're not on the street anymore, Calvin. The courtroom is a war of words, and you have almost none at your own disposal. The days back on the street corner, when a vocabulary of two hundred words could get you by, are long gone."

"Two hundred words are enough for a confession," said Eddy.

"Yes," groaned Jesse, "enough for that, confession. One final thing, Calvin. You and I and Eddy are gonna have a secret sign language, just between us. It's like the signals that soldiers use in the field. It's like a code. We will begin using this sign language at our next interview. Now, look at me and pay close attention. There are five signs that you will have to recognize and learn to follow. I'll write them down for you. When I fold my arms like this it means you are talking too much, shut up. That's the first sign. And"—Jesse smiled—"it's my favorite.

"When I run my hand through my hair like this, it means that I want you to explain further, to elaborate. You will find out what that word means later. When I rub my nose with my left hand it means you are becoming too emotional, too angry. If I rub my nose with the right hand it means I want you to become emotional, I want you to cry."

A startled look came over Calvin's face. Despite the fact that he had just cried in his cell, he did not consider himself a crier. He did not cry. Calvin opened his mouth to protest, but Jesse quickly folded his arms.

"You'll cry when I tell you to cry, Calvin. Piss on your damned pride! Otherwise we'll both be crying when they sentence you. Do you know what a sentence of life without possibility of parole means, Biscuit Boy? I'll tell you what it means. A long, long time from now in a prison that has yet to be built, a young prison guard will rap on your cell door to see if you've taken your medications. By then you'll be on heart medicines and kidney dialysis and you'll have an artificial liver. You won't move, so he'll unlock your cell door and discover that you've died of old age. Well, Calvin, that young prison guard's grandfather hasn't been born yet."

Eddy winced at the story. He looked into Calvin's eyes and knew that the boy had not really understood the story. Jesse had seen it, too.

"Now, there's one final sign. When I stand up, it means you're volunteering information. It means you're not listening to the question. You need to listen to the question and answer just the question that was asked and nothing more. Five simple signs, do you think you can remember them?"

Calvin nodded.

"Good," said Jesse with a tired voice. "You're gonna get a lot of practice and I'm gonna jump on your ass every time you fuck up."

Jesse leaned forward, toward his client. It was clear to him that the boy was months away from even the most basic understanding of the true danger of his situation. He would keep trying to find an example that would hit home.

"The courtroom is like an orphanage, Calvin, and the jurors are there to pore over all of the children and choose one to adopt . . . which witness to believe. Do you know who it is that people adopt?"

Calvin shook his head, no.

"They adopt a child that looks like themselves. People want a child who matches their own skin color and eye color. If they can't have that, they take a child that they can mold in their own image. Everyone takes the infants and the toddlers and passes over the older children, who already have fixed tendencies and personalities. In the end, the most needy kids are always the least likely to be chosen.

"There will be twelve white people on the jury, Calvin, and they will all be looking right past you, right past a person who doesn't look a thing like themselves. They'll adopt that nice boy-next-door prosecutor or that handsome cop, but not you. Even if you speak the truth, they won't hear it if it has an accent or comes from thick, black lips. They certainly won't hear it if it's filled with sidewalk jargon and street slang."

Jesse was silent for a moment as he pondered his own words.

"Don't worry, Calvin. They don't listen to poetry either. Listen," said Jesse in a calmer voice, "don't talk to the police. You probably don't know it yet, but that police inspector on that tape had you for lunch. He made that confession for you. Never talk to anyone in your cellblock about your case. Above all, don't talk to that Little Reggie if he or one of his boys comes to visit you." Both Jesse and Eddy noticed the fear in Biscuit Boy's face at the mention of Little Reggie's name.

"In a couple of weeks I'll let you speak. Then you can tell me why they call you Biscuit Boy."

A small smile crossed Calvin's face, but disappeared just as quickly as it had arrived. Jesse yawned, then nodded toward his sleepy investigator, who immediately began packing his briefcase to leave. The two men stood up and stretched, then Jesse signaled to the deputy at post eight that the interview was over. As Calvin was being led back to his cell, Jesse turned toward his investigator and whispered, "Little Reggie Harp sure has that boy scared to death."

"He probably threatened to kill someone in Calvin's family," answered Eddy. "The cops can't find him. He's just disappeared."

"You'll find him," said Jesse. "Just make sure he doesn't know you're looking for him. Everyone says he's cold-blooded."

Eddy nodded, then asked his friend a question.

"What do you think the jury is going to do tomorrow in the Vung case?" He was referring to a case that had gone to the jury for deliberations just two days before.

"I think they'll have a verdict. Tomorrow's Friday and they'll want to go home and not have to come back on Monday. More than three days on that kind of evidence is hoping for too much. I'm praying for a manslaughter," said Jesse, "but, as you know, I've got a bad feeling about this one. I only wish that stupid Vung had allowed us to help him. I've never done a trial where the defendant has refused to say a single word to me."

"Or to me," added Eddy solemnly. "This is the first time I've ever had to deal with the Vietnamese community. They're an insular bunch."

"If he hadn't threatened all of the witnesses and their families, we might have been able to find out what really happened at that party. It's how they handled cases back in the old country: scare the shit out of the witnesses and say nothing to the lawyers. No, I think tomorrow morning we'll be counting papers."

A confused look came over his investigator's face as the two men stepped into the elevator.

"The jury has to work its way from first-degree murder downward, so if the foreman hands the judge three pieces of paper it means we've got a voluntary manslaughter, not guilty of first- and second-degree. It could also be an acquittal, but I don't expect that. If he hands him two sheets, it's got to be a second-degree murder. They don't have to fill out the third sheet. In my dreams I've been seeing just a single piece of paper. I wake up two or three times a night, covered in sweat."

Eddy knew what Jesse wasn't saying about those dreams—that they were mild disturbances compared with the other dreams that tormented him every night of his life. On trips to other jurisdictions, when the two had shared a hotel room, Eddy had witnessed the savage impact of those nightmares.

"*Ay Dios mio*, that Bao Vung is one hardheaded Vietnamese dude.

Cabeza de piedra. He won't even talk to the interpreter." Jesse's voice dropped to a whisper. "He reminds me of someone I met over twenty-five years ago in Vietnam."

Jesse's mind flew backward twenty-nine years to one of the two dreams that tortured him each night. Both dreams always left him bathed in sweat, though one was a cacophonous orchestra and the other a quiet duet. One ravaged his sleep, while the other seduced him, made him follow hopefully, before stabbing him from the shadows. One was a counterpoint to the other. Every night of his life there was a man in his dreams.

As he walked from the elevator, Jesse knew that tonight would be no different from any other night. One of the two dreams would seize him in the dark, reach out from the grave and ambush him in the small hours of the morning.

For years it would take him hours to fall asleep afterward. Over time he lost some of his fear of these visits from beyond life. In a perverse sort of way he actually began to look forward to them. Two men who had perished long, long ago had become Jesse's most intimate acquaintances. He had met one of the men in Dong Ha and the other in a prison camp in Da Nang. The first was an African-American staff sergeant.

The other had been an enemy soldier.

4

french lessons

A ghastly line of bodies had been hastily arranged by the side of the road. Some clean-shaven troops from psychological operations had dumped them there in the burning heat of midday for the edification of the villagers. The word had been put out that they had all been killed in a firefight. A small dog and two war correspondents in tailored combat fatigues, ignoring the swarm of flies, were moving up and down the row of the dead like careful browsers at a weekend garage sale. The skinny, friendless dog would nuzzle here and there for something loose and organic.

Every now and then one of the human shoppers would spot a potential gem and bend down to squint at it, to place it within a frame, to consider it through a zoom lens. Here was a featureless grimace, gaping and frozen forever by a tide of napalm. There was a genderless, timeless gray child whose body might have been pulled from the ashes of Pompeii. A small eruption had just opened near the child's belly and liquid secrets had begun to boil out. The rest were the generic indigenous dead, their bodies twisted and insulted by a variety of high-speed metals and phosphors.

The photographer from the *Stars and Stripes* finally gave in to the reality of his constituency and backed away to take a long, sterile shot. His newspaper was not interested in photojournalism, only in raw numbers and morale-boosting photos. The slender woman from *Paris Match* lingered pensively over the child, the smoke from her cigarette curling up and around the body of her camera and into her face. An ash from her Gaulois fell and melted into the child's body. Her eyes scanned the charred form for an unburned clearing in the landscape, for a poignant contrast, a mole or a birthmark or a single indication of gender.

Across the road from the spectacle was a group of silent children, orphans dressed in torn and dusty clothing. The face of death was nothing new to them. There were black flies crawling in their living eyes, and their bloodstreams were teeming with malarial beasties. The security of family and village had been torn away from them at just that tender time when their minds would be wholly preoccupied with play. Still possessed by curiosity, they had all come to marvel at the woman's long blond hair. In an hour or so they would begin again to worry about food.

A third man joined the photographers. He was a soldier, a buck sergeant in the U.S. Army. Without hesitation he moved directly to the end of the line and to the body of a particular young man. He moved with such speed and purpose that the two correspondents took note of it and lowered their lenses to watch him. They both sensed that something unusual was happening. Why would an American NCO be interested in the corpse of a North Vietnamese regular? Was he one of those wild-eyed, catatonic GIs who collected ears?

After staring downward at the corpse for a long moment, the buck sergeant stepped forward. He inspected the pants and the sandals, then knelt down and carefully began to undo the buttons on the man's tunic. There were two entry holes in the man's chest but there was no blood, not on his skin or on his shirt. The soldier moved his face to within mere inches of the other's. He noticed that there were deep wrinkles on the forehead and about the open eyes of the dead man. These signs of severe distress were new.

The sergeant placed his hands on either side of the man's face and tried to turn the head to the left, but it wouldn't move; rigor mortis had already set in. So he turned the entire body onto its side, then bent forward to inspect something closely. Their faces were so close that he could smell what had once been the breath of the other. Something he saw there made him shiver and sigh. He exhaled deeply, then let the body drop. He buttoned the shirt, stood up, and walked slowly away.

Could that be sadness in his eyes? *C'était impossible.* The dead man was the enemy. Did this soldier kill the other? Could they have known each other? Should they interview him? He had a name tag but neither had caught his name. The photographers watched him as he walked past them, then suddenly, becoming aware of each other and of their own confusion at what they had just witnessed, they clumsily glanced downward to check their shutter speeds. Squinting to consider the fading light, they quickly stooped to adjust and re-adjust their f-stops until the moment of awkwardness had passed.

"Monsieur sergeant, connaissez-vous le soldat?" the tall, blond woman ventured. Then, remembering herself, she said, "Do you know this soldier?"

Just one week before, the corpse at the end of the line had been alive. Sergeant Jesse Pasadoble had been waiting for a flight up to the compound at Dong Ha. From there he would be going on to some godforsaken outpost near the Laotian border. He had three or four days to kill before the chopper lifted from the tarmac. A close friend of his, a staff sergeant, had chosen him for a special assignment and had talked him into coming along.

"Well, Sergeant Pasadoble, you still hanging around Dong Ha?" the staff sergeant had asked in a chiding tone. "You think you ain't in the world? You think this is the asshole and the armpit of civiliza-tion? There's gonna be a special operation soon. If you want to see the real Nam, you best come along. *Venez avec moi, mon ami.* You've got some in-country R&R coming. Go on down to Da Nang and get yourself some real food, and maybe even catch a movie. After that, come with me. *Venez avec moi.*"

Sergeant Pasadoble had been wandering around the secured area of Da Nang and had stumbled upon an enclosed and heavily guarded prison yard. Surrounding the enclosure was a twelve-foot Cyclone fence topped with thick loops of razor wire. There were three heavily armed guard towers, and military police everywhere. Ser-geant Pasadoble noticed that except for one prisoner, the yard was empty.

He was in the exact center of the yard. The man was sitting shirt-less in the boiling sunlight, his brown legs crossed and his un-blinking eyes staring straight ahead. The entire contents of a box of c-rations were arrayed in a semicircle that began with his left knee and ended at his right. He was sitting there alone. All his fellow pris-oners were gathered in small groups, smoking Kools and Salems in the shaded areas provided for them at each end of the long yard. Now and then, one of them would nod or point toward him and the rest of the men would laugh out loud.

The sergeant walked toward the Cyclone fence and stopped only when a voice above him called out rudely, "Hey, man, what do you think you're doing?" He turned to see a flabby, oafish-looking PFC staring down at him from a guard tower, his M-60 machine gun canted downward.

"What do you think I'm doing?" Jesse answered. "I've never seen an NVA this close and alive." North Vietnamese Army regulars did not usually accept capture, or so the story went.

"You can look at the slimy bastard," the private first class answered, "but pull out your magazine. We can't have you snuffing out one of our charges, now, can we? Not that any of us would really give a flying shit." He laughed and winked as he lit a cigarette with his Vietnam edition Zippo. As the guard was speaking, the mute man sitting in the center of the prison yard had stopped gazing at the infinite and had begun to stare at the visitor. He watched as the sergeant walked to the foot of the guard tower and leaned his M-16 against one of its wooden legs. The guard overhead nodded his approval.

"Go ahead, look at gooks all you want, sarge, but don't touch the wire. Touching the fucking wire is number ten, you bic?"

Before walking back toward the fence Sergeant Pasadoble removed his helmet and flak vest. As he neared the fence, the North Vietnamese regular rose to his feet, then gathered his rations into a pile and placed them on a light shirt that had been spread out on the dirt beneath him. Without taking his eyes from those of the American soldier, he lifted the sleeves and the tails of his shirt and with his makeshift bag began walking directly toward him.

To his right and his left his fellow prisoners suddenly ceased their animated gestures and their conversations and focused all their attention on the two soldiers meeting at the fence. Both men could feel the eyes of the guards staring downward at them. The sergeant could hear the voice of the PFC explaining into the radio that everything was okay, he just wanted to see a gook soldier up close and breathing. What had been a noisy, raucous yard a moment ago was now as silent as a Buddhist monastery.

Jesse stopped just short of the fence and watched in silence as the enemy walked toward him. So this was the man he had glimpsed through the lens of a starlight scope. This was the man who could run full speed in the highland blackness with a rocket launcher on his back. Here was the man who ate next to nothing, who sent no letters home and received none. Here was the man with the better mythology: Americans are sent here to fight against an evil and undefinable thing called Communism; to fight for blue jeans and convertibles and full-color foldouts of big-breasted blondes. This man was sent here to die—to expel the Japanese, the French, the Americans from the soil of his ancestors. His mythology contained less myth.

He was wearing black thongs and had the wide feet of a farmer. He wore the dark-brown pants that were the standard issue in Hanoi. They were threadbare and soaked with sweat. His body was thin and muscular, his face angular and wide. His nostrils had an indignant, almost arrogant flare and the skin around and above his eyes was as smooth as porcelain. His complexion was darker than that of most Vietnamese and his hair was black and curly above a high and almost regal forehead.

When he got within five feet of the fence, one of the ARVN guards screamed something into a bullhorn, and the man froze in his tracks. He raised both arms into the air, took another step forward, then squatted down, indicating that he would go no further. After a long moment of immobile silence on both sides of the wire, the NVA soldier smiled broadly, almost childishly, then reached up to grab a shock of his own hair. With his other hand he pointed at the American sergeant.

"You same-same me," he said in pidgin. His voice was high-pitched and musical. War had not altered his civilian timbre. He released his hair, then ran his fingers over the brown skin of his cheek, then over his brown, sunburned forearm. "You same-same me," he repeated.

Having used all of his pidgin language, he asked a question in Vietnamese. Sergeant Pasadoble shrugged, then shook his head. There was a look of intensity mixed with frustration in his face. "No bic," he said, indicating that he did not understand. Neither man had bothered to learn much of the enemy's language. Both knew a few cruel and derogatory phrases, a few crude words of command or interrogation, but not much more.

"You," said the NVA, still trying his pidgin, "*không den, không trang; no negro, ni blanco.* You Español?"

"*Habla Usted Español?*" said Jesse excitedly.

"No. *Poco, poco. Beaucoup Españoles en Marseille.*"

"*Marseille? Français? Parlez-vous Français?*"

"*Mais oui,*" said the regular, his smooth face suddenly transformed by an electric intensity. "*Etes-vous Español?*" he asked.

"*Non,*" answered Sergeant Pasadoble, immediately caught up in the common language, "*Je suis Mexican, Mexican-American.* Do you know where Mexico is?"

The regular nodded his head, yes. "I've seen it on the maps, but I am ashamed to admit that I know nothing of it. But I have noticed that many of your troops speak Spanish."

"*C'est un pays de sang melé.* It is a land of mixed blood, Spanish and Indian. It is just south of the United States. Contrary to popular thought, it was the Mexican people who crossed the land bridge thousands of years ago and populated China and the rest of Asia."

The Vietnamese laughed with his whole face and body. Behind him, his fellow prisoners were buzzing with suspicion. The flabby PFC up above spat with disgust.

"So it is you who are responsible for *les Chinois*, the Chinese! I have always wondered who to blame for that."

Sergeant Pasadoble and the NVA soldier laughed loudly at the joke, for a moment forgetting the war that had brought them together as combatants. The sudden burst of laughter turned heads from one end of the compound to the other. Suddenly a voice boomed out over the loudspeakers: "Sergeant, this visit is unauthorized and must terminate immediately."

Jesse stepped back from the wire and walked toward the guard tower.

"Who is the commanding officer of this compound?" he asked the oafish PFC. When the answer was shouted down to him, Jesse grabbed his gear and walked in the direction of a heavily fortified hooch just north of the compound. In half an hour he returned to the tower with a piece of paper signed by the company commander. He waved the document at the PFC and shouted, "I can talk to him for one hour a day for the next three days."

"Whatever turns you on, sarge," answered the PFC. "Personally, I'd rather visit the bar girls on China Beach. I love that Saigon tea."

On the fourth and last visit, the Vietnamese soldier seemed unwilling to limit the conversation to the lighter subjects that had dominated the first three visits. After a few passing remarks about Mexican food, American jazz, and Brazilian soccer, the man behind the wire grew quiet. The smile on his face faded as the enemy soldier asked something that he had always wanted to ask an American.

"I am sorry to ask this question, *mon ami*, but I must. I know that we will never meet again, and I believe you to be an honest man. So I must ask. In the north of my country, the children are told in school that all the people of color in the United States live in a separate country. They are told that white Americans are rich and they throw thousands of gallons of milk into the ocean to spite the poor of the world. They are taught that teachers are not allowed to teach their students. *Ces choses-là, sont-elles vraies?* Are these things true?"

After considering the question for a few minutes, the sergeant answered, "It is true that dairy farmers in America have been known to pour milk into the gutters when an overabundance has driven prices down. It is also true that there are many hungry people in America who could drink that milk. Schoolteachers are sometimes forced to go on strike when the classrooms grow too large or their paycheck has become too small. It is both a protest and a labor tactic. Their strikes do not fare well, because teachers are not as respected as they should be. So I guess what your children have been taught is true, but it is not the truth."

The North Vietnamese soldier nodded his understanding. The truth no longer surprised him.

"And do you live in a separate country?"

Sergeant Pasadoble placed his right index finger on the center of his own forehead. "We do," he said.

"Ah," sighed the regular, *"je comprends!"* He nodded his head. "I am a Chàm," he said. "Some people say we came from India long, long ago. Some say we came from Indonesia. We have a completely different way of writing and we speak a dialect that is like no other in Southeast Asia. Any radio communications between our troops—if we have a radio—is done in Chàm, since no Vietnamese, north or south, can decode it. Centuries ago we were conquered and then subjugated by the Vietnamese. Since that time we have never had an equal place in this country.

"Because I am Chàm, I must sit alone in this yard." Just before his smile died away, he replenished it when he suddenly remembered an obvious courtesy that had been completely ignored. *"Pardonez-moi.*

Je m'appelle Hong Trac." He bowed as he said his name. "I have known you for four days and I have not given you my name. I am so sorry."

After repeating Hong Trac's full name several times until the enemy soldier nodded enthusiastically that the pronunciation was correct, the sergeant countered with, "*Me llamo, Je m'appelle Jesse Pasadoble. A sus ordenes.*"

Hong found the name Jesse easy to pronounce. "Do you know where we are, Jesse?"

The sergeant looked around himself and shook his head, not really. In Vietnam, all Americans lived in a separate country. Few, if any, GIs tried the local food or bothered to learn any of the language. Most passed their entire tours without ever speaking with a Vietnamese.

"This area is called Thành Bình." Hong used his hands to indicate the area outside the compound. "The name means 'peaceful place.' As a child I lived not three blocks in that direction, on Thanh Long Street, the street of the Blue Dragon. Have you been to Marseille, Jesse?" asked Hong.

Jesse shook his head, no.

"I once lived in Marseille for two wonderful years. I love that city more than any other on earth. The last time I was there I met the woman I was destined to marry. As a child, I was fortunate enough to have parents who could send me to lycée in the Bouches du Rhône. How is it that you speak French?"

"I have always dreamed of traveling," said Jesse. "Since my Spanish isn't too bad, I took French in high school." Jesse hesitated for a moment, then added, "I had a girlfriend who spoke French. She was from Quebec. And I figured with three languages I could go just about anywhere in the world."

"*Vous avez raison.* You're right about that," said Hong. "But you must go to Marseille someday. The port is magnificent. From the hills above the sea it is easy to imagine the Crusaders leaving in their wooden boats for the Holy Land. Sit in the coffee shops or on one of those green benches on the Canebière and just listen . . . just listen.

"Marseille is great simply because of all the people like you and I who must go there. It is beautiful because emissaries of separate countries have conferences at every café. There are cultural exchanges in every doorway. Besides," he smiled, "Paris is too cold for dark people like you and me."

As he said it, Hong was smelling the sweet steam of bubbling bouillabaisse, nursing a cup of hot espresso, and listening for a moment to the conversations that once surrounded him: the sharp and muffled snapping and cooing of a lovers' quarrel here; the directions to an address near the Château d'If over there; at this table a lonely old man is openly disgusted with the writings of Jean Genet; at that one two Belgian students are worshiping Miles Davis. In Hong's nostrils was the acrid odor of African tobacco and the haughty, self-conscious scent of Swiss perfume.

"What are you taught about us?" he said with a calm and distracted air.

"In America they say that you Vietnamese do not value life."

Hong laughed a dark, sardonic laugh.

"If that is true, then why do I fear death so much?"

As he spoke, memories of diving Huey gunships and B-52 strikes filled his mind. Of the hundred and sixty men in his original company, only five were left.

"When the bombs fall, I curl up like a trembling child and I pray that death will be painless. No, Jesse, life is a valuable thing. I know that I will soon be losing mine." Grief suddenly began to cloud Hong's large eyes. "I will never see Marseille again. Even now my dear wife Hoa is waiting there for me."

"You're not going to die," said Jesse. "You're a captive and the rules are specific regarding prisoners of war. For you this conflict is over. You'll get three square meals a day, a shower, and a place to sleep. You just have to wait it out, then go home."

Hong smiled patiently.

"Do you see those men behind me, Jesse? Soon one of them will be taken away to be questioned. That one will quickly decide that the loss of a Chàm is a small price to pay for his own survival. So he will tell them my title: that I am a high-ranking infantry officer. They will come for me in another day, perhaps two days."

"They kill prisoners out in the bush, Hong, but not here in a secured area."

There was a sad desperation in Jesse's voice. The anonymity and heat of combat were one thing, but to kill an unarmed prisoner in a secured area was murder. There was no hot blood here.

"They don't shoot people here, Hong. They won't shoot you. You can take my word for it."

"You're right, Jesse," said Hong with even more patience.

"There is a soft and fat South Vietnamese colonel in that metal building"—he pointed to a Quonset hut just outside the compound—"and he has a good friend who is an intelligence agent from your army. I've seen them drinking Korean beer together. It is said that they have a very special way of torturing prisoners. They use a *tournevis*. It is just a rumor; no one can say for sure because no one ever comes back from an interrogation."

Jesse culled through his French vocabulary for the meaning of the word *tournevis* but found nothing. At the same time, he wasn't sure that he wanted to know.

"They place it into the ear and drive it through the brain with a carpenter's hammer."

As he said it, Hong placed a cupped left hand over his left ear. He wondered which of his precious memories would die first. Would it be his memories of childhood on the Street of the Blue Dragon or his memories of lovely Hoa in Marseille? Then there was that very special memory of a night in Orléans. It had been their first night of nakedness.

For days he had been sitting alone in the prison yard using all of his powers of concentration to shift his memories around so that the first to go as the hammer fell would be his days as an officer, his rousing, stupid days of ambition and war lust. He had passed the few last hours just before meeting Jesse by weighing his recollections, determining their priority, then arranging the stages of his military career along a straight line from ear to ear. All of his other memories were dispersed to other countries, other continents of the mind, far from that line.

When the *tournevis* was driven in behind his eye sockets toward his right ear, the muscles of his face and the airy tendons of his spirit would strain to protect an ember, to shelter a single flicker of light and hide it safe in the ruin and wreckage of his soul. He would be there once again, looking up from a coffee-stained volume of Baudelaire to see her for the very first time, her jacket and arms closed desperately around a stack of falling books and her large eyes casting back and forth for a place to sit, a dry, safe place out of the rain. Hoa's gaze would meet Hong's in that small instant and life would truly begin.

Without uttering another word, Hong rose up from his squatting position and dropped to his knees as he fully embraced that moment so long ago. All at once his head fell forward and he wrenched his arms behind his own back as though they were being rudely bound.

"Hong," cried Jesse, "*écoutez-moi!*"

"What's the matter with him?" called out the oafish PFC. "Is he dinky-dau?"

No matter how hard Jesse tried, Hong would say no more; he would answer no more questions. Jesse pleaded with Hong, but the regular would not respond. The words and visions in his mind were too scrambled now for communication with the living. He had spoken his last words.

"*Connaissez-vous le soldat?*" the French photographer asked Jesse one week later, as she stood among the dead. Then remembering herself she said, "Do you know this soldier?"

Jesse stopped walking when he heard the question. He turned to face the two correspondents, the dog, the orphans, and the line of dusty corpses.

"The one on the end, his name is Hong Trac!" he screamed at them with his arm extended and his finger pointing.

There were bullet holes in his body but they were bloodless and had been put there long after death. They were meant to simulate the effects of a firefight somewhere out in the bush. In Hong's left ear there was a narrow rectangular slot; an empty mineshaft that plunged downward through soft cartilage into the auditory canal, and from there it sliced and severed the optic nerve and pons, blunting memory after memory like a ravenous disease of the aged.

"His name was Hong Trac!" he said again, quietly this time, but with the same intensity. He then turned to walk away but stopped in midstep. Without turning to face her, he asked the Frenchwoman with the long blond hair, "*Que veut dire le mot 'tournevis'?* What does it mean?"

A confused look came over her pretty face, but she shrugged and decided to answer the question, but only in exchange for one of her own. As she spoke the sergeant was already walking away.

"Did you know him, sergeant?" she asked in a raised voice. "Did you know that man?"

"No," said Jesse to no one. "But he surely knew me."

"A *tournevis*? Why would you ask such a question in a place like this?" she called out after him in her lovely French accent. "*Qu'est-ce que c'est que le mot en Anglais* . . . what is it? Oh, yes, I know. It is what you call a screwdriver."

The buck sergeant walked for hours. With his head down and his rifle slung uselessly across his back, he walked alone and far into the night, the living and the dead face of Hong flooding his mind. An old woman on the sidewalk preparing *canh chua*, fish soup, looked into his eyes as he approached. She shivered at what she saw and quickly turned away.

"*Chào bá,*" he spoke softly as he passed.

The old woman lifted her head at the sound of the greeting. "*Chào em,*" she answered with a smile. Then she shook her head as she watched him disappearing into the dark of Công Húa Street. Between here and China Beach there would be dozens of snipers who would gladly put a bullet through his head. She said a silent prayer for the foreign buck sergeant as she stoked her small cooking fire. He was from the other side, but tonight he was not the enemy. She had been fooled at first, but his voice had told her that the simmering redness in his eyes had not been hatred.

"*Chào em,*" she repeated as he disappeared into the darkness.

At daybreak Jesse Pasadoble would lift off on a gunship headed to the DMZ. From there he would fly on a Chinook to a small hill near the Loatian border. Grunts on the Ch-47 noted with derision that he spoke to no one and kept to himself.

Jesse stood staring through a small window as the chopper filled with cigarette smoke and aimless, nervous chatter. Visions of Hong and his wife in Marseille still crowded his mind. Through the dirty glass porthole the buck sergeant who kept to himself saw images of southern France—villages, bicyclettes, and boulevards—and not the endless gray and green of the Central Highlands of Vietnam.

When Jesse finally sat down in the chopper, he felt a strange sense of anticipation. Despite reports of heavy contact near the hill, he felt eager to get there. The thoughts weighing upon his soul were far too much to bear alone. Whether or not he would ever confide in them, there were two friends waiting for him on that hill, a black staff sergeant named A. B. Flyer and a new friend, a man of letters and of sensibilities . . . an army chaplain.

5

the infamous blue ballet

For endless hours the remote and elevated jungle garden had been battered mercilessly by brutal shards of blinding light. A calamitous din had followed closely behind each flash—discordant jumbles of shattering impact and sharp, desperate shouts. Creatures formed in the image of God had staggered backward from the western perimeter in strobe-lit steps, as the powerful slam of a rocket-propelled grenade collapsed a sandbag bunker.

Each trip flare that had flashed in the yellow darkness had drawn the bullets of a dozen riflemen. Shaped mines had been detonated sequentially, sending wide, overlapping arcs of shrapnel into the forest and into squads of bewildered, then suffering men. Red tracer rounds flowed out in lazy, lethal sweeps. Above it all there had been the occasional yellow glare of star shells drifting serenely beneath their tiny silk parachutes. Everywhere, below curling plumes of smoke, there had been countless cries for help in a dozen separate tongues.

In the darkness, ephemeral flowers of concussive flame like red trumpet vines had flashed into bloom, then had receded, to quickly wither shut in accelerated time, in savage salvos of impossible time. In the air, callous leaden spores had burst forth from their casings, seeking out the perfect bodies of young foot soldiers. The fruits of physics had been harvested here.

In the first light of day and far into the descending heat of evening, the small hill remained stunned, shivering, and confused. Somehow the age-old laws of geological time had been reversed in an unnatural, confounding instant. Molten magma had poured from the sky and splashed down onto a perplexed earth, fiery calderas had cracked open everywhere, cinder cones and vents had erupted with no pressure from below. Above its ruptured topsoils, the hill was spiteful and suffering beneath its freshly wounded crust. The crest was smoke-enshrouded, and down below, in its deepest bedrock, the hill had been rudely torn away from the ancient comfort of tectonic, subterranean rhythms.

Two groups of men had met on one face of this hill, and their savage intentions had left every tree limb and twig disfigured. Unwatered since the last monsoon rains, the small hill of dry and cracked earth had been sickened to nausea by this forced feeding of burned sulfur and human fluids. Here and there intrepid flowers persisted between fissures and foxholes, their soft petals and thin stems choked shut by the savage spray, the crimson effluence of exit wounds. Against their will, the living poppies masqueraded as roses.

In one place, a ragged patch of hair follicles and skin soiled the stigma and stamens of a weeping blue blossom, repelling bee after bee. In another, scores of red seeds had erupted from human bodies, bursting violently through the drabness of cloth and skin—seed of stomach, seed of lung, hopeless grains set onto the wind. Everywhere, shell casings littered the garden like brazen chaff.

Among the wide spray of innards was a slice of cerebellum, a single sliver of mind, thrown yards from its previous owner. On a stem of wild lemon grass hung a taste for grape soda and shepherd's pie, the memory of her goodbye, even the newborn baby's impulse to cry when the world was upside down. On a leaf of wild lemon grass specks of sense were stranded and fading—three digits of a phone number, a single syllable from the second verse of a cherished song, and half a glimpse of a woman's entire face.

At the top of the hill, drying in the sunlight, was an array of green pods: plastic bags snapped shut and steaming from within. A chaplain crawled among them, calling out to God and screaming the names of the newly dead at the top of his lungs. His body shook with palsy as he went from bag to bag retrieving a dog tag and their personal effects and marking soiled paperwork with their names and the date of their death.

A sergeant by his side was helping him with the grisly duty. Below them, grunts were laying out more concertina wire, setting new trip flares, and replanting the hill with claymore mines. Behind the landing pad, the bunkers that protected the radio emplacement were being rebuilt by a gaggle of shirtless, wordless men.

"Try to calm down, padre," said the black sergeant. "Tonight's gonna be our last night in this place. I'm sure of that." He had a smooth and soothing Southern accent. His voice was a round baritone with a burnish of gentleness that belied his muscular build and serious eyes. A hint of both French and of Dixieland seasoned every sentence he spoke.

"I just talked to battalion. I gave them a sit-rep from hell and they won't dare leave us hanging like last night. You have my word on that. Now, take some deep breaths, padre. Otherwise you're gonna bust your heart wide open. I've seen it happen. Like the boys always say, keep your shit wired tight."

The sergeant's words were slurred. He had almost bitten his tongue in two during the last mortar barrage. It was a terrible habit that, perversely, the sergeant had grown to love. The feel of bloating and the taste of blood in his mouth meant that he had survived once again.

"After tonight we can blow all this equipment and di-di back to Dong Ha. I can get me a cold beer and a *Playboy* magazine and you can go on down to Da Nang and rip off some of that sacramental wine and talk philosophy with that captain friend of yours. Da Nang will calm you down. It's surrounded by beaucoup marines, Special Forces, and the Ameri-Cal. As for me, I don't mind Dong Ha. Sure, it's a damn toilet, but there ain't nothing to worry about in Dong Ha except them eight-foot rockets and them nightly probes by Victor Charlie."

The black sergeant was smiling and softening his language for the chaplain's sake. There was nothing to smile about. The only words appropriate to this place were obscenities. He deeply regretted talking his friend Jesse into joining him on this mission. The air support last night had been gravely inadequate: two Huey gunships and a single pass by a pair of fast movers. The jets had shot their wads, then had streaked home for a pizza and some Korean beer. Because of the distance from here to their home base, they had no loiter time over the target. Someone in Da Nang thought this hill had a low priority.

"I can't stay another night," moaned the chaplain. "I just can't stay another night on this hill. I can't hold it together. I hate the holes on this hill. We're digging our own graves. I hate living in this grass. I hate living in holes, and I hate hills and I hate all the insects in this godforsaken country."

The look of profound anguish that had settled into his eyes during the night hovered on his entire face like a permanent shadow. Inhaling deeply, then holding his breath, he snapped open the last body bag and began to sob uncontrollably once again. It was the Russian boy from New Jersey, the one that had "John Wayne" written in large script on his helmet and tattooed on his right arm.

"Someone ought to shoot John Wayne," whispered the chaplain, his voice breaking and a small trickle of blood moving downward from his left nostril to the notch of his upper lip, where it mixed with the smelling salts he had smeared on earlier.

"Yeah," sighed the sergeant, "for someone who never picked up a real gun, he's sure gotten a lot of American boys killed."

They both stared downward at the muddy white face of the handsome Russian boy. His face had once been beautiful. Now there were swatches of torn skin spread from shoulder to shoulder like leaves on a pillow. There was insect predation already visible. He was a naturalized citizen with an unpronounceable name. His buddies had simply called him Roosky. Neither dared open the snaps any farther. There was little left below the chest. His tattoos and his birthmarks had been liquefied by a mortar round, a direct hit. The contents of the bottom half of the bag would never be shown in any war movie. No actor would ever suffer these wounds.

Last night had been a heartless flurry of extremes; straight lines of inexorable energy had moved oblivious to topologies, ignoring the palm of a hand or the curve of a tree. Vectors had burst randomly as planned. War had happened last night: the sensate had been placed in the same space as the senseless.

The chaplain checked the boy's dog tag for a religious preference. His fingers shook as he lifted the small neck chain, then pulled at it to view the tag. The words No Preference were engraved into the burned metal. Using his thumb, the chaplain made a cross on the boy's forehead. Behind the boy's body bag his helmet was perched atop his M-16, its muzzle pushed down into the dirt. An hour ago his platoon had stood down to honor him and the others.

Hours ago the padre had become heart-sickened at the ticklish rubbing of his own selfish and cowardly lips against the earlobes of the dying. Despite all his best efforts, he had puked at the sight of open chest and stomach wounds, at the fragile plumbing, the crimson jellies and brackish rivulets just beneath the skin. He had never been able to stare at God's secret baggage without revulsion, and that revulsion had degraded his prayers until they were little more than feckless mumblings. His sickened face had, itself, become a profound betrayal, a ruthless mirror that showed pleading, desperate boys that there was no prayer in heaven or on earth that could keep them or their image alive.

"I have to close his eyes," whimpered the padre. "I've got to close his eyes."

"Why?" asked the sergeant. "He slid out of his mother's sack face up with his eyes open. Now he's slid back into a sack. Let the poor bastard see where he's going."

It had occurred to the young chaplain this morning that a man's intestines and kidneys looked remarkably like wet plastic bags filled with ocher and purplish fluids. Fibrous plastic bags filled with putrid juices seemed so carelessly jammed into the tightest spots beneath the ribs. He chuckled painfully at the thought of people dressed up and out on dates carrying those bags inside of them; they spoke of classic beauty and sighed at the depth of love while those hideous bags gushed and gurgled inside of them.

"All we love is skin!" he screamed.

The sergeant beside him said nothing. Trench madness was something he had seen before. He had experienced it himself. Some folks still called it the thousand-yard stare or combat fatigue, stupid euphemisms for the effects of unrelenting terror. The sergeant hated euphemisms. In a place where battles were seldom won by anyone, the number crunchers and accountants in Saigon had gone crazy with them. Casualties had evolved into "acceptable losses" and from there to "limited breakage" or projected "spillage." There was even a set of words for civilian deaths caused by military operations: "overspray" and "overkill."

"Love songs were written for intact skin!" muttered the chaplain, who sobbed uncontrollably as he spoke. "I am a fucking fraud."

At another time he would have winced at the vulgarity of his own words. He had recited the Extreme Unction into the ears of scores of eighteen-year-olds and he had never once had the strength to "sell the prayer," as they called it at chaplain's school. How on earth can you be a thespian when a severed artery is spurting all over your script, when desperation is always stepping on your lines? Out of craven fear he had rushed his prayers. Like a drunken, harried actor he had mumbled his way through his forgotten lines. He had ushered his boys—his flock—off to eternity with a shoddy, extemporaneous supplication ringing in their ears.

The padre raised his eyes to the horizon. In a single night he had acquired the combat veteran's hardened eyes and numbed face. Out there somewhere, the sermons were already being said for the Russian boy. The swing shift at graves registration in Da Nang would already be generating an inventory of his parts and categorizing his remains as unviewable. Apprentice morticians would scurry for a shot at his corpse. A forklift at a warehouse near China Beach would be taking his aluminum casket down from the high, shining stacks. It had been made for him. The metal had been smelted, stressed, and formed especially for him. Before the Russian boy was born, the aluminum ore had been dug from the ground just for him.

Forms would be filled out in duplicate directing that other forms be filled out in triplicate. In some Quonset hut in Da Nang the boilerplate notice of death and letter of condolence were being cut by a clerk-typist, a private first class with just one month in country. Somewhere else a bored captain whose short-timer calendar was almost completely filled would sign a tall stack of such letters using a rubber stamp of his signature.

In just a few days Roosky's mother would find the dreaded letter in her mailbox. She would wait long, terrible hours before opening it. Her unheard wails would assail the walls of her little home with unremitting grief. In one instant her soul would flood with every bedspread that she had straightened for him, every bowl of borscht and every meat pie that she had ever cooked for him, every laughing sigh at his seeming inability to change his dirty underwear. Someday, somewhere, his two brothers were lying awake at night straining to recall the features of his face. Someday, somewhere, fingers were already reaching out to touch cold, dark marble, to follow the deep, chiseled letters of his engraved name. Somewhere a flag was being folded, corner to corner to corner. Now it is being placed into the hands of a woman.

"I am the resurrection and the life. . . ." The chaplain groaned, using his forearms to cover his own contorted face. Hours ago he had tried his best to speak into this boy's ear, but the sight of a perfectly formed concha and an unstained lobe amidst all of the ruin had overcome him once again. The sweaty, bloody boy had expired without forgiveness.

"Combat makes the skin permeable, doesn't it? Doesn't it, sergeant? Everyone here is covered with blood and sweat and piss. That's what it's about, isn't it? We're protecting our innermost fluids while trying to cause leaks in the skin of the enemy. There's even a technical word for it, isn't there? An ugly acronym: SLUD. Salivation, lacrimation, urination, and defecation."

"Padre," said the black sergeant patiently, "can I tell you something? *Ecoutez-moi un moment.*" The padre nodded without uncovering his sickened face.

"After this, after what you've seen here, your old life is nothing but a lie."

After a moment of silence the chaplain responded weakly, "What do you mean?" The statement had struck its mark at the very center of the chaplain's soul. His own life was truly nothing but a lie.

"When you was back in the world, there was happiness and sadness, of course—car accidents, promotions, demotions, tragic illnesses, and birthdays. Sometimes you was sick, but mostly you was feeling *trés bien*, feeling pretty good."

The chaplain nodded weakly. His eyes were still dilated and his skin was clammy and gray with shock. His former life now seemed like a dream.

"Now and again a close relative passes on; someone who seemed happy turns around and blows their brains out and some completely unworthy fool goes and wins the lottery. Remember the world, padre? Now, padre, let's say that your old life was a car with a nice, big speedometer on the dashboard. When you was happy, you would be cruising along at sixty. Top speed was around seventy miles an hour. When you was sad, your life would be pokin' along at ten miles an hour or sometimes even slower."

The chaplain dropped his arms and opened his eyes, squinting at the unbelievable ugliness around him. In the clearing at the base of the hill, a suffering North Vietnamese soldier lifted his arm straight into the air. From somewhere to the right a shot rang out and the North Vietnamese soldier slumped and died, his final request granted.

"Please forgive me, but I don't understand what it is you're trying to say."

"Padre," continued the sergeant calmly, "since you been to the Nam, since you been on this red dirt hill, that old speedometer of yours has just got to be tossed out. It's outdated. It's junk. Now you understand that there's happiness far beyond sixty miles an hour, and there's sadness and grief way, way down below zero. Do you remember how happy you were this morning when the dinks who breached the western perimeter were stopped and the incoming ceased and you found yourself in one piece?"

The padre nodded. There was extreme joy and a hint of shame in his nod. His relief at having survived was an ecstasy beyond expression and beyond measure. His relief had been beyond holy.

"Think about how sad you are right now about that boy's death, about all of their deaths. You're feelin' it now, padre. That old life of yours back in the world was a lie. You had a small speedometer, padre. A tiny, pathetic little gauge up there on the dashboard of your existence. Until something goes terribly wrong, everyone back home is idling in first gear. All of them are asleep. Before you came here, padre, you was idling, too."

There was simmering anger in the sergeant's voice. " 'War' was just a word in some politician's mouth. 'Combat' was a word that bartenders and sportscasters used to describe a football game. 'Sudden death' was something that jocks looked forward to in a game that's gone into overtime. 'Next of kin' was just a phrase, just a bunch of faceless people back in the world. It was all a judas-goat lie, like John Wayne wading through Japanese soldiers on Iwo Jima, and them recruitment posters."

The two men moved to the last body bag. Beneath the flap and closures was the decimated face of a brand new first lieutenant. He had been platoon leader for exactly two days. The chaplain shook his head violently, so the sergeant opened the bag and removed the dog tags. He tore one tag from its small chain, then placed the other one into the mouth of the dead soldier. The first tag was handed to the chaplain. The sergeant lifted the first lieutenant's jaw to close it, then snapped the bag shut. The tag was designed to be wedged into the matching gaps in the upper and lower front teeth, then the jaw would be jammed shut by shoving the chin. But the sergeant had never been able to do it.

"Remember all those folks that come on the television after surviving an airplane crash? They all say that their life has been changed forever, that they're really gonna appreciate their life after coming so close to losing it. The grunts over here, the boys with their asses in the grass, they go through a plane crash every fucking day, sometimes every hour. No matter how much preparation you do or how much equipment you got, when there's contact with Charlie everything falls to shit, it's one terrible accident after another.

"I don't give a good goddamn about all them fancy plans and code names them brass-plated idiots over in Da Nang dream up—it all falls apart out here. *Je les emmerde!* But out here, no airline sends a team of psychologists to help them." He pointed to a group of troops below. "Nobody will ever give a shit. No one will ever come along to readjust their speedometers. If they get out of here alive, they will always be running at a different speed. A normal day back in the world won't even register on their instruments. The world won't move them no more. Whether you live or die, once you been here you become invisible to normal people. The ones that live ain't never the same." The sergeant paused. "There ain't no justice out here, man, there's just us."

The sergeant placed an arm on the chaplain's shoulder.

"Look here at these young ones, padre." The sergeant gestured down the hill toward another group of men. "Shit, they ain't figured out how to undo a brassiere or how to ask a woman for a date yet, and some of them will never get that chance. And here they're supposed to solve the great mystery! Don't none of them even know what the question is, and here they've got a face-to-face look at the final answer. They're the toughest motherfuckers on earth, but they're just boys, bedwetters and jackoffs. You'd think a fair God would let 'em have one fuck before they get blown apart, just one little old mercy fuck."

A new flood of perspiration had broken out on the sergeant's face. It was not the salty sheen of hard labor or the oily slick generated by fear. It was the pure, plaintive sweat of helplessness, the sweat of a childhood fever.

"These boys are fighting a two-front war, padre. That was the mistake the Germans made in World War Two. They're fighting the Vietnamese and they're fighting America, too. For most of these black kids the army is the first time they have ever been allowed to sit and eat with whites—at least they can in this platoon. Back in the world, you never see what you're looking at right now: Mexican kids talking with blacks. It's rare, even here. Shit, I've seen platoons that are as segregated as Selma. Some of these boys from the reservations ain't never seen a white man except on television, and here they're fighting for him. Shit, this fucking police action ain't nothing but a turf war. Today it's ours, tomorrow it'll be theirs."

The sergeant dropped his head and was silent for a moment. Beads of sweat fell from his forehead and nose.

"Did you notice, lieutenant, that beside some of those Montagnards over there, you and me and the skipper over in HQ are the only grown-up men here? Shit, some of them zips that breached the wire last night don't even have pubic hair yet. *C'est un ballet bleu infame!* That's what this is, *un ballet bleu infame.*"

The padre's contorted face somehow managed a look of confusion.

"The infamous blue ballet," translated the sergeant. "The infamous blue ballet is a French phrase that means lewd acts with underage boys. That's exactly how it's described in the French penal code. That's all this fucking war adds up to, lieutenant: lewd acts with boys."

The sergeant whimpered, then drew his sleeve across his face and cheeks. He wondered why he had waited so long to speak his mind. He had been a good soldier for so long that he had never seen the good in thinking about the bigger picture. Down below, in a bunker on the northeastern quadrant of the perimeter, a grizzled old Montagnard corporal repeated the sergeant's phrase: "*Ban vũ balê xanh nõi tiếng.*" The infamous blue ballet. His old eyes had seen the French boys in these same trenches, and the Japanese before them. He had heard the phrase before. He had witnessed this same form of pornography time and time again.

"You've heard their crazy philosophy discussions, haven't you, their supposings?" asked the sergeant. "I know you've taken part in some of their bull sessions, I've heard you. These boys have two choices out here, either give in to the obscenity or do something to try to keep their sanity. Kids that see this kind of shit always got a lifetime's worth of questions to ask. Death don't just brush by you out here, it takes your head in its jaws and sticks its thick tongue clear down your throat. It's the French kiss from hell. You have to give a shit, padre. It's your job to give a shit about these guys. Please excuse my French, but, shit, right now is the first time that you're really capable of it. *C'est la* goddamn *verité*. That's the God's truth."

Behind them, on the range of high hills that hid Laos from view, the sun was just setting. The clear sky was beginning to fill with stars at its western edge, and fingers of amber were shooting up toward the Southern Cross.

"Now you know what terror feels like, padre." The sergeant lit a cigarette. He had quit smoking on his last trip home, but out here, cancer didn't mean shit. "I could never have explained it to you before. The old elephant came and sat on your chest, didn't he? The lightning bolt went through your asshole and up your spine. The electricity is still there, ain't it? It'll burn for years."

The chaplain nodded. The sparks were still dancing on his spinal column. The fear had been overwhelming, suffocating, completely debilitating. The fear had been bestial. He had been paralyzed by the desperate, selfish need to survive. Even hours afterward, his muscles were still quaking spasmodically, coming down from a deluge of adrenaline. The muscles of his jaw were swollen from clenching, his teeth hurt, and his intestines ached from the internal pressure. His mouth and gums burned with the tides of bile that had risen, then fallen in his esophagus all night long. His ears were still ringing from the reports of a hundred rifles, and his knees ached. He had probably crawled ten miles over the face of this hill following the medic from wound to terrible wound.

"You've met the beast, padre. You peeked into the dungeon and caught a glimpse at the secret. Now you know what those boys know. To live, you would run with spiked boots on a sidewalk made of newborn babies. You would step on your dear sweet mother's face to keep from getting dismembered, to keep from having your nuts shot off. You've learned that every bullet Charlie takes raises your odds of leaving here alive. But it ain't all bad. Amazing as it seems, padre, there is one benefit to having your brains and stomach slow-cooked by hatred and fear."

The sergeant turned to face the sunset. The chaplain watched, relieved to be distracted from the body bags. The Creole sergeant tossed his cigarette away, then unbuttoned the top button of his sweat-stained tunic and leaned forward while exhaling a blast of warm air. His face almost touched the ground as his lungs emptied. He then began to unwind slowly, inhaling deeply but with consummate control. The padre watched as amber strands from the sunset seemed to dive down from the sky, coalesce into a small aurora borealis, then flow into the sergeant's mouth and down into his lungs. The whites of the Creole soldier's eyes began to glow with the inner light.

"Once you been here, padre," whispered the sergeant as he held his breath, "you can taste a sunset. Everyday air will feel like liquid water on your teeth and tongue. Even the smallest moments, the tiniest ideas, will have their own special flavor. Nothing is ever the same again. *Jamais la même.* Nothing. Back in the world they will think you are crazy. If you make it back to the world, you'll find that you ain't got a home no more." The sergeant exhaled the sun as he spoke.

"Do you have a family, sergeant?" asked the padre, amazed by the display.

"I have a beautiful wife who I don't deserve," answered the sergeant with some reluctance. Suddenly a thought stung him, a poignant thought that carried with it a bitter taste. Why had he never inhaled her? Why had he never sucked in her words just as they left her lips? There had been a time when his eager tongue had probed her throat for the merest possibility of a syllable. Why had he never inhaled her?

He had gone home between tours but found that he couldn't be alone with her anymore. He couldn't sit and smooch or watch television or choose a restaurant for Saturday night dinner. He had been distracted and unable to sleep, incapable of small talk, but worst of all he had been a liar. He could make love to his wife, but he couldn't love her. There had been physical relief in their bed, but no passion.

Pensively, he exhaled another chest full of golden light. He and his wife had made some business plans, but his heart hadn't been in it. He had brought the war home with him along with his luggage and the jungle rot in his crotch and shoes. Here in Vietnam was where he belonged, but even here he had made mistakes.

"Hey, padre, let's play us a game of suppose," said the sergeant, wanting to distract himself from the memories of his wife and the horror at hand. He knew that the chaplain had long, outrageous conversations with some of the men in which they collectively rearranged history, and the world and its laws.

"Let's you and me talk about a different kind of world. You might call it philosophizing, but with these boys, it's called supposing. Let's suppose this. Let's suppose that. Suppose you tell me what you and Jesse and them were supposing yesterday."

"Cornelius wondered what America would be like if there had never been any African slaves," answered the chaplain after closing his eyes and inhaling slowly to collect himself and his thoughts.

The sergeant laughed. "That's some supposin'! What answer did they come up with for that one?"

"They had some remarkable ideas. They supposed that there would be no jazz in America, which also means that the blues and rock-and-roll would never have happened in the States. Jesse and Cornelius supposed that jazz would have been born in Morocco, where French, Spanish, and African rhythms would have collided. Billie Holiday, under another name, would've sung her songs in French."

"*Alors!*" cried the sergeant. "*Mademoiselle Billie Jour de Fête.* She would have sounded so good in French!"

"They further extrapolated that the collision of African music and Welsh-Irish that became rock music would have taken place on the Normandy coast, where Celtic roots are still very strong. Jesse supposed that because of the immense popularity of Moroccan jazz and Afro-Celtic rock-and-roll, French would be the predominant language in the world today rather than English. French ballet, not yet set in its ways, would have been transformed by Africans into improvisational and fusion ballet. They would be tap-dancing in Calais. It seems that everything turns on jazz."

"That Jesse's got some strange notions. *C'est vrai. Il est original,*" mused the sergeant, who realized in the same instant that he seldom lapsed into French these days. "Everything turns on jazz, eh? I kinda like that one. Everything turns on jazz."

The old Montagnard corporal down below echoed the phrase, "*Moì thú dêù lên nhac jazz.*"

The sergeant rose from his knees and shaded his eyes to survey the western perimeter, his platoon's area of responsibility.

"Well, the bunkers are back together and the perimeter is as good as we can get it," he said, still shaking the persistent image of his wife from his mind. He noticed that each position had been dug in deeper than usual. "After last night, none of these boys will be digging any bullshit bunkers. Still it's not much of a night defensive position. If we put listening posts thirty meters out, we'd be shaking hands with Charlie. Because of all the brush down there the killing zone is real shallow. Too damn shallow. The LZ ain't really secure, but it won't get no better than this. Thank goodness the fifty-calibers are working. If we get some support, we'll be all right. I wish to hell the chain of command up here wasn't so green."

He looked downward at the chaplain, who was still kneeling. On any other day the frightened face before him would have angered him. On any other day he would have given the platoon leader's bullshit speech about fear being the true enemy. But the tears on the padre's face had become the tears of his wife, his face had become hers. He saw her piercing eyes beneath his brow. She had seen through everything. Even on that last night in San Francisco, she had seen his distracted and dying heart.

"The dustoff choppers will be here in a little while," he said in a strangely gentle voice. "If there's room after they load these here bodies and the walking wounded, you can go back to battalion. I know you won't fire a gun, padre, so it don't matter to me what you decide to do. I need guns up here, not religion. But no one should have to die for this shitty mission. Before you leave, padre, I'll tell you a little something about this mission. I guarantee you're gonna love it. I sure hope the choppers brought some resupply, more gun juice and more star shells. We can't work without light."

A shiver ran down the length of the sergeant's back as he anticipated what would happen without resupply and reinforcement. The NVA in this sector was a disciplined corps, while his own troops were like a pickup band in Harlem, players from everywhere. The sergeant took a heavy, hard step and the dust on his boots rose like a cloud of steam around his bloused trousers. It was a step of resignation, of acceptance. The LZ wasn't really secure. His wife had been right.

Down below the sad array of green pods, below the Creole

sergeant and the frightened chaplain, a group of young men had gathered to smoke and to calm one another down. Except for a swatch of olive drab here and there, they were all the same color as the clinging red dust around them. They moved and spoke awkwardly, sleepwalking their way through wave after wave of inexpressible grief and fatigue. The hair on the napes of their necks would be standing for hours, their semipermeable skin would crawl for days.

The ground around them was littered with shell casings, claymore bags, ration cans, discarded harnesses, and torn rucksacks. There were broken sandbags everywhere, smoke grenades, and the ominous wrappings that had once held field bandages. Here and there were the empty pith helmets of the North Vietnamese.

"Jesse," said Cornelius, a young black man from Oakland, "how come a college-boy pogue like you is here with his ass in the grass like all us illiterate grunts? You ain't eleven-bravo, is you?"

Cornelius was referring to the military occupational specialty number for an infantryman.

"You too smart for eleven-bravo. Is you one of those spooky crypto dudes?"

Cornelius was tall and thin, impossibly thin. His skin color had gone past black and looked purple in the sun. All of his classmates at Castlemont High School had been unmerciful with him for four full years. Back home at chicken dinners with his family, his mother had set aside all the gizzards and chicken skins for him to eat, but it had never made any difference in his weight. She'd made rice and gravy just for him using nothing but rice, flour, and pure bacon drippings, but the boy never gained a pound. She made him suck on spoons full of Crisco, but his skin remained stuck to his ribcage. No one knew where he got the strength to lug an M-60 machine gun around. An extra barrel and belt of cartridges were strapped across his narrow back. The letters FTA were written on every square inch of Cornelius's clothing, flak vest, and helmet. Fuck The Army.

"I went to Berkeley for one year, two semesters," sneered Jesse with a distracted, stunned air, "and I'm here because I'm a fucking idiot." His voice was raspy and brittle. He could not keep his teeth from chattering. Death's tongue had reached down into his small intestines. He removed his flak vest as he spoke, then used his T-shirt to wipe the mud and sweat from his face. He didn't mind the questioning. No one did. Conversations after great sorrow were now a necessity of life. They often took strange and unforeseeable twists. The discussions had a life of their own. They had to.

"Jesus," Jesse said softly, "I think I aged ten years last night. I never, ever want to go through that again. My teeth are all loose from the stress. My gums are black. I've had enough of this."

"Now, even I know you ain't no idiot," said Cornelius. "First time I talked with you I could tell that right off. Word is you coulda been the driver for a full-bird colonel." He placed both hands on an imaginary steering wheel and managed a smile as he spoke. "Now, that would surely be the gravy train." He smiled. "Colonels don't get shot in this here war. A man who drives for a colonel done fell into a real fat spot."

"Shit," said Jesse, trying hard to shake the fear and shock from his thoughts, "that's ancient history. They offered me that job way down in Bien Hoa when I was still pissin' stateside water. The colonel almost shit when I turned him down. They got so pissed at me that they sent me up to the DMZ, to Dong Ha, the armpit of the fucking world. The day I got there the Tết offensive kicked off. I swear to God, the second I stepped off that chopper some sappers hit the ammo dump. The zips were probing and pounding that place for weeks."

"You avoidin' the question, my man," insisted Cornelius. "I've heard you talkin' that *parlez-vous* French with them Montagnards and talkin' that Mexican lingo with Mendez and Lopez. You must've done something real bad to end up here with all the bloods and spics. How did you get on this hill? And why the fuck are we up here guarding a fucking radio installation in the first place? And why the hell does Charlie give a shit about this place when I sure as shit don't?"

"We're a communications relay," answered Jesse in a hollow and mechanical voice. "Something is happening out there past the free-fire zone and across the border—air strikes, black operations. You saw the crypto guys that they airlifted out of here yesterday?"

"Yeah, just before the feces come into contact with the fan," said Cornelius with a disdainful laugh. He hated army intelligence. They were never right, and they never stuck around to see what happened when they were wrong. Last night they had fallen all over themselves in their mad dash for the safety of the choppers, all the while assuring field command on the hill that there were no NVA units in the area larger than platoon strength. The chicken-shits left behind most of their equipment, two half-full cups of warm coffee, and three battalions of seasoned North Vietnamese regulars with mortars and heavy armor just beyond the treeline.

"Those army intelligence officers sure know how to stand by their predictions," sneered Jesse as he recalled the special treatment that had been given those men. They had been hustled off like a gaggle of spoiled, self-indulgent celebrities. By now they would be buying Saigon tea for some half-naked bar girls in Da Nang. Right now they could be eating slices of pepperoni pizza at the Special Forces compound or swimming at the Air Force pool near China Beach. Jesse shook his head in anger. They didn't draft college kids, and the boys with the lowest test scores in boot camp were stuck in the infantry. It was always the sons of the poor who ended up on hills like this.

"I think we're a conduit into Laos from I Corps command in Da Nang, that's why we have both a tropospheric scatter dish and a line-of-sight relay system," explained Jesse.

"*Jesus, hijo de Dios!*" moaned a voice with a Mexican accent. Someone wanted a translation of that last sentence.

"Someone very far away is talking to somebody just on the other side of the Laotian border," explained Jesse. "It's all scrambled when it comes through here, and they're rotating codes and frequencies every twenty minutes. Everything's in code. Top-secret shit."

"Shit is right," said Cornelius. "It's them CIA fuckups again. I shoulda known it. I shoulda known! I bet the spooks is sticking them poor South Vietnamese rangers in there again, trying to infiltrate the troops that is coming down old Ho's trail. It never fucking works," said Cornelius disgustedly. "Poor bastards always get caught and the CIA always leaves them twisting in the breeze, pretending it never happened. I tell you, if the CIA ever wants my black ass to do anything, I wants the money up front, in small unmarked bills. Talk about the gravy train, all their fuckups are a secret."

"Yeah," said Jesse, "I've heard it described as an insertion operation. I've been told that the spooks have been pouring money and guns into some turncoat Pathet Lao cadre. They're supposed to help with the infiltration. They've been doing the same thing above the

DMZ for years. But hell, for all I know, everything I've heard is bullshit. But getting back to your question about how I got here, the staff sergeant over there convinced me to come. He said that my ass needed to be farther out in the grass, that Dong Ha was easy street compared to the bush. He knew that in my confused heart, I wanted to come and see what the grunts were up to. I know how to fix all the radio equipment up there, and you needed a second RTO, so here I am."

Jesse pointed toward the PRC-25 at his feet, a radio the size of a large rucksack that had a very conspicuous antenna. The first radiotelephone operator was lying in one of the body bags at the top of the hill.

"I speak *pocho* Spanish because I'm Chicano, and passable French because I once had a girlfriend from Quebec. She was one sweet thing. I haven't had much opportunity to speak French until I came to the Nam. A lot of the older folks here still *parlent Français*; some of the Montagnards, some of the bar girls, and all of the Catholic nuns do. Sometimes the Sarge and I practice our French on each other. It comes in handy over here."

As he spoke, the image of Hong Trac's cold body lying by a roadside back in Da Nang pushed its way back into his mind's eye. He could hear the sharp clicking of the photographer's camera. The blond hair of the French woman was the last image to fade from his mind.

"But that's all I'm going to say about my past. It's really not very interesting. Right now all I want is to be any place on earth but here, but I'll settle for a Thai stick, a bath, and two weeks in Singapore. This boonie shit ain't for my ass. I can't believe I volunteered for this." He held his hands out as he spoke. They were still shaking violently. They had been shaking for hours.

"Hit on this," said a voice behind the glowing ash of a joint that had been extended to Jesse. It was Jim-Earl, the Shoshone from the Wind River Reservation. Almost every Indian that had enlisted or who had been drafted by the army had been put directly into the infantry.

Jesse took the cigarette, inhaled deeply, then held his breath for a few seconds before speaking. "Now you guys have to answer a question for me. What was your asshole pucker factor last night? I need some sort of gauge for future reference—just in case there is a future."

"Mine was a definite ten." Cornelius laughed and reached around with his right hand and rubbed his ass. It had leaked. "Good thing this here underwear is green." He reached around and checked the front of his pants, too. "Seems I done leaked from every damn hole. I'll tell you, the army sure has been good for my sex life. Every time I turn around, I'm gettin' fucked."

"It was a definite eleven," said another voice. "Fuck, it still is," added the voice. There was a look of distance and horror in the speaker's eyes. He was a new grunt, a boy from Nevada who had a pronounced overbite and one slow eye.

"That's good to hear. I feel better now." Jesse sighed. "But I really don't think my asshole will ever open again. The damn thing is sealed shut. I didn't know there was that much fear anywhere in the universe. It's been hours and I'm still shaking from it. My heart won't slow down and I'm so numb I can't feel my fingers and my feet. I have deep cuts everywhere and I don't know how or when I got them."

He exhaled deeply as he probed a dozen new lacerations and abrasions. Now he started to feel the pain. Jesse couldn't know it as he spoke, but his voice was no longer the same. Around each forced word that left his lips was a deathly host of sullen harmonics, echoes of savagery, second- and third-order resonances of screams and sighs, sights of explicit mortality and images of incredible courage that had settled in to infect and to bless each day for the rest of his life.

"Join the club," said a Midwestern voice. "I went my whole first tour of duty without ever getting this close to Charlie. I can't believe it, last night the fuckin' dinks was running right between our bunkers. I could hear 'em talking. I could see their faces. Jesus, I thought I was dead."

"I felt like there were lead weights all over me," continued Jesse, who somehow felt compelled to keep talking, "like I was moving in Jell-O. At first I was too afraid to pull the trigger, then I was too scared to stop. If there had been a Southern Baptist church choir in front of me, I would have shot it to pieces." He turned to gaze at the body bags lined up at the crest of the hill.

"Human life is only worth what we agree it's worth. There's no intrinsic value." Jesse's voice almost broke as he spoke. He had dared to say the ancient secret out loud.

"I don't know what you just said, but you're one of us now, man," said Cornelius. "You sho nuff meat just like us," he smiled, using his best Alabama–East Oakland drawl.

Jim-Earl grunted his laconic agreement. The other Indians said nothing. They were huddled together, lighting up still another gigantic joint. The Midwestern voice was silent. After a few minutes, the voice from Iowa said, "I thought I joined up to be a soldier. Hell, I ain't nothing but a chauffeur for this here rifle. How come they don't use robots for this here job?"

"Because there have to be casualties." It was the padre, who had seemingly appeared from nowhere. "You can't keep score without casualties."

"Charlie ain't keepin' score," said Cornelius softly. "We're runnin' it up on him and he keeps on comin'."

"*Orale,*" said a Mexican voice. "Let these *Norteños* and the *Sureños* kill each other off. I don't give a shit about either side."

Just then the breeze shifted, bringing with it the hot air that had been languishing above the row of body bags. Some troops bent over with dry heaves, some held their breath and closed their eyes until the stench passed. It was the smell of meat. The rancid meat of friends. The graying meat of a second lieutenant who had lost his face. The meat of a Russian boy who went berserk just before the mortar round hit him. It was the scent of the secret. After holding his breath for half a minute, Jesse was the first to test the air. He inhaled the lingering remnants of tragedy.

"Last night, when the zips started using RPGs on us, I heard someone yell out, 'Hide in your asshole!' "

"The troopers' anthem!" shouted the Midwestern voice.

"How is it that you guys say to hide in your assholes when they've been squeezed shut by a maximum pucker factor?"

"Holy shit, I never thought of that one," said Cornelius. "Is we gone and mixed our muthafuckin' metaphors?" he asked in a terribly rendered British accent.

"Grunts' homilies are certainly anomalies," mused Jesse.

"*Jesus-Santo,*" said the same Mexican voice. It was Tiburcio Mendez, an enlistee from Tijuana who joined the U.S. Army to get his American citizenship. Enlistment was a way of getting across the

Rio Grande that the Border Patrol didn't seem to care about. No idiot gringos were crying out for a greater INS presence at the recruitment centers.

"Don't worry, Mendez," said Cornelius, "I didn't understand it either. In fact, I'm not even sure it was English. Tell me, Jesse, will I be able to talk like that after two semesters?"

Cornelius's voice always had a calming effect on his buddies. It was a lovely tenor voice that had been polished and tuned in a tiny Baptist church choir in East Oakland. It was Cornelius who sang "Asleep in the Arms of the Lord," the little-known lyrics to "Taps" whenever there was a stand-down for fallen comrades. His clear, pure voice would rise above the benediction like a wish rising from an orphan.

As the sun set, Mendez's brown eyes had been glued to the darkening horizon. It was not the same expanse of sky he had always seen down in Mexico. As he compulsively rubbed a large silver crucifix that hung from his neck, his eyes spotted an object moving in the sky. Beneath his thumb the body of Christ had eventually gone from white metal to a dull gray. One arm of the cross had been completely eroded away. The wound to His side was no more.

"Is that one of those . . . *como se dice* . . . *satélite* . . . *uno de los esputniks?*"

Some necks craned upward to look. A few tired eyes pulled away from the dull green light of starlight scopes and lifted to the heavens. Few of them would ever notice that the constellations were different in this sky, that the distant stars were impossibly bright against the black felt of an unpolluted atmosphere. But they all saw what Tiburcio Mendez had seen: it was a bright ball that moved unswervingly across night sky.

"It's a spy plane," said a voice in the darkness.

"No spy plane goes that fast," said the Shoshone voice. "Besides, what spy plane is gonna advertise itself like that?"

There was a strange desperation in the two voices in the dark, a desperation generated by the impending disappearance of the flying object. When it dove into the horizon, this human pause, this moment of normalcy would go with it. Their eyes would have to return to the specter of North Vietnamese troops moving out there in the blackness.

"B-52's don't fly alone," said another voice, "maybe it is a satellite.

It don't have to be Sputnik; it could be one of ours. For a time back there, those Russians were sure kickin' our asses up there in space. Is Jesse still here? Ask him what he thinks."

"Yeah," said another voice filled with friendly derision, "let's ask the college-boy radio whiz."

Other voices laughed nervously in the dark, then waited for an answer from Jesse. Someone's eye went back to his scope for a second or two to verify that nothing in the darkness had changed. They were still out there, digging spider holes, dragging their killed and wounded into the forest. They were busy diagramming the new claymore placements on the hill and calculating the fields of fire that had thinned out since their last assault. They were out there, totally aware of the fact that wounded and dead Americans and Montagnards had been airlifted away but no replacements had arrived.

"I think Mendez is right," said a voice that was a distance away from the others yet clearly audible. It was Jesse's voice. He had moved away from the group, suddenly groggy from the marijuana. "It's too high and too fast for any airplane."

"Shit, Mendez," said a Midwestern voice, "you finally got something right."

There was silence from Mendez.

"Hey, chatterbox, you got nothing to say?"

Mendez was silent, ruminating over a question he had always wanted to ask someone but had never gotten up the courage for.

"What keeps that thing up there?" asked the Midwestern voice, happy to talk about anything but the small, surrounded hill that at once exposed him and protected him.

"It's not high enough to be truly beyond earth's gravity," said Jesse's distant voice, "but it has enough lateral velocity so that it keeps missing the earth as it falls. Essentially, it keeps falling toward something that it will never hit."

"Sounds just like my life," said another, much more disturbed voice. It was the chaplain. There were still remnants of terror in his voice box. His body and soul were still buzzing with horror. It had taken hours for his battered heart to return to a rate that was only twice normal. He couldn't know it but every capillary in his eyes had burst; even in the relative calm of evening, his eyes and ears were bleeding. "Sounds like my life," he repeated.

"*Todavía está loco, el padre?*" whispered another, even more distant voice. It was Lopez, using Spanish to compound the courtesy of a lowered voice. People from his village would never dishonor a priest. Julio Lopez shivered as he spoke into the dark. Below his face, his fingers were moving like fleshy machines. Even in pitch blackness he could clean his rifle again and again, then load and reload each magazine. Each round was drawn across his forehead to lubricate it before it was placed into a magazine. Julio Lopez's rifle was never going to jam.

Sometime during the night a cold chill, as sharp as a knife, had suddenly penetrated his flak jacket and shoved its honed and frigid fingers down his perpetually sweating back. In a moment of both insight and panic, Lopez understood that he had to speak to the padre, whether he was insane or not. There wasn't much time left. There were sins to confess. *"Está fuera de sus sesos?"* he asked.

"Shit, he's in his right mind," said a Southern black voice that was breaking silence. It had the nasal, snarling vowels of the Mississippi Delta. It was a voice that slid effortlessly up and down in pitch, like a polished bottleneck on wooden frets. "It's this shit that's crazy. It's the Nam that's crazy."

He had been scanning the horizon with his scope. Suddenly his eye settled on a single target.

"Shit, do you know what them zips are doing? I can see 'em up there in the trees cutting down them poor fuckers that got blown up into the canopy. I sure do love them gunships. I can see two of them out there eating something. It looks like they're eating rocks! What the hell could it be?"

The voice of a Montagnard soldier rang out. He had heard the question and was answering it with his beautiful, incomprehensible dialect. No one but his own countrymen would ever understand his words. The importance of his statement would be lost forever: "They are eating green rocks. Can't you fools see? They are swallowing green rocks. They seek out the power in jade."

"Jesse, amigo." It was Mendez, finally breaking his own pouting silence. *"Pienses que algún día habrán Mexicanos en espacio? Mexicanos en las galaxias?"* A long, silent interval passed before he had the courage to translate the passage. "Do you suppose that there will ever be Mexicanos in space?"

There was laughter everywhere. Grunts who had been on the brink of despondency or fatigued beyond description began to chuckle at the absurdity of the question and the insane images it had created in their minds. A hundred yards away North Vietnamese regulars lifted their heads when the laughter reached them. The glow from their horridly bitter Chinese cigarettes was visible at a hundred meters. Some even laughed mockingly, while others wondered why the GIs weren't more afraid.

"Pancho Villa on Venus." Cornelius giggled. His was a tentative, restrained form of laughter. He had heard the North Vietnamese. They sounded cocky. "The Frito Bandito versus Emperor Ming on Jupiter."

"*Mi vida loca* on Mercury," said Lopez.

"How the hell do you jump-start a rocket ship?" asked the voice from the Mississippi Delta.

Within the perimeter, only the Montagnards failed to laugh. They were busy cleaning their antique rifles while speaking their strange language, drinking bark tea, and taking bites out of dried balls of rice that contained slices of roasted monkey meat and a few morsels of vegetable.

"Mendez, you been at the morphine again?" asked the medic. "You better save your feel-good Syrettes for the beast, my man."

Mendez was silent. When the laughter died down, the grunts somehow realized that Jesse, though silent, was actually pondering the ridiculous question. It was the chaplain who spoke next. With the particulars of his crazed and sweating face fading away in the darkness, he repeated Mendez's odd query.

"Do you suppose there will ever be Mexicans in space?"

"Yeah," joined in Cornelius, eager to discuss anything but the Nam. "Let's do some more supposin'! Let's suppose on something real crazy, something wild as shit, like a bunch of Mexicans flying around in outer space! Low-rider rockets and pachucos on Pluto. Jesse, listen here, man . . ."

Cornelius had just caught a whiff of gook Camels, those bitter NVA cigarettes. It was a strong and disconcerting smell. As his eyes scanned the perimeter, he finished his question slowly.

". . . do you suppose there will ever be Mexicans in space?"

6

mexicans in space

The sound of movement beyond the outer holes and the far tree-line was growing louder and louder. There were so many enemy troops out there that they didn't give a shit whether the boys on the hill heard them.

"*Supongamos, mis amigos!*" cried Jesse with a tone of forced enthusiasm mixed with desperation. He had to speak up to be heard over the disdainful sound of enemy voices not a hundred yards away.

"*Supongamos, amigos.* You've never heard of the exploits of *los estrellanauts*? You've never heard of MASA?" said Jesse with a feigned look of pained astonishment, "the Mexican Aeronautical and Space Agency? Frankly, I am appalled at your unforgivable ignorance. Personally, I've always believed that Mexicans should have been in outer space decades ago, maybe a century ago."

As he spoke, Jesse did not notice that the background noise beyond the outer berm had all but disappeared.

"Hey!" It was Lopez who had gone back to his starlight scope. "I can't see any of them. Maybe the zips pulled out." His voice was filled with hope.

"*Ojalá que sí!*" sighed Mendez, who crossed himself twice.

"They're gone, but the little fuckers will be back."

It was the voice of the black sergeant, who had just left the Salon des Refusés, the huge metal cargo container that held the long-distance radio equipment. He knew something. He had good information, and it wasn't from any of those fools from army intelligence.

"I've been scanning the frequencies up in the Salon. There's *beaucoup* contact about thirty clicks to the east. They've got zips in battalion strength coming at them. Sounds like our boys are catching some heavy shit." What he didn't say was that it was an identical radio installation and LZ that was being hit. What he didn't say was that the installation had gone down and that this hill was the only working relay now. Things had not gone according to plan. They never did.

"God willing, we'll di-di outta here long before the zips know we're gone. In the meantime, keep your hats on. There are snipers out there." The sergeant was glad that the dark skies and his dark complexion had worked together to hide his concerns, his fear. He composed himself, then grinned a wide, visible grin.

"*Mais dîtes-moi, mon frère*, how in hell could Mexicans be in space?"

Despite his own warning, the sergeant had removed his helmet and was pouring potable water from a canteen over his face and neck. Like the others, his skin was raw with heat rash and his arms and hands were covered with scars and open cuts. Even after sundown it was over one hundred degrees. He toweled himself dry, then began to dust himself with antifungal powder. In the few moments that he had his arms exposed, more than a dozen mosquitoes had landed and were plumbing his skin for a meal. Just then a new breeze came up from the south and every face turned into the blessed liquid force of it.

The breeze grew into a severe gust of wind that rattled the sergeant's precious hand-painted sign above the door of the radio installation. One of the wires gave way and the sign dangled from a single corner. The sergeant sighed. He would have to rehang the "Salon des Refusés."

"There's your answer, sergeant," said Jesse. "The wind."

Jesse lifted his sweating face to catch the full effect of the breeze, then he loosened his belt and zipped down his fly to allow the cool air to circulate inside his pants. He sighed gratefully as the eternal burn of crotch rot subsided for a few precious moments.

"Suppose the wind had been blowing just right back in the sixteenth and seventeenth centuries. The world would have been a very different place today."

In anticipation of Jesse's story, new, extra-large joints had been hand-rolled and fired up. They looked like Cuban cigars. Taut shoulders, tight with savvy, were allowed to slump a bit. There was *beaucoup* contact going on thirty kilometers to the east. That could mean a quiet night here. For a moment, young men were no longer soldiers. For a moment they were all gathered like enthusiastic students around a noisy table in a coffee shop in Berkeley.

"Just imagine what would have happened if Hernán Cortez and his men had been blown far off course and landed at Plymouth Rock instead of Veracruz. On the other hand, imagine that the pilgrims had been blown south by a terrific gale and the *Mayflower* had run aground in the Yucatán peninsula."

"What would be different?" asked the chaplain, suddenly intrigued by the unusual scenario.

"Think about it, padre. What is the primary difference between Mexico and the United States today?" countered Jesse. He waited a moment before answering his own question. No one spoke.

"Mexico is a mestizo culture, a racially mixed *cultura* and the United States is not. Both the Roman Catholics and the Puritans had their stupid debates about whether or not the indigenous people were human, but in the meantime the Catholic soldiers went ahead and got it on with the native girls anyway.

"Those conquistadors were damned sex fiends, and they went nuts over all those bare-breasted women! Hell, it was Magellan's dick that got his ass killed. He got caught messing around with Lapu-Lapu's wife. To a man, the Spanish soldiers asked themselves, 'Why should the pope have all the fun?' "

There was a general consensus among the grunts that the horny Spaniards had posed a supremely logical and valid question. After all, there were so many beautiful women here in the Nam. Everywhere in this country there seemed to be slender, dark-eyed women lifting their blouses for passing GIs while begging for C-rations.

"The Puritans, on the other hand, were revolted by the carefree spirit and nakedness of the Indians." Jesse smiled in the direction of the Indian troops. "So much so that they made it a capital crime to have sex with them. Since they believed that everything earthly was necessarily evil, they believed that people close to the earth must be evil, too. So it must be all right with God to take land away from evil people, to let evil heathens suffer disease and starve to death.

"Just after the Puritans massacred the entire Pequot tribe, they held a prayer meeting! They could've been killing vermin or termites instead of women and children. Those people saw everything in terms of their stern, joyless beliefs. They interpreted cultural difference as religious difference. So the prayers of an Indian priest became heresy."

In the dark the Indian soldiers were moving in closer to hear. Wary of snipers, they cupped their enormous joints in their hands or beneath their helmets as they passed them back and forth.

"You mean to say we ain't a melting pot?" sneered Jim-Earl sarcastically.

"There was melting, all right," said the Creole sergeant with a laugh. "All them European folks melted into white."

"This simple idea of cultural difference as blasphemy is the very foundation of American racism. It wasn't much of a leap from the Puritans to the Aryan Nation. It wasn't much of a leap from their laws against consorting with the Indians to the Jim Crow laws in the South and the antimiscegenation laws in the West. You see, back in the world, racism is a sacred thing."

"You know," said the Creole sergeant thoughtfully, "a large percentage of the membership of the Ku Klux Klan in the forties and fifties was made up of preachers and pastors. I think I read that each chapter has its own chaplain. I think they call him a Kludd. I imagine the name comes from the sound that shit makes when it hits the floor."

There was laughter from everywhere on the hill. Other groups of men had ceased their talking to listen.

"What are you saying, Jesse," asked the chaplain, "that the sixteenth-century Catholics were benevolent degenerates?"

"Hell, no, padre!" answered Jesse. "I think they were more civilized than the Puritans, but only a little more. The difference was that the Spaniards believed that all the sins of the flesh could be forgiven in the end. During your life you could lust and get laid all you wanted. All you needed to get into heaven was an act of repentance before you died. It was a perfect system. Check out all those celibate popes with their Vatican concubines and scores of illegitimate kids.

Think about it, padre, you're out here giving the Last Rites to men who have probably just killed another man.

"The Puritans, on the other hand, abstained from just about everything that was any fun at all: tobacco, cigarettes, coffee, dancing, singing. They believed that forgiveness and redemption lay in the next life, not this one."

"They should have abstained from long ocean voyages," said Jim-Earl, while exhaling a thick curtain of smoke. The other Indians grunted.

"They believed that if you tortured the body into submission," continued Jesse, "the soul would certainly follow. It was the complete reverse of the Catholics. The same naked Indian girls that drove the Spaniards wild with longing were branded as satanic by the Puritans. One group was oversexed; the other was totally repressed. We drew the short straw on that one. We got the repressed group. That's why America is filled with an equal number of censors and sex fiends. It is both compelled and repelled by breasts."

"Fucking-A," said a voice in the dark. "I love breasts."

"The confessions of a serial masturbator!" said the voice of a buddha-head, a kid from Hawaii that the troopers called Spam Boy.

"Last night, Jesse, when things were bad, when you were scared, did you say a prayer?"

It was the chaplain. After the last two days on this hill, his own religious education had begun to seem naive and insulated. Even here, in hell, he needed some reassurance. Jesse said nothing. Silence was his answer.

"Isn't it lonely?" added the chaplain.

"If I get out of here alive," said Jesse quietly, "then someone else doesn't." He nodded toward the small, burned harness and rucksack of a North Vietnamese soldier. "I'm no better than him. The God that built that sky up there, padre, does not choose between people down here. If I survive, it's because of these guys right here." There was a gesture in the dark that no one needed to see in order to understand. "If we get out of here, it will be because we lucked out."

Jesse's face lit up as he pulled on the burning mota. Fuck the snipers. He smiled as he acknowledged its beneficent effect on his brain and his speech.

"So anyway," he began again, dispelling the lull that the padre's question had caused, "the *Mayflower* washes up onto the beach at

Veracruz and those cold-blooded pilgrims suddenly find themselves
in a genuine tropical paradise. This sure as hell ain't England, and it
ain't the Netherlands. There are no snowdrifts here, no frozen toes,
no begging from the Indians . . . and no Thanksgiving. Now they're
really pissed off because there's nothing there that they can use to
mortify the flesh. After months at sea they find themselves in the
garden of Eden and the damn place is filled with brown people."

"There goes the neighborhood." Cornelius laughed.

"Now they're completely at a loss for what to do. They came here
to live the New Testament, and they find themselves in the first pages
of Genesis. How could they possibly bemoan their lot in life in this
land of milk and honey? Ah, but the Puritans were resourceful folks.
They considered their options. They could import tons of snow or
set sail for the frigid shores of Iceland or they could reach out and
pick some of the fruit that's hanging everywhere around them.

"They might have heard the same rumors that Cortez had heard
about a city of gold, but they lacked the military power and experience to strike inland for Tenochtitlán and the land of the Aztecs. So
they would have convened a prayer meeting, killed a few of the locals
who had come to visit, and finally decided to stay where they were.
Maybe they would even move out to Isla Mujeres to escape all those
sex-crazed Mayans. Only now the natives would call it Isla de los
Lerdos."

Mendez, Lopez, and the other Latinos broke out laughing at the
name. Island of the dullards.

"*Isla de los pendejos,*" one of them said spitefully.

"Do you remember the story of La Malinche?" Only the two
Mexicans nodded their heads.

"She was the Indian woman who became Cortez's sugar mama.
She cooked for him, gave him kids, and incidentally, helped him to
betray and annihilate her own people."

"Then he left her for another woman," said Tiburcio Mendez
with a smirk.

"There's no way that La Malinche would have fallen for a sexually
repressed, tight-assed pilgrim," said Jesse. "No way! Pocahontas
must've been blind or really hard up to fall for a wimp like John
Rolfe. Anyway, the Puritans would have done well for themselves
out there on the island. More pilgrims would have arrived and today
there would be a huge self-mortification theme park on the island

and a body of water to keep the dreariness and the Protestant work ethic away from the shores of Quintana Roo. The Mexicans would have established a Border Patrol to keep those stern, pasty-faced people at bay."

"Keep those bastards from taking jobs away from the Mexicans!" exclaimed Mendez.

"Meanwhile, up at Plymouth Rock our boy Cortez has landed and in his push westward runs smack dab into the five tribes of the Iroquois Confederacy. Now, these folks are certainly not the Aztecs. They don't have a king who makes Hamlet look decisive, and they don't have a mythology that says that white gods with beards will appear from out of the east. The Spaniards would never have lulled the Iroquois Nation into complacency with Bible studies and false pacifism. There would have been beaucoup shit coming down."

"Them Iroquois are cold," said Jim-Earl the Shoshone, his voice filled with deep respect.

"Damn right," said Jesse. "The way I figure it, five or six divisions of Iroquois regulars told old Powhatan to get out of the way, then they wiped Cortez out."

"But not before sodomizing him," said a Cherokee voice.

"*Coño! En las nalgas,*" said Mendez with a jerk of his hips.

Jesse laughed. The padre blinked his eyes in confusion. His seminary training and his doctorate in divinity had not prepared him for this sort of discussion.

"The Indians would have been put on notice as to the true intentions of the Europeans. Jamestown would have never happened. Lung cancer would have to be invented somewhere else."

"The Kola would've had their war ponies decades earlier," said an excited Indian voice.

"With those horses, their cavalry could have repelled the Dutch merchants and the French Jesuits, and the entire Huron Nation would still be alive today. North America would be Russian-Indian and French-Indian today," concluded Jesse.

"Why wouldn't they kill off the Russians and the French?" asked the chaplain, who was surprised by his own question, asked in earnest. For a moment he had forgotten about the war that raged around him. This "supposing" stuff actually worked, he thought to himself.

"Because they came for the pelts, for the furs," said Jesse. "They didn't take away the Indians' land and their livelihoods. A lot of them took Indian wives. Indians can understand lustiness, it's self-deprivation that confounds them. Today everything west of the Mississippi and north of Texas would be called Russo-Aztlán; everything east would be called Kola-Quebec. It is my supposition, after the benefit of much marijuana, that Mexico would have the same name as today because it's derived from the word Mejica, the Aztec name for themselves."

Jesse smiled. He loved these speculations. Thoughts like these were always bubbling up in his overactive mind. He often used historical scenarios such as these to help himself fall asleep when marijuana didn't work. It didn't matter that no two scenarios ever had the same result.

"Say, man," said Cornelius, suddenly caught up in the fantasy, "there wouldn't be no slavery in Russo-Aztlán and Kola-Quebec, because there wouldn't be no Spaniards and no Englishmen!"

"Right on," said a twelve-string voice from Mississippi.

"No fucking missionaries in Hawaii," spat Spam Boy.

"That's right," said Jesse, "and old Moctezoma, down in Mexico, would have learned of the defeat of Cortez and eventually realized that the bearded people were not gods. He would have seen the necessity of preparing for future invasions from Europe. Having firsthand knowledge of the insanity of the English—remember, the Puritans are camped out on the Island of Dullards—he would have sought help from the mortal enemies of both the English and the Spaniards.

"I think he would have sent his royal emissaries to Dublin and Edinburgh to speak to all of the clan chieftains of the Irish and the Scots. Other Aztec emissaries would have gone off to Paris. All of indigenous America would have been spared Moctezoma's imperial foolishness and his terrible defeat at the hands of Hernán Cortez."

Jesse took a deep drag off another joint that had been shoved into his face by an unknown grunt. Now his entire brain was bathed in warmth. This daydream felt good.

"Alexander Graham Bell and James Watt would have been born in Cuernavaca. Their fathers would have married Mixtec women. The Industrial Revolution would have begun in the wide streets of Tenochtitlán City. And listen to this. . . ." Jesse grinned with glee. "In the seventeenth century, thirty thousand Aztec soldiers would have joined the Irish for an invasion of England. Oliver Cromwell would have been soundly defeated at the great Battle of the Isle of Man. An Aztec soldier would have torn Cromwell's heart from his body."

"*Andale pues!*" said Lopez excitedly. "*Qué madre!* Corn, beef fajitas, and cabbage!"

"England would finally have some decent food," said the padre, "and no gold bullion coming in from Mexico would have meant the end of the Inquisition in Spain. Without the Inquisition, Spain might have experienced the Renaissance. Who knows, maybe Generalissimo Franco would never have existed."

"Now you've got it, padre!" said Jesse enthusiastically.

"And we wouldn't be standing here in Indian country," spat Jim-Earl, completely aware of the irony in his words. The Seminoles were out there, huddling and skulking beyond the berm. The long knives, having run out of Indians and elbow room in North America, had crossed the Pacific Ocean.

"What about me and my family?" It was the Midwestern voice.

"Your name is Dutch, isn't it?" asked Jesse. "That would make you a Dutch Kola-Quebequois, unless your family managed to get across the big river."

"That's way better than honky," said the Mississippi voice.

"You would have a real culture. White don't mean any more than black does," added the Creole sergeant.

"You could be crossing the Rio Grande at night, trying to get work in Mexico," said Lopez.

Abruptly, the sound of inbound choppers in the far distance brought a sudden end to the dreaming and to the discussion. The conversation would begin again, somewhere else in another province, in another ville, in another calm moment after great turbulence.

The sergeant had already gone to organize the removal of the bodies and the wounded who hadn't been airlifted earlier. As the trio of helicopters came closer to the small landing zone behind the radio dishes, a stream of red tracers rose up from the forest darkness to meet them. Some North Vietnamese were still out there. A lot of them were still out there.

The single gunship peeled off to return fire, while the slick ships kept coming, the saucers of their rotors almost touching. From the high pitch of the blades, it was clear that the Hueys were empty.

Even as they set down in a swirling cloud of dust, the tracer rounds followed them down. The young, gum-chewing warrant officers at their controls moved deliberately, almost slowly, and with unearthly courage despite the deadly rain of bullets piercing the skin of their ship. Within their huge headsets was a torrent of words, controlled jargon in a cold monotone, practiced words hovering at the very edge of sheer panic.

Without saying a thing, the chaplain got up and ran at full speed to the top of the hill, falling three or four times before he reached the landing zone. Behind him, Julio Lopez was calling after him, crying out that death was coming for him and that he needed to make one last confession. The chaplain heard Julio's voice but kept running. He hurriedly helped someone place the Russian boy's bag into a chopper. Two wounded boys needed help climbing in.

One of them, a traumatic amputee, was hit again as he was lifted up. The bullet slammed into his remaining leg. It had flown toward his body at over three thousand feet per second and the dark spray it created filled the air inside the helicopter. Everyone inside was breathing pieces of a friend. A chopper on the pad was an easy target.

The legless boy's screams went unheard as the chaplain climbed in with him and crouched down near the transmission housing. He covered his own contorted face with his hands as rounds tore into the chopper's body. As he did so, the door gunner noticed that the padre was not getting out and said something into his radio. The copilot looked back toward the hellhole area of his ship to survey the chaplain hiding there.

For an instant there was eye contact between the two. Without a word he turned his head toward his console and the chopper lifted from the pad. The air was cooling and thick and so the rotors had bite. Climbing would be easy, even with an extra man aboard. In mere seconds the firing stopped and the chaplain glanced cautiously through the door. The hill was gone.

"Sit down, lieutenant. Can I get you a stiff drink? I've got whiskey, vodka, and some tequila. I've got it all, and there are some real ice cubes in that refrigerator over there. Maybe you want a cigarette? Winston? Camels?"

The younger man shook his head, no. As he did so, beads of sweat poured from his forehead and his matted hairline. He had been standing in a posture that only slightly resembled attention, his field cap in his hand. There was darkened blood caked into the folds of his knuckles. The whites of his eyes were crimson. Now and again his body would be racked by a seismic quivering that would be punctuated by a small whimper.

"Go ahead, sit down. Take a few deep breaths, and for God's sake, try to pull yourself together."

The older, taller man lit a cigarette, exhaled, and coughed. His free hand was gesturing toward a chair. Even as he made the gesture, the colonel was appreciating the ancient, symbolic nature of the open hand, palm up, and the placid extension of wrist. He winced inwardly as he noticed the purplish line on his ring finger. He hoped that the lieutenant hadn't noticed the missing wedding band. The colonel above the extended palm considered his own sin something less than adultery if his wedding ring was not present during the act.

The eyes above the palm never left those of the junior officer, whose own frenzied eyes never seemed to settle anywhere. The younger man did not even look down to see the chair as he lowered himself into it. He had, however, seen the missing ring.

The colonel closed his hand. He had seen the symptoms before, back in Korea and now here. Wild eyes, uncontrollable sweating, and soiled trousers were the classic signs that the flight response had triumphed over the will to stand and fight. We are fighters in every sense of the word, thought the pensive colonel, though we are technically noncombatants. The senior officer at the desk opened a manila file and began to peruse the contents.

On the wall behind his head were photographs of Lyndon Johnson and Generals Westmoreland and Ky. The only color photo on the wall was a poster of Anita Bryant in a bathing suit. On a contiguous wall was a huge, faded reproduction of the Florentine artist Andrea Mantegna's painting *The Agony in the Garden*.

"I know you had a special relationship with Captain Gregory, but right now he's on R and R, somewhere in the wilds of Sydney or Melbourne. He's probably getting himself a little round-eyed nookie even as we speak." The colonel winked a naughty little wink. "He's a fine chaplain. I'm holding down the fort while he's gone. Oh, by the way, my name is Colonel Urban—Kelvin Urban Junior, or Urban the Second as the boys in seminary used to say, and I hope you can speak with me with as much comfort and confidence as you spoke to

Captain Gregory. By the way, did you hear the big news?" He smiled, then reached behind himself to grab a water glass and a bottle of whiskey.

"That colored preacher got his today. Some guy went and gunned down that Martin Luther King character. Imagine—a Negro fellow named after Martin Luther! I really can't say I'm sorry that it happened." He grinned while lifting his glass in a mocking toast. "I can't stand how them colored Southern Baptists hand out those doctorates of divinity like they were free tickets to a Saturday movie. Only problem is, everybody's real worried that the colored soldiers won't fight when they hear about it. Hell, if the colored grunts refuse to fight, the Mexicans might follow, then the goddamn Indians.

"Now, let's see, it says here that your place of birth is unknown. Your ethnic origin seems to be a bit muddled. Now, let's see the bottom line—you're a Unitarian?"

The lieutenant nodded his head slowly in the affirmative as the interval between sobs grew a bit longer with each passing moment.

"So you're formally noncommittal." The colonel laughed. It was an old joke in the chaplains' corps. "What are you really? Or shall I put it this way, what were you before you decided to become a Unitarian?"

"I was a Catholic, sir," said the lieutenant in a voice that was barely audible. It was a lie, but it was an old, established lie, and it was better than the truth. "I was a Catholic, sir," said the lieutenant once more, completely unaware that he had just repeated himself. Even after he said the words, his lips kept forming them over and over again, a physical echo. His boiling mind was elsewhere, racing far behind and far ahead of both the question and the answer.

"I was a Catholic, sir."

"Well," said the colonel, "I must admit that I do consider the Unitarians to be a step up from the Roman Catholics. It's a small prejudice that I guess most Lutherans share." There was a small, insincere smile that flickered and died on the colonel's face. "It says here you have master's degrees in theology and history. Is there any period that you favor?"

"The Crusades," whispered the young chaplain, whose face had fallen forward and was now being cradled by his dirty, shaking hands. "The Middle Ages and the Crusades," he repeated, but the words had been inaudible. He had spoken them into his palms, into the deltas formed by the intersection of his life lines and his heart lines.

"A glorious period!" exclaimed the colonel, his voice rising with enthusiasm. "I so love the era of the Christian soldier. The era of worldwide mobilization against the infidel. No ifs, ands, or buts back then. No protestors, no flag burnings, no Jane Fondas."

He dropped a single ice cube into a water glass, then poured two fingers of amber whiskey over the cube. "Personally, I love to read about the Middle Ages before the Crusades. Now, there was a period of piety. The entire world was the City of God. Back then there was no real difference between a colonel and a bishop."

The colonel sighed wistfully.

"But this is all beside the point, isn't it? Now, let's get down to those proverbial brass tacks, lieutenant. While I was praying in chapel this morning, I was informed of something that I found to be quite disturbing. I was told that one of our most promising chaplains had abandoned his field post, not to mention his flock, and high-tailed it on home without orders and without communicating with a superior officer. Now, I know the job's a bitch, but this is something we just can't have."

The lieutenant wasn't listening. He struggled to keep his jaw from quaking as it had on that long ride back on the chopper. His teeth had been chattering so badly that he'd bitten his tongue and lips in a dozen places. He closed his eyes, an act that somehow permitted another small note of grief to escape from his stomach and fill his gorge.

Because of his fear, a soldier had expired in that Huey without benefit of a chaplain, a chaplain who had been cowering less than a yard away. There had been no confession, no Extreme Unction. The colonel stopped speaking long enough to look up and see the lieutenant slumping to the floor. The young man's face was slick with sweat and tears.

The colonel rose angrily to his feet, walked around his desk, and grabbed the lieutenant by his collar. Grunting angrily, he lifted the young chaplain up off his chair, slammed him down, then leaned forward until they were nose to nose.

"Maybe you noncommittal, so-called intellectual Unitarians don't know this," said the colonel in a transformed voice, "but Jehovah God is a heat seeker." The smile on the colonel's face had disappeared completely, leaving behind the angular, arid chin and thin lips of a professional soldier . . . a lifer.

"Time to stop beating around the burning bush," growled the colonel. Courtesy and social grace had now given way completely to the dark power of the lifer: the power of inertia, the power to keep any boat from rocking, the ability to turn the smallest duty into a drudgery, and that drudgery into a litany of grumblings and reams of paper. Buried beneath this power, the smallest task became impossible. The course of least resistance ensured that nothing was ever done and no one was ever responsible for failing to do it. All lifers dutifully followed the rules of planetary motion.

"Open the Bible, son," said the colonel, striking an elliptical posture, "and show me a chapter that's filled with nice little parishes, tea socials, and contented congregations. Show me the fucking page where everyone's happy and yellow cowards like you prosper and die surrounded by immediate family. The Holy Bible, chapter and verse, is one war after another. After all that begetting and begatting came the smiting and the slaying and the plagues, just like clockwork, just like Exodus follows Genesis.

"Do you think them damn Jews are the only ones who can carry God in an ark at the head of their column, smiting down their enemies and leveling their lands? Well, we've got God fighting for us, too, right here in Vietnam. After all, isn't the Pentateuch a story about the bitterness of a divided nation, lieutenant, just like the Nam?"

The colonel released his hold on the chaplain's jacket. He had used more energy on this useless conversation than he had expended on his entire first tour of duty. He sat down. A body at rest.

"For all your supposed faith, you don't really want to meet your maker, do you? It got too hot for you out on that hilltop position, didn't it?"

The lieutenant nodded slowly. A desolate groan left his throat.

"Do you remember the story of Elijah, chaplain?" the colonel said. He would expend one last erg of energy on this worthless Unitarian. Actually, it wouldn't take even that much effort. He was about to deliver an old, well-worn sermon.

"Do you know the story about King Ahab and his pagan wife Jezebel? Now, there was a lovely and seductive woman, but the trouble was, she worshiped pagan deities and imported her own pagan priests. Now, this made the prophet Elijah real mad. So Elijah summoned King Ahab and his wife and all of her prophets to Mount Carmel for a contest, a final showdown between Yahweh and her god, Baal. The story goes that two bullocks were placed on two separate altars, and Elijah challenged the priests of Baal to implore their god to send down a heavenly fire to consume their bullock. You know what happened, don't you?"

The young chaplain nodded. He knew the story. He had seen the fire on the hill. He had once lived on a hill.

"That's right, son, nothing at all happened. The skies were stone silent. Then Elijah called upon his God, our God, and lo and behold, dark clouds gathered from horizon to horizon, then glorious flames filled the skies. In seconds, that bullock was charred to cinders."

The colonel lit another cigarette then paused a moment to let the import of his sermon sink in.

"You are part of a great tradition, my boy. Moses, Aaron, David, Solomon, and Elijah; there's always a man of God at the head of the column with the warriors and the generals. In the best of all worlds it is the men of God who lead the crusaders. Remember Saint Bernard?"

It was the colonel who closed his eyes now, remembering his own glorious days of combat in Korea. Once he had even been close enough to the fighting that he could see men dying, both Red Chinese and Americans. It was General Douglas MacArthur himself who had lent him his own personal binoculars. The colonel shook his head. The general had had such a messianic caritas, such immense power over men. He could have been a king, or even better, a medieval pope. One of the general's favorite mottoes had been engraved onto the body of those binoculars: *Flavit Jehovah et disipati sunt.* God breathed on them and they were dispersed.

"There's always been a prophet standing right there in the drop zone when the fire from heaven comes down to turn the bull to smoking ashes. Don't you see? Old Elijah was a FAC, a forward air controller, calling in a fire mission to the Lord."

The colonel, who had risen and taken three steps backward, now walked back to his desk and sat down. The smile had faded from his face.

"There's a chopper leaving from pad alpha at fifteen-thirty hours. You be on it or I'll have your ass court-martialed. Maybe Captain

Gregory had more time to sit around and philosophize with you, but I don't. You have a job to do. We all have a job to do. What you experienced up on your hill was just another small siege in a small anonymous place."

"You know what happened back on the hill?" asked the padre, a surprised and animated look appearing on his face. "You know about the spiders and the secrets and the young boys being molested?"

"There's been some talk," answered the colonel, who had a confused look on his face. "Command is aware of the situation."

"I can't lie to them anymore," mumbled the lieutenant in a feeble but growing voice. "I can't lie to them. They're paying the highest price and they're getting nothing for it, and I don't have the will or the stomach to tell them any different. Do you know what the grunts say, colonel?" For the first time his eyes were glued to those of the colonel. "They say, 'It don't mean nothing.' That's their answer when things are beyond reason and beyond hope. 'It don't mean nothing.' And they're right! Those grunts aren't stupid. None of this means nothing. None of this hellhole adds up to democracy, and none of this means God."

The colonel was quiet for a moment, then broke into laughter. He reached for his pack of cigarettes and once again offered one to the lieutenant, who refused at first, then took one. It would be his first cigarette in years. As he lit both cigarettes, the colonel continued his uncontrolled, cynical laughter. High over their heads another flight of Phantom jets was leaving for points north. The sound of their engines was deafening. They were loaded with snake and nape, missiles and napalm, to burn the bullock.

"Your poor Okie fruit-picking parents up in Oregon or your minimum-wage colored parents down in Watts don't want a reason for their dear son's death, they want a rationale." The colonel exhaled a thick, righteous cloud of filtered and mentholated death. "Now, there is a huge difference between a reason and a rationale, young lieutenant."

He refilled his water glass. Then, splurging a bit, he dropped in another precious ice cube.

"A rationale is something that can be included in a prayer; it's something you can put into a sermon. It's a benediction!"

He upended his glass and drained it into his throat. The ice cube disappeared into his mouth. This time there was no pretense. This man needed his liquor.

"Think about it, what are you gonna say to those people? What are you going to say to some simpleminded Southern Baptist or a Jehovah's Witness who doesn't even have a week of training in the seminary? There's millions of barrels of oil beneath the soil here? We need to keep Red China under control? Do we tell them we need to demonstrate all of these newfangled weapons for all of those buyers in the Persian Gulf, Iran, and Central America? Hell, there's a billion pristine lungs sucking oxygen in China. Do we tell them that we're fighting here so that our tobacco companies can open up these markets? Hell, no!

"You give them democracy and God! Now, that's the stuff of prayers. That's the stuff they can repeat on Veterans' Day and Memorial Day. You tell them their son died bravely and with a movie star's sneer on his lips. You don't tell them their dear boy became some kind of poet-warrior in his final days. And you, my young chaplain, are part of the rationale, not part of the reason. The reason for being here does not include you."

"And the troops?" asked the lieutenant weakly.

"One of these days they'll get a statue or something. The survivors will organize themselves into VFW chapters and tell stories to kids who'll ignore them. Now, get back to that goddamn hill. Do your job! Take part in their facile foxhole philosophies."

"It's called 'supposing,'" muttered the younger chaplain.

"Whatever," sneered the colonel. "You were specially trained to conduct field services and symposiums. As it happens, I've taught some of those courses myself. My paper on the fallacies of Sartre is still being used at my seminary."

The colonel's face flushed with pride.

"An intellectual like yourself should have no trouble answering their naive questions about sex before marriage and the meaning of life. Don't let it get any more complicated than that. If you get too complicated, folks in the chaplains' corps will begin to think you're one of them effete papists who's lapsed into linguistics . . . or maybe they'll think you're a Jew."

"Can you answer questions about Mexicans in space?" asked the padre defiantly. "Can you? Do you know anything about spider holes?"

The lieutenant rose to his feet and was standing with his thighs against the colonel's desk. There was a growing disdain in the lieutenant's voice that the colonel did not appreciate.

"Can you speak a single goddamn word of Gaelo-Aztecan? Can you? Do you have any idea what happened to Oliver Cromwell's heart? Did you know that I was never a Catholic? I am an insect. That is my denomination! Does someone like you know the first thing about Moroccan jazz? Can you write a poem in Ladino? I didn't think you could. I was never a Catholic, sir. I was never a Mennonite. I was a spider. It's a blue ballet out there, colonel, and it's men like you who are the perverts."

"What? What the hell are you talking about? Are you crazy?"

The chaplain did not answer. There was a haughty look on his raving face. He had just made several key points that had not been refuted.

"Just help them write their letters," said the colonel, ignoring the look of smug satisfaction that had appeared on his underling's face. "Ease their way into the next world. Help our boys kill the Hun."

"A lot of North Vietnamese soldiers are Catholics," said the lieutenant. "They have rosary beads wrapped around their rifles. I've heard them saying the Lord's Prayer in Vietnamese."

"Like I said"—the colonel smiled—"you gotta help our boys kill the Hun. Policies change, lieutenant. No more secure duties for us soldiers of God. No more hanging around the hospitals and loitering in canvas chapels. We're out in the field now, where we belong."

The colonel put down his newest cold drink and pointed a quivering finger toward the lieutenant.

"You be on that chopper at fifteen-thirty hours or I'll start organizing a firing squad for your yellow Unitarian, intellectual ass. You flake out again and I'll snatch your bars so fast it'll make your head spin."

The lieutenant saluted weakly then turned and walked to the door. As he opened the door the white light and oppressive heat of Da Nang rushed into the air-conditioned room. There had been a forty-degree difference in temperature between the colonel's office and the air of Vietnam. Riding piggyback on the thick waves of heat were the sickening scent of jet fuel and the numbing cacophony of the largest airport in the world.

"Close that goddamn door, lieutenant!" roared the colonel, "it'll take an hour to get this room back down to seventy degrees. Do you remember what happened to the prophets of Baal, lieutenant?"

The chaplain stepped through the door without answering his superior officer. The prophets had been taken from the top of the hill into a nearby valley where they had been slaughtered, one by one. It had not really been a contest. It had been a trap.

"And may God be with you," the colonel had called out as the door slammed shut.

When the young chaplain last saw the colonel he had been sitting behind his desk polishing the brass crucifix on his clean, dustless helmet and sneaking a quick peek at a pair of brigadier general's stars that he kept hidden in his desk, just in case the rumors from Command were true.

The chopper was blessedly clean. The ground crew had washed and sterilized it. It was a "slick," a lightly armed troop carrier and the very same helicopter that had brought the chaplain to Da Nang just hours earlier. The lieutenant peeked cautiously into the doorway, then sighed. The ground crew had used a high pressure water hose to remove the blood and body parts. A wave of nausea washed over the chaplain's face as he remembered last night's flight, and the young soldier who had flown back with him. The grunt had been cradling his own helmet in his shaking arms as the chopper lifted from the hill. In the webbing of the helmet was the young man's own right kneecap.

"They can sew it back on, can't they?"

The young soldier had repeated that question over and over. They couldn't. The leg it had come from was out there, somewhere below the dark canopy of tree limbs. But beyond the sadness that the chaplain had felt for the young man, there was something else, something deviated and twisted. He had experienced the strange, almost overpowering desire to touch the kneecap. It had been so perverse. It was certainly something he would never have wanted to do while it was still attached to a living leg.

Once the compulsion to touch the kneecap had seized him, the chaplain had heard nothing during the flight, not the beating of the rotors, not the door gunner slashing the muzzle of his machine gun from side to side. He had not heard the soldiers' questions nor their pleas to administer the last rites to the legless boy.

The delirium that had begun on the hill had intensified beyond measure when finally the young lieutenant reached out with his right hand toward a cradled helmet, and with a shaking index finger touched disembodied cartilage, graying skin and a cold, ragged piece of vastus medialis.

When the chopper began its descent to the hill, the padre moved to the door to look downward. From the descending chopper his view had been obscured at first by dust and smoke. What was it that he saw below? Was it high Masada or ravaged Antioch? Was it the charred summit of Mount Carmel? As the Huey neared the LZ, the chaplain bit his lip. There were more green bags stacked at the top of the hill.

The hill below had been completely blackened all the way to its crest. There were unfamiliar blisters and newly cut gashes in the crust of the earth. Smoke was seeping from deep fissures. The jungle around the base of the hill had been completely razed. More terrible things had happened during the night.

The padre fought back the competing desires to scream or burst into tears. If what he saw below had happened in Central Park, it would be considered an American tragedy. The newspapers would be filled with this story for weeks. If a New York–to–Saigon passenger jet had gone down in the Sheep Meadow, every ambulance from five boroughs would be down below, parked helter-skelter, their doors ajar, their blinding, blinking lights flashing madly, urgently.

The phone lines would be jammed with calls from terrified families and still hopeful loved ones. The coroner's office would spend weeks checking reams of dental records. Anguished family members would have to be carried away after identifying the body. Camera shots would be averted in deference. There would be candles and prayers in scores of churches and Buddhist temples. Human beings had been transformed into sacks of skin dripping crimson. Blame would have to be assigned, lawyers retained, culpability alleged in a hundred lawsuits.

But here, on the Laotian border, the survivors' sorrow would be deferred for decades. The families of these victims would never be able to imagine the deaths of their loved ones. Responsibility would be dissolved in the acid solution of patriotism. Agony would be soothed by the sweet balm of loyalty. What the padre saw below was not the Sheep Meadow. It was nothing at all. Just the end of a minor siege in an anonymous place.

The metal containers that held the radio equipment looked strange. He was not able to focus his eyes on them. They seemed distorted, misshapen, as if drawn in sfumato. Their color had gone from drab green to a dark, streaked gray. As he stepped from the chopper, the chaplain noticed that some of the troops were standing silently by the larger container box, the Salon des Refusés.

They stood in a half circle at the crest of the hill, their hats off and their necks craned at the same identical angle. Their rifles were somewhere else entirely, dropped or discarded, but almost certainly forgotten for the moment. There were mortar tubes, canteens, helmets, and bandoliers left here and there in give-a-shit randomness. Every square inch of scorched ground around them was littered with Claymore sacks and ammo boxes.

The chaplain took his place among the boys, who were unaware of him and of one another as they stood and stared. They were slumping in a semicircle; rubber-legged, breathing heavily and barely conscious. They stood in that way that troopers stand when, for some unknown and unknowable reason, death has brushed against them, then shoved against them, then left them untouched as it moved on to fully embrace someone else. Their bodies, still vibrating with terror, sagged within their soaked clothing as they stared in common disbelief.

Young men who could believe in little more than pneumatics, ballistics, and small superstitions were struck dumb by what they saw. What they saw was a phenomenon, like a planet with a slightly erratic orbit, thereby proving the presence of yet another body. What they were seeing was something even more intriguing than Sputnik. They were witnessing a true miracle in a land otherwise administered by the laws of physics and governed by the rules of probability, and they called others over to see it.

"Come here, man, and look at this!"

"*Amigos, ven acá. Míralo. La mierda! Míralo!*"

"Shit, you gotta see this!"

Another man joined them as they all peered at a small, shining object. Unlike the others, he had dragged his rifle with him, and its flash suppressor dug a line in the mud beside him as he walked. He

moved to the half circle and took his place in a gap between two soldiers. He stood next to the padre. It was Jesse, still living. Jesse bent
down to look at the object more carefully, then fell to one knee.

It was indeed a miracle. He was seeing a miracle. The chaplain
noticed a sort of Kirlian aura around Jesse's head. Was it evidence of
a phantom life that had been traumatically torn away or was it simply
the heat that was generated when a young life changes too fast?

On the outside skin of the metal wall of the container box, a dog
tag hung from its small, fragile chain. The dog tag was shining and
perfect, and the chain, as far as was visible, was perfectly intact.
There was a small slot in the outer wall of the box, a slot that was precisely the same size as the edge of the metal tag. The tag had been
blown through two layers of corrugated, reinforced steel, and neither the chain nor the tag had been broken or marked in any manner.

There it was, the wafer-thin tag materializing through metal,
walking through walls and putting the terrible force of plastique to
shame. There it was, hanging like a weed daring to grow in a fissure
of steel, like a tender vine pushing itself through a crack in the
mortar of a stone fence. It was an absurd act of life, this name and serial number pressed through to the world of the living from the hell
that existed on the other side.

The frail chain was unbroken. Had it passed through the substance of a human neck? Or did the terrible explosion carefully lift it
off the neck and guide it over the head, being careful not to let it
catch on the ears? Without saying a word, the man on his knee stood,
then reached up and pulled the door open even farther. The canvas
bag that had carried the explosive was little more than a layer of tan
dust. The sapper's brown feet were still there, just inside the door.
Between his sandaled feet was the single green and black boot of an
American soldier. None of the feet were connected to legs. Nothing
else of the two men could be seen.

"Supposing there is a God," said someone. "Supposing He really
gives a shit?"

Had their bodies liquefied and commingled with the sandbags,
the PSP, and all the electronic equipment? Had someone already removed the American's body and flown it back to Da Nang? Did
more than one NVA get this far when they overran the hill last
night? Could they have retrieved their comrade's body? Everything
within the container was seared black and melting together. The in-

terior walls and the roof of the reefer bulged outward, a ghastly black circle of striated and smoking steel. The Salon des Refusés's sign had been blown a hundred yards down the hill.

Jesse then moved back to the tiny altar hanging on the side of the box. Now even more soldiers had gathered to see it. An Indian soldier stared silently. He was smoking a joint in broad daylight. The brass wouldn't have approved, but the brass was dead. Tiburcio Mendez crossed himself and dropped down to one knee to stare.

"*Qué milagro,*" whispered Mendez solemnly. His true voice was veiled with sadness. The mere sight of the dog tag had brought him some small measure of relief. His best friend Julio Lopez was up there in one of the body bags. Mendez had been at his side when blood orchids had blossomed on his upper chest and neck. Mendez laughed a crying laugh. He had actually seen flowers instead of exit wounds. Maybe it had been a sign. Perhaps this *milagro* meant that Lopez's wounds, in the hallowed presence of El Señor, would soon be transformed into bright, spreading bouquets.

There was a small relief in their eyes. Perhaps the war wasn't just physics, after all. Perhaps they weren't just anonymous bodies being smashed together in a linear accelerator where predictable pieces flew off and energy was released in the form of human souls. Ineffable, unreasonable things still happened. There was still a place on this earth for mystery. Jesse reached for the dog tag, and before anyone could stop him he pulled it from its chain and dropped it into his pocket.

The men around him groaned, then returned slowly to their tasks. The spell had been broken. There were three or four bodies still to be tagged and bagged, radio equipment and crypto logs to be destroyed. The tall body of the boy from Mississippi had to be carried up the hill to the LZ. The medevac choppers would fly him to Da Nang, where his large intestines would be sterilized then reinserted into the cavity below his stomach. Then his wounds would be sewn shut, but it would be too late. No one would know that he had been shot and killed in the same instant that his hero, Martin Luther King, had turned to ask a question at the windy back door of room 306 of the Lorraine Hotel.

"Do I really need a coat?"

It would be four full days before his brothers in the field would find out about the assassination in Memphis. They would be told by Hanoi Radio.

"African-American soldiers, why are you fighting for a country that kills your greatest leader? Why are you fighting for a country that will not let you eat at a lunch counter with whites?"

"Is Dr. King really dead?" a thousand GI voices would say. "Man, is the King of love really dead? It was a white man that killed him, wasn't it? Jesus Christ! Oh, Jesus fucking Christ! Why the fuck am I shooting at zips? They ain't never did me no wrong, never called me nigger. I should be back home shooting at the man, shooting at the Klan!"

Following orders from the Pentagon, Armed Forces Radio would delay the story for fear that black soldiers would riot, for fear that they would lay down their arms and refuse to kill men of color. In a few hours the hill would be given back to the NVA and to the jungle. Somewhere down the slope the chaplain had left the altar to poke and prod at the rubble in an effort to locate his personal Bible. Jesse watched as the chaplain suddenly stood bolt upright, dropping the charred Bible to the ground.

The padre had inadvertently focused his eyes on the burned objects around his feet. He had walked into the middle of the objects assuming they were tree stumps or blackened sandbags. He had inhaled the smoke. But they weren't tree stumps at all. They were bodies, charcoal and purple bodies eternally locked in the familiar pugilist's contraction; the blanched, yellow bones beneath the simmering embers cracked open by the enormous force of muscles contracting violently in the heat—the usual reaction to napalm.

Now the padre had surely seen enough. Now he had touched far more than a kneecap. Jesse watched him as the chaplain began to stagger like a drunkard toward the southern base of the hill. Somehow Jesse knew that he would not be coming back.

"Where are you going, padre?" called Jesse frantically as he ran down the hill toward the chaplain. "You know the sergeant is dead, don't you?" said Jesse, his voice cracking. "I found a right foot in the container box. Jesus, I think it's his. It's so damn heavy. Do you know how heavy a foot is? They listed him as missing, but I know he's dead. Do you know if medevac got him? Do you think he could be one of these bodies out here? Are any of these bodies missing a foot?"

Jesse's crazed words were spilling out of his mouth.

"You know that Lopez and Cornelius are dead, don't you? They were good boys, good friends. Who is going to sing 'Taps' now? I don't know the goddamn words!"

Though tears were streaming down Jesse's face, he would never believe that the mere presence of liquid meant that he must be crying. Crying was a release and a relief. These were silent tears of mourning that came not from his eyes but from deep in his muscles and bones. He would weep, but Jesse would never cry.

"Dirty sons of bitches!" he screamed at the burned bodies around him. He kicked the body nearest him, sending a faceless head rolling down the hill. Only the severed stem of the neck was pink. Jesse saw it and groaned. His speedometer was reading three hundred miles an hour.

"Where the fuck were you last night, padre?" Jesse screamed even louder. "Lopez said his last confessions to me and I'm no priest! Lopez wanted you, padre. He had to settle for me! He wanted to tell you that he stole money from his mother when he was ten, and that he used to spy on his younger sister when she was naked in the shower! Her name is Yolanda. One time he even masturbated while she douched. Some deep confessions, huh? He was a real bad one, huh? A real sinner! You let them down! Where were you, padre? Spam Boy is gone, too. He spoke Hawaiian. It's a feminine language, isn't it? It's full of vowels. You let them all down!"

"I know, Jesse. I know," said the lieutenant in a desolate voice. "But please tell me what happened here last night. What happened to you, Jesse?" said the padre, who was now staring into Jesse's burning, flooded eyes. The Kirlian light around his face was even more intense than just minutes before. "It should have happened to me, too. You're not the same. I can see you're not the same. I don't know why, but I can see it. I know I should've been here. I know I should've been here. Please tell me what happened here last night."

"I can't tell you, padre. I can't tell you what happened." Jesse used his filthy forearm to wipe the mud and tears from his face. He sank to his knees and began to shiver uncontrollably.

"I don't ever want to think about it again. Never again! I will die before I ever think about this place again! Where the fuck do you think you are going?" Jesse demanded as he rose to his feet and grabbed the chaplain's shoulder, forcing him to stop moving for a moment. His grip on the chaplain's jacket was rough and painful, but there was no complaint.

"That way," said the chaplain, pointing directly ahead.

He was pointing toward the southwest. Jesse released his grip and removed his hand from the padre's shoulder. He looked into the man's eyes and saw that the padre was no longer a part of anyone's army, not God's, not America's. He was no longer a part of this war. The sweet, sooty smell of burning humans had finally released his tenuous mind from this agonized plane of reality.

No one on the hill would try to stop him as he walked away. It was his personal right. There were a whole lot of guys over here who had shot themselves in the foot to get out. It happened all the time. The young padre had just chosen to shoot himself in a far more vulnerable spot.

"Do you know that the sergeant told me something about this mission, Jesse?" said the padre as he walked away. His voice had darkened into a slur and his face had taken on a sinister look. The chaplain had decided to let one last communication flow from his closing mind. Jesse ran a few steps to catch up.

"He told me that this hill installation was a decoy. Isn't that something? That other relay station thirty clicks to the east was the real thing. We were a decoy. We were never supposed to carry a signal. Those crypto machines were turned off. When the other installation went down, we had to take up the communications. The sergeant had to fire up this installation all by himself. He said that some deskbound full-bird colonel over at command came up with this bright idea. He said that the bastard's probably calling his wife back home in Ohio right now, and is telling her about his promotion."

"The North Vietnamese just hit both positions," said Jesse with a tone of wonderment. It began to dawn on the young sergeant what exactly had happened. The chaplain nodded.

"They used most of their troops and heavy armor on the real radio repeater," continued Jesse, "then they came back here for us. Somehow they knew which one was real. They knew it would take time for this one to get on line. By that time, the insertion teams in Cambodia would be fucked. This whole installation don't mean nothing. They did this to us, padre, because they wanted us to know that they could do it."

The chaplain was nodding his head knowingly and giggling hysterically as he walked.

"Where are you going from here, Jesse? What are you going to do now?"

"Supposing I get out of here in one piece, padre," Jesse answered through clenched, chattering teeth and a seething breath. "Supposing I don't lose my fucking mind like you did, I'm going to live in France . . . in Marseille. I'll go and live in France, where the women wear no pants. I've never been there, but someone back in Da Nang told me that it's real nice. A friend told me it was where I should go. I don't belong back home anymore. I don't ever want to go back there. I'm gonna sit in a café in Marseille and think crazy, fucked-up thoughts and write bad poems. I want to drink coffee and read my bad stanzas out loud."

Suddenly the full implication of the padre's revelation sank in even deeper.

"We were a decoy, padre? Cornelius and Sarge and Roosky were fucking decoys? The Indians were a decoy?" Jesse fell silent for a long moment. His eyes scanned the death at his feet and the burned ground that stretched out for half a mile.

"I suppose what I really want is some justice, padre. Fuck all these lifers and their fucking war. Fuck the domino theory! There must be some fucking place on this earth where the right thing gets done, where there's no bullshit. I just want some justice."

Jesse suddenly stopped walking. His bleary gaze settled upon the NVA head that he had kicked. The spinal cord was still pink and glistening at the center of the charcoal rubble that had been the neck. The head looked like a geode cracked open to expose the blazing rose crystal within. Jesse walked a few steps toward the head, then bent down when he noticed that something had fallen out of the dead mouth. He picked the object up. It was a piece of green jade. He moved to a second charred body and probed in the dead mouth with his finger. Another sliver of jade fell out.

He moved from body to body, checking for the presence of the strange stone. No other bodies contained the jade. Somehow Jesse noticed that the two bodies where he had found the green stones had been smaller than all the rest.

"They eat jade, padre!" he said in a voice that was a mixture of pain and mystery. "Why the fuck do they eat jade?"

"'Be careful, Jesse, too much thinking will make you crazy."

The padre had not heard Jesse's question. "I've seen it in you, in those weird daydreams and supposings of yours. Just look at me," the padre raved. "It's made me crazy. It stole my faith. How many times in one life can a faith be stolen?"

The padre was thirty yards away now and yelling.

"This cruel place could seduce you, Jesse. It's so damned seductive! It could make you believe that ice is fire." The chaplain was laughing now, a sharp, hideous cackle. The padre used both arms in a sweeping gesture, from horizon to horizon.

"This place can steal your soul as well as your life. Someday a long time from now, you could find yourself loving these moments of horror, embracing them. You could begin to believe that this is true life, that everything slower than three hundred miles an hour is a lie. *Furta sacra*, Jesse. *Furta sacra*."

The padre continued speaking as he walked, though no one heard his words. He mumbled on about sacred theft as he walked, the sacking of Jerusalem, the burning of Byzantium, the sacking of the Dome of the Rock by the crusaders, the craven act of thievery in the holy name of God—the act of stealing the youth from a boy's skin and marrow, the act of stealing the thoughts from his mind and the pulse from right out of his arm. He walked away with tides of bitterness breaking beneath his sullen tongue.

Making invisible Catholic crosses with his Unitarian right hand, he spoke into the ear of dead Cornelius as he walked. He blessed those limp, sleepy hands of his, and those large, plum-colored, expressive lips that were almost feminine. He blessed the Baptist soul of the tall Creole sergeant whose hair was wispy and nut brown at the temples. He blessed the dear sergeant's wife, wherever she was and wherever her life took her.

He blessed poor, innocent Julio Lopez, who always seemed more comfortable moving sideways. His wide, pigeon-toed feet should have been straightened while he was still an infant back in Juarez. He finished his belated, failed blessings, then passed silently through the outer perimeter and was walking by the decimated bunkers of the enemy when the boys on the hill lost sight of him.

The padre, with his last sane thought, supposed that he would never again bother his own God with a prayer. He would never again pretend to interpret the ineffable. What good was prayer anyway?

The priests of Baal had gone back to the drawing board and returned with F-14s and laser-guided bombs.

"What mean ye," he cried out in the words of the prophets to the scorched trees above his head, "what mean ye that ye beat my people to pieces?"

If only he had turned back to look upward at the blistered hill, he might have kept some small hope sequestered within. He might have clung to the other reality a few days more. Above him were boys stunned by great pain yet gathering together again to smoke dope and to suppose an alternate world.

"Suppose men did not kill the things they love."

Above him was a young Chicano sergeant, who, in his own moment of madness, was placing a piece of jade on his tongue.

Above him were boys cut open by hatred, cleansed by fire, stitched shut by grief; boys at world's end probing that fearful perimeter for a single fleeting sight of love divine.

In the end, only Tiburcio Mendez strained his eyes for a final glimpse of the padre. He wondered how far he would make it. Would he die in the Mekong Delta? If, by some miracle, the Viet Cong or the North Vietnamese regulars didn't kill him, he would probably drown in the Mekong River or the South China Sea. He had no chance of survival. When the chaplain disappeared into the distance, Mendez rubbed his crucifix and once again turned his eyes to the heavens.

Far above all of their heads, far above both the living and the dead, miles above the airless ionosphere in the cold silence of space, a Scotch-Irish and Mexican satellite spun its way between the stars.

7

on tourette's hill

Bruce McMurtry, the bailiff in Superior Court department 23, put away his girlie magazine and signaled emphatically to Jesse Pasadoble as the lawyer entered the empty courtroom. In his meaty hand, uplifted triumphantly, the bailiff held a single sheet of folded paper. It had to be a note from the jury. Jesse read the note quickly, then shook his head slowly. Bruce smiled as he watched for a reaction in Jesse's face.

Of course, the bailiff already knew what the jury was going to do. Every time he had entered the jury room to take them to lunch, he had snagged some juicy snippets of their conversations, the tail end of a heated exchange, and even the total, tearful collapse of a once resolute will to resist. He enjoyed watching the worried lawyers squirming over issues and questions that had, long ago, been resolved in the minds of all but one or two jurors. This particular note indicated that the foreman wanted the judge to reinstruct them on the definition of malice aforethought, and on premeditation and deliberation.

"They asked for sandwiches and cold drinks. They want to work right through lunch on the People of the State of California versus Bao Vung." Bruce smiled sadistically. "They're real close." He knew how hard this time was for the lawyers, and he loved to witness it. He reached behind his desk and produced the suit that Bao had worn throughout the trial.

"I called in Hong Ha, the Vietnamese interpreter. He'll be here in a minute. I brought the defendant down from the jail and I'm putting the suit on him right now," said Bruce. "They're real close."

"They're stuck between first- and second-degree," said a voice from the doorway. It was Peter Cling, the prosecutor.

Jesse concurred with a nod. It was Friday and the jury had decided against going to a nearby restaurant for a leisurely, convivial lunch. The thrill of being thrown into a windowless room with eleven complete strangers had long since worn off. The warm glow of mutual humanity and exploration in the trial phase had been snuffed out by the time deliberations began, blown away by sudden exposure to the harsh light of buried bias and entrenched opinion, by the power of cherished prejudice. They were hard at it now. The honeymoon had ended the moment a foreperson had been chosen. The clock on the wall was moving toward the end of the workday. Five o'clock on Friday was always a bad time for defense lawyers.

The prosecutor's analysis was probably right, but still, there was the smallest of possibilities that they were discarding first-degree murder, then moving on to choose between second-degree murder and manslaughter, a killing while in the heat of passion or during a sudden quarrel. The question could have been sent out to appease a single juror who was holding out for first-degree. There was also the remote possibility that the jury could be deadlocked on the issue of premeditation: whether the intent to kill was turned over in Bao Vung's mind before he acted. The whole case might have to be tried again. That would be a win for the defense.

"Has the judge seen this?" Jesse asked the district attorney.

"He wants to see both of us in chambers," said Cling.

Peter Cling was a curly-haired, square-jawed Irishman. Despite himself, Jesse liked him. He was tough and tenacious, and he took losing the same way he took winning: he walked out of the courtroom and got ready for the next case. He had won too many murder trials to care what the jurors or anyone else thought about him after the case was through.

When other, less experienced prosecutors gloated over their own imagined prowess after a victory, he understood how high the deck was stacked against the defendant and his lawyer. Despite the burden

of proof: beyond a reasonable doubt, most potential jurors walked
into the courtroom absolutely convinced of their own impartiality,
but in their hidden hearts they came prepared to convict, and both
Peter and Jesse knew it well.

The two men walked together into the chambers of the Honor-
able Judge Harris Taback. The judge was seated behind his desk, a
look of sheer rapture on his face. It was lunchtime and the moon of a
face that surrounded his wire-rimmed spectacles was in perpetual
motion; from forehead to mandible, every muscle above the neck
was hard at work. His fingers, pink and cherubic, were clustered in
front of his face. His pinkie ring was smeared with condiments. The
judge looked like a black-robed praying mantis mauling an aphid.
He was devouring a huge pastrami sandwich, two pounds of spiced
meat flanked by mere suggestions of bread. His lap was littered with
crumbs of rye and dollops of horseradish.

"I had this flown in just this morning from Cantor's down on
Fairfax Boulevard in Los Angeles. My hand to God, this is the
original manna."

He took another bite.

"You can keep the Carnegie Deli. You can have Saul's and
Shensen's. That Eric Safire and what's-his-face, Marvin Rous both
like that Shensen's drek, but what do they know? They're sephardim!
What do they know from kosher? They're Jaime-come-latelys to the
West Coast. Don't even mention Brother's Restaurant in Redwood
City or wherever. They've got Korean cooks! Did you hear me? Ko-
reans! Next to this, it's all trayf."

The judge smiled and spoke while he ate, the tan mash of masti-
cated meat and bread was a shapeless, speckled mass of putty on his
tongue and teeth. In between his sentences, like an excited, preoccupied child, he hummed a senseless, repetitive refrain. Now and again
he would retrieve a scrap of food from his lap and stick it back into
the sandwich as though it were a folded prayer shoved into a crack
in the Wailing Wall.

"And Jesus Christ, the Atomic horseradish they got down there is
the best on the entire goddamn earth. The stuff will grow hair, I
swear to God, the E'mes. Atomic horseradish is better than Ro-
gaine." He removed one hand from his sandwich just long enough to
point to the bald spot on the top of his head. "This is what you get
from wearing a yarmulke for forty years."

Once again his smile dove into the business end of the sandwich. Jesse noticed that when the judge bit into the pastrami, his eyes rolled back in their sockets, just like a shark's. From the other end of the sandwich, through the pores of the rye bread and between the slices of spiced, oily meat, and finally, from the spaces between his slick, stubby fingers, muffled words nonetheless emerged.

"Come to think of it, they made a helluva pastrami at the Eden Roc Hotel in Miami Beach. A helluva sandwich! Jesus, my father took me there as a child to see Louis Prima and Keely Smith in the Mediterranean Lounge. Can you believe it, they had to play the lounge? A class act like that had to play the small room!"

A small, wistful shadow of sadness passed across the judge's face for a fleeting instant. He had once had a powerful boyhood crush on Keely Smith. In fact, his overwhelming feelings for the woman had required six years of postadolescent therapy to straighten out. To this day he demanded that his wife Lavon dye her hair raven black and wear a pixie cut. Even as he lapsed momentarily into a familiar, lifelong love for Keely, his lips moved silently to the words of her hit song "Sweet and Lovely."

"What does the jury want this time?" he said, bursting from his precious revery. "A bunch of kvetching yekls, I swear to God. Somebody read me the damn note already."

Peter Cling obliged. After hearing the contents of the note, the judge swigged down a bottle of Cel-Ray and announced that he would send the pertinent instructions directly into the jury room and they could read about premeditation for themselves.

"I should have to drag them out here and read it to them again? The first time they didn't hear it? Sorry to say this, Pasadoble, but a verdict they should've come back with two days ago. Your boy is a shmuck, Jesse. And this was a slam-dunk for you, Peter. Shame on you! I tell you, it's that guy in the first row wearing the Birkenstocks and white socks; you never should have left him on the jury. He's a fashion catastrophe! He's a goddamn artichoke, a momzer! The rest are nuchshleppers, goyim . . . present company excepted, of course. God, such a panel they sent us! Half of them have been victims of violent crimes and the other two-thirds were molested by a parent. Now look here."

He signaled with both grease-covered hands that the two lawyers should move closer.

"Approach the bimmeh, my friends. Both of you guys are pros. Enough said about that. You both know that it's never too late to settle this case. Enough said?" He lowered his voice to intensify the air of sincerity. "Jesse, would your client take a voluntary manslaughter if Peter offered it right now, this very moment? We all know that this jury could hang up. You could be exposed to a homicide all over again."

"Peter is never going to offer a voluntary," said Jesse, looking at the prosecutor, who said nothing but who fully concurred by his silence. "Besides, the only plea bargain my client would take is a full apology from the state and a free taxi ride home."

"Bruce!" The judge yelled out to his bailiff, who appeared in the doorway almost instantaneously. He had been on his way into chambers when he was called.

"We have an instruction to send into the jury room," said Judge Taback. "I've written my comments on the bottom," he said while pointing with the remnants of his sandwich.

"Too late," said Bruce with a wide smile, "they have a verdict."

"Oh, Jesus!" said Jesse. No matter how many trials he had done, those words always sent a chill down his spine. Reflexively, he reached into his pocket and pulled out his key chain. Instead of a fob, the chain held two dog tags side by side. One of them was his own. He ran his thumb over the raised letters of the two tags, feeling the letters and words that had been burned into his mind for decades. The tags calmed him. They reminded him that there were far worse things on this earth than jury trials and verdicts. No matter how difficult this experience was, it was only an asshole pucker factor of three, maybe four.

The judge smiled broadly. He could go home early today. He really needed a deep massage and a double martini. There was a new masseuse at the club Concordia Argonaut, a raven-haired Sephardi from Morocco who had the strongest fingers in San Francisco. The judge's shoulder muscles twitched at the thought. His pet name for her was Keely.

The prosecutor's only visible reaction was to grind his teeth nervously beneath his ruddy cheeks. The defendant had made it easy for him, but anything could happen in a court of law and he knew it. He knew from experience. Sympathy or anger could send a jury reeling sideways into completely illogical verdicts. They could hate the judge's dandruff or be disgusted by an attorney's choice of tie. If they didn't like the way you looked, they ignored what you had to say.

A working-class jury despised anyone wearing expensive Italian suits. Well-to-do jurors sneered at the audacity and pretense of someone wearing the same Italian suits. Every jury hated any sign of smugness in a district attorney. They didn't mind it in a defense lawyer. Defense attorneys were expected to have transformed their desperation into poise and polish and into the ability to do the unexpected. Jurors wanted to be entertained by defense lawyers, but if by chance they were, they felt sure that they had somehow been tricked, defrauded.

Jesse waited nervously in the back hallway while his client finished putting on the baggy, wrinkled blue suit. He had changed into his jail clothing when the jury had begun its deliberations. The defendant did a pathetic job tying his tie, but Jesse let it go. Bao Vung could use the sympathy. When they walked into the courtroom, the jury had already been seated and everything was silent and tense. Only Bruce the bailiff was smiling.

Jesse looked into the faces of the jurors. No one returned his inquisitive stare. They were looking everywhere but at one another or at the defense table. It was a bad sign. They felt guilty about rushing their verdict. He moved his eyes from one juror to the next. Still no response, not even from the young, progressive lesbian in the second row.

Jesse's stomach began to tighten. His dark-blue suit felt tight and ill fitting. A thin film of sweat had appeared on his forehead. With all of his strength he forced his hands to stay absolutely still. His key chain and dog tags had been making a racket. Beneath his thumb he felt his own name, a serial number, a blood type, and the words No Preference.

There were two gay men and a lesbian on the jury. The gay men owned property in the Castro district and were definitely for the prosecution, thought Jesse. Jesse regretted keeping them on the panel, but the jury pool had been so thin. The judge was wrong about the man in the Birkenstocks. Jesse guessed that it had been the lesbian who had held out. The rest of the jury had been blue-hairs, retirees who had nothing better to do with their time than sit on a jury. Jesse sighed. For them, this was as good as a soap opera.

The entire jury pool had been a travesty, nothing but blue-hairs, sweaty bicycle messengers with rings in their noses, conservative, older Asians who had heard the rumor that all you had to do to get out of jury duty was shrug and answer in Cantonese. The venire had included two or three Filipino clerks who wanted only to be excused from jury duty altogether or be allowed to vote guilty and go home. There had been a smattering of tall, white-haired bank executives clutching their portfolios and cursing that foolish day when they had registered to vote. There had been a few Barbie doll people, young socialites with surgically sculpted faces and new sweaters draped over their shoulders.

There had been no Latinos on the panel. Immigrants from Nicaragua and El Salvador were so distrustful of government that they never voted; they never registered, either at the polling booth or the Department of Motor Vehicles. Older Mexicans who had voted south of the border believed that every election was surely rigged, that every cop was on the take. Younger Mexicanos would register their cars, but they would use aliases and false addresses. They had learned from their elders, and didn't want to be picked up for all of their outstanding traffic warrants. Russian Jews knew better than to voluntarily place their true names onto a piece of paper.

Jesse had used all his peremptory challenges on this jury. He had never been satisfied with it. In the entire voir-dire process he had not heard a single answer that rang true. In desperation he had even reached into his pocket and placed the sliver of jade he had found almost thirty years ago onto the tip of his tongue. But it hadn't helped; he'd heard nothing. Every mind on the panel had slammed shut the instant the judge had read the charges against the Vietnamese defendant: ". . . did intentionally and with malice aforethought murder a human being . . ."

He had kicked off every older Asian juror in hopes that the prosecutor would move for a mistrial based upon Jesse's exercise of racially motivated challenges to a set of jurors. The court would be forced to bring in a whole new panel. Any other prosecutor in this building would have jumped to his or her feet and objected strenuously, righteously, and mechanically. Peter Cling wouldn't fall for it. His case was too good. He'd given Jesse all the peremptory challenges he wanted. He knew what Jesse knew: other than juror number seven, the lesbian, there had been no freethinkers on this panel, no artichokes.

"May the record reflect that all parties are present in the matter of the State of California versus Bao Han Vung. Madame foreperson," asked Judge Taback, "does the jury have a verdict?" There were stray pieces of pastrami in his teeth and shining beads of perspiration breaking out on his forehead as the follicles and pores of his crown responded to the magic Atomic horseradish.

"Yes, we do," said the foreperson. She rose and handed two pieces of paper to the court clerk. The judge, the prosecutor, and the defense lawyer knew immediately that the verdict had to be a second-degree murder. Judge Taback smiled knowingly at both the prosecutor and the defense attorney. Better than a first-degree, sighed the defense lawyer to himself. His thumb stopped moving over the dog tags. Better than a voluntary manslaughter, thought the prosecutor, whose jaw had loosened up perceptibly.

"Feh!" muttered the judge to himself as he perused the forms. This was a farshtinkener jury panel. They could've done this two days ago. He glanced at his gold watch. He was about an hour away from that martini and those unbelievable fingers. A smile appeared on his face as he imagined the sweet pain. The jurors saw the smile and surmised, with great satisfaction, that his honor was quite pleased with their verdict. One day in the future, two of these jurors, while hearing another case, would vote for guilt simply to please the judge.

"Will the defendant rise."

Jesse rose with his client.

"Will madame clerk please read the verdicts."

"We the jury in the above stated cause do hereby find the defendant Bao Han Vung not guilty of count one, murder in the first degree."

Though Jesse knew that this was coming, he still loved to hear the words "not guilty." It helped cushion the blow that was sure to follow. Bao Han Vung, not knowing the significance of two sheets of paper, smiled confidently.

"We the jury in the above stated cause find the defendant Bao Vung guilty of count two, murder in the second degree. Further, we find the allegation to be true, that in the commission of the above crime he did personally use a firearm."

"*Caí này nghĩa là gì?* What this mean?"

Jesse could not believe his ears. Since he had been appointed to represent this defendant, more than a year ago, the man had stubbornly refused to speak to anyone—not his lawyer, not his family. Jesse had sent various Vietnamese interpreters into the jail and even a Buddhist monk from the defendant's hometown, but Bao Vung had maintained his cold silence. And now he was speaking out loud, and in passable English.

"What this mean?" he repeated.

"It means," whispered Jesse, "that you will get fifteen years to life for murder in the second degree. You will also get a mandatory consecutive term of three, five, or ten years for use of a weapon. It means the judge could give you a maximum of fifteen years to life, plus ten years consecutive."

As the lawyer and his client spoke for the first time, the judge was thanking the jury for their service and excusing them from any further duty. As he spoke to them, the jury was treated to a glimpse of scattered remnants of the judge's lunch still clinging to his teeth. Before filing out of the courtroom and into the hallway, the departing jurors had all hazarded a last backward glance at the defendant.

"Well, what do you think?" asked the lesbian juror audibly as she slowly put on a jacket. There was a disturbed, pensive look on her pretty face. The young woman was clearly shaken by the whole experience.

"I'm not really sure," answered another juror, "but I think it was pastrami."

When the door closed behind the last juror Vung spoke again.

"The gun not belong me. I took from Ky."

"You took it from the victim?" asked Jesse angrily. He reached out for his client and grabbed a lapel of his suit. He jerked the defendant's face toward his own. Bruce, the bailiff, rose quickly from his seat, shrugged, then sat back down. A lawyer was attacking his own client? He had seen the reverse often enough. This situation just wasn't covered in his job description.

"You took the gun from the victim?" The fingers of Jesse's free hand were moving furiously over the dog tags now. "When did you do that? If you say the night of the killing I'll kick the shit out of you right here and now."

"I took one from Ky just before he die. He had two gun." Vung meekly held up two fingers and repeated his comment in Vietnamese. Hong Ha, the interpreter, repeated in English, "Ky had two guns."

"I've been trying to get you to talk to me for over a year. Your wife has been begging you to talk to me or to Eddy. Why are you bothering to tell me this today, thirty seconds after the damn verdict? It's too late, man."

Jesse turned away from his client. The enormity of his client's foolishness was almost overwhelming.

"Your brilliant strategy sure paid off, didn't it, asshole? First you got your boys to scare off all of the witnesses by threatening to kidnap their grandparents and children. Then you threaten all of their extended families with death, and what happened? They all waltzed in here, one right after the other, and testified against you, pointed you out in the courtroom.

"Did you see them up there? They were shaking with fear and that jury was hanging on their every word. If the victim did have a gun in his hand, none of those witnesses was going to say it. Your terror tactics made sure of that. This is not Vietnam, Vung. You should've told me."

Hong Ha, the Vietnamese interpreter, reached out and touched Jesse's wrist. "Calm down, Mr. Pasadoble," he said gently. "Vung will suffer for his stupidity."

"We didn't get at the truth in this trial, Hong," said Jesse. "Vung should be sentenced for the truth of his crime, not for his stupidity."

Vung turned to the Vietnamese interpreter. There was a word that he could not say in English.

"Appeal?" said the translator.

"Appeal what?" asked Jesse, now even angrier than before. "Newly discovered evidence? The victim had a gun in his hand? Vung, it has to be evidence that we couldn't have discovered at the time of trial, even with due diligence. I don't think it applies to evidence that the defendant himself decides his attorney shouldn't have. We couldn't investigate a self-defense because you wouldn't let us!"

There was a soft overlay of Vietnamese above Jesse's English as he spoke. Hong Ha's lips moved no farther than five inches from the defendant's ear as he translated.

"You told all those witnesses out there not to talk to me or my investigator. You did that, Vung. It was you. You made me try this case in a straitjacket. I know that this jury suspected that something else was happening at that party, that's why they compromised on their verdict. If we had been allowed to work on this case, who knows what they might have done? You could be free today."

Vung turned toward the interpreter and whispered a full sentence in Vietnamese.

"He says," began the interpreter, "that the guns are in the lake in Golden Gate Park."

Jesse's head fell into the palms of his hands. Long ago he had learned to respect the tough single-mindedness of men like Vung. Short, small-boned men like him had once ridden down the Ho Chi Minh trail on bicycles, carrying dismantled artillery pieces or enormous bags of rice on their sweating, breaking backs.

"Vung, you number-ten dinky-dau."

"Vung," repeated the interpreter, "you are worthless and crazy."

Jesse turned to face the interpreter. Generalized, diffuse anger was beginning to focus, to acquire direction.

"I want you to translate this word for word."

The interpreter nodded solemnly.

"Look at me, Vung."

Vung raised his eyes to meet those of his lawyer. It was the first time the two had ever made eye contact. In the jail the prisoner had steadfastly refused to look at his lawyer's face. He had spent long, silent hours feigning bored deafness and staring at the Formica tabletop or at the ceiling of the interview room.

"Bao Vung, you are a stupid son of a bitch. And now you are a sorry bastard with a whole lot of time on your hands. I will file your appeal. I will file a declaration saying that I messed up your case. My investigator will file a second declaration of his own. He will say that he failed to investigate the possibility of a second gun. I will prepare a motion for a new trial based on newly discovered evidence and ineffective assistance of counsel.

"I will do whatever I can. I was ready to do just that over a year ago. I want you to know that if it would do any good, I would beat you to a pulp right now for what you've done to yourself. It's what I feel like doing."

Jesse held a clenched fist in front of his client's face. There were tears in Vung's eyes, and he turned away from both the interpreter and his lawyer.

"He's got to go now," said Bruce, the bailiff, sternly. Manny Valenzuela, a second bailiff, had joined him.

Just then Jesse caught a glimpse of two forms seated in the back of the courtroom. It was Eddy Oasa, his investigator, and Carolina, his ex-girlfriend, sitting silently and respectfully in the last row of seats. They had heard the verdict and smatterings of the conversation afterward. Jesse waved them forward, but only Eddy rose and walked to the defense table.

"I'm very sorry, man," said Eddy. "You did the best you could for him. He sunk himself."

"I must love pain," said Jesse wearily. "I must really love it. Did you hear what he just told me?" Eddy shook his head, no. As he watched his client being escorted from the room, Jesse spoke in a restrained, controlled voice. "He told me that Ky had a gun. He just told me that the two guns are at the bottom of a lake in Golden Gate Park."

Eddy slumped visibly as he listened. For this trial he had interviewed scores of terrified witnesses. Over time he had come to believe that Ky had been carrying a gun, but he could never prove it. No witness had answered any of his questions without first having a heated discussion in Vietnamese with his family or the elders of his community. Only a few small merchants had talked, and they had said that Ky ran a protection racket and was never without his gun. Eddy looked to the front of the courtroom and watched as Bruce and Manny took Vung on the very first steps of his twenty-five-year journey.

Soon enough this courtroom, the color of the oak paneling, and the dry taste of the recycled air would be lost in the mists of his diminished life, a life that would become a grinding gray monotony of restraints, manacles, hobbles, Cyclone fences, razor wire, and bars. Over the years, time would distort everything that had happened today.

Bao Vung's recollections of this trial would be reduced, boiled down to a few faint flashes: a tearful witness, a standing foreperson, the fearsome, echoing words of a court clerk, and the brown and red face of an angry lawyer. Awash in an ocean of years, he would soon forget the insignificant slice of an instant when an index finger tickled a hair trigger, that single drop in a swelling sea of time when a firing pin moved forward to strike a center-fire cartridge.

The bailiffs were leading him toward a world without butter, forks, knives, or shoestrings; a world devoid of spices, French coffees, or Vietnamese food. It would be almost three decades before he would slurp a bowl of noodles or savor the taste of lemon grass and mint. The heavy door slammed behind Bao Vung and he began to move through a dark maze of cramped, barred rooms, through a quarter century of stainless-steel commodes, waxy single-ply toilet paper, stupid tattooed cellmates, and televisions with tiny nine-inch screens. Before he next saw the sunlight he would smoke twenty-three thousand packs of Salems and Kools, receive six thousand letters, and write five times as many.

A man who may well have fired a gun in self-defense had made the fateful decision to let his chain-smoking, Elvis-haired hoodlum friends intimidate all the witnesses. Appeals would be filed in vain. On the day of his release from prison, he would qualify for Social Security.

"What's happening, Eddy?" asked Jesse, who was also staring toward the holding cell. The image of Bao Vung disappearing into the jail elevator was now burned into his memory.

"You know how the cops have been trying to find Little Reggie Harp?" said Eddy excitedly. "Well, they found him."

"Where?" asked Jesse, suddenly diverted from his sadness. "Was it the Hayward cops? He has a cousin in Hayward, doesn't he?" As he spoke he glanced toward the back of the courtroom where Carolina sat silently. She is so beautiful, but demanding, excessively demanding, thought Jesse. She wants a normal, healthy, loving relationship. Her presence in this part of his life made him uncomfortable.

"No, man," continued Eddy excitedly. "They found him in the projects. He never left Tourette's Hill." There was an incredible intensity in his voice.

"Has he given a statement?" asked Jesse, suddenly unaware of Bao Vung, who was now four floors overhead and sobbing in his cell. "Did he mention Calvin?"

"He ain't never going to talk again."

"Oh no!" shouted Jesse. "How long?"

"A week, maybe ten days. It was hard to tell. The homicide inspectors think there were four or five generations of insect predation present. He could have been put into the ground two days after the killings at the Amazon Luncheonette. But get this. He had a note on his body from someone we both know and love. It was a death threat. They found it in one of his pockets."

"Biscuit Boy can write? Calvin writes notes? Did you see the paragraph he sent me about the book he's reading? He's on his third rewrite. The spelling and penmanship are below high school level."

As he spoke Jesse removed a sheet of paper from his briefcase and handed it to Eddy, who glanced at it briefly.

"He sure wrote this one," said Eddy, "and he signed it for good measure. The lab found his fingerprints all over the note. I've heard from the cops that it says Little Reggie is a dead man. Unless it was smuggled out of the jail, Calvin must have written it before his arrest. But listen, Jesse, you ain't heard the best part. They're digging up the whole damn hill. Tourette's Hill looks like Swiss cheese."

"Where is this Tourette's Hill?" asked Jesse impatiently.

"Potrero Hill, man," said Eddy. "Ain't you down with the new lingo?"

"Are they looking for the murder weapon, the gun?"

"No, man. It's bigger than that. Someone called in a bomb threat. The anonymous caller said that there was a pipe bomb buried near a wrecked car just below the projects, so the bomb squad brought in a metal detector, a robot arm and a dog. There wasn't any bomb, but the dog started digging behind a Dumpster and found Little Reggie. While homicide detail and the coroner were securing the first crime scene, the dog went running up the hillside about thirty feet or so and found another one. They've found three bodies so far and they're looking for more."

"Jesus, let's go!" said Jesse. "Any identities on the other two?"

"Not yet, but they're all young NMAs, Negro male adults. It's strange that no one ever reported any of those boys as missing. Word up on the hill is that kids have been disappearing up there for several months now."

"This is bad," said Jesse as he shoved Vung's thick case files into a briefcase. "This is very bad. Now there's no one else to prosecute for the Flyer and Adrong murders except Calvin Thibault. The jury won't like us blaming the crimes on a moldering corpse. Juries always want to punish a living human being."

Jesse walked to the back of the courtroom as Eddy read the sheet of paper that Jesse had handed him.

"Hello, Carolina," said Jesse as he stopped at the last row of seats.

If he felt something, his voice gave no indication. Carolina stood up and took one step toward him. She was not surprised at his tone of voice. Jesse Pasadoble was always protecting himself.

"I'm sorry about your client. I need to talk to you," she said. She tried to smile but gave up. She seemed distracted for a second, then regained her focus, reclaiming her inner strength.

"I don't have a lot of time today—"

"I don't mean right now," interrupted Carolina. "It doesn't have to be right now. I knew this wouldn't be a good time—not that I knew what the verdict would be, but Eddy told me you'd be here. I don't want to do this, but if I don't . . . ." She caught herself, inhaled deeply, and began again. "Come by when you can sit and communicate with me . . . just talk with me. That's all I want. I'll cook something for you—and I swear to the dark virgin that it won't be a veggie burger." She smiled a wistful, awkward smile, then quickly left the courtroom. "Goodbye, Eddy," she called out after the swinging doors had closed behind her.

"The dark virgin?" asked Eddy after waving goodbye to Carolina.

"La Morena," answered Jesse with only the hint of a smile, "is the patron saint of Mexican food. Carolina is one of those health-food fanatics. You know, ninety-grain breads and drinks made from crab-grass and yeast."

Jesse and Eddy walked from the courtroom into the large tiled hallway that ran the length of the third floor. Thankfully, there were no jurors lingering on the benches—they had all dissolved into the weekend and back into their own lives. Any reservations they had about their verdict had dissipated into space by the time they reached their homes. Farther down the hallway Carolina had stopped at a kiosk to buy a juice.

"Eddy, can I meet you at Tourette's Hill in about twenty minutes?"

Eddy noticed Carolina in line at the kiosk, smiled, then nodded at Jesse. He snapped open his sunglasses, adjusted them on his nose and ears, then disappeared through an exit door. Jesse walked down the hallway, all the while watching the woman who was now extending her hand to receive change. Carolina was having an intense conversation with the concessionaire. Making friends always came easy to her. She was probably trying to convince the poor guy behind the counter to stock more health foods. Jesse laughed to himself. The bottle in her left hand probably contained a dull gray mixture of free-range organic carrot juice and herbal teas that had been lovingly fertilized with the sterilized droppings of silent, celibate monks.

He sat down on a bench behind her. He could tell that she hadn't noticed him. He used the opportunity to look closely at her face and hair, her huge brown eyes. She was wearing baggy clothes: men's overalls and a heavy fatigue jacket. Had he ever really seen her? He had known so many women and had failed to love any of them. All of those relationships had ended with Jesse's wondering why the woman was so sad, so angry. When the initial passion was gone, what was left? Jesse had always taken his leave at the same time: when sexual demands gave way to emotional demands. He had warned Carolina. He had told her what to expect. He furrowed his brow in consternation. Why was this the first and only relationship that felt like a failure?

Despite her present manner of dress, she was a beautiful Spanish and Italian woman from Berkeley, who, at the age of seven, had decided that her primary ambition in life was to be a Chicana. Her father had been a sailor in the Second World War and had met her mother Rose on the island of Trinidad.

Her given name had been Giselle, but what Chicana could tolerate or even pronounce that name? For a time she had used the name Carole, but had abandoned it in favor of the Spanish version, Carolina. In truth, it was her second mother, her Italian wet nurse and babysitter, who gave her the name. Signora Stella Trovato, a woman who had spent her youth singing and dancing in the bars and bistros of San Miguel de Allende, had filled the child's mouth with macaroni and menudo, and her ears with old Italian sayings and the lyrics to a hundred Mexican songs.

Carolina spent her days at work listening to the Trio los Panchos and laboring quietly in her photographic studio or in her darkroom. She loved to work all day and into the smallest hours of the morning, choosing backdrops and lighting for the next shoot. In the winter she labored as a temporary secretary in one of those huge, dreary law offices downtown.

Summertime was her favorite time of year. Each June she would quit her office job and drive out to her storage unit on César Chávez Street. She would pour a tablespoon of gasoline into the carburetor of an ancient, dented, decal-ridden Ford Stepvan, start it up, and drive it to the nearest carwash. Carolina spent each summer driving up and down the streets of Bernal Heights and the Mission District, selling cherry popsicles, "drumsticks," and ice cream sandwiches to tiny Mexican and Guatemalan kids.

This year, the loudspeaker on the roof of her van played "Somewhere My Love," over and over again. The first time she had ever seen Jesse Pasadoble he had been standing in line with the kiddies, waiting to buy a grape Missile. The lawyer had purchased her entire stock that day, enough for the seventy kids at a nearby playground. Selling *paletas* was fun, but someday she hoped to be like Manuel Bravo or Graciela Iturbide and make a living with her photography.

In her studio she kept a small navy surplus cot beneath her shelves of chemicals, her bottles of developer and stop bath. It was where she slept when Jesse was not sleeping beside her. Lately she had been sleeping there every night. Her queen-sized bed upstairs had been undisturbed for almost five weeks.

"Señorita Carolina, there is a man behind you who seems very interested in you. He has been staring at you for some time now." The old man who ran the kiosk made a slight nod toward the oak bench behind Carolina.

"Is he a Chicano carrying a beat-up leather briefcase and wearing a red and blue tie?"

"Sí, señorita. That is him."

"What do you think of him, señor?" she said without turning to look behind herself.

"Oh, I have seen many men like him back in Mexico. They think that love, *el amor,* will turn them into someone else, someone they would not respect. *¡Pendejo!* I tell you, if I was twenty years younger, he would have to fight me for you." The old man raised one fist into the air in a gesture of both defiance and chivalry.

"*Pero, tengo una pregunta para tí.* Why do you hide your beauty? Why do you hide behind your clothing? Even an old man can see what you are doing."

"What am I doing?" asked Carolina, a stricken look on her face.

"You are trying to keep time from passing by." The old man raised both arms as he spoke. "You are trying to stop the natural way of things. You hide from the eyes of other men because he is the one you want. But most of all you hide because it makes you more like him." He nodded toward Jesse.

Carolina stood silent for a moment, stunned by the old fellow's words. As a young girl she had been mortified by the mere idea of makeup, by the thought of wanting to be looked at. Over time she had come to think of beauty as a personal weakness. Perhaps this is what kept Jesse away. In the last few months her manner of dress had become less and less feminine. Skirts and blouses had given way to canvas and denim from the local surplus store. Had she purposefully chosen a man who could not love? Was she testing him, trying to determine whether he could love her soul? It all seemed so crazy.

"Gracias," she whispered as she disappeared through the door and down the cement stairs. There was a look of desperate confusion on her face. She walked away without looking back at either Jesse or the old señor.

Behind her Jesse remained on the bench for ten silent minutes. Carolina was unlike any other woman he had ever known. Jesse suddenly realized that he missed seeing her . . . touching her.

"'Hey, Jesse," said deputy Jeri Pietrelli, "you'll never guess what's happening here. Milton Salteeno is in trial!" At the courtroom entrance nearest the bench, a female bailiff was using a portable metal detector to scan anyone who entered.

"You're kidding!" said Jesse, a look of stark disbelief on his face. He rose from the bench. Thoughts of Carolina would have to wait for another time. There was too much to do. Besides, nothing had changed. She still wanted something from him that he just couldn't give.

"Salteeno hasn't had a trial in twenty years!" exclaimed Jesse. "Have the newspapers been notified? Has someone called a press conference? Have they picked a jury yet?"

"'Not yet," said the bailiff.

"Ten bucks says it folds before lunch," sneered Jesse. The bailiff shook her head, her long hair landing first on one shoulder, then the other. She wanted nothing to do with that bet.

"Who is Milton Salteeno?" asked Hong Ha, the interpreter, as he descended the stairway with Jesse on his way to the first floor.

"You've never heard of him? He is the world-famous Panamanian plea artist," replied Jesse. "If plea bargains were paint, this guy would be Jan Vermeer or Pablo Picasso. His problem is that none of the prosecutors are afraid of him—they all know he isn't going to trial. So the deals he gets for his clients are lousy. You'll recognize him as soon as you see him. He's always out here in the hall bluffing and strutting with that empty briefcase of his. He's the only man I know who can fake an orgasm.

"He was at the very height of his powers during his Afro-Latino period. He's almost single-handedly sent half the black and brown men in this city down the river. In fact, a whole wing at Folsom Prison is named in his honor. His intimates and confidants report that for Christmas last year he gave each one of his own kids a suspended sentence and a term of supervised probation."

"I guess you don't like him." Hong was laughing.

"I hate him and everyone like him," spat Jesse. His eyes were becoming red again. "He should get out of the business. You can smell that man's fear of trial right through those expensive suits of his. The defendants can smell it, too. It's a stench that is a blend of aftershave, terror, and apathy. With that *cagatinta* as your lawyer, the decision whether or not to fight the case has nothing to do with the strengths or weaknesses of the evidence. That man's ass has never been in the grass."

"Mister Pasadoble, I have a question that I must ask you. Back in the courtroom I saw you with that small piece of jade," said Hong. "To my amazement you placed it into your mouth. I have not seen that done in many years. I didn't think anyone believed in that anymore, especially here in America."

Jesse looked at Hong, then reached into his pocket for the sliver of jade.

"I first put this stone into my mouth almost thirty years ago. Back then something unbelievable happened to me as soon as I closed my lips around this stone. It has never happened since, but I keep trying."

"It works on very few men," said Hong softly, "and for those for whom it works, it does so only under very special circumstances."

"Do you know what they are?" asked Jesse, his voice rising with hope.

"I had hoped that you could tell me," smiled Hong. The interpreter reached into his own pocket and retrieved his own piece of jade. "My father gave this to me." He smiled. "He told me that it was used against the French. He always said that the jade will only work for women, certain priests, or for men who are drowning. It has never worked for me."

Jesse left the building and walked to his car. Just yards behind them, the jury panel that had been assigned to Milton Salteeno's case was filing out of the building and spreading into the parking lot. This time the case had not folded as Jesse had predicted. This time, when the judge had announced the name of the case as the People of the State of California versus Virgilio Madrugada, the defendant had risen on his own behalf and announced that his name was Artemio Sanchez and that this man seated next to him was not his lawyer. When the defense attorney was asked by the judge whether he recognized his client, it had become apparent to all present that Milton Salteeno had never interviewed Virgilio Madrugada, had never seen his face.

As Jesse drove south down Highway 280 and made the exit at Potrero Hill, his troubled mind was, once again, climbing another hill, one that rose up in his thoughts a dozen times a day from a time long ago and a place half a world away. Sometimes Jesse truly believed that the hill near Laos was the true, concrete world of the present, while the lawyer and his cases in San Francisco were merely wishful phantasms—the fabricated, desperate dreams of a frightened soldier.

The lawyer's thumb had begun to rub the dog tags once again, but this time with even greater intensity. Jesse detested hills, and he worked in a city filled with them. That hill near Laos was far more than a memory. It was lodged in his mind like a formless, massless tumor. Moments from those nights almost three decades ago had long ago invaded his cells and callously mined his cytoplasm with indelible pangs. Shouts, cries, and whispers in the present were paltry counterpoints and halftones to those in the distant past. Every word in the present was but a pale copy of the truest utterances. Every laughing voice, in Jesse's ears, eventually melted into a death rattle. Every lovely, vital face, in Jesse's eyes, had already begun to molder.

He had stopped resisting these things long, long ago. How could he ever explain this to Carolina . . . to anyone? The painful memories had evolved into a cold, quizzical passacaglia, eternal notes in basso profundo and in unbreakable code. Someday he would solve the riddle of it. Someday he would live one sweet, mortal moment without the constant accompaniment of percussive anger and a grinding bass line of grief. Until that day, Jesse hated hills.

Even in broad daylight the hill was difficult to see. The mounds of discards and heaps of trash on the hillside had begun to fuse with the industrial rubble down below to form a wide, formless mass of fast-food wrappers, rusted metal, plastics and paper soaked in rainwater, and engine oil.

Above this ruin, the dreary rows of buildings had been painted with a muddy, battleship-gray enamel that had been donated by the naval shipyard just before it was shut down. That unsightly coating had been augmented over time by the work of hundreds of graffiti artists. The result was a perfect camouflage that no military techni-cian could ever duplicate. For all intents and purposes these housing projects were completely invisible to the uncaring eye.

This hill, affronted by neglect and veiled by the muddled human haze of five hundred marginal lives, was being savaged once more. Now strangers had come to cut and probe at the hillside, to unearth the refuse and disturb the residue of squandered, half-lived lives.

Emergency vehicles were parked everywhere on the hill, their doors ajar, their red and blue lights flashing, and their radios squawk-ing intermittently. The police had delineated the entire eastern perimeter of the hillside below the projects with a long line of wide yellow tape. Work crews were scattered on the eastern face of the hill, gingerly digging ominous, shallow holes into the firmament. Somber men were kneeling beside those holes, first recoiling, then photographing, then collecting the things that lay below. Eddy Oasa had parked just outside the police line. Upon seeing Jesse, he exited his car and joined his friend.

To the right, on the north side of the hill, Jesse and Eddy could see the beautiful back yard and the newly shingled blue roof of the Amazon Luncheonette. The police had nailed one end of their yellow tape to the fence that surrounded Persephone Flyer's lovely garden. Suddenly Jesse noticed a solitary figure moving between the garden boxes and trellises and glancing every now and then in the di-rection of the macabre activity on the hill.

"Who is that?" asked Jesse.

"Oh, that's Mr. Homeless. That's what the boys up here on the hill call him. There are a lot of homeless guys living up here in aban-doned trailers and drainage ditches, but he's the only one the kids will talk to. All of the gangbangers and druggies up here complain that he's a real pest, always asking them weird questions and trying to talk them out of using guns and drugs. But the kids like him because he's got some strange, exotic stories to tell. He probably belongs in a mental hospital. There's an entire encampment of them at the base of the hill, and under that overpass."

Jesse turned to look in a northeasterly direction. Beneath a huge structure of asphalt and cement he could see a dozen cardboard and corrugated-tin hovels built up against a straining, deformed stretch of Cyclone fence. Holes in the sides of these hapless, flimsy shanties had been plugged with rags, many of which were olive drab. Near the center of this collection of poor homes was a silent pack of dusty dogs and the telltale heat waves that rose from a small, hidden campfire.

"They live near the projects because the cops don't bother them here. There are just too many guns on this hill. It's just too well forti-fied. No one ventures up here, not the Mormons or the Jehovah's Witnesses, not the United Parcel Service, not even the pizza delivery people come up here. As far as I know, Mr. Homeless is the only one of them that has a name, the rest are nameless. He seems to have free run of the projects. For some reason all the gangs leave him alone. I've already tried to ask him some questions, but he won't say a word."

"Like Bao Vung," said Jesse in a voice just above a whisper. "You've got to try him again. Someone like him could see and hear everything that happens up here." Jesse handed Eddy three twenty-dollar bills. "Buy him lunch up at Klein's deli. Better yet, get him enough gift certificates for one full meal a day for two or three weeks. But no booze."

Jesse and Eddy moved around the yellow tape to the crime scene nearest a large gray Dumpster. Two of the bodies were already wrapped up and ready for transport. A third was lying in the back of the coroner's white van. They were three recumbent males—two of them virtually weightless and indistinguishable from soil and a third still heavy but tight with rigor mortis.

They looked so much smaller than life under the white cloth and the ridiculous restraining belts that covered them. Eddy pointed to a shallow trench that ran parallel to the Dumpster. A stand of grass hid its dimensions.

"That's where they found Little Reggie," said Eddy. "There was only two or three inches of soil on top of him. Somebody just kicked some dirt over him. The homicide detective said that he had been strangled, but he didn't find any signs of a struggle. The ligature was still around his neck. There was a lot of excitement over the ligature—it wasn't the usual extension cord or curtain pull. It was a woven rope. The coroner thinks it might be ceremonial. Whatever it is, it's very old.

"The heels of his shoes were badly scraped. It's pretty clear that he was dragged here from somewhere else. The other two bodies were found up there on that slope. They were both shot in the head at close range with a nine-millimeter weapon."

"How do they know that?" asked Jesse, suddenly recalling the expended round that had been found on Persephone Flyer's breast.

"The other two bodies are pretty decomposed. The slugs just dropped to the ground beneath the skeletons."

"And Little Reggie Harp was the only one who was strangled," mumbled Jesse to himself. "Shooters don't strangle, it's too personal. Have they found Little Reggie's gun yet?"

Eddy shook his head in the negative. Suddenly all the officers and lab technicians that had been working the crime scenes dropped what they were doing and converged noisily at a fourth location. This one was much closer to the project buildings themselves. Eddy and Jesse scrambled up the slope in hopes of getting a better look.

As two burly officers pulled at a large slab of cement, the others turned away violently and grabbed at their jackets and shirts to shield their mouths and noses from the stench. One green-faced officer raised his hand to signal the photographer. They had found another one. Jesse and Eddy ducked under the perimeter tape and walked toward the newest dig.

In this impoverished crypt, only the athletic footwear was still intact and untouched by decay. The geometrically sculpted gray soles of the shoes, pliable medals of stealth and virility, looked as though they had never been burdened by living weight. The padded uppers still looked unused, their garish stripes and glib hieroglyphic logos still charged with portent and prowess.

The shirt and pants, on the other hand, had collapsed as the human within had deflated. The arms were bent upward at the elbows. The fingers had grasped the soil with infinite patience until the soil had finally returned the embrace. The facial features of the boy had already resolved into a colorless expression made of soft shadows of sediment. Flesh had settled into layers of loam and sand.

A dying grimace on the lips had merged with the remnants of a tap-root. The teeth, cracked and separated, had been sown into the earth, into a hollow beneath the left shoe.

Jesse closed his eyes to compose himself. Like so many young men in his memory, this one had been spoiled, smoke-damaged, broken. There must be a million such shoddy graves in Vietnam and Cambodia. This boy had suffered two of the grunts' greatest terrors: the first was a bullet in the testicles. Then this boy had also been shot in the mouth, causing the teeth to be sprayed back through the brain and sideways through the cheeks.

At the top of the hill, on the litter-blighted street that ran just below the ugly rows of buildings on the crest, a long line of youthful spectators had gathered to watch the diggers down below. Like brooding, dark-skinned Egyptians, they resented the presence of pale outlanders on their soil, foreigners who were digging at their private past and carrying away the mummies and artifacts of their lives.

A common, silent sigh rose up from these onlookers as a fourth deflated and desiccated body was revealed to the open air. Another pair of sacred shoes would be manhandled and studied, defiled by in-fidels. Their secret rites of passage would now be exposed to a cynical, unschooled outside world.

Every child born on this hill had entered this world without the slightest chance to succeed. That chance had been ritually excised at birth, as routinely as excess umbilical cord, as routinely as the re-moval of the foreskin.

Having suffered that mutilation ceremony, every child had been given rights to an automatic weapon, a pair of oversized shoes made by Indonesian slave labor, and a personal saint—a celebrity athlete who had "gotten out," a patron point man who had scouted out the invisible path to the other world and would soon return to lead the way there.

According to ghetto mythology, this mystic pathway of escape would be marked not with mere bread crumbs on the sidewalk or with cryptic ciphers cut into the stumps of trees, but by a never-ending assortment of white, balding, television sports announcers and by a complete line of coordinated designer sports clothing. All of the boys on this hill were wearing their uniforms and waiting for a mission.

Jesse shook his head at the throng of aimless boys at the top of the hill. As they stood side by side, their colorful clothing seemed to join together to form one huge advertising billboard. Over the years one or two of their predecessors had managed to use their athletic abilities to escape this place, only to become transformed into strutting, megalomaniacal Judas goats for various clothing and fortified beer companies. They were the new John Waynes, peddling the myth.

Jesse turned away from the human billboard. His old friend Cornelius, a machine-gunner who had died at the age of eighteen, had come from a place like this one. He reminded himself that hope, like despondency, could find you no matter where you lived. The youngsters up above had fallen silent for a moment as the last body was raised from the ground. A boy who once weighed one hundred and fifty pounds was lifted with ease by a single man. In another age, in another place, a communal song of loss would have risen from these onlookers' throats.

Behind these bystanders, inside three separate apartments, three mothers were deep in mourning. All three women were without husbands. All three had hearts that had been completely untouched by the love of a man but whose striated wombs had been stretched and shrunken time and again by the burgeoning squirm of new life.

There had been men, of course—brown amphibians who slid easily from the firm soil of one woman into the salt waters of another; wriggling, slippery eels between the sheets, these men grew legs whenever the weather changed. They rose up and walked away when the tremor in the loins transmuted into family; when hot, writhing women became mothers.

These mothers would not have to be told the identities of the shriveled corpses. These three had known all along, yet they had steadfastly hoped beyond hope that their wayward sons had run away or were somewhere in the city's seedy Tenderloin district, passed out from quarts of old English 800, anesthetized by crack cocaine or, the good Lord willing, comatose with tar heroin. Or just maybe their three missing boys had gone searching in Oakland or in the Marin City projects, and had chanced to run across their shiftless, good-for-nothing biological fathers.

Three fearful mothers had prayed fervently that perhaps their dear missing sons were languishing in a jail in some distant county, that maybe some racist cop was refusing to let them call home. On this hill the American Dream was out there beyond the yellow tape. On this hill the most that their children could do was not very much at all, but like mothers everywhere, they had all been hoping for the best.

The fourth mother did not mourn. Worry brought worry lines and crows' feet. Worry changed the body's chemistry and led to body odor and malodorous sweating. Mourning only weighed the body down, distorting the posture and bearing.

The fourth mother did not mourn. Nor did she worry. When the official word came down about her son's death, the fourth mother took an express bus to Union Square, where she purchased some skin conditioner imported from Paris, got a pedicure at a Vietnamese shop, and bought a new pair of shoes. Believing that no one was watching, the fourth mother had dashed out on a moonlit night dressed only in a towel . . . and danced naked in her dead boy's grave. This time it was empty.

8

the ballet rose

"Let's go up," said Jesse, who had just caught the syrup, salt, and acid scent of death. The breeze had shifted and carried the horrid odor southward. He recognized it immediately and reflexively held his breath. Almost thirty years had passed and still it smelled precisely the same. It smelled like boys that he had once known; people like Roosky and Cornelius. It had the odor of his dreams. He stopped holding his breath, inhaled deeply to honor his old friends, then started the long climb toward the buildings.

"Are you kidding?" asked Eddy, who suddenly seemed very nervous. "You can't just go waltzing up there. That's Tourette's Hill. Haven't you heard the stories about that place? Why they call it Tourette's Hill? If that place gets a grip on you, you'll wind up doing an armed robbery in Pacific Heights or a drive-by shooting in the Fillmore. Then it'll be sayonara and goodbye to your law practice."

Jesse searched Eddy's face for some trace of sarcasm or humor. There was none. Eddy was deadly serious.

"The word is that the paramedics and ambulance drivers from San Francisco General Hospital came up with that name: Tourette's Hill. The closer you get to the top of this terrain, the less control you'll have over your faculties, your senses, even your conscience. More often than not, whenever there's an emergency out here they've had to send a second ambulance crew to rescue the first. Even pizza delivery won't come up here."

"I'll bet you Giles de la Tourette never had a place like this in mind," said Jesse, laughing at Eddy's words. There was a grin of smug skepticism on his face when he stepped under the yellow tape onto the road that led to the first row of projects. Eddy shook his head, then followed closely behind, his beard quivering with worry and expectation.

As they reached the first intersection, Jesse began to feel that a sharp, involuntary twitch had developed in his right hand. It began as a small tug on his wrist muscles but soon grew into a violent, twitching spasm that contorted the muscles of his upper arm. Jesse gritted his teeth and grabbed his right hand with his left. No matter how much force he exerted he was unable to control it.

Suddenly the word "shit" burst from his tensed lips, then "mother-fucker!" Jesse had no idea what impulse might have prompted those words. He had not been angry, or even excited. The words seemed to have no connection whatsoever to his aching wrist. Behind him he saw Eddy doubled over and laughing knowingly, his own left arm convulsing uncontrollably.

"Shit, I told you," said Eddy, stuttering as he tried to resist the impulse to curse. "First you get these involuntary tics, then hundreds and hundreds of goddamn words drop from your motherfucking vocabulary like so many flakes of dandruff. Then you get the overwhelming urge to wear huge tennis shoes and sell drugs. Fuck, if we're going to talk about this, we have to go back down the hill a little fucking distance."

The two men backtracked thirty or forty feet down the hill in staggering steps until they reached the precise point where their extremities had begun quaking.

"Jesus, what on earth was that?" said Jesse, still using his left hand to control his right. He spat toward the ground, trying to rid his tongue of unwanted expletives.

"That was urban Tourette's syndrome," answered a breathless Eddy. "I tried to warn you."

"What an experience!" exclaimed Jesse. "I was cursing like a soldier. For a few moments up there I actually cared about the NBA championships, and I even believed that big-time wrestling wasn't rigged. I kept trying to tell you something but didn't have the words with which to say it. Then, all of a sudden, I had the overpowering desire to carry a loaded gun. What the hell is urban Tourette's?"

"Look up there at that intersection. Tell me what you see."

Jesse squinted toward the intersection above. The kids had dispersed and now were on every corner, forming spastic, mercantile gestures with their faces and hands, holding up plastic bags of rock cocaine for sale and crying out spasmodically at passing cars. Among the drug dealers were a dusty pair of white men wearing the soiled uniforms of a local ambulance company. Two medics from the lowlands had succumbed and gone over to the enemy.

On the northwest street corner one young man was screaming a convulsive stream of obscenities into his cellular phone. When Jesse turned his gaze to the opposite corner, he realized that those obscenities were being directed to another cellular phone just across the street, not forty feet away.

"Fuck you!"

"No, fuck you very much! Wait a minute, muthufucka, somebody's paging me. Shit, it's just my mother. Where was I? Oh, yeah. Fuck you very much! Don't mean nothin'. Okay, talk to you later, man."

On every corner there were kids with cellular phones stuck to their ears and pagers beeping on their belts. They were peddling drugs and cursing one another vociferously at the very same time.

Dozens of kids with huge pants and even larger coats were standing next to uninsured BMW convertibles with empty gas tanks. Beneath the driver's seat of every car there was an unlicensed or stolen semi-automatic handgun. Jesse could feel the presence of weaponry. A metal detector on this hill would burn out in ten minutes. Within thirty yards of the lawyer and his investigator were two Beretta 92s, one Ruger Mark II, an UZI SMG, five Mac 10s, one stainless steel Walther and two Glock 26s. Chained to the driver's seats, guarding each car, was an angry, unfed, pit bull.

All subtlety had been wrung from these boys. No stranger who stood at this crossroads could imagine any of them ever whispering to any other. The women here had abrasive, cutting voices like brass horns or wailing banshees, while the young men shrieked and grunted to themselves, to one another, and to no one.

Every gesture, every motive, every word and every response to a word was an expression or an application of personal force—a gesture of violence, possession, control, or aggression. On this hill, the powerless were obsessed with power. Jesse turned his gaze to the east, toward the bay and the distant hills of Piedmont and Montclair. Beyond those towns were Concord, Vallejo, and Walnut Creek, all the bedroom communities of the East Bay. The blight of identical tract homes was still spreading, as whites fled toward the flatlands of Brentwood and the Delta.

Loud, martialistic music with snarling, petulant lyrics poured from every apartment and vehicle at the crest of the hill. Every open door revealed an eternally blaring television. There were no books or magazines in this place. In this place, Johnny Hartman and Duke Ellington were truly dead. No one here had ever heard of Ornette Coleman or John Coltrane. A few of the apartments featured computer screens filled with loud, blazing, stupefying war games of eternally repetitive violence: space marines killing aliens; ninja assassins assailing a Mandarin emperor. Gigabytes of memory for kilobyte lives.

Here, where Biscuit Boy was born and raised, was a free fire zone, open season on any moment of calm. Like the Middle Ages, this was a place of basic oral communication only. An oligarchy of sports and movie celebrities ruled over a new consumer peasantry. Like poor soldier serfs, these children built their lives around the imaginary castles of athletes and actors. In this land of functional illiteracy, there were icons everywhere, sports icons, icons of status, icons on the computer screen. There were icons on every television urging children to buy denim icons for their legs and canvas icons for their feet. As a new medieval era dawned, iconography, cryptography, and feudal impotence merged and now held sway.

Amazingly, here, too, was the cutting edge of modern mass culture in America. The high-fives and low-fives of a celebrating Brazilian basketball team began here as back-street gestures of satisfaction or recognition. America's hairstyles began here, too. Even barbers in faraway Kansas had been forced to learn how to cut a fade into the hair of freckle-faced, blue-eyed boys. Ghetto and barrio fashions, sources of probable cause for arrest in Oakland, would, in time, be found draped over the long, lithe bodies of starving French models. Oozing importance, feigning hostility, and sporting plastic pistols, they would glide to and fro down a runway in New York City.

"The doctors over at General," continued Eddy, "think that

urban Tourette's is, in part, the result of radon gases from all this concrete mixing with hamburger wrappers and the tons of cocaine residue that have fallen onto the roadway. This compound ferments underfoot and is then bombarded by that dead blue light that pours out of television screens.

"The result is an insidious chemical gas that slowly leaches the human spirit out of these kids. It attacks and destroys the hippocampus so that these kids have no future and no cultural memory. Without a hippocampus they are forced to live in the eternal now. The same thing happens to all the young vatos in the Mission. The gas robs all of them of their souls."

"Like soldiers in extremis," mused Jesse.

"Jesse, these kids are incapable of abstraction. Everything in their lives is physical and in the immediate present. They need to own things now; they need to react to insults now. They need to retaliate now. Hell, half the boys that were raised in this place are already in state prison. When the union movement was murdered in America, the bodies were thrown here and a thousand places like this."

"Damn," said Jesse, amazed at the depth of Eddy's feelings. "I thought I was angry. Now, tell me, my man, just how do we get up that hill without ending up like those ambulance drivers?"

"You have to climb up a few feet at a time, then rest a bit. Otherwise you'll get the spiritual bends. Bubbles of Tourette's gas will form in your blood and in your joints if you move too fast. Did you know that I charge you extra for coming up here? Hazardous-duty pay."

The two men walked up the hill and through the incredible din of boom boxes, maundering dope fiends, and narcotics hawkers at the street corners.

"You cops?" one young man asked threateningly through a set of expensive gold teeth. He was wearing a tattered Domino's pizza uniform, a paper hat with matching jacket.

"No," said Jesse, "I am Biscuit Boy's lawyer and this is his investigator."

"Is the Biscuit in trouble?" said the young man. "He ain't that kind of boy, I'll tell you that much. Fact is, he a chicken-chested wimp. He don't know how to do no drama. He ain't even strapped. How he gonna do a drama?" As he said it he proudly opened his Chicago Bulls jacket to show Jesse and Eddy the Mac-10 semi-automatic he had tucked into his belt. It was the nine-millimeter model. The young man smiled.

"Have you ever considered a membership in the National Rifle Association?" asked Eddy sarcastically. "They worship projectiles just like you do."

"Ain't they the enemy?" answered the boy after scratching his head for a moment.

"Can you tell me something more about Calvin?" said Jesse impatiently.

"The Biscuit Boy don't use no drugs, didn't never hardly drink, don't do nothin' but steal biscuits. He kind of a sissy. Hey, do you want to buy a twenty-shot?" He opened his mouth to display two off-white rocks on his tongue. "Say, was you my lawyer once?"

"I don't recognize you," said Jesse. "What's your name?"

"I know I seen you someplace," said the young man without answering the question. "I seen you, too," he said pointing toward Eddy. "Is you here from the pizza parlor? I swear I didn't steal that van!" He pointed to a van that was parked halfway up the hill. It had been put up on blocks and stripped clean. Only the plastic pizza on the roof of the van was left intact. With a confused look lingering on his face he turned toward Jesse. "I think I remember something about a pizza parlor. Maybe I worked there. Was you my boss?"

"I told you, I'm Calvin's lawyer. Do you know who those kids were?" said Jesse, pointing downward to the four empty graves on the hillside.

"Yeah, I know," said the young man who turned away suddenly and began to punch in a number on his tiny cellular phone, his long curving fingernails savagely entering the digits. Evidently, Jesse's conversation with him was over. A phone not thirty feet away began to ring. The young man screamed "Fuck you" twice into the phone then pulled the instrument away from his lips. "Now I remember you. You done Mark Ballinger's cases, didn't you?"

Jesse nodded. The young man's lips returned to his phone.

"Biscuit's got that Mexican lawyer who done them cases for Baby Strange. No, not that Baby Strange. We talkin' about his son, little Baby Strange with them three murder beefs. Remember, he touched up them two dudes from Valencia Gardens and he did a touch-up on that one-eyed dude from the Fillmore? Baby Strange beat the gas chamber."

"I've never been very religious," sighed Jesse to his investigator, "but I think I could be a born-again Luddite."

The young boy terminated his conversation with an expletive that was yet another synonym for intercourse, then turned to Jesse and Eddy.

"You okay up here. You can come on up."

Jesse realized that this seeming buffoon had just transmitted the lawyer and the investigator's identities and credentials across the entire hill, and in code, to boot: "These two are not the enemy." He was an RTO and cryptographer combined.

"People will talk to you now, but you can't subpoena nobody. Nobody up here will take a subpoena," the young man cautioned. Jesse noticed that the young man's voice had changed. There was a deeper, more authoritative tenor in his words.

"That's some tired shit you're peddling. It's gaffle, man," spat Jesse angrily. "Everybody in the projects is always crying and moaning that they can't get no justice in the courts, but no one ever wants to help. These people don't want to be subpoenaed because they have warrants for traffic and petty theft. Biscuit could be charged with six murders! Do you understand that? Scream that into your damned phone!"

The investigator laughed at Jesse's frustration while he turned to a page of his notes. The young man walked slowly, mechanically toward the van and stood next to it, touching the metal, probing it as though it held a secret

"Calvin's mother lives in 27D," said Eddy. "I spoke to her on the phone this morning. She'll be home. According to Calvin she's always home."

A small window in the door opened a crack, just enough for a pair of dark eyes to peek outside. The room behind that eye was black, lit only by the numbing flicker of a cathode-ray tube. Above the insipid drone of an announcer's voice, the sound of a half dozen deadbolts could be heard as they were removed, one after the next, like a jagged line of old iron sutures.

A small woman used one thin arm to usher the men into her tidy, dark home. The other arm was raised to cover her eyes. She seemed like a woman who should have been blind. She was stunned by brightness; her awkward, offset eyes announced that her true life's vocation was to be found in sleep. Jesse remarked to himself that except for the eyes, Calvin looked just like his mother.

Without asking for her permission, Jesse began to walk slowly from room to room. He opened cabinets and closet doors as he moved. He touched fabric and linen and the gaudy white oak veneer that had been glued onto every visible surface of her cheap, particle-board furnishings. He moved to the tiny kitchen, to the stovetop, where a shriveled pork chop languished in a puddle of cold grease. He would have to describe Calvin's home to the jury, describe his life. Jesse was struck by the fact that Mrs. Thibault had so few possessions.

There was no shortage of knickknacks but nothing of any size—doilies, handmade dolls, a cluster of bottles with colored water, and a gaggle of ceramic figurines. On the wall was a single black velvet painting of Martin Luther King. There were old circus tickets taped to the refrigerator. There was a tiny gathering of photographs on top of the television.

"There, Calvin in that one. He just ten year old. That my daughter Beulah. She doing real good. She got a job at the school of cosmetology over in Oakland. She even got a credit card now. That my Marvin. He be killed in a drive-by shooting last year. At least we found his body right off and buried him proper. Not like them boys out there. Thank Jesus God for that."

She pointed to the school photo that was taped to the wall, above the rest. "That one be my youngest boy, Angelo. We call him Pickle 'cause he a real sourpuss. He out there somewhere on the hill sellin' gaffle."

"Gaffle?" said Eddy.

"It's the latest word for bunk," answered Jesse with a smile, referring to fake cocaine. "Ain't you up on the lingo? Some kids are out there selling instant mashed potato buds in place of crack. That's a dangerous business, Mrs. Thibault. Those crackheads can get really mad if they aren't unconscious by noon."

"I told him that, but I can't make him stay home. No matter what I do, he won't stay home and he won't go to school. At least he be safe now," she said softly.

"Safe from Little Reggie," ventured Eddy.

Mrs. Thibault slumped to the couch, then nodded her head twice, then let it fall wearily into her lap. She put her hands behind her head and laced her fingers together. Her thin knuckles were bony and worn. Now Jesse knew why she stayed indoors, a prisoner of her apartment. She was surrounded by a world on fire and she had resigned herself to the fact that she was nothing more than kindling.

"Everybody knew they was dead," she said softly as she lifted her head. "Them poor mamas . . ." She was crying. "Them poor mamas. Their poor boys died alone, without so much as a Christian burial." The television was still blaring, so Eddy reached for the remote and turned it off. Surprisingly, Mrs. Thibault did not seem to notice. In her life, television was a loyal, mindless, and undemanding companion, an endless drone of product-objects and product-people, a semihuman machine that automatically transformed itself into a night light at two in the morning.

"Everybody so afraid of Little Reggie that didn't no one say nothing about them boys being missing. They went one at a time, a couple of months or so apart. We all heard the shots. Even the boys' mothers didn't say nothing. They got other kids, you know. Little Reggie could hurt them, too. He said he would. That Little Reggie always been real bad. I been scared to death about Pickle since Calvin been arrested."

"Did anyone see Little Reggie do these killings?" asked Eddy. "Are there any witnesses to any of the shootings?"

"No, but he steady be saying he done it. He always be bragging on it to everybody, waving that big gun around. Mind you, as sure as there's a devil, that boy be Satan hisself. A bad seed. And his mama's so nice and all. She a real pretty woman. She magazine pretty. She be light-skinned and she's got that good hair . . . real straight. She coulda been Miss America back in 1977, did you know that? I think it was '76 or '77. She was Miss Alabama, but something happened. Something bad happened. She a nice lady. She sure deserve better than all this. Last week she braided my hair."

She used one hand to primp her braids.

"Do you know anything about a note that Calvin supposedly wrote to Little Reggie?" asked Jesse. "It's said to contain a death threat."

"My boy couldn't death-threat nobody," said Mrs. Thibault weakly. "And if he did, it's about time he stood up to that fool. He was all the time making Calvin do things."

"What kind of things?" asked Eddy, pressing down the top of his ballpoint pen. Mrs. Thibault found the clicking sound disquieting, disconcerting. People in the projects always suffered whenever a stranger came by and wrote things down.

"I don't know," she answered cautiously, "but Calvin used to come home crying and say that Little Reggie went and did something real mean to somebody, or made him watch while Reggie done some crazy things. I don't know, but I'm glad that boy be dead. God help me I'm glad. His mama live right over there in the next building. She glad, too. I can tell. Is you ever seen Little Reggie?"

Neither the lawyer nor the investigator answered the question.

"He favors his mama, except for them eyes. He be a pretty boy, but he got them yellow, catfish eyes. Mean, swampy eyes. He look at you and you know there's no use talkin' with him. He don't feel nothin'. He empty inside. Something to do with his father. He be cursed or got the evil eye or something."

Mrs. Thibault fell quiet. For a few moments the apartment experienced a rare spell of silence.

"The folks on the hill say the devil raped Mrs. Harp and she gave birth to Reggie just a week later. I seen them police diggin' up Little Reggie's body. He look for all the world like he be sleepin'. Too damn mean to rot."

Mrs. Thibault daubed her eyes with a tissue. "Death threat," she whispered indignantly. "My boy can't even write."

At that Eddy walked to the refrigerator, removed a small magnet from the door, and used it to hang up the piece of paper that Jesse had given him in the courtroom. It was Biscuit Boy's assignment, his paragraph about "A Gathering of Old Men."

They be this one man so black that he be blu. An he proud that they be no white blood in him. He all blu-black. He strong an he African and he laff at niggas want strate hair and lit skin.

"How did Calvin get his nickname? How did he come to be called the Biscuit Boy?" asked Jesse.

Mrs. Thibault's face lit up with one of the few smiles that she allotted herself on any given day.

"It was that poor Vietnamese girl over to the luncheonette that went and name him. God rest her soul. Calvin be sweet on her. He be real sweet on her. Here she be my age and all, and he be sweet on her. I must admit, she pretty." She pulled her hair back with the finger of one hand. "Me . . . I look twenty years older than that woman, maybe more. Calvin ain't never killed nobody, much less someone he be sweet on. That boy use to stay up on that street just to get one look at that woman. If he did, he come home all smilin' and singin'."

Just then there was a loud knock on the door. Mrs. Thibault rose to answer it, but two men stepped inside before she could take a step. It was Inspector Normandie and a uniformed officer.

"Good day, ma'am," he said with a perfunctory nod. His red face was sweaty and his facial expression was caught somewhere between social awkwardness and a barely subdued look of glee.

"I saw your son's lawyer walking up here, ma'am, so I took the liberty of letting myself in. I hope I'm not intruding. This is Sergeant Thompson." The uniformed officer nodded without smiling. "If you don't mind, ma'am, I'd like to speak with Mr. Pasadoble for a moment." The inspector then looked in the direction of the lawyer and said, "We can step outside."

The inspector and the lawyer stepped onto the front porch and shut the door behind them. Jesse noticed that the sergeant had remained behind. Inside, Eddy and the sergeant were eyeing each other at a discreet distance. Mrs. Thibault had turned on the television.

"You're a Potrero Hill virgin, ain't you, a cherry?" grinned the inspector. Jesse's expression made it clear that he did not understand the comment.

"This is your first time on this anonymous little hill, isn't it? I saw you cussing up a storm and shaking like a leaf on the way up here. It takes a long time to get used to this place. Took me a couple of years. I've got something to show you, counselor. I don't think the prosecutor will mind if I let you get an early peek at this."

He reached inside his overcoat and pulled out a zip-top plastic bag that contained a small, folded piece of paper. With the tip of a wooden pencil, the inspector reached inside the bag and carefully unfolded the small sheet. He then handed the bag to the lawyer. He smiled as Jesse lifted the note to his eyes. The inspector was enjoying himself.

"Reggie, you is gonna die jest like the rest of them," read Jesse aloud. "I swear you be a dead man. Calvin."

"We haven't told Mrs. Thibault yet, but we're pretty sure we're going to find Angelo the Pickle out there, too." He nodded toward the hillside and the four open graves.

"We know he's been missing for a few days now. I must say, counselor, your boy is the worst case I've seen in this town since the Night Stalker. As soon as we find that nine-millimeter gun with Calvin's fingerprints all over it, we'll have our ballistics tests and we'll have our special circumstances. The Biscuit Boy is going to fry. Oh, excuse me. I misspoke. We're doing lethal injections in California now, aren't we? I hate them goddamn federal courts."

"You're crazy if you think Calvin killed these boys," said a dazed, angered Jesse. "You're even crazier if you think he would kill his own brother. You and I both know that Little Reggie Harp is the killer."

"Then who did Reggie?" smiled the Inspector. "Who touched up my man Reggie? Do you think it was a strangulation suicide? As a matter of fact we're beginning to think that Calvin is the brains behind the killings at the Amazon Luncheonette. It's true, we haven't found the gun yet, but that won't hurt our case and you know it. Shit, the less hard evidence we have, the better off we are. The jury's just gonna love the cold-blooded execution of two pretty women. All of that bra and panty and bullet testimony . . . you get my drift.

"Even if he hasn't got any criminal history, five or six murders will get him the leather restraints and the hypodermic needle. Remember, counselor, the eyewitnesses may not be able to point to a killer, but they do say that two black boys did it and one of those boys is named Calvin."

Jesse pushed open the door of the apartment and waved Eddy outside. He then reached into the pocket of his coat and removed a tiny recorder. As Eddy said goodbye to Mrs. Thibault, Jesse switched the recorder on, then stated the exact time, date, and location of this conversation as well as the identities of those present.

"Eddy Oasa is present, as well as Inspector Saxon Normandie of San Francisco homicide detail. Inspector Normandie, do you object to my recording this conversation?"

"Hell yes, I do!" shouted the inspector.

"Good!" laughed Jesse, "because you have just verified your presence with that answer. Inspector, I hereby forbid you as well as any member of the homicide detail to have any contact with Calvin

Thibault. I forbid anyone to speak to him at your behest. Any hand-writing exemplars or physical evidence from his person must be ob-tained by court order and with notice to me."

He turned off the recorder, then, after signaling for Eddy to fol-low, began walking away from the inspector and toward the Amazon Luncheonette. They had gone only about thirty feet when the figure of a woman appeared in a distant doorway. Without knowing why, Jesse walked toward her. As Jesse got closer to the woman in the doorway, the reddish and alabaster blur of her image resolved into the incredible form of a woman wearing a pink strapless evening gown and matching shoes.

Her long, straight hair was done in a combination bubble and flip. From a distance she looked like a middle-aged Josephine Baker or Lena Horne. Up close she looked even better. One leg was straight while the other was just bent at the knee. Her feet were at a perfect ninety-degree angle to one another.

"For your information, counselor, that is Mrs. Harp, the mother of Little Reggie," shouted the departing inspector, nodding toward the woman. "She's quite a celebrity around here. Folks say she's a real Jezebel. Now, I'm as close-minded as the next male chauvinist redneck"—the inspector smiled—"but I sure as hell wouldn't mind dippin' my pen in some of that black ink."

"Jesus!" said Eddy, who shook his head with disgust at the police officer as he turned away. Jesse and his investigator walked toward the woman, stopping at the base of her front porch.

"May we speak with you, ma'am?" said Eddy with uncommon deference. The inspector's crude comments were still ringing in his ears.

Without a word, but lifting her slender arm to direct their atten-tion, the woman backed gracefully away from the door to allow the men to enter. What Jesse and Eddy saw inside her apartment stunned them into five long minutes of rapt and complete silence. In every nook and on every wall were row upon row of professional photographs of a young Mrs. Harp. Here she is a prom queen; there she is Miss Montgomery 1976. In another photo she is kissing the winner of a stock car race at the Macon county fair. In another she is shaking hands with Ed Sullivan.

She is everywhere, lounging like a sleepy kitten on the hood of a shiny new Corvette; posing next to a brand new Kelvinator washing machine. Her professional name was once Tawny Mae Harp. Her true name—her maiden name—was Princess Sabine Johnson. In a corner of the kitchen where a stove should have been, there was a locked display case filled with ribbons, trophies, and long-winded testimonials.

"Harp is not my true name. I was never married to Mister Anvil Harp," she said quietly, allowing her guests to thoroughly peruse every photo. "He was a mistake." Her voice was breathy and her red lips enunciated every word perfectly. "He was an . . . Reggie's father was an indiscretion."

She moved easily out of one posture and into another, posing in front of photo after photo, gliding to each as if her stiletto heels were sliding on panes of oiled glass. At the same time her hand was up-lifted demurely to indicate a particular photograph without actually pointing directly at it. Her raised elbow, slightly bent wrist, and re-laxed fingers performed in concert to form a polite suggestion, a mere implication of an indication. Anything more would have been uncouth, unprofessional.

Jesse noticed that there were no photographs of her family or her children anywhere in the home. Except for a selection of emcees and judges in tuxedos and an autographed photo of Bert Parks, no photos of a child or of an adult male were anywhere present.

"I'm sorry about your son," he heard himself saying.

"This is a photograph from a rodeo in Mobile." It seemed as though Princess Sabine Johnson Harp had not heard Jesse's condo-lences. "It was quite something for a black woman . . . for a woman of color to be the queen of a rodeo back in 1973. As far as I know, it hadn't happened before and it hasn't happened since."

"I'm sorry about Little Reggie," repeated Jesse in a forceful but respectful voice. It was something he wanted to express to this woman before asking her any questions. "I'm sorry about your son."

Her posture slumped; the perfectly held spine and shoulders col-lapsed visibly. The politely curved elbow drooped; the bent wrist straightened and fell downward. The once arching breasts dipped below the brim of the bodice. The demure smile on Sabine's perfect face evaporated completely, leaving behind the bare residue of a pro-fessional persona.

"I don't want to talk about Little Reggie Harp," she said harshly. "There has to be an end to mourning, doesn't there? Now, gentlemen"—she sighed with exasperation—"pray, let's continue our tour, shall we?"

Her studied, prize-winning composure returned to her almost immediately. Neither Jesse nor Eddy had seen an iota of grief in her eyes. Perhaps Little Reggie had savaged her along with everyone else on this hill.

"Here I am on the cover of *Ebony* magazine, and here on the cover of *Jet*. My, but I do look rather fatigued in that photo, don't I? Probably a late dinner and soirée the night before. I was Miss Pike County in 1975 and Miss Coffee Brown in 1974. Why, I was no more than a child when I started winning swimsuit competitions. This is a brand-new shopping center in Tuscaloosa, where I got to cut the ribbon with the mayor, and I shoveled the very first spadeful of dirt. Lord help me, I think I buried His Honor's left shoe."

She laughed sweetly and tossed her head to sweep a face full of soft, straight hair to the side and out of her lovely eyes. For the first time she looked directly at the two men who were standing in her hallway. They did not seem to appreciate her awards, her honors. The brilliant smile faded, then disappeared as a look of firm resolve took its place.

She led the two men to a back bedroom that had been converted into a large walk-in closet. Jesse noticed that the unit had originally been designed to be a two-bedroom apartment, yet there was only one bed. He also noticed the bathroom. There was a thin strip of paper stretched across the toilet seat that read "Guaranteed Freshness." The water glasses on the sink were wrapped in small plastic bags. The tiny soaps were in their wrappers, still unopened. The towels hanging on her racks were all from the Grand Montgomery Hotel.

Near the mirror was a small, two-cup coffeemaker. Jesse looked at Eddy, who had also seen the bathroom. Sabine slid open a door and turned on an overhead light fixture that lit the entire contents of the closet. There were hundreds of dresses, costumes, and bathing suits on rotating racks. One entire wall of the room was hidden behind stack after stack of shoe boxes. Every label was French or Italian. There were no coats or warm jackets. Her entire wardrobe was summer.

"Did Reggie live with you, Mrs. Harp?" asked Eddy. "There is nothing in this apartment that would belong to a man . . . or a boy. Nothing that I can see."

Her jaw became tense and jutting. She quickly pulled a bathing suit from its rack and stared at it intently. Slowly, the concern on her face began to melt away.

"Of course he lived here," she said in an absentminded whisper. "I'm his mother, aren't I?"

She smiled at the bathing suit as she spoke. It was strictly regulation, one-piece with absolutely no padding in the breast area, not even a smidgen. Completely unmindful of the men in her dressing room, she imagined herself stripping naked and pulling the tight bathing suit onto her body. The image sent chills down her spine. All these years later and it would still fit.

"I can't help it if he chooses to sleep here and there. I can't control him anymore." She smiled mechanically while glancing downward toward her ample breasts. From the time that those two hills had been mere bumps beneath her T-shirts she had wished and cajoled her mammary glands into being. It was clear to both Jesse and Eddy that this woman's downcast glance at the geography of her chest was one of her favorite views. It was also clear that Sabine had just referred to her dead son in the present tense.

"Did you know any of the other boys who died?" asked Jesse, remembering the task at hand. "Were they friends of Little Reggie?"

"I don't mix with the people up here," Sabine answered with impatience and indignation. "This is only a temporary situation. I'll be leaving here soon. I really don't belong up here . . . never belonged up here. Please don't judge me by this place. People up here are trash."

The last sentence flew from her mouth like spittle. Seemingly embarrassed by her outburst, Princess Sabine smiled meekly then returned her attention to the bathing suit. She carefully inspected the leg holes, and a look of pride filled her face. Most of the other girls would put two-sided tape in the leg holes to keep the suit from riding up on the thighs. Not Princess Sabine—never.

Most contestants used tape to lift their boobs as high as they could without having the nipples pop out. Not Sabine Johnson. Little Reggie's mother smiled as she recalled how the bodice would strain over her breasts. Without knowing it, she smiled broadly at the two men who were questioning her and ran her tongue over her upper teeth. There was no Vaseline on those teeth to keep the lips from sticking to them. No caps, no white dye on her teeth or collagen in her lips. She was purely organic, natural, one of God's favored creatures.

Sabine stood before her latest audience of leering men. Their mouths were moving, but she could not hear them. Even as Jesse repeated a question, Princess Sabine was walking a runway at some distant county fair with a hundred hungry eyes staring at her.

"Do you know how those boys died? Did you hear any gunshots? Did you know any of the boys personally?"

The disturbing sentences seemed to be coming from the crowd at the county fair. Or was it one of the judges who was asking those disconcerting questions? They were most certainly not proper questions for a beauty contest! Princess Sabine stomped her foot angrily. There would be no prizes today, no first runner-up.

"Why don't you people just go away and leave me alone?" she began screaming. "Just leave me alone! I don't deserve any of this. I don't know what happened to Reggie and those other boys. Things happened to them, to all of them. There are winners and losers in everything. Things happen!"

Sabine stopped suddenly, placing a hand over her mouth.

"I don't know anything," she said in a new voice, one that Jesse and Eddy had not heard before. Gone was the mother and the beauty queen. The woman standing before them now was far from beautiful. She had a palsied, feverish face and eyes narrowed to glowing slits. With one quivering, extended hand she showed Jesse and Eddy the door.

"My father Butler Johnson would kill you both for the insinuations you've made against his little daughter today. He would kill you. Why on earth would I have a personal relationship with anyone up on this hill? I told you, everyone up here is trash." As she enunciated each syllable, Sabine coated it with bile, placed it on her tongue, and spat it at the two men.

"My father was a gentleman. You two could do far worse than emulate Butler Johnson, but of course you have no breeding. It's what I do every day of my life—emulate that dear man. My father brought me up with love and devotion," she hissed. "I brought Reggie up the very same way. He's a well-bred boy. How dare you come here with all your questions. Now, leave me alone!" Princess Sabine slammed the front door. "I have nothing more to say to you."

As Jesse and Eddy walked down the hill toward the scene of La Massacre des Amazons, the investigator reached into his pocket and handed something to Jesse. It was an object contained within a crumpled manila envelope.

"I forgot to give this to you. I just got it today. It's a taped copy of the 911 call that was made from the phone booth across from the Amazon Luncheonette."

"What's on it?"

"I don't know," answered Eddy. "I thought you should listen to it first. I do know one thing. The guy at police communications said that one of the victims' voices is on that tape. He said that there is also the barely audible sound of a second, much more distant voice. He said that you can hear two gunshots, clear as a bell on the recording. There were some other sounds on the tape, but he couldn't make them out. In all honesty, I guess I didn't play it because I just wasn't ready to hear it, Jesse. The communications officer told me that she said only one word into the mouthpiece."

"One word?" repeated Jesse in a barely audible voice.

The thought of hearing a single word from the lips of a dying woman sent a cold chill down Jesse's back. Long ago he had heard just such a word in one of the ugliest and most beautiful moments he had ever endured. It had been an unclouded, crystalline, and razor-edged moment free of self-consciousness and free of all shame. He had held a dying boy's head until that precise instant, that slice of a moment when the nuclei of a billion cells in the center of his eye went dim in unison. He had seen the white of an eye shift subtly to gray. He had detected what he thought was a moment of weightlessness in the body of Julio Lopez.

He had felt the sum and the subtraction of it: that faint shift of inner light, that instant when all of the muscles of his warm body quit idling and stalled out forever—that split second of a moment when the last five neurons flickered and faded away.

"Padre!" said Jesse aloud, echoing the very word that had escaped his lips as Julio had succumbed, almost thirty years before.

"What was that? Did you say 'padre'?" asked Eddy.

"It was nothing," responded Jesse, as he turned down the small walkway that led to the front door of the Amazon Luncheonette. His

voice was a mixture of confusion and embarrassment. He stopped
halfway to the door, then continued at a more respectful pace. He
turned to face Eddy.

"I had a friend once, a padre, an infantry chaplain. He went insane . . . or maybe he went sane back in 1968. One day he just walked
away from the war."

A shiver lingered between his shoulder blades as he turned to peer
through the glass of the luncheonette. He focused his eyes; pro-
gramming them to ignore all reflections. Suddenly the frozen dis-
array resolved itself into view. There were jars filled with spices and
sauces strewn on the floor and a stovetop covered with unwashed
pots. Through the back window of the narrow restaurant Jesse had a
clear view of the bedroom beyond. The rear window framed the hill
and housing projects. There were signs of ambition, industry, and
hope everywhere. The hours and days before their death must've
been happy ones, thought Jesse.

The women had run through this door, crossed the street, and
moved diagonally toward the phone booth on the other side of the
street. No blood had been found in the restaurant. Jesse pushed at
the new glass door. Despite the band of yellow police tape and a notice from the district attorney's office, the door opened easily. The
cops had forgotten to lock the place after they left. Jesse pushed the
door open and the two men walked in slowly.

"Look."

Eddy was pointing to the industrial refrigerator. The doors had
been left ajar. Jesse pulled out his tiny recorder and began his entry
by stating the new time and the full date and location.

"I am present with my investigator Edmund Kazuso Oasa. Using
a fork retrieved from the sink, I am opening the door further. There
is a streak of blood on the door approximately seven inches long.
The streak culminates in a single fingerprint. The streak seems intact. No samples were taken. I don't believe that the police have seen
this. There are scratch marks on the inside of the metal door and on
the surface behind it. Someone was in here. It should be noted that
the shelves have yet to be placed in their respective positions. They
are still in a carton to the left of the refrigerator. We are now photographing the door and the interior of the box."

Eddy stepped forward and focused on the door. "A flash will wipe
this out," he said, then he walked to the front wall and turned on the

bank of overhead lights. He switched off his flash unit. The Pentax clicked, then clicked again.

"I'll tell the DA about this tomorrow morning," said Jesse as he dropped his recorder into a pocket. "You've got to get in touch with this guy Anvil Harp, Eddy. Find out why he didn't bother to marry a Miss America contestant! Perhaps he never asked her. Maybe she didn't want him. Find out what really happened. Why was he an indiscretion? I want to know where Little Reggie lived. There was absolutely no evidence of him anywhere in her apartment.

"I want to know why she's living all alone in a housing project," continued Jesse. "There were no flowers, no gifts anywhere. There's no evidence of a man in her life. I want to know why she's built a motel around herself. Why would someone who should have buckets of money and dozens of suitors have little more than a room full of Italian shoes and a few mementos?"

The investigator was nodding and frantically scribbling notes into his binder. Eddy was wondering where in America these questions would send him.

"Hell, in 1977 in the South, she must have been Helen of Troy," said Jesse. "She must have been African-American royalty back in Selma and Atlantic City. Did you see her? Did you see her entire life on those walls? How could such a woman possibly fail? How on earth can beauty fail?"

Eddy could not answer the question. Princess Sabine had what every woman allegedly wanted, yet she had nothing at all. The world was ignoring her. Worse yet, the world had forgotten her.

"I'll get on Mister Harp tomorrow afternoon," he said quietly. "There can't be more than one or two Anvil Harps in all of North America. It's an unusual first name. If he's written a check or applied for credit in the last ten years, the databases will have him. I'll do it as soon as I get back from Tracy. According to Bernard Skelley's sister Margie Dixon, Bernard's brother Richard used to live in the Fruitvale District with his family. He moved from there to the acorn projects. The locals call the place 'ghost town.'"

"Did Minnie, the little girl who says she was molested by the supreme being, live with Richard in West Oakland?" asked Jesse. "Did Minnie Skelley live in the Fruitvale, too?"

"All of them lived together. Richard had a steady job at a local auto dismantler until it closed. Now he's a carny again and the family is split up. A lot of their stuff is in storage.

"Margie says he worked as a carny about ten years ago. He runs a game booth in a parking-lot carnival that's working down in the Central Valley right now. It's real small-time, there's only seven mechanical rides, two tents, and two or three hot food stands. The carnival is due in Hayward next weekend, so I'll get a close look at Richard. When the supreme being was in town he used to stay at his brother's house in Oakland. Margie is going to give me the rundown on the entire family history."

"Why is Margie talking to you?" asked Jesse.

"The Skelley family has disowned her. They haven't spoken to her in years. Her ex-husband, Wallace Dixon, is a black man who drives for Alameda County Transit. I spoke to him on the phone. Seems like a decent sort. He pays his alimony right on time. Now she's running around with an eccentric English professor from Stanislaus Junior College. His name is Eric Caine. I ran them both in the database and superior court records. Neither of them has a rap sheet. I'll do phone interviews with them tonight."

"A black man and an English professor, eh?" Jesse laughed. "Which one does the Skelley family hate more?"

When they reached the phone booth, both Jesse and Eddy were suddenly aware of the dozens of eyes watching them. Without knowing it, they had become aware of the cumulative breeze that is created when a dozen sheer curtains are moved cautiously aside. Without hearing it, they sensed the sum of a dozen sighs. The witnesses to the murders had gone back to their windows to watch as a neighborhood wound was reopened.

There had been no rain since the shooting, and spots of dried blood were still visible on the sidewalk. The telephone had been removed because it had been losing money since the night of the killings. In truth, not a single soul had used it since that night. There were bare wires hanging down from a hole in the wall. Before leaving the area, Jesse had nervously pulled at the wires. Had these strands of copper and plastic felt the desperation in Persephone Flyer's voice?

As he drove down Mississippi Street toward the Hall of Justice, Jesse wondered what that single word on the tape would be? He opened the envelope and pushed the cassette into his car radio, then he waved at Eddy, who was driving toward the Bay Bridge in his own car. The radio was turned off so that the 911 tape wouldn't begin playing until Jesse was perfectly ready to hear it.

After a long thoughtful pause at a stop sign, he turned his car down Sixteenth Street, turned left on Market, and began driving toward Twin Peaks. It was then that he realized that he needed to decide what his destination was before driving any farther. He could go to Glen Park, where Carolina would be having her dinner and watching the news, or he could drive across the Golden Gate Bridge and spend the night alone in the little room he kept at the Sonoma Inn Motel. This might be as good a night as any to "communicate" with her. He winced at the thought of it. Those conversations always ended the same way: with a paralyzed and mute Jesse leaving in the middle of a vegetarian meal, and with Carolina frustrated and sobbing. Might as well get it over with, he thought, though he couldn't decide which he dreaded more, the communication or the tofu. Suddenly his fingers reached for the radio and turned it on.

He fully expected to hear Benny Green, the Modern Jazz Quartet, or the Horace Silver quintet. The question of where to sleep had caused him to forget for an instant that there was a tape lodged in the radio, ready to play. What he heard first was the monotone voice of the communications technician as he announced the date and the exact time of the incoming call. Then Jesse heard the single spoken word: a long airy vowel, a soft consonant of pressed lips, a short and guttural vowel, and, finally, a moment of sibilance that faded off to eternity. He began to finger his dog tags once again as he heard the consonants and vowels that would serve to punctuate a lifetime, the single word that would have to suffice.

He sped past Carolina's house, up Sloat Boulevard, down Nineteenth Avenue, and back toward the city. She had been home, her front room lights had been on. She was probably in her darkroom wondering when, if ever, he was going to come by. Jesse could see her in his mind's eye, carefully rinsing a photograph, the acrid scents of acetic acid and melancholy filling her lovely nose.

He drove erratically and carelessly, crossing double lines and running stop signs as he played and replayed that single word. When the sound of two gunshots filled his ears for the fifth time he pulled to the side of the road to compose himself before driving on. He passed Balboa Street, turning down Geary, and pulled over at the Dublin City Bar, leaving his car running and the driver's door wide open. He ran into the bar and stood impatiently at the cash register, his face glistening with sweat. His old friend Hollis had seen him come in and greeted him with a wide smile.

"Hollis, get me a bottle of mezcal and a six-pack of Mexican beer," he shouted, ignoring the other patrons seated at the counter. Hollis the bartender nodded at Jesse. He pulled a tall bottle from the shelf above his head, then reached into a nearby refrigerator for the six-pack. It took some time to move all the Irish beers aside so that he could reach the Mexican beers.

"What's the hurry, Jesse?" asked the bartender. "We haven't talked about old times in two or three months. Why not have a seat and join the living? Two pints for two poets, eh?" Even as he asked, Hollis saw the negative answers to his friendly inquiries written on Jesse's frenzied and pallid face. "Some other time, eh, sarge? Some other time."

Jesse nodded both impatiently and apologetically as he tossed twenty dollars onto the counter. Then he grabbed the liquor and ran out of the bar. As he drove off, Jesse knew that Hollis would understand such a rude entry and departure. Hollis understood everything—he had fought at Ia Drang. He had reenlisted twice and had done three tours in Vietnam. He had done heroin, cocaine, and transcendental meditation. He would not need an explanation.

On the road north Jesse played the tape over and over again, his hand shaking with internal resistance each time he reached up to rewind the cassette. By the time he reached the motel he had downed half the bottle. With each swig his lips came closer and closer to the pink *gusano*, the worm that crawls toward everyone's bedsheet. Is that what the Mexicans meant by their tradition? wondered Jesse. Was it good luck to swallow death? To taste it while still alive? Hadn't he already done that? All at once the thought of eating the *gusano* was no longer repugnant. He had tasted death before.

He swallowed the worm just as his car skidded into the parking lot of his motel. In a moment of lucidity he realized that he had no memory whatsoever of having driven across the Golden Gate Bridge. He opened the trunk of his car to retrieve a small cassette player, then staggered to his room, leaving the trunk wide open.

That night he finally fell asleep at six in the morning. By daybreak he had thrown up twice, the first time on the sheets. He had finished the bottle and tossed it heedlessly onto the floor. He had followed a liter of mezcal with five bottles of Corona. He had sobbed each time he heard that voice and that single word. The soft sound of air passing through Persephone's larynx, over her palatine tonsil, and past her lips had staggered Jesse, jolted him like a bolt of ball lightning down his spine.

Persephone had not cried out for help. In fact, there had been no hint of fear in her voice. Her tone had been one of quiet supplication, almost prayerlike. The final word to resonate in her nasal conchas was a name, the name of a man: Amos.

"Amos Flyer!" Jesse had screamed at the spinning walls of his motel room. The sleepy motel clerk at the front desk had been deluged with angry calls complaining about the horrid noises coming from within room 27. Jesse knew Amos Flyer. Why hadn't he made the connection before? He knew Amos Flyer! He loved Amos Flyer! And even more than that, he knew precisely what the second voice had been screaming just after the first gunshot and just before the second.

She hadn't been screaming "ten lands," as one of the witnesses had stated. She had been screaming words that Jesse had heard once before, words that had been burned into his memory. Those words had certainly been Mai Adrong's final words as she ran forward to embrace her dear friend. Both women had done what they had to do, and neither had been afraid. Jesse's tumbling mind seethed with a hundred ironies.

When he finally lost consciousness, Jesse dreamed a dream unlike any before—the hardest dream, the cruelest, the kind that contains no mystery at all, no deep meanings sequestered within vague and skewed symbols. Rolling and sweltering, his closed eyes dancing madly beneath his lids, Jesse whimpered while knitting a smoky skein of siege and embrace beneath his brow. The man's body tossed wildly as the wounded mind of the seventeen-year-old soldier came forward once more: the boy assuming command of the man. He came forward beseeching all impostors, piling calumnies upon every lover, balking at any splendor, and leering madly at the lustrous deafening of guns.

Jesse lay his head down where there were two ghostly hills, one upon the other, the hardest pillows on earth. They were eerie hillsides of shanties and sorties where tender, practiced movements of arabesque and grand jeté were set to the billowing, profane music of battle. Between his ears grew the tumult of toe shoes beneath a callow rank of pale-blue dancers suddenly cut down by combustion. The troupe performed in a florid grotto where the sweet lure of jeopardy is effaced by chagrin, endless braids of chagrin. At stage left the grace of bedlam was chained to couplets of dalliance.

There were soldiers coming up the rise, and screaming in the yellow light of drifting flares. The faceless had faces. There were young soldiers coming up, flaunting their last instant of human wholeness for carefully positioned machine guns. Jesse fired madly through the hotel room's plaster ceiling, through the roof and through the universe. One of the enemy soldiers refused to die.

Down below, there were sudden, wet plumes of crimson, spreading out like horizontal geysers. Chiaroscuro: a canvas of innards covered his hotel bed; his legs were lathered in bile and acid. There was hot distemper in his dreams, sordid squalls of dismay. There was a maelstrom upon his sheets, body counts a world and decades apart. A friend gone insane is walking toward the Mekong River. Jesse buckled violently as a screwdriver coldly disengaged his mind. The stabbing pain was replaced by a vision of bodies arrayed, shredded and cooling, bodies all craving the mundane. Boys once so addicted to breath were all craving the mundane.

Then there was the dying voice of Julio Lopez speaking from below the bed. Jesse saw that his slender brown body was just beneath his own, sewn into the mattress, sealed in and suffocating. Cotton filled Julio's mouth as he tried to speak. A sorrowful dance step and its entangled shadow, the man's variation moved across the stage, followed by the woman's, claustrophobic and clutching and moribund. There was a slavish dance in his dreams: a woeful pas de deux on two separate stages, one upon the other, years apart.

A mad elopement of pariahs commingled an ablution of yeast and opium. A line of green boys, prescient and listless, circled his forlorn bed in a tight and noiseless three-meter spread. On Jesse's pillow, his bile-ridden sweat smelled of the ancient docks at Marseille. His shoulders beneath his shirt and tie were galled by straps and web belts and by the weight of canteens and taped magazines.

Finally, at the darkest part of the morning, Jesse dreamed of the young padre who had walked through a minefield and away from a war.

"What mean ye that ye beat my people to pieces?"

Clutched in Jesse's fingers were two dog tags, his own and the one that had emerged from the surface of a metal wall in the same way that Japanese carp break the surface of a pond, the dog tag that once hung on the neck of a Creole sergeant named Amos Flyer.

At the first blush of dusk, just minutes before merciful sleep, the radio alarm came on. Jesse heard nothing. There was a sweet coda on a radio, a soulful rendition of "L'Amour Suprême" performed by Jean Jacques Kainji, the magnificent French-Nigerian saxophonist who, in another world and in another time, would have been named John Coltrane. There was the late-breaking news flash that the Martian probe sent into space by the United States almost a year before had landed on the surface of the red planet.

The first photos from the surface would shock the entire world. There on the surface, hastily left by the side of one of the canals, were six empty bottles of cerveza Bohemia, a giant, unopened bag of chicharrón, eleven cigarette butts, and three discarded tin cans that had once contained menudo.

9

the spider's banquet

It begins in the frozen grasses and rarefied air of Tibet as a small, thirsting spring. Its small visage at that altitude is pure and infantile. Little more than a feeble trickle, it is helplessly swaddled in lichens and moss. Up here, a jackboot could stifle it. A tank tread could reroute it. A thirsty bulrush could swallow it whole. Here at the roof of the world it is just one of many supplicant springs, mere novice flows tugging at the hemline of lofty snow, suckling there at frost and here at lowly sleet.

It learns to toddle in these highlands and begins to walk where the yak, a tiny bullock, is slaughtered reverently and is so fiercely venerated. It gathers its strength in southern China and becomes a wide flow as it skirts the Zadoi temple of Jingding, where celestial prayers rise up like startled larks and naked Buddhist monks and Hui Muslims go down in silent droves to bathe. It begins to darken and deepen near the Golden Triangle, where it hears the voices, feels the hulls, feeds the children of the people called Blang, Kongge, Han, Van, and Aku.

It passes by brimming ladles of rice wine, lime-green papayas sautéed with peanuts, hidden caches of fermenting fish heads, and mile upon green mile of poppy fields fringed by irrigation ditches and the bending people who tend them. Beyond these are endless fields of tea, mint, and lemon grass. Behind those are the never-

ending patchwork of rice paddies, the serenity and steam of countless tea ceremonies, and the davening, clouded mutters of a legion of
heroin addicts.

Hidden within fields such as these, spread out in an unnatural
array, are skulking squads of Pathet Lao, Khmer Rouge cadres, platoons of Vietcong, and battalions of North Vietnamese regulars.
They are all venerable orders, replenished each day by newly sewn
uniforms covering newly recruited flesh. The grassy fields are littered with the rusted paraphernalia of a dozen wars. As with all
armies, the barked commands and the cold machines always outlive
the men.

New to these grasses and valleys are razor-wired encampments of
ARVN from the Army of the Republic of Vietnam, and . . . there are
Americans—noisy, brash, and brimming with slick and polished
mythologies of good and evil and tales of technical invincibility.

The river that flows beneath American gunboats has seen the
Mongols, the Burmans, the Toungoo and Chakri dynasties. It has
heard the names beneath the names: ancient Upper Chenla, Lower
Chenla and the eternal Kingdom of Champa. Now it has heard of
Watts, Echo Park, Buttermilk Bottom, and Staten Island. Now the
river has heard Janis Joplin and Smokey Robinson.

The crystalline head of this river is twenty-five hundred miles
from its murky, splayed legs. In south China, its given name is Lan-
cang, the force of a million gray elephants that rampage and rumble
headlong into Laos. There, its huge belly is replenished by Luang,
the monster dragon who spits torrents of fresh rain. At full strength
it flows by the ruins of Angkor Wat and blithely sloughs off Tonle
Sap, a tiny tributary that soon becomes a great lake where Cham and
Khmer fishermen gracefully cast their white butterfly nets, pulling
back generation after generation of slippery, brown wives and flapping children, harvesting century after century of life.

It listens to prayers as it travels; it has always listened to prayers.
There are gentle Cao Dai sentiments sunk deep in its sediment, and
Christian prayers clinging like fervent froth to its wide banks. Its re-
sponsive face is ever changing in reaction to endless Taoist chants.
Its waves have heaved and sighed forever, moved by the birth of
mountains; moved by the words of the Koran. Unlike all other rivers
on earth, this one is driven down to the sea by the dew and sweat of
orchids, by the unceasing hopes of men.

Each trough is a cruel frailty, each crest an anonymous act of morality. This river was busily flooding the banks of Southeast Asia for ten kilometers on either side when the ancient schism between Mahayana and Theravada split the heart of Asia.

Miles downriver the Mekong divides twice. It becomes the Tien Giang and the Hua Giang long before it flays itself into the nineheaded serpent of the delta called Cong Cuu Long. He is the dragon who is doomed to do eternal, elemental battle with the sea. For hundreds of miles up the delta, salt water invades the flow of rain and melted snow.

The color of this conflict is a bluish-green whose deepest moods are black as obsidian. It is here that the floating markets flourish, clotting small harbors like giant, woven water lilies. It is here in the humid delta that the trees of the mangrove forests interlace their roots and thicken into impenetrability.

The lieutenant from the Chaplain's Corps walked, then ran, then staggered toward this river. With the voice of a young Chicano sergeant still ringing in his ears and the sad, confused gaze of Tiburcio Mendez probing at his back, he walked heedlessly through a minefield, his senseless feet setting off trip flares as he moved. He crossed a small ravine and then staggered past a hastily hidden pile of NVA dead. They had been dragged from the field of battle in order to skew the enemy's body count.

It was obvious that they had been moved from the scene in a frenzy of fear and disrespect; bloodless cheeks had been torn and scuffed by rocks, and sightless eyes had been punctured by exposed roots. Their bodies had been stripped of weapons and food. Any insignia of rank had been torn away. More than anything else, they looked like a cord of expressive firewood or a gothic frieze depicting the everlasting pain of Hades. The bitter, cloying scent of the rotting corpses wafted into his nose, enraging his nerve endings, but it did not enter into his soul.

The lieutenant blessed them all with a sweeping motion of his hand. It was not a learned but an uncommitted wave. That would have been a staunchly Unitarian gesture. The pain behind the movement of the hand was not the staid, bloodless echo of an ancient passion—it certainly was not Catholic. Rather, it was a calm gesture of recognition, a gesture of acknowledgment and acceptance—as though the horror of these fields was little more than yet another blow struck by an old, familiar foe. For some unknown reason the chaplain felt like singing, but singing was not the word that properly described his desire. He wished to chant. There was a dyslexic song of stilted, unfamiliar rhythms and unrhymed words that stuck in his gorge and could not rise.

Minutes later he stepped into a deep crater, suddenly falling waist-deep into soft, collapsing soil. Around his rooted legs was a large, circular depression that was all that remained of an extensive underground hospital complex. There were muted groans just yards beneath his feet, painful sighs of hope and surrender that invaded his consciousness as if in a dream. His ears heard muffled, suffocating cries for help, but his mind did not. The blaring sounds within his own skull were much too deafening.

If he had gazed downward, he would have seen traces of a ruined enemy medical installation—unsterilized needles and ragged bandages, the splinters of handmade surgical tools. A once enormous complex of rooms cut deep into the soil had been instantly transformed into an endless maze of catacombs. A bomb had found its target.

He walked until the sun set once more, stopping only because the night was as profoundly black as total blindness. Though the sky was ablaze with stars, he could see nothing at all below the horizon. Considering neither safety nor comfort, he found a small depression in a grassy hillside and dropped down to wait for morning. He may have slept. He may have dreamed. How could he know? Even in the deep quiet of midnight, the eclipse of reason behind his eyes raised a sheen of sweat on his brow and tightened the muscles of his jaw into an eternal grimace.

Sometime during the night a herd of tiny, spotted deer wandered in, heading for the river. They had stopped to graze on a knoll just below the padre's depression. One of the deer, a fawn just two hands high, had spotted the padre's salt-laden boots and was happily chewing on their green canvas. At that very moment the man began to believe he was one with the wild weeds and grasses beneath him, his life gone fallow. Memories and conceits sprouted and died within his mind in random but natural order, flowering in a single instant, and gone to seed in the next. He did not feel it when the canvas gave way and his foot began to bleed.

Days and nights passed this way until the limping lieutenant reached the river at Nong Khai. It was here that the chaplain lost landfall and tumbled headfirst into the mighty Mekong. The mad lieutenant never sensed the water or the pain of the fall. Without knowing it, he coughed and vomited, clearing his lungs of algae and murky water. Blind to the world, he flailed his arms wildly until they caught on a passing log. Immobile and blanched white, he joined the torpid parade of floating dead, the fetid regatta of bobbing soldiers and murdered civilians that has always enjoyed free run of the river.

That hill was far behind him now, that desperate, defaced elevation. Far behind him was Jesse Pasadoble bending in that eerie Martian landscape to touch a smoking corpse and scream a question that would forever be unheard. Were the padre in his right mind, he could have recalled his own impression that the young sergeant had seemed little more than a puppet, a living effigy of himself. He had looked as though he were actually hanging from the clouds of thick smoke that hugged the hillside, the shoulders of his fatigues pinned to the curling air and his legs dangling beneath his waist.

In a single night all life's comfort had been stripped from the young sergeant, leaving only endless longing and aimless passion. His world back home in America was a land obsessed with comfort; with the avoidance of pain . . . at any cost. America was the chaplain's adopted country. There, everyone who can afford it dashes headlong into comfort, into barricades and behind walls for a life without disease and agony—hiding from both risk and passion alike.

In Vietnam, there was no comfort, nor would there ever be. The Creole sergeant had been right. Those boys, like the slaves from Africa, like the hopeless Indians, like true artists and the poor, had been chosen to bear the discomfort of their country, to bear the loss. If nothing else, the lieutenant understood loss. He was intimate with it. After all, the Unitarian had been born in Mexico, a land whose primary sensibility is that of profound loss. Everyone in Mexico felt it. The sense of loss had its roots in the time of the conquest: the loss of a hundred native religions, the loss of an entire race of peoples.

In the United States, there were many peoples who felt this same loss: the Apache and Papago felt it, as well as the great-grandchildren of slaves. Yet white America sensed only gain: the taming of the West meant gain; the defeat of the Mexican Army meant gain. The subjugation of the redwoods and the spotted owl meant progress. Is it any wonder that when those who feel loss utter the word "justice," it

cannot possibly mean the same thing as when that word is spoken by
those who know only gain? Hadn't the Creole sergeant back on that
hill said something about justice? Hadn't the Chicano sergeant said
something?

The boys back on the hill had repelled an NVA battalion time and
time again but felt no joy in it, no gain from it. The entire U.S. Army
had a sense of loss wriggling in its arteries, lurking in its veins like a
malarial parasite hiding within its mechanistic passion for destruction. Back home, hamburgers were still being fried and vodka martinis were still being shaken and poured. There was no gas rationing
in Trenton; there were no victory gardens in Boise.

America had fully expected to win without suffering, without loss.
The boys on the hill knew differently. The American Dream—the
two-bedroom house with a white picket fence—had always been
built on a graveyard. It had always been built at the expense of the
Huron Nation, at the expense of the bison, and at the expense of the
Vietnamese. It had always been built on a hill.

One hundred kilometers behind the floating padre were the deep
brown eyes of Corporal Tiburcio Mendez scanning the heavens
above for some absurd object—for some insane reason. The Salon
des Refusés was there, bloated and bent beyond recognition. Poor
Cornelius was there, impossibly still, lying and drying in his chrysalis next to the stiffening body bags of a Midwestern boy and Jim-
Earl, the Shoshone.

Both boys had been cracked open, their scrambled innards draped,
painting the dirt a deep aubergine and red. Both had suffered ter-
ribly before finding the ultimate comfort. All the colored boys, the
Okies, and the spics were far behind, still fighting Vietnam and
America at the same time. Tall, white-haired officers and officials on
two continents were busily barking orders into their ears—Lester
Maddox, George Wallace, and Generals Ky and Westmoreland.
Back on the hill there were charred bullocks sprawled everywhere.

The padre's legs danced involuntarily as a final image of the
Creole sergeant and his troops flashed into his mind. From his sub-
merged eye, a single tear welled up and rushed down to join the
river. Now he numbly realized that he loved those volatile children
on the hill. The unexploded gunpowder in their groins should have
gone off on mattresses. Those missing hands were meant to stroke
the hair of a lover. Those traumatically avulsed feet should have

stepped onto a dance floor. Their senseless eyes should have been allowed to seek out and choose a single face among a million faces, then in three score years and ten, in failing sight, watch that beloved face age and die.

Were these new thoughts? wondered the living flotsam. Were these thoughts new or had he heard them back at seminary? Had there been brandy and late-night coffee, and early morning interlude of alcohol, caffeine, and philosophy? What was the ancient lesson? He seemed to recall that there was an ancient lesson. The opposite of comfort is wilderness. Oh, yes, the New Testament. The opposite of comfort is wilderness. Was this another way of saying that everything turns on jazz?

The padre was free of it all now, his flimsy legs and knees striking an occasional rock or tree stump. His wild, confused, and careening mind—even more turbulent than the water—was far, far away from the Mekong River and that unspeakable war. As hour after hour passed he became as sentient flotsam, dreaming in crests and troughs, hearing in undulations and eddies. Among the myriad sounds that both haunt and attend a river, the padre heard something else. It was the faintest strain—the thread of a sound. It was a prayer, sequestered among psalms that were split at the heart, spoken in one language but always answered in another. It was a whispered, breath-driven tide of supplication that carried with it the scent of candle wax, the crisp, wet smell of apple orchards, and an image of acre upon acre of the waving green grasses of the state of Chihuahua. Slowly, the trembling and tenuous mind of the floating man was wholly transformed from the high grasses that lined the banks of the Mekong River into the grasses of his youth in Mexico.

"What is more placid than tall grass; untended, unmatted; a shivering edge of life to match, gust for gust, the precocious wind—to give it shape?"

The living flotsam spoke its words upward toward the trees that shaded the river. A family of spider monkeys listened closely. He gazed upward at them and saw fauns, dryads, satyrs, all charmed by Orfeo's spoken aria.

"The truth of grass is in its power to stand out of sight regardless of eyes; to be unmeasured, uncounted; to be among so many and so remain unchosen . . . undistinguished. No matter who is moving through the earth's hair, nothing new ever happens here.

Yes, it is true that the jaguar and the fawn hide here. In Chiapas and Guatemala, soldiers hide here, set man traps, and bury their fallen here."

The drowned man, soaked to his soul but for a few dozen raging and rhapsodizing neurons, passed through a forest that had been defoliated. He wondered as he stared at a sky of Kirlian leaves whether the living trunks, in spring, still felt the weight of phantom fruit. He wondered if, someday, someone would come to revive these stumps—help them live on. As he spoke aloud to no one, he imagined a glade of prosthetic limbs.

"I am grass, and here in Chihuahua young girls in the first heat of womanhood lie curling and unfurling here, their ardor ankle-deep in my soil. Loving couples roll and thrash here fervidly, upending shoots and tearing at tender roots. Mexican butchers kill their trusting cattle here. Grass like me is full of words, full of secretive spiders and flirting moths. Everything happens in grass like me. But never anything new.

"Let's suppose."

Above his head a new family of spider monkeys ceased their grooming to hear his words. The padre saw them turning their heads to see him as he passed below. He lifted an arm and pointed a finger at them.

"*Supongamos*, as someone once said. Supposing I say to you that my own story begins on the hallowed hinge of a chrysalis, an exquisite cocoon that dangles between truth and fable. But before I begin my mad weaving, there are certain things that I suppose I must confess to you. I cannot be an omniscient narrator, so don't expect me to have the answers to everything, and don't expect me to see every facet as though I had a hundred insect eyes."

The family of monkeys blinked their mutual confusion, then returned to their search for ticks, hair lice, and fleas.

"I suppose that I must have been chosen to spin my own part of this tale. Chosen not by a conscious mind but by the odds, by chance . . . by destinies. Why was I chosen? Why me, since I am no one at all? Well, I am something of a sort: a coward who has run away from war and from my own past. That is my single qualification. I am a wayward shepherd who has left all his flock behind. But I certainly don't mind the question. I must have been chosen because I know it all from beginning to end. I am certainly not the story itself. I am only the grass that tattles on the wind."

On the shore a sniper followed the padre's progress, framing the floating man's head in the rear sight of his rifle. The man's wild gestures above the waves had caught the sniper's eye.

"Don't get me wrong"—the padre continued his sermon to no one. "As I have said, I am far from omniscient and still farther away from perfect. In fact, my only true strength is my ability to see the ends of things. You see, I am obsessed with endings. I am insane with endings. To be sure, they have ruled my life. Endings are the captain of my soul. Why else would I turn my back on my calling, abandon everything, even death on that hill near Laos? Who one earth can abandon death?"

The sniper on the bank lowered his weapon and clicked on the safety. He was a soldier—not a butcher of the insane, of the already dead.

"Maybe I shouldn't be telling you this. Perhaps I should make an end and simply float away on the Mekong and die waterlogged and anonymous. I doubt you'll listen to me anyway. I'm really not in mint condition, you see. Never was. But don't you see how adrift we are? We're down here and God's way up there."

The chaplain pointed toward the clouds that were gathering above him. All at once a squall sent sheets of dark water rushing downward. The padre's first impulse was to seek shelter from the rain, but the absurdity of that soon had him laughing madly.

"The real omniscient narrator is always way up there. I tell you, believing in God is exactly like living downstairs from a boy genius who has been stricken with polio. I had to do that once, you know. I was a kid then, back in Mexico. I could hear that poor, sickly boy scuffling and stumbling around upstairs, that angry, envious little Mennonite boy.

"I remember him, inching his way down the stairs and clinging tightly to the railings. There was always black ink on his tongue and on his fingertips. The boy passed his days turning the pages of a book. He always smelled like bedsheets, like mounds of tossed linen in an airless room. I remember thinking that he was a prisoner of linen—a secret slave to detergents, disinfectants, and bleaches. He always smelled the way a mother should smell, like fawning kisses, like fumes of guilt and medication. He smelled like a mother's tears on clean laundry.

"My God, he was such an angry boy, fed up with adoration. All he ever wanted was to be able to move around on his own, without someone downstairs always apologizing for his absence, always listening for his halting steps or divining the cause and effect of every cough. I apologize for this manner of speaking. Though now I am little more than a sheaf of grass stems that has been tossed upon the waters; I was once an ardent seminarian.

"Maybe I shouldn't be telling you any of this. Who am I to comment on God. I'm not in mint condition. Maybe you don't really need to know about the buzzing cruelty and the webs that I have come to understand as life. But please pardon me. Here I am telling you about endings when my poor life's story must have a starting place.

"We certainly won't start with me. That would be insane. But perhaps, by the end of my sermon, you can tell me who I am or who I have become. You see, I've forgotten completely."

The chaplain suddenly stopped his monologue. Because of the rain, he had been shouting. Now the rain had stopped and the silence around him was stunning, thrilling, as though the Mekong River was resting.

"I was once a man," he continued in a lower voice. "I was once a combat chaplain, I do know that. I was someone who trod the fields down alongside the troops. Now I am only grass, and look here, there are even drops of blood on my face. But have a care! If you think my story is about death, you have another think coming."

The chaplain's body, saturated by water to within an inch of his bones, traversed a small rapids, his back and chest striking several sharp rocks. A rib cracked beneath his fatigue jacket. Like so many other injuries, this wound would not heal for years. Perhaps it would never heal.

The Mennonites of his youth refused to tell him of his origins, nor would the disdainful nuns and priests of the local cathedral. But the old men and old women who spent their last days in front of or within the local cantinas were more than willing to speak.

As he bobbed in the wake and backwash of a passing rice boat, the lieutenant wondered if the pain he was feeling was the deep ache of a broken rib bone or the sad pang of memory.

* * *

In a land of heat and distance, in a land where even the most obvious things are hidden, each moment that lapses into the past lapses into legend. In the tiny towns and villages of Chihuahua, legend has it that the boy was left alone to work for his keep with an insular, hermetic community of Mexican Mennonites. It was said that he was left completely alone to unravel the knotty intricacies of English and German from his small Spanish perch. Some seemed to recall that a seemingly impoverished cripple abandoned him on the front porch of a German family that had made its way south from Pennsylvania. Still others relate that the child was dragged against his will to an apple farm north of Pedernales and left to be the houseboy for an old-maid sister of the order.

The padre's true father was a man called Papa Guillermo, after his own father, the venerable Tata Guillermo Calavera. *Los dos*, both grandfather and father, were reputed to be *ermitaños y avoros muy famosos*, famous hermit-misers that pretended to suffering abject poverty but who in reality possessed wealth beyond Midas. Old Tata was said to be one of those fabled Mexican dirt farmers whose niggardly peso-pinching eventually resulted in the accumulation of a vast fortune. They say that he hid his wealth in the steep, grassy land around his farmhouse. His savage distrust of the banks eventually metastasized into a hoarding disease of staggering proportion. In time the disease became congenital.

Old Tata had never drawn a map of his treasures. That *viejito* was far too *cauteloso*, far too wary for that. That rumor was quite incorrect. Using a sharpened ice pick, the old man had scratched the precious map onto the lenses of his only pair of reading glasses. When reposing in the outhouse, in one of his famous marathon bowel movements, the *viejito* would sit with his chin resting on the heels of his hands, his lungs and lower abdomen burning with exertion. From this position, he could see the precise location of each treasure trove. The left lens spied upon the north side of the hill and the right lens covered the south, the line of demarcation running down the center of his nose.

Unfortunately, the old man passed away in that outhouse, his withered body falling down through the wooden toilet seat into thirty-five years' accumulation of human waste. The secret glasses with their cryptic message went with him, never to be found.

After his death, his only son, Papa Guillermo, kept the farm going for a few years, but local mythology has it that he finally gave in to the persistent tales of buried gold and silver coinage. He auctioned off all his bags of seed and his draft animals. He sold the entire grassy lowlands to those stupid Mennonite farmers. Papa told himself that the bottom land was far too rocky to farm and the soil far too acidic. No corn or lettuce would ever grow there. He took great pride in the fact that he had driven a hard bargain for that useless, barren land.

All that he kept for himself and his family was the small hill that overlooked the parcels and the rights to the stream that ran along its base. Papa Guillermo would dedicate himself instead to a life of excavation. The family home had always been precariously perched at the top of the hill. After years of incessant digging, its foundation had tilted severely to the northeast. Anything placed on the floor would roll or slide to the north side of the house. In an effort to maintain some semblance of stability, all the chairs and the tables had to be nailed down to the floorboards. The last thirty years of Papa's life were spent cutting and reinforcing a thousand sinkholes and the narrow, water-filled tunnels that ran beneath the family homestead. Old *revolucionarios* would swig on pulque and whoop at Papa's ingenuity, his military genius. To defend his secret gold mine from legions of claim jumpers, the old man had crisscrossed the entire surface of the hill with a web of strings and wires on which were hung bottles and empty cans that clinked and tinkled in the smallest breeze.

"No one would ever sneak up on him," whispered the old *soldados*, their voices filled with grudging respect, "not even the wind."

Two hundred miles down the Mekong the wind had pushed the lieutenant toward the bank, where he was rudely prodded by oars. He responded with half-groans and semi-gestures that spoke the whole truth about war. It was his death moans that would shield him from the curious. The living would abandon him to the currents and allow him to float out to landless sea with all the other dead. In the South China Sea there would be floating islands of once living persons who had turned to clay—coves, peninsulas, and archipelagos of flesh bobbing on foam, shaken loose from life by unwitnessed forces. Above all the bodies were the pungent, swirling fumes of remembrance. A bird landed on the chaplain's forehead and began to peck

at insects that clung to his hairline, and still, the padre dreamed of
Chihuahua. . . .

But even all those cruel whispers and twisted tales about his family
were not the end. More arcane and slanted rumors began to circulate
about the chaplain's ancestors. The gossips in the Pedernales *lavan-
dería* swore that, in truth, Tata and Papa Guillermo Calavera were
not even human at all. If the truth be told, the two men had begun
life as lowly *insectos*, as burrowing spiders, *arañas* who had been mag-
ically transformed into fully grown human men only after having
made an unbreakable pact with Satanás, the devil himself.

In exchange for this miraculous transformation, the two spiders
had, in turn, agreed to live lives of depressing loneliness and to years
of digging in the soil. In their original form—the form that God
intended—both men had been what modern entomologists call a
Mexican brown recluse, a small nondescript arachnid that spends its
entire life spinning its silken traps in the hollows of trees and in
earthen holes.

But even this dark slander was not the worst of the malicious
tongue-wagging. It was said that both men, though by no means
handsome specimens, had somehow managed to woo and to marry
women who were renowned throughout the land for their stunning
physical and spiritual beauty. The same savage tongues that went on
and on about brown spiders recounted in whispers that the two men
had trapped the women in their hideous webs, then dragged them,
kicking and screaming, down into the darkness of their subterranean
lives.

Both of these beautiful women had once been delicate *mariposas*,
butterflies, lovely Mexican painted ladies. It was whispered that both
women, at their wedding ceremonies, had been adorned with voluminous, flowing gowns in order to hide the eye spots beneath their
armpits and the wide red bands than ran across their lovely breasts.

The world just below the Rio Grande had been both revolted and
amazed when the younger set of mismatched *insectos* somehow gave
birth to a human son. He looked like a child in every way, but could
the boy truly be human? Madre de Dios! Beneath his skin, wasn't he
little more than an *abominacíon*, a creation of *mágico obscuro*, black
magic? One midwife whispered that this bawling infant had never

seen the inside of a womb, but rather had been a wriggling pupa carried in a bag beneath his mother's dress.

There were those treasure hunters in the village who swore on the blessed eyes of their departed mothers that they had penetrated the perimeter of the hill and slid soundlessly past the sensitive web. These people proclaimed over and over that they had heard the occupants of the house on the hill humming and buzzing an insect's babble. There had been ear-splitting, sibilant sounds like the ones that sprang from the legs of giant crickets and the mandibles of the largest butterflies.

Some had actually glimpsed the man and the woman levitating and dropping down to the floor inside their dining room. They related that the woman, like her sisters the monarch and the moth, was drawn again and again to a flickering line of golden candlesticks that dominated the room. And in the darkest corner of that room the boy's bed hung from the ceiling like a gigantic egg sac, swaying back and forth to the high strains of an unearthly music. It seemed to all who had eyes to see and ears to hear that the Calavera boy had descended from a line of insects . . . and now he has gone to live with unsuspecting Mennonites. If the gossips only knew. The truth behind all their suspicions was far more bizarre.

The chaplain floated past banks of torched homes and tiny villages that had been ravaged by one side or the other. There were hungry hollow-eyed people everywhere, quietly cleaning up the mess left behind by the warriors. At times he was joined on his journey by travel mates. For a while a dead girl kept him company, but she sternly refused to share his upended view of the world. She preferred instead to stare downward at the muddy riverbed, her unblinking eyes forsaking the sky altogether.

Once a beheaded Korean ranger joined him, and for a time the two were trapped in a shallow whirlpool, circling endlessly with the shards of a boat rudder, slivers of a broken oar, plastic bottles, and a burned flotation device from a downed helicopter. The two became caught up in a hopeless discussion. While the chaplain's mind swam with bullocks, butterflies, arks, and shattered tablets, the Korean had few original thoughts, if any at all. Their trip together ended abruptly when the wash of a passing gunboat released the living man to follow the river.

Tides of considerations, like brine, rose and fell upon the half-drowned man, slapping his body and wearing away his outer layers of skin. He slowly began to find in the river new beliefs to believe: the sperm in the fallopian tube will defeat the loaded mortar. The hoe will surely slaughter the tank. The glance between lovers will rebuild all that radar and artillery can detect and destroy. He came to believe that someday, a legion of one-legged men will proclaim the fields of grass to be free of land mines, their absent limbs the first step into the future. It would be armless girls who would undo the tangled nets of war. Somewhere between a tiny rope bridge and a small, isolated colony of lepers, the chaplain came to believe in all of the small people who would come out to rebuild when the machines of war were stilled.

Five hundred miles downriver his body was used for target practice by a newly formed platoon of Viet Cong. One bullet pierced his bloated thigh, but exited without drawing blood. A thousand miles and a million thoughts later, his body chanced to foul a fishing net, and an exasperated, cursing fisherman was forced to haul the carcass on board. Now released from the waters, the padre was free to dream of the years beyond Chihuahua, beyond the hill near Laos, and he dreamed of a long sea voyage in an overcrowded boat. He had visions of salt burning in his wounds, of thin chicken broth, wretched seasickness, and the acrid smell of living bodies pressed one against another.

He dreamed of urine and rice, the cry of a child that decayed from an embittered wail, past a delirious whimper, and finally, into stark silence. He dreamed of breasts drained dry and of burials at sea. He dreamed in color and saw the red rash and bright pus of his own wounded thigh. He suffered an unending nightmare of concertina wire and tents, of overseers and of the overseen. Somewhere he heard the careless rip of clothing and saw the cruel dominion of male flesh over female flesh.

He had lied to the colonel in Da Nang. He had never really been a Unitarian. He had never been a Mennonite or a Catholic. Had he confessed as much? There had never been gold nuggets and silver coins hidden in the hill of his childhood back in Chihuahua. His ancestors had not been misers. It had all been a ruse, a decoy.

Things of much greater value had been buried up on that precious hill. But most important of all, he had never been a *recluso*

Mexicano, a spider. When, after an unknowable time had elapsed—perhaps months or perhaps years—and he finally woke from his drowning dream, he was sweating, naked, and breathless, his erect male member inside a woman who called herself Cassandra.

"Why did you stop?" Her large eyes were open now, her heavy breathing had slowed. "Vô Dahn, please don't stop. Vô Dahn, what is it? I was getting so close."

The man above her stared downward at the lovely face of the woman beneath him—at her rising and falling breasts, at the glistening patches on her skin where their sweat had mixed. He raised his head to look around the room. He recognized nothing at all—not the paintings, not the furniture, not even the remains of a meal for two. He rose from the bed and walked to the window, spreading wide the curtains despite his nakedness.

He looked downward at the harbor and the bay and the construction cranes and gray high-rise buildings that glutted the skyline to his left. He wondered if he was in San Francisco or Seattle. There were signs down below written in Cantonese. He shook his head. How did he know it was Cantonese? He could be on Stockton Street, looking toward Oakland. His eyes returned to the distant bay. The very sight of water left him cold.

After a moment of silence he moved back to the bed but did not rejoin the woman lying there. He sat down in a blue chair that had been draped with hastily tossed clothing. He lifted a man's shirt to eye level, then let it drop. The shirt slumped to the floor, disappointed, deflated, unrecognized.

"Vô Dahn, *mon cher*, you're beginning to remember things, aren't you? I can't tell you how many times I've prayed for this moment, even though I knew it might mean that you could forget us, what we've meant to each other."

She lay on the bed as she spoke, her eyes still gazing upward and her legs still open and receptive. There was a trembling on the surface of her skin. At last, she was living the moment that she had both dreaded and longed for. Now that the time had finally come, she felt relieved.

"Now I've become a liar," she sighed. "Now I've become a liar. *Maintenant, je suis une menteuse.*"

"It seems that remembering means forgetting," whispered Vô

Dahn. He hadn't heard her last words. "Somehow, remembering means forgetting." He raised his head to look at the beautiful woman on the bed. "You called me Vô Dahn. How did I get the name Vô Dahn?"

"You got that name by forgetting your own true name. As long as I've known you, you've been without a name. *Vô Dahn* means nameless. You have been called Vô Dahn for at least three years. It was I who named you."

"What year is this? Where am I? What have I been doing? Do we live here together? Are we lovers, you and I?"

The woman sat upright on the bed. The man noticed for the first time the flawless, almost alabaster skin that covered the last layer of her soul's temple. Only a blurring tattoo on her forearm marred the perfection of her skin. He canted his head to read the words written there, then his eyes returned to her face and hair. She had long black hair that fell almost to her waist. Her face was unwrinkled and unmarred by worry, but there was such grief in her eyes.

She swung her legs over the edge of the bed and jumped down to a soft woven mat. Her legs seemed as smooth as marble. It was clear that their lovemaking session was over. Perhaps they would never make love again. A sigh of disappointment escaped the man's lips as she threw a loose robe around her body, covering her thighs and her breasts. The sigh was familiar to her, so she smiled. Not everything had been lost.

"I have been lying about you to myself for years, Vô Dahn. But since you have always insisted that you are no one, I never thought of it as a lie. As long as you were my lover, I knew that someday I could tell my husband that I made love to no one."

"You have a husband?" asked the man.

"I am married." She exhaled deeply. He could taste her breath. Its flavor calmed him. "He might be dead—he's probably dead, but I still have hopes. As his wife it is my duty. Every day I hope." She walked toward the sitting man and let her hair touch his shoulder and his bowed and confused head.

"My name is Cassandra. At least that's my English name. I've had a dozen names in the last few years. But it is Cassandra who knows that her husband is dead. It is Cassandra who knows that today is the end of our love affair—that the time has come for me to begin my search for someone. *Mon cher*, you and I met five years ago. For three years you and I have taken care of each other. You have been more to me than a husband. You may not know it and you may never know it, but for a year or two, perhaps more, you were a very happy man."

The man who had raised his head to listen to her now dropped it back down, as a thousand thoughts fought for access to a single throat and tongue.

"My name was once William Calvert," he said, in exchange for her revelation.

"This is our apartment, Vô Dahn—I mean, William Calvert. We met in a refugee camp in Thon Buri, Thailand. If you think hard, you will find that you speak some Chinese, French, Vietnamese, and Thai."

The two were speaking just above a whisper. They were rank strangers now, risen up from a warm bed of intimacy. He rose from the chair and placed his hands upon her waist as if to lift her. The woman was confused: should she embrace him or not?

My name is a lie, he thought to himself as looked down at the woman before him. Now he remembered that the useless land the Mennonites had purchased from his father had turned them into rich apple growers. It made them gentleman farmers, and to assuage their guilt, they had given the poor Mexican boy a luxurious name in repayment. They had always known the real value of the property and had paid his father next to nothing for it. When some of their children returned to the United Sates for a proper advanced education, he had been allowed to go with them. *Quelle folie!* Vô Dahn suited him well.

"The city outside that window is Hong Kong. We live in a small apartment on a small hill just north of Boundary Street. Kowloon is in that direction and Kai Tak airport is in the other direction." After a moment of hesitation she ventured her bravest question.

"Do you know who you really are, Vô Dahn?"

"The name my father gave me was Guillermo Calavera, but that name is a lie, too, like everything else in my life."

He inhaled as his muscles swelled. His hands tightened on her tiny midriff. She flexed her lovely legs. Still confused and a bit awkward with her own nakedness beneath the robe, she turned first to the right and then to the left, *une pirouette dehors.* Her long hair leapt from one shoulder to the other. Then, following the force of his hands, she jumped straight up. He carried her back to the bed and laid her down once more.

"My name is not really Cassandra. I've had a Thai name, a Chinese name . . . so many names. But I want to say that our life together is not a lie."

"Me llamo . . . my true name is Guillermo Moises Carvajal. I was a chaplain for the U.S. Army in Vietnam. My life alone has been nothing but lies!"

"I was a whore for the Thai guards."

A tone of indescribable grief settled into Cassandra's voice as she forced the sentences from her mouth.

"It was an ugly camp—they were all ugly camps. I had no other choice. If I hadn't surrendered my body to them they would have taken the little girls. I couldn't bear the thought of that. It was you who gave me the strength to endure it. It was you.

"Since then I have cleaned bilges and outhouses in Bangkok and Macao and waited on tables in Victoria. Now I am a maid in one of those British hotels over there. They make me wear very short dresses. You are a taxi driver for the English and the Germans. You know every street on the Heights and on the Island. Your taxicab is down in the street below. It's that little green Toyota with the front fender missing. There is your coat and hat."

She pointed to a closet on the other side of the bed. He turned to see, but only as a gesture. Like the woman, his entire being was flailing desperately at the words that filled the room. It was as though the words had always been there, hovering in that small apartment, waiting patiently for the two mouths that would, at last, come speak them. Each word was tinged with frenzy and relief, glad that their human conduits had finally arrived.

"It was a hill—it wasn't just terrain," said the still naked man through clenched teeth. "Cassandra, there were young men out there—not just ground units, grunts. There were trees, stands of elephant grass and deep ravines—living things, not goddamn lines of fire and killing zones. They were not just soldiers, they were my flock. What became of them, Cassandra? Where are they now?"

"The North Vietnamese have marched into Saigon." The woman sighed, then knelt down before the man in the blue chair. She took his hand and gave it the kiss that haunts.

"The land is filled with reeducation, revenge, and the ghosts of millions of my people. Your flock has gone back home to a country that is fighting itself. Many soldiers are living in Lisbon and Paris. A few of them have become senators or congressmen, but many more are drug addicts or living under bridges. I've seen them on the television news. They are lost in their own homeland."

"Do they still need me?" asked the padre. There was pain in his voice. "Do you think my flock needs me now?"

"Back in Thailand, Vô Dahn—Guillermo, you would whisper into my ear late at night. I remember, your lips right next to my ear, words of hope carried upon your breath. You never let me lose hope. You tended to the women who gave their bodies, and to the children. When the young girls found the first stains of blood in their underclothing, when they knew the Thai soldiers would be coming for them, you told them what was love and what was not love. You taught us all how to suppose, and we passed so many nights supposing world upon world, better worlds than this one. Don't you remember that? Vô Dahn, my dear, you were the strongest one of all. I am sure they need you, Vô Dahn. I am sure of it."

The chaplain closed his eyes and fell backward into the chair. His dance with Cassandra had not ended. It would never end. But Vô Dahn, William, Guillermo had no idea what steps, what movements came next in this bumbling, self-conscious pas de deux.

"One night, on the boat that finally brought us to Hong Kong, you told me little things about the Mennonites in Chihuahua. I hope I pronounced it right. After years together, you finally shared with me some of the story of your parents. You once even told me about the insects and about a little boy with polio. It was then that I put that beautiful painting on your back. It is the only tattoo I have ever made. An old Laotian woman helped me to do it. Why did you make me put it there, Vô Dahn? At first I understood so little of it. The boy was upstairs, the boy was like God. You have been sick so often that I thought you were dreaming. Over time, I came to understand. It was you who taught me English."

Cassandra reached upward with her right hand, touching the familiar chest and belly of her ex-lover. The skin beneath her touch burned with a different, unfamiliar fever. This heat was a stranger.

"Once when I was a child, there were a series of particularly heavy storms raging in northeastern Mexico." There was a hint of detachment in the padre's voice. He could not speak of these things without drifting.

"Chihuahua had never seen such torrents of water and wind. One of my grandfather's hidden treasures saw the light of day during one of those storms. I stumbled upon it on my way to the outhouse. I saw the tip of a canvas bag sticking out from the soil and the high grass. I dug it up and found another buried beneath it.

"I brought them both into our tilted home. When I opened the first one, I slowly began to understand why my father and grandfather had fostered, even encouraged all of those strange rumors about our family. He was protecting us . . . all those years he had been protecting us.

"I hid the bags in the basement and visited them each time the Mennonites allowed me to return home. Later I would visit the bags when the semester was over at seminary. My brothers at the seminary couldn't understand why I didn't vacation in the Grand Tetons or visit New York City. Something always brought me back to Mexico.

"At night I would cautiously remove the contents from the bags, then unwrap layer upon layer of protective cloth. Even as a boy I could tell that the old paper in the center of the larger bag was somehow sacred, precious. Within the second bag was the lyrical heart of my history. Even then I knew my family was different, Cassandra. In the years since then the truth has been at my door, begging to be let in. So often I have turned it away. I have never had the courage to speak the truth aloud. Secrecy has been my birthright."

He pounded his skull—pummeled his *calavera* with his fists, banging his knuckles against the hidden meaning of words.

"Vô Dahn, while you have spent these years removing names, I have spent them covering one name with another. Are we going our separate ways, my love? I know that I must go to America! I believe that there is someone there who might answer my most heartfelt question. I must find her."

She wrapped her thin fingers around the man's wrist.

"I have loved no one. *Regardez-moi. Ecoutez-moi, mon amour.* Look at me, Vô Dahn. My God, I have loved no one so much," she whispered. She leaned toward him and kissed his hand. "*Vĩnh viễn,*" she said softly. The Vietnamese words for forever.

"*Kerereti*, Cassandra. *Te quiero*. Something deep inside me loves you more than I can say. But I have to go back to a hill and find my lost flock, or what's left of it. I abandoned them all, Cassandra. I walked away when they needed me the most. Will they ever forgive me? They are all back in America—the ones who survived. I know they are all back in the world."

The chaplain closed his eyes, his face distorted with pain.

"*Kerereti*," he muttered.

He rose from the chair and led her back to the bed.

"It is a word in Ladino—one half of the language of spiders. The other half is a smattering of Yiddish. You said that I can also speak French, Vietnamese, and Thai? Perhaps I needed all of these tongues just to speak a single honest thing. It was a copy of the Torah that I found, Cassandra, and a beautiful book of the Psalms. Both had been printed by hand on parchment and protected by the skin of lambs. I once said that I was nobody. *Tôi không là gì cả*. It isn't true. I once played the fiddle in secret. I am a Mexican brown recluse. No, I am a violin spider. No, no, I am a Jew."

The chaplain's lips quivered as they pronounced a forbidden sentence. Cassandra released his wrist. He walked back to the chair and began to dress. She knew as she watched him that they would never make love again, that they would never sleep in the same bed again. Her delirious and desperate fingers would never reach around her lover's back to touch the painted violin—to accompany her own orgasms with pizzicato.

She wondered if he would ever remember that they had slept together in pigpens and beneath woodpiles, that they had kept each other alive by stealing rice and by killing rats for food. Would he ever recall the night that they had slept curled up together in a sewer pipe near the harbor at Macao? A tear reached her lovely eye as she realized that his soft lips would never again brush against her cheeks and her neck.

"Will either of us love again?" she said.

He did not respond, but turned his back to the mirror, then twisted his neck and upper body to inspect the wonderful tattoo that he had never seen. He nodded silently, then winced as he tightened the belt around his waist. An old wound to his ribs had never healed. He pulled the shirt on, walked toward the door, then turned to face the beautiful woman who was crying softly on the bed. Now he truly understood what that buzzing in his childhood cellar had been.

It had been the soaring and driving intonations of his father's voice. It had been the resin and horsehairs of the ancient fiddle. There had been secret services in that basement for other spider families. There had been weddings and bar mitzvahs and silent seders. Now he remembered those slaps to his face whenever the family was in the midst of strangers and an odd, foreign word inadvertently leapt from his mouth.

Now he knew that *tesoro* meant Torah. *Caser* meant kosher. The old well on his father's farm, the *aguada*, had, in truth, been the hiding place of the Haggadah. Culture had been buried in those holes, artifacts of the chosen. Joyous music had been muffled for centuries. His whole family line had been skilled cryptographers, codemakers, beginning in the darkest years of the seventeenth century. Hiding had been passed down in the blood, as had the ability to spin homonyms in three languages.

He faced the door, turned the knob, and pulled it open to reveal a dimly lit hallway that he had never seen before. His right hand reached up automatically to touch the nonexistent archstone of a cheap wooden casement. It would be the first of a thousand such empty hallways, common areas filled with shadows and tender theory. He turned toward her one last time.

He tried to memorize her beauty. God's breath was dispersing them. She was as striking as Tirza, as bright as Jerusalem. Her breasts were like twin fawns feeding among the water lilies. Slowly, she lowered her eyes for fear of making him tremble.

"*Hob mich vainik lieb, nor hob mir lang lieb,*" he said to her in the second language of the violin spider. "It's all right, Cassandra, if you should love me a little less tomorrow and a little less the day after that. I'll understand."

He turned to walk away, never asking for her true name.

"Love me less, but please, love me forever."

10

gods go begging

There was a stirring in the silence. A soft breeze of stale, dank air escaped from the room as though the weathered seal of a long-forgotten vacuum had, at last, been broken. A sudden shaft of glaring light appeared, flanked by sharp shards of shadow. Curtains had been moved aside and a window was forced open. A human being, once in deep, tormented half-sleep, was now awake. He had forced himself to stagger through a minefield of empty bottles to suck in the light and air of the harsh present.

Jesse shook his unresponsive head, stirring up the mezcal and nightmares of last night and this morning. There was an uneasy moment of disorientation and dizziness as he stood unsteadily before the open window, first one knee then the other almost giving way. The skin of his face still vibrated with the pain of those horrid dreams, with the ever-echoing enunciation from Persephone Flyer's lips. Jesse shuddered, shaking his head and body in an effort to come back to the here and now. The dreams of Vietnam had always been with him, but never before with such ferocious and unrelenting intensity.

Jesse knew that the terror of last night had been much more than a mere dream. That hill near the Laotian border had always been haunted, possessed by the restless ghosts of hundreds, perhaps thousands of young men. Last night his own living spirit had been kidnapped from this room and taken there, not for a reunion but for a quick object lesson, a reminder that his soul would never leave that hill, no matter where his body went. No bachelor's degree, no law degree, no jungle grasses could hope to cover the impossible fear and anguish that still lingered there; no roots could ever leach from that soil the grief and blood, and the sorrowful shouts that had been sown there.

While his sweating, drunken body had been pinned to a bed in a motel room, his soul had been forced to revisit a time when, no matter where Jesse's gaze had fallen, he had witnessed something he could not bear to see. Last night it had been raining in Vietnam; the monsoons had been in full swing. The swollen cloud of death that hung eternally over that hill had poured down a steady stream of regrets. Top soil had been washed away in torrents, leaving yellow bones exposed. The spirits of those killed in war were always helpless in the dry season. They needed to ride down on weather, to come down with the rain. In Jesse's dreams there was always rain.

Without thinking, Jesse mumbled a line from a poem. Perhaps the sound of his own voice—his own mortal, living voice—could chase away the lingering vestiges of the night before. He repeated the line as he left the hotel room and fell into the driver's seat of his car, attempting to speak each word carefully and precisely. He found that enunciation was extremely difficult because of his dry mouth and his buzzing, pounding brain.

From what I've tasted of desire I hold with those who favor fire.

He seldom climbed out of bed without thinking of Robert Frost's enigmatic poem "Fire and Ice." He drove down Highway 101 South toward the Golden Gate Bridge. He turned his rearview mirror for a look at his own face. He was hungover and disheveled. His teeth were unbrushed and his hair uncombed. There was blood on his incisors. Sometime during the night, he had bitten his tongue. All in all, the weary face in the mirror was a perfect reflection of his soul.

He cast a final glace at the mirror as he crossed over Richardson Bay. The eyes were the same. They had always been the same, constants in a changing face and a changing world. Jesse shook his head in utter frustration and confusion. Who was seeing whom in that mirror? Was it the young soldier gazing at his own future countenance or was it the middle-aged lawyer looking back through the pupil and the iris at the tormented boy? His mind was not working well enough to be asking such questions. He turned his eyes to the road just in time to slam on his brakes and barely avoid colliding with a truck.

When Jesse reached Nineteenth Avenue he took a sudden right on Lake Street and pulled over. He closed his eyes and rested his head on the steering wheel. His hangover was killing him. The last face he had seen in his dreams was the face of Carolina. Could she ever understand the whirlwind of his mind? Could she ever understand why he had failed her again and again, why he would always fail?

Suddenly his hands were flailing at the driver's door in an attempt to locate the door handle. After a seeming eternity it flew open and Jesse heaved a torrent of fluids out into the street. After wiping his mouth and chin with his sleeve he started the car and headed down Geary Boulevard toward the Dublin City Bar. Hollis would have the antidote for this agony. Somewhere in all of those brightly colored bottles behind the bar was the cure for what ailed Jesse Pasadoble.

"Do you know how it feels, man, knowing you're gonna die?" The customer raised his voice for a second salvo. "Do you have any idea how it feels? My wife doesn't give a shit. None of my kids give a damn about me, either. They're all computer-literate. Wouldn't know a transistor from a turd but they're computer-literate!"

"It's too early in the day to be so damn drunk," said Hollis. "That drink you have there in your hand is your last pour from this bar. So move along, my friend. Go home and get some rest and I'll see you tomorrow."

"You've got no heart, Hollis," said the drunkard as he staggered from the stool and out into the sunlight. "You've got no heart at all."

"Jesse!" cried Hollis. "Jesus, boy, you look like shit. You look like a self-propelled Howitzer run over you. Come in, come in. Light 'em up if you got 'em. I'll make you a coffee, one of them newfangled café mochas. We've got this here shiny new machine, one of those Italian gadgets. Personally, I don't think they belong in an Irish bar."

"No thanks, man," said Jesse, his voice filled with troubled desperation. "Just get me some mezcal."

"Bullshit," shouted Hollis. "That old hair-of-the-dog crap holds about as much water as the fuckin' domino theory. I'll make you a coffee that'll have your hair standin' on end. You'll drink it and like it." Hollis smiled.

Jesse sat on the first stool and watched wearily as Hollis attempted to manipulate the new Italian coffeemaker. Despite his obvious disdain for the machine, his scarred hands moved in a slow, deliberate manner. Even while swathed in nausea, Jesse understood that Hollis was a kind of miracle. He had done three tours in Vietnam. The injuries that he had sustained while in the Airborne were everywhere on his body: both legs, both arms; there were metal fragments in every muscle of his upper torso and a patch of plastic mesh sewn into his forehead.

Oddly enough, the cumulative effect of all those wounds was one of perfect balance. What should have been a severe limp in his left leg was little more than an almost imperceptible twitch, as it compensated for the twisted knee and ankle of the right leg, the right leg itself compensating for a mass of mangled back muscles that had healed in such a way that his posture seemed perfect, almost imperious. Hollis didn't limp, he simply moved much slower than most people. Those who didn't know his history misconstrued it as a surfeit of patience and reserve.

"So how's it going?" asked Jesse, his feeble voice barely audible across the bar.

"Is that my friend askin' the question, or is that my lawyer askin' the question?"

"Both," said Jesse.

"Well, sarge, I been keepin' up with my probation officer, if that's what you mean. I've tested clean every time. I've kept this here job now for . . . eleven months, longest I've ever worked in one place. I've made lots of new friends here. There are beautiful girls in here every night." Hollis winked. "I emcee the wet T-shirt contest on Friday and Saturday. I'll tell you, I'm staying right here. No more streets for me."

Jesse stared at his old friend as he fumbled with the new espresso machine. Jesse had met him years ago, when Hollis was making a living stealing cars to pay for an ancient drug habit. Then a young public defender, Jesse had been given all of Hollis's cases. In five minutes' time they had become fast friends. Like so many other boys, Hollis had been flash-frozen by war when he was still so very much in love with his own life and the world around him. He had enlisted at the age of sixteen. At the age of seventeen—in the space of a few days—he had become sickened with experience, gagging on the slice of life that had been given him. Hell, he was still choking, and taking his first real breaths almost thirty years after that war. Jesse could never understand why Hollis had reenlisted twice.

"Here's your coffee. Drink up, now, there's more where this here came from."

Jesse drank from the mug, then covered his mouth with his hand, trying not to spit up.

"Shit!" he screamed after swallowing a scalding mouthful. "That's not coffee, that's tar!"

"Sure woke you up," said Hollis, whose face suddenly took on a pensive look. He hesitated for a moment, then asked, "Have you seen Carolina? She was in here the other day looking for you. She sat in that seat and drank a lemonade. She never said a word about you, but I know why she was here. Is it her, or is it the Nam?"

"You, more than any other man, know that there's no difference between the two," said Jesse quietly. After a moment of thought, he repeated Hollis's question. "Is it her, or is it the Nam? Hell if I know. What the hell do I know about anything?"

Hollis stopped washing glasses for a moment; the wineglass and the sponge were frozen in midair.

"Do you ever ask for forgiveness?" asked Hollis.

"I am the only one who has never forgiven me," said Jesse in a sickly monotone.

"You're the only one who can," said Hollis, who had abandoned the dishes and was now attempting to make himself a caffé latté.

"Over the years I've been able to get by," mumbled Jesse. "You know what it's like, Hollis. I cover my friends' backs and I can hump it around the courtrooms pretty well."

"You're a hell of a lawyer," interjected Hollis.

"I've even had my share of girlfriends," continued Jesse, his voice almost breathless. "But I've never really been there for any of them. I've never been . . . in the moment, never existing with any woman in the same time and place."

Jesse diluted his viscous coffee with a half cup of hot milk. Hollis nodded sympathetically. He understood all too well.

"So many would-be lovers have ended up pounding on my chest in sheer frustration, begging to know where I was, pleading to know why I was never really present for them. I can barely accept love, Hollis, and I am even worse at giving it. Jesus, sometimes it feels like

my soul has turned gray with freezer burn. I don't know how any of
them ever tolerated me. And now it's Carolina's turn. If I really cared
about her, I would walk out of her life today. I would give her the
chance to find someone, some normal guy who is capable of loving
her."

Jesse shook his head sadly.

"Can I have my mezcal now?" he asked plaintively.

"You ain't answered my question, Jesse," said Hollis as he tasted
his latest creation. "Answer my goddamn question!"

"Forgiveness?" Jesse shrugged with an air of hopelessness. "Forgiveness," he repeated into the coffee mug at his lips. The tarry substance burned its way down his gorge.

"You see, I think there is something here much more important
than forgiveness," whispered Hollis while putting a finger to his lips,
indicating that he was in possession of a secret. This was something
that he had thought about for a long time. For years the question had
ridden his veins on a streak of heroin; it had slipped into his mind
every night on a puff of crack cocaine.

"Foolishness and risk are more important," he said, his eyes
burning with certainty. "Them things come way before forgiveness.
You've gone and skipped the first two steps, Jesse."

Jesse sat quietly, thinking about his friend's statement, his battered mind rebelling against every attempt at concentration.

"Is there something that you care most about?" asked Jesse, who
had shoved the glass of coffee to one side and was resting his head
and arms on the counter. A wave of weariness washed over his eyes.

"You are like me," said Jesse. "You don't trust happiness. You have
the same horrible dreams. What is it that a man like you—a man
who's seen what you've seen—cares about?"

Hollis listened to the question, put his coffee on the counter, then
walked around it to sit on the stool next to his friend. He bit his lip as
the question sank in. It was a question that he desperately wanted to
answer.

"I had this wife . . ."

With that single phrase, the oppressive fatigue that had filled
Jesse's mind and body began to dissipate; the chill that had been de-
posited in his bones by those horrid dreams was instantly dispelled.
The empty bar filled with empty stools was no more. A layer of
warmth seemed to settle in, as though the room had suddenly been

transformed into a home. Even the harsh sounds of the street seemed moderated, muffled to a calm and civil softness by the presence of cushions, throw rugs, and curtains.

Jesse had never known that Hollis had once been married. He had never mentioned it once in fifteen years. No matter how hard Jesse tried, he could not imagine it. No tuxedo could ever have been draped on that body; no vows of love could have formed in that mouth.

"Sometimes my Evie, my wife—I married her after my second tour of duty—she would make this here hot tamale pie. You know, the kind with that cornmeal crust and lots of spiced meat and onions, and smothered with Mexican peppers and melted processed cheese. You know, them hot peppers from south of the border down in old Mexico. Anyway, she'd whip that up—all the time humming in the kitchen—and then, while the pie was in the oven, she'd go and make me up a big pitcher of lemonade. Hand-squeezed, mind you. In the pitcher there'd be these square ice cubes, top to bottom, and slices of lemon rind. I hate those round, automated ice cubes, you know. Now, that there was food. That there was food for sure. She'd set it all out and, God help me, I'd eat every damn crumb."

Now his voice dropped down to a point just above audibility.

"You know, Jesse, I couldn't never thank her for making that pie. I couldn't never just open this goddamn, stupid mouth and say a simple thank-you."

He balled his right hand into a tight fist and slammed his knuckles twice against the counter. The blows brought a trickle of blood from two or three of his knuckles.

"Thank you, Evie," he sighed. "Thank you, wife."

He grabbed a cloth from behind the counter and dabbed at the blood on his hand. The sight of his own blood made him angry. He had been seriously wounded a half dozen times during the war, and each time he had wanted so badly to live. How could someone who craves life be so good at wasting it? He touched the cloth to his lips. He could taste the salton sign of life.

"After dinner she'd take a long bath and I'd peek in and see her buck naked; her right arm would be lying on the rim of the tub and her titties would be floatin' in the suds. I'd want so damn much to just reach out and touch her, all nice like, but I never, ever did. Shit . . ." Hollis's voice began to break. "Shit, I had to go and hit her before I could climb up on her. I had to smack her around. Jesus! I'd beat her black and blue and force her to do what she already wanted to do anyways."

Hollis took another sip of coffee. His hands shook as he put the rim of the cup to his lips.

"Black and blue . . . What I would give," said Hollis, with a hard-ened tone of stark intensity, "to be back there for one day. What I would give to be back there on a hot-tamale-pie-and-lemonade day. I could eat that whole pie, wash it all down with a big glass of hand-squeezed lemonade, then lick that plate clean. Then, after dinner, after a couple of hours of television, she would be there in the bathtub, buck naked. What I would give to be there, to just reach out and just caress her skin."

Hollis extended one arm as he spoke, stroking the air with a hand. The savage pain in his face eased a bit as his hand touched an imagi-nary breast.

The image of Carolina drifted into Jesse's mind. She was probably much prettier than Evie, but just as lonely. After a moment of silence Hollis shivered, then composed himself.

"I thought that war let me see the real things about who we are. It was like all the truth you could handle—not like living in the world, back here where nothin's true. But I don't want it no more, Jesse. I would trade it all for her. If I had the chance, I swear to God I would melt right into her, come inside her legs and melt right into her skin like that lavender hand lotion that she loved. I would suck her titties so hard that I could taste the milk that she didn't never make for the children I didn't never give her. I would talk sweet nothing stuff into her ear. She always wanted that, my lips against her ear. She always said how she wanted that. I knew what was right, but it seemed so foolish, so weak."

Jesse reached out with his right hand and touched the trembling shoulder of his friend.

"I've been frozen solid even longer than you have been," said Hollis. "I've been frozen stiff, walking the streets and sleeping on sidewalks. I was once so afraid of being a cripple or an amputee, so scared that my next breath would be my last breath, that I slowly learned to love every second of this here life in a really crippled way. Here, inside me," he placed a palm on his chest, "I love things, I love lots of things, but I never can reach out for them. I got no arms for that. I love music and rhythms, but the foolishness of dancin' makes me paralyzed. I got no legs for that. Even when I get lucky, I can't even make love with the lights on. Shit, I see the death in everything even more than the life."

Jesse ran the fingers of both hands through his hair as he listened. There was a thick residue of sweat lingering there from the night before. Hollis grabbed Jesse's mug of coffee with one hand and his own glass with the other. He walked to a nearby garbage can and dumped the two drinks into it. He walked behind the counter and grabbed a bottle of El Presidente Tequila Añejo and two water glasses.

"Time for the real thing," he said as he poured two drinks, six fingers high.

"I see it everywhere," said Jesse, "even in the courtroom. When I look into the twelve faces of the jury, I feel so much more inside of me, and inside of them. But I can never seem to break through, to say what I feel and what they need to hear. I know what I need to do, but I just can't do it. I'm trapped inside this callused skin of mine. It's even worse with Carolina."

"Vietnam was supposed to be a place where the boys who made it got to go home and screw everything in skirts," said Hollis. "It was supposed to make us into men, but it turned us all into stone."

Hollis was speaking to no one now. His eyes focused on a point in space. He grabbed the glass of tequila, threw his head back, and swallowed it all.

"You might be right, Hollis, love in the abstract is the best we can do. Maybe the power to risk is as close as we ever come to God, as close as we come." Jesse's voice was still slurred and thick. "You and I can sight down a rifle barrel and pull the trigger, but neither of us can kiss with our eyes closed. It's the cold that will kill us all. Maybe it's only that leap out of the cold that can save us, the leap toward the fire. I know I can't do it yet, and shit, I'll probably never get the chance to do it. And you, the man who could just reach out and caress your Evie's skin, would never have needed a lawyer. That man wouldn't have reenlisted for a third tour. You could be right, risk is as close as we get to God."

The two men sat staring at each other in silence. One mind was hovering around a treeless trailer court down in Bakersfield, while the other was standing at the front door of a small house in Glen

Park. Evie had long since divorced and remarried. Hollis had heard through the grapevine that she had met a dark-skinned Hindu fellow in Boron, and when she found out that he owned a trailer court and laundromat, she quickly became Mrs. Evie Patel. The two had run off to Las Vegas and tied the knot in a country-and-western chapel. A minister dressed like Hank Williams had performed the services. Kitty Wells had been the witness.

But the bartender couldn't know that her new husband would never eat tamale pie, and when he climbed on top of her at night, there were no pent-up waters seething behind a coldhearted dam. Nothing ever burst and ran rampant, spilling over her in pang after pang of pain and pleasure.

Nowadays, gasping for breath, she mixed the ingredients for the tamale pie with her left hand, the right hand sunk deep into her wet pink panties. These days she stood next to the stove for heat, and sometimes she would—almost accidentally—walk repeatedly into the sharp edge of a kitchen counter and raise hot bruises on her skin—a silent, solo bacchanal of abuse. At night, when her new husband would reach out for her, she would sigh apologetically, her head swooning with cluster migraines and dimming visions of Hollis. She would babble incoherently until the little brown Hindu abandoned his shy overtures, the maiden feigning madness.

Jesse's mind was on Carolina. He winced as he recalled their last night together. He drained the glass of tequila, then slammed it down on the bar. Carolina had told him that she was tired of their perfunctory sex and wanted some tenderness, just a little tenderness. She wanted to make love in the way that women meant when they used the phrase "make love."

Naked and tearful on the edge of the bed, she had demanded it as she had so many times before. Jesse had stood there, frozen. He had stood there allowing sorrow to transmute into anger at the impossible depth of her demand. He had done nothing in response. There had been an ultimatum. She would never again sleep in this bed or in this bedroom without love.

"You are a strange lover, Jesse, so full of emotion, but no one ever gets to see it. I know it's there, but I never get any of it. You love life, but you're certainly not living in it. Sometimes it's like you're not alive at all. It's like you're haunting your own living body."

Carolina, who wore wire-rimmed bifocals at the age of thirty-three, put them on to watch him dress and walk silently out of the room. For half an hour she sat staring at the closed door. Without her glasses she was nearly as blind as some small subterranean creature. Jesse had given her the name of Topo, which is the Spanish word for a small, burrowing mole. Sometimes her names crossed and became Topolina.

After Jesse left the room, Topolina waited for the bedroom door to slam and for his body heat to fade away before she dared move. Tonight his mute intensity had scared her. She had never tried to photograph Jesse. She realized that she was deathly afraid of what the camera might see. She had ruined her eyesight by looking at things too closely. Now she had ruined her life by loving a man who could not love in return.

"Maybe your worst fear is true," she shouted through the closed door. "Maybe you did die back there on that precious fucking hill of yours." It was a spiteful sentence that she sorely regretted as soon as she had uttered it.

"I didn't mean that! I didn't mean it!" she screamed. In despair, she tore off her glasses and threw them against the door. The thick lenses shattered, mining her carpet with a thousand tiny weapons.

Twenty minutes passed before either Hollis or Jesse moved from his stool in the Dublin City Bar. The two mute men had sat like bookends pressing memories between them.

"I loved her," said Hollis. He poured another drink for the both of them. "Hair of the dog," he said.

"To fools," said Jesse as he raised his glass. All at once the poem made sense to him. Robert Frost had been writing about the process of poetry itself, about the process of creation. It is desire that creates poetry, that sparks into flame those incredibly rare moments of humanity in our mundane and selfish human lives.

Such an irony! Was it possible that a part of something could be larger than the whole? Those lonely and desolate ghost soldiers on that hill in Vietnam had been trying to tell him something. All at once it was clear to him what they had been saying: the end of desire was a greater tragedy than the end of life itself. Ice keeps the hand from reaching out. It is ice that keeps the rhythmic soul from dancing, from improvising. Desire could never be the agent that ends the world.

"You're gonna make it, Hollis," said Jesse with a smile.

"Don't mean nothin'," said Hollis.

Jesse stood up. The bartender sighed, then stood up too, clearly disappointed that Jesse was leaving so soon. The men hugged each other, each one less angry and more hopeful than he was just an hour before. As his friend walked through the door and out into the sunlight, Hollis found a clean rag and began polishing the espresso machine. A soft whistle signaled a new relationship between the bartender and the contraption.

Jesse drove down Geary Boulevard and headed back toward the motel. As he crossed the bridge he was aware of an ocean and a sky that were the same shade of blue. He felt so much better now. Hollis and Evie's story had replaced all the nightmares and the delirium of the night before. When Jesse arrived at the motel, both Topolina and Eddy were standing in the parking lot waiting for him. Neither was smiling as he parked his car and exited.

"You missed four court appearances this morning," said Eddy, with a confused and worried look on his face. "You'd better call the courts and massage the judges or they're going to hold you in contempt of court. Judge Taback had a fit."

"I didn't have any court appearances today," responded Jesse as he reached into his jacket for his calendar. "Those four court appearances are for Thursday, the seventeenth. I'm sure of it."

"That's today," said Carolina impatiently. She did not look at Jesse as she spoke. "Today is the seventeenth. Where the hell were you yesterday?"

There was anger and disappointment in her voice.

"What did you do yesterday? You didn't go to your office. You didn't call anyone. You didn't bother to call me. No one could get in touch with you. I had to call Eddy."

Jesse closed his eyes as the realization hit him. After all of that mezcal and beer he had slept right through an entire day and into another night. Twenty-four hours had been lost. He unlocked the door, walked into his motel room, then began calling the courts.

Carolina and Eddy followed but stopped at the front door. The room smelled of sweat, alcohol, and vomit. There was a disconcerting haze in the air, the palpable residue of nightmares. Neither Carolina nor Eddy would step through it. Carolina, who had never been baptized a Catholic, crossed herself at the threshold. She lifted a nonexistent crucifix to her lips and kissed it.

"*Qué barbaroto!*" she muttered.

"Everything has been put over until Monday," said Jesse, hanging up the phone. "Judge Saldamando and Judge Louie really didn't give a damn about my failure to appear. Jack Berman didn't even notice that I wasn't there. He sent my guy to a drug program, then left to play tennis. Hell, I haven't missed a court appearance in over ten years. But I did have to remind that sanctimonious Judge Taback about those two mornings during our last trial when he overslept and the jury had to be sent home for the day. He claimed it was the flu, but I jogged his memory a little. He should stick to Manischewitz and give up those double martinis."

"None of that excuses you," said Carolina angrily.

Jesse nodded curtly at her. She wasn't looking back at him. He then turned quickly toward his investigator.

"I heard the tape, Eddy!" There was a strange intensity in his voice. "I heard the tape! She said just one solitary word to the 911 operator. She said, 'Amos.' I knew Amos Flyer, Eddy! I knew the man!"

His hand dove into his pocket as he spoke. He felt for the dog tag, the miraculous one that had pierced the wall of the Salon des Refusés. In an instant the excitement in his voice died away. Images of the Creole sergeant's death were filling his mind, displacing tamale pie and lemonade.

"In a way, I think I knew her, too. I've known her for years. I don't know why she was killed, but I think I know why Persephone Flyer died. I know it all sounds impossible. I know it's hard to believe, Eddy, but I understand why. If I'm not mistaken, Mai Adrong died for the same reason. We've got to talk to Mr. Homeless. When can I talk to him? I've got a feeling about that guy."

"I gave him the food money," said Eddy. "He's had at least two or three good meals at Klein's Deli by now. I told the people at the deli not to sell him any alcohol. Anyway, I've got something to show you. It can't wait. I went out to Tracy and talked to Margie Dixon about the Supreme Being and her other brother, Richard. The woman had a lot to say. There's something you've got to see. I haven't seen it yet, but if Margie is right about this, the supreme being could walk away free from this beef."

"What is it?" asked Jesse excitedly, his thumb rubbing the raised letters of Sergeant Amos Flyer's name.

"We've got to go see it. Just trust me on this," said Eddy. There was excitement in his eyes. No description could do justice to this.

"If Margie's description is correct, it could be a complete defense to all the charges. It's over in Modesto, in some old barn or warehouse. Margie has the location and the keys to the place. We're supposed to pick her up in Tracy in about two hours. She's waiting for us at some hamburger stand called Chez Boeuf. I don't know what *boeuf* is so I brought some Hawaiian food with me in case we get hungry. I've got two bento boxes of spam musubi with egg."

Jesse looked toward Carolina, whose large dark eyes were refusing to meet his. He was going to Tracy and she knew it. There would be no talking today, no explanations today, and she was more than angry about it. He walked toward her, stopping just in front of her. Using both hands, he reached out, cupping her pouting face in his palms, his thumbs caressing her lips.

"Topolina," he whispered softly. Lifting her face he kissed her gently, then walked to his car. Eddy touched Carolina's hand and followed Jesse. When they turned Eddy's car onto highway 101 South, they could see her, still standing in the middle of the motel parking lot, her face filled with tears of utter disbelief.

"I've never seen you kiss her," said Eddy quietly. "I've never seen you kiss her."

Margie Skelley Dixon was nothing at all like her brother Bernard. She was tiny and delicate, with strawberry-blond hair and long, elastic fingers that seemed double-jointed. Her wrists, her ears, and the flesh of her neck were almost transparent. Her smile was soft and humane. Premature worry lines had already pleated the corners of her eyes, eyes that were clear blue and direct evidence of an inquisitive, agile mind. Using her dreams as cement, and huge, hardbound editions of Dickens and Joyce as bricks, she spent her days and nights building a wall of books between herself and her appointed destiny.

Genetics and the suffocating limitations of Tracy had joined forces and doomed her to a future in a trailer court or a stark tract home somewhere in the Central Valley, to a life of television and tabloids and preparing meals in which every organic object is mummified with batter, then chicken-fried and smothered with white gravy.

Through the mail she ordered cookbooks from all over the world and spent long evenings memorizing their contents and imagining the exotic flavors while touching the photos with her fingertips. In time she would be able to discern the spices present in any given recipe simply by caressing a photograph of the final dish. It was her fervent hope that the recipes for coquilles St.-Jacques and ratatouille Provençale would eventually displace the constant impulse to stuff a hot dog with Velveeta and then wrap it with bacon. She prayed that saltimboca would jump into her mouth and dislodge her taste for lard. Her bookshelves were crammed with Berlitz courses in nine different languages. The walls of her bedroom were a collage of maps and travel guides.

Every chance she got, she would drive the fifty-five miles into San Francisco to savor pad Thai, caldo de camarones, and ziti Tartufo. She would spend endless hours at the aquatic park listening to the African drummers and basking in the sound of exotic tongues. Using will power alone, she hoped against hope to plug the holes in the cultural sieve that was her heritage—her hillbilly heart. This woman labored against providence with every breath she took.

"*Nous sommes ici,*" sang Margie as the car pulled onto a dusty dirt road on the outskirts of Modesto. Her lilting voice belied the growing terror in her heart. She exited the car and walked slowly toward a large, weathered barn. She walked as though she were on the surface of Jupiter; the weight of her own reticence coupled with the weight of her determination had caused her shoulders and hips to sag visibly. In front of her the wide front door of the barn had been chained and padlocked.

"*¿Dónde están las llaves?*" she muttered as she pored through her crowded purse. After opening the lock, she pulled at the huge door but was unable to move it. Eddy and Jesse had to lift the door, then tug on it in unison before it finally yawned open.

"When he lost his job, he sold almost everything," Margie said as she led the way into the barn. "He even sold his rider lawn mower, his precious John Deere, and he didn't even have a lawn. But some things he just couldn't sell."

Jesse and his investigator stood awestricken at what they saw. Covering every wall was an array of weaponry that only the best-equipped armies could match. In the far corner of the barn was a deuce-and-a-half truck, and behind that was a battered armored personnel carrier, probably of Korean War vintage. The back wall of the barn was covered with an array of semi-automatic weapons, including old M-1s and M-14s, and at least three .38-calibre "grease guns."

There was a rack of M-16s to the left, a crate of hand grenades, and one ancient mortar tube. The mortar rounds were lying next to it like a pile of discarded soda bottles. The ground to the right was covered with ammunition boxes, tent halves, entrenching tools, and one M-60 machine gun. Hanging from the rafters were huge Confederate and Nazi flags. Behind the flags hung a cheap tapestry depicting the Last Supper. Judas's face had been painted black and a large nose had been added.

"My brothers, Bernard and Richard, are in the local militia," whispered Margie. "This is their company headquarters."

There was a table near the door that was covered with yellowed periodicals—tracts from the Posse Comitatus, an SS action team in Michigan, and a worn copy of the Turner Diaries. Margie ran her fingers over the photos on the front page of one of the tracts. "Tasteless," she said to no one.

A chill went down Jesse's spine as he stared at the weaponry around him. Not even the San Francisco Police Department had this kind of armory. Eddy walked cautiously outside to see if anyone was lurking nearby.

"Don't worry," said Margie, "they won't come out here today. They're on maneuvers in Manteca." Margie's face contorted as she spoke the Spanish word for lard.

"Maneuvers?" asked Jesse.

"They take about three hours putting on jungle fatigues and their camouflage makeup, then they crawl around in the dirt for about five minutes before they pull a muscle or puke their breakfast. Then they break out the beer and hot dogs and tell phony war stories. It's truly ridiculous. They use walkie-talkies to talk between the picnic tables. 'Apache One to Apache Niner; you got any mayonnaise on your table? Over.'"

Margie laughed at her own imitation of her brother Richard's voice. As her laughter slowly died, she walked toward a large object that was covered with a dusty tarp. It had been placed into the far right corner of the barn. With one hand she grabbed a corner of the tarp and began to pull. As the object was slowly revealed, Jesse and Eddy stared in anxious anticipation. There was a wry smile on Eddy's face as the canvas tarp moved across the midsection of the object. It was a huge, wooden bed. The large, thick quilt that covered the mattress was made from an American flag. Soon, all that remained hidden by the tarp was the headboard.

"Are you ready? *Están listos?*" said Margie. Jesse assumed that her sense of the dramatic was showing, but quickly changed his mind. There was something else in her voice—a cold and cutting edge. "Are you ready?" she repeated, as though those three words were the only possible words appropriate for this moment. No one answered, so she quickly pulled the tarp to the floor. "It was never Bernard," whispered Margie as the object came into view. "It was always Richard."

Jesse's stare immediately turned to glee.

"Photograph it, Eddy!" he screamed, laughing and walking in circles, unable to contain his joy. "Photograph it, then let's remove the headboard! We're gonna lash it to the car. Come here, Margie."

He threw his arms around Margie Skelley Dixon, lifting her off the floor with the force of his embrace.

"Eddy," exclaimed Jesse, "remind me to call Chez Panisse on the way back to San Francisco. I'll make reservations for six. Are you still seeing that English professor from Merced?"

Margie nodded.

"I'm going to buy you the best dinner you ever had. We'll drink two bottles of Margaux, Premier Grand Cru." Then Jesse noticed that the same hint of sadness had returned to her face. He lowered her to her feet. With a hand on each of her shoulders, he held her at arm's length and forced her to look into his eyes.

"Listen, Margie, you're not choosing between brothers. That's not what you're doing. You're making sure that the truth is known. You're bringing just a little bit of justice to a world that needs it very badly."

"That's not why I'm sad," said Margie softly. "I always knew this day was coming. I always knew there was something wrong with my niece Minnie. The little girl was never, ever happy. The poor thing was never given the chance to be a child. She's never wanted to have a doll or to play house. God!" sighed Margie. "She was having sex years before she got her period. That son of a bitch took away her first childhood crush, her first prom, the nervous joy of her wedding night. I'm sad because I suspected this long ago and did absolutely nothing about it. I didn't want to believe it was happening to her."

"Minnie's just a child," said Eddy. "There's still hope for her. Children can heal."

"Her mother is not going to be there for her," added Jesse in his softest voice. "She's probably known what her husband has been doing all these years and closed her eyes to it. But little Minnie will have an aunt, an aunt who understands this kind of pain very well, and who, in spite of it, has managed to fall in love twice."

Margie turned to face the lawyer.

"How did you know?" she asked.

"I don't know how I knew," said Jesse, unaware of the fact that he had placed the jade stone beneath his tongue. "But I know that you're running away. All those arcane books, all those languages you speak . . . I've never seen anyone run so hard. You're trying to escape from far more than just Spam kabobs and Velveeta pick-me-ups."

"Will I have to testify against my own brother?"

"You might not have to," answered Jesse. "This bed and the DNA testing that I'm going to order might be enough. It's Minnie that I'm worried about. To this day she hasn't had the courage to name her true assailant. She's given a description that could fit either brother and she's pointed to a picture of the supreme being, but she might have been pointing to the eagle. She's never given a name. She has never spoken the name out loud. She's going to have to see this headboard again and have the courage to tell the whole truth. I'm sure she's scared to death of her father."

"I know I was," whispered Margie.

"If she refuses to name him, we may have to put this case in front of twelve people. If the prosecutor is hardheaded, you might have to take the stand. A jury will have to decide which of the two eagles has savaged little girls—this one or the one on Bernard's chest. To my mind, this bedstead is enough for a reasonable doubt. I know it'll shatter Minnie's world into a thousand pieces, but it may be a world that needs shattering. It won't be easy, but you can help her make it. You are her family now, Margie."

Jesse smiled at Margie.

"Have you ever eaten at Chez Panisse?"

Margie shook her head but smiled. To her, Chez Panisse was Mecca, the farthest place on earth from Chez Boeuf. Jesse reached into his coat for the tiny recorder and began by entering the day and date, location, exact time, and those present. Then he began to describe the bed.

"It is a handmade, queen-size, pine bed—a four-poster. The bedspread is a quilt made from pieces of American flags. The large headboard is hand-carved and hand-painted in red, white, and blue. There is a globe that is crossed at its center by a banner that reads 'U.S. Marines, Semper Fidelis.' On the surface of the globe is a map of Vietnam. Above the globe and clutching it in its talons is a huge American eagle in bas-relief. The wings of the eagle span the entire headboard, the white wing tips touching the twin posts. A child lying on this bed, her father's bed, would see an eagle spreading its wings over her head. She would see this eagle whether or not her father was present. . . ."

The recording ended abruptly as Margie ran sobbing from the barn. The cold specificity of Jesse's description had summoned up old and painful memories.

"Margie . . . was on this bed, too," said Eddy who slapped his right palm against his forehead. He had finally grasped the meaning of Jesse's comments to Margie. He winced with disgust, then turned his face away from Jesse. There were tears in his eyes. Suddenly recalling that little Minnie had stated that she could not see the eagle during the rapes, Eddy blurted out a sentence filled with pain. "She couldn't see an eagle because his big perverted ass completely covered her tiny body."

Jesse nodded his agreement.

"They ought to hang that son of a bitch from a telephone pole—by his nuts."

"That would be too good for him," said Jesse as he walked toward the bed. He placed his hand on the quilt. It was a bed of living, waking nightmares, a mattress of cold fusion, a machine built to destroy the budding hippocampus and create girls who have no memory—girls who live in an eternal present that is their only defense against a terrible past, little girls devoid of romance.

Jesse's voice dropped down to less than a whisper. Girls like Margie and little Minnie had seen war and would live to share the nightmare.

"Besides, the perverted bastard might like it."

Jesse and Eddy dismantled the bed and strapped the eagle to the roof of the car. Then both men walked to the side of the barn, where they found a water faucet. Ten minutes of vigorous rubbing beneath the spigot could not wash away the vileness that clung to their hands. The ride back to San Francisco would be a quiet and painful one. A hellish wooden harpy would be flying just above their heads, and in the back seat, where Margie lay silently, the world would be turned upside-down.

For the first time in years she was once again lying beneath Southeast Asia, the odd pain of familiar blood pinning her to the sheets, the pain of rambling and senseless consanguinity pelting her thighs, battering her small legs, stunning her ears with the misshapen drek that rode upon her brother's breath.

"Are you ready?"

As the car left the Modesto city limits, Margie writhed and shivered in the arctic wastes of the backseat. She bit her wrist to drive her brother Richard's voice from her mind. A warm flow of blood across her palm was just enough warmth to keep her from freezing solid. Even after her memories were suppressed, the weight of the wings above her head forced tears to her eyes. Wings like those lifted no one, carried no one to heaven. It had been years before she learned that those strange, upside-down, and reversed words meant "always faithful."

Nothing more was said on the trip back to San Francisco. As Jesse drove, Eddy chewed absentmindedly on his Spam musubi. The odor of seaweed and pork shoulder began to fill the car. Just a few miles from the Bay Bridge, Jesse thought he heard the high-pitched voice of a little girl coming from the blackness of the backseat.

"God is watching."

11

the women's chorus

Eight eyes and seven breasts—Persephone and her three sisters gathered together at the family home perched on the outskirts of Alexandria. None of the women lived in town anymore. It was 1978, and all four had taken husbands and were living elsewhere. The house was *une trés petite maison*, a small wooden house filled with tiny, warm bedrooms and a single great room: the kitchen. The women were seated in a circle near the stove, the chairs having been purloined from the huge table in the center of the room.

The home was set in a quiet neighborhood with narrow cobbled streets completely shaded by maple trees. Each shade tree was flattered by the cloying, loving arms of a Chinese wisteria. Each wisteria vine was caressed by bees.

The chorus of women sat in the great room surrounded by memories and photographs of their magnificent mother. Though all four sisters were powerful women in their own right, none of them could hold a candle to their mother. It was she who had turned the tide in the thirties, when it looked as though the Depression would wash them all away.

Lysistrata, a small Creole village on the fringe of Alexandria, had been named by Lizzie Boudreaux, their mother. It was she who had seen that the town had been mapped out and incorporated, that a proper library had been built, and that the patch of land was named after her favorite Greek play. It was she who had the strength to demand that all the new husbands refrain from joining the military. It was she who had given the sisters unity and direction when the foolish men enlisted anyway. If each sister had been a point of the compass, she had been their magnetic north.

On every wall of the great room was a photograph or a painting of Miss Lizzie, her long arms outstretched and so lithe and blithely weightless, her toes ever en point. She was the only Creole or black woman ever to dance prima ballerina at the Atlanta Ballet. Here she is a sylphid in flashing white; there she is a sloe-eyed *gitana* in somber red and insolent gold; here she sits, surrounded by daughters; there she is flanked by the entire corps de ballet. In one small photograph, she is sleeping in a casket, her once weightless legs now leaden. There are flowers enough—cast onstage by wild and inconsolable admirers—to hide the metal bier and the gaping hole beside it.

The four women sat quietly in the kitchen, readying themselves for the strange task at hand. Their father, Priapus Boudreaux, was seated—stiff and erect—in a wooden chair in the middle of the room, surrounded by his daughters. Out in the parlor, a group of their father's friends was waiting to see the final product. A chorus of old men, they were bedecked with medals and ribbons from the Great War. Nostalgia sagged from their faces like a second layer of old skin.

Shy and sheepish now, Priapus was once the largest man in the county, a man who could outpull a mule. Gray and bent and self-effacing now, he was once the proud consort to terpsichorean royalty. His dinner jacket, tattered and passé, is covered with a pink towel, and the old man has removed his thick glasses. Without his lenses, he had no power whatsoever. Tonight, as he did on every other night of his married life, he had surrendered to the women of his family.

One of the sisters, Cleonice Fontenot—the one with a single breast—began to cut the old man's graying hair, while the other sisters remarked, one after another, upon the still-handsome man who was their father.

"Leave enough hair for me to work with," said the fourth sister. Her name was Lampi Le Jeune. Her full first name was something that she will never disclose.

"Just because they cut your left breast off don't mean you have to cut off all of the hair on that side of his head! You're not the reason that the world is tilted on its axis."

Cleonice laughed, then squinted to inspect her work. It was true. She had ignored the entire right side of his head. She sighed with the realization that she was not as strong as she had thought. She cared what the world saw when it looked at her chest. She cared that her husband's fondling hands had one less option. Lately she had been using her left hand more and more. She laughed a sinister laugh. Her comb and snapping scissors moved reluctantly to the other side of his head.

The second sister, Myrinne Thibideau, walked to the sink and began mixing the ingredients for the elixir that would restore the old man's lost youth and his sexual desire. When the thick compound was thoroughly mixed, she rubbed some of it on her finger and tested it for color against her own dark hair. In moments she was spreading the concoction over Priapus's scalp and newly trimmed locks. As she did, she realized that it had been decades since she had touched her father. She rubbed his scalp thoughtfully, feeling the memories just beneath her fingertips and the single foolish hope that was sequestered among them.

Her father groaned under the wet weight of anticipation. There was discomfort in his eyes as his second daughter worked. Could she feel the deception beneath the deception? The second sister wrapped a towel around her father's newly blackened head, then returned to her seat. The gray hairs would be invisible for a few months. Her job was almost done.

The old man sat quietly though impatiently in his chair; the linoleum tiles around his feet were littered with flecks of his grayness here and with whole clumps of his grizzled years there. Specks of age had fallen onto his precious brown wingtips. The kitchen floor beneath his chair resembled a fossil bed. He looked down at the proof of autumn on his very own boughs and prayed silently for just one more printemps—a single hard-legged spring; for another warrior's summer to come invade his life and conquer this impending winter.

He swooned in his chair as a lovely Frenchwoman from out of the distant past threw her arms around his black body as he and his colored comrades marched through Normandy. He had been walking behind a Sherman tank when she burst out of the crowd and ran toward him. For an instant there were flowers at his feet and loose petals clinging to his youthful sweat. Why was the nearness of death so much like the nearness of love? he wondered in enraptured confusion.

Persephone Flyer, the third sister, rose from her chair and with a treezers began to pull the disgusting hairs from her father's nose and ears. With each disinterment of a follicle the old man's right leg kicked out reflexively from beneath his chair. How he hated those hairs and the efforts required to remove them. Each violent kick was followed by a wail of relief that contained within itself odd-order harmonics of pleasurable pain. It had been the same in 1944—the wonderful pain of illicit, forbidden love.

The Frenchwoman's husband and every member of the local resistance had been exposed by traitors and executed by the Germans. On a single blissful evening, all of her terrible grief and exulting joy had been impaled upon Negro corporal Priapus Boudreaux in the grassy field behind her home. Creole sweat had met with perfume and sat glistening in commingled beads upon Alsatian skin.

So the old man sat in the kitchen, a feeble partner among four prima donnas. He sat denying *le temps passé*, denying the passing years, and longing fervently for the turgid power of war.

"*Ayez soin!*" he screamed at his daughter. "Be careful with those damned tweezers, *ma fille!*"

"*Taisez-vous, mon père,*" hissed Persephone. "It's a shameful day when a veteran of World War Two is wounded by tweezers. Each hair means one day discarded. Look at all of the days scattered around your shoes. Count yourself among the lucky, *mon vieilliard*. Each discarded hair is one day that can be lived again."

"Listen to your daughter, you old fool!" shouted the men from the parlor.

Even as the chorus spoke, the fourth sister rose from her chair and began preparing for her solo. First she swept up the hair. In a few moments, in response to the subtlest cue, she would take her turn to perform. As a cosmetologist, she would be the one to remove the excess dye from his hair, to sculpt a new, more modern hairdo, and to soften the scars that time and concern had left on his face. It was a formidable task.

She stood back for a moment, looking carefully at her father. Had she ever really seen his face? She walked toward the doorway and flicked on another light. To her amazement, his eyes were deeper than she remembered, more shadowed with need than she wished to acknowledge. She turned away to avoid the inevitable, to keep from thinking the next thought: a living person had been buried in this home. Now his daughters were preparing his body for the next life.

He had always lived in the shadow of his wife. In time the man had been completely eclipsed by his own love—by his choice of lover and eventually by his female progeny. But Miss Lizzie had been dead for years now, all but one set of her costumes and toe shoes had been put up in the attic.

What a night that had been, that long night at the mortuary when all four daughters had dressed their mother's body. They had put her in her favorite costume, that of the dying swan, even as they passed that long night telling stories of her vital beauty and grace. Now the girls were all married off and had moved away. Now it was time for their father to find a companion for his last years, perhaps an old maid or a widow to cook for him and to walk with him in the evening. This house had become a tomb, a mausoleum, and he had become its doddering caretaker. Enough was enough.

The old man had evolved a plan to cure his loneliness, to reverse the direction of his life. He would buy a new double-breasted suit and new shoes. He would dust off his bronze star and his purple heart with clusters, and take a bus over to Savannah, then hire a motorboat to one of the small sea islands just off the coast. It had all been arranged and paid for in advance. On that island were rising hills of sand and stands of tall, verdant grass that hid enfeebled, elevated walkways and tiny, wood-plank houses held up by rotting stilts.

There were families out there in that grass, families with a powerful linguistic memory of the Côte d'Ivoire and the Costa de los Esclavos still lingering on their tongues. Glottal stops were hidden within their exclamations and their sobs. Families lived out there in small shacks crowded with numbing despair and starving children. Their lives were lived just above the whim of the tides.

There were working men out there who did battle with the infertile soils and with the murky, fishless waters, men who had no work to do, and young but never youthful mothers out there whose hips bore both the agony and ennui of those men. There were human bodies out there, striated and worn. There were children out there—fecund girl children who were available for marriage, but at a price.

The sweet daughter of Cinesias Williams was out there. The old man's right hand reached down into his coat pocket. He felt the manila envelope there, enough money for an unemployed father to buy a motorboat. Enough money for Cinesias to abandon his wife, those children, and those godforsaken islands forever.

"So tell us about this woman," said Persephone. "You said she comes from Atlanta and her family owns a grocery store."

"A couple of stores, maybe even a chain of them," retorted the old man angrily. It was a bald-faced lie and he sensed that Persephone knew it.

"She don't need my money, if that's what you're thinking. *Elle est trés riche. Trés beaucoup d'argent!* She don't need a single red cent from me. Not a red cent."

The old man pulled a cigar from his jacket pocket and lit it with indignation. Persephone reached for a nearby spray bottle and doused the flame with equal fervor.

"We're just curious, Papa," said Persephone. "You never say anything about this mystery lady, not a single word. She must be somewhat younger than you are or you wouldn't have asked us to do this rather extensive makeover for you. *Comment s'appelle? Quelle âge? Racontez, vite!* Is she sixty-five, seventy?"

"Leave him be!" cried the chorus of old men.

"Mind your own business," retorted the chorus of women.

The old man said nothing. The soggy cigar hung limp from his teeth. Persephone tilted his head to the left, then grabbed an entire bunch of ear hairs with the tweezers. She jerked them out of his head like so many radishes from the ground and he reacted by whimpering and pulling his head away. She was angry at her father, but grabbed a towel to dab at the blood in his ear. She then leaned down to whisper.

"*Je t'aime, Papa.* We all love you. Don't you think we have a right to know?"

"You'll meet her when the time comes," said the old man, who turned his ear away from his daughter's lips. In truth, he hoped that the time would never come. He was sure it never would. These daughters of his departed wife would be unmerciful in their disgust and revulsion if they ever found out their father had taken a child bride. They would make his life into living hell if they ever discovered that he'd paid money for her.

He sighed anxiously to himself. There was a growing feeling of finality to this gathering. If he was lucky, these four domineering daughters would never again visit him in this lifetime. They would go back to Athens, Georgia, and to Sparta, New York. They were just like their dear mother, and thank God, their mother was dead. For good and all, he was through with strong women.

As Persephone softly rubbed away the furrows that had appeared on his brow, the old man closed his eyes and began once more to dream of the Frenchwoman. He had always intended to return to France to find her, but never did. The memory of that glorious day had almost died away. In order to spark an accurate picture of her in the remaining neurons of his mind, he began, once again, to dream a dream of war.

Persephone Flyer would be flying back to San Francisco in the morning. All four sisters had left their father to his new hair and face, and were gathered around the kitchen table to both celebrate and mourn her departure.

Meanwhile, the old man was off with his comrades. They were in the parlor drinking, recalling battles in the French countryside and passing around a photo of the girl-child of Cinesias Williams. The old men were giggling and snickering over the length of her knobby legs and the merest hint of breasts beneath a flour-sack dress. Priapus Boudreaux cast a nervous glance toward his youngest daughter. It was Persephone whom he feared the most.

In the kitchen, Persephone felt her father's probing glance, but her mind was elsewhere. In the left cup of Persephone's brassiere were two envelopes. She had forgotten about them for most of the evening, but now they chafed her skin as the anticipation grew. She had carried them on the plane from the West Coast. The postmark on the first letter indicated that it had been mailed from Seattle.

The second was an official dispatch from the Department of the Army. Would this be their final letter to her? Had they at last located his body? Had some Vietnamese farmer run across his Creole rib cage and his dog tags while plowing a field? For some reason she hadn't wanted to read them until she was safely in the family home and surrounded by her own flesh and blood.

With her sisters beside her, silent and breathless, she carefully opened the first envelope. At first she tried to open it along the flap, but she grew impatient, and in a fit of pique, tore it open. The letter inside was the second carbon copy. The original was in Washington. The third and fourth carbons were suffocating somewhere in the bowels of some far-flung army post that was charged with generating such documents.

"He's still listed as missing in action." She sighed. She considered crying but held back her tears. It was certainly far better than a "killed in action" designation, or a "missing in action and presumed dead." Years from now, other letters would come bearing just those designations. Her sisters moved about her, touching her shoulders and kissing her cheek with delicacy and experience. It was better than killed in action, their fingers and lips repeated. Better than KIA.

"Good-for-nothing man will be back on your front porch in no time," said one of the sisters. "Pretty soon you'll wish he was back in the army. When he comes back, tell him he ain't never gonna get none of that good loving of yours if he stays a soldier."

"That's right," echoed another sister. "Don't give him no sexual favors unless he swears on the Good Book to stay home with you. Be as cold as ice to him, and never stir a limb. He'll stay home. You better believe he will."

"He's missing, that's all, just missing," said the sister with one breast. "All you need is one good letter. The next letter will be better. It'll be the news you're waiting for. Who is the second letter from?"

"There's no return address," answered Persephone, "but this handwriting has to be a woman's."

She sniffed the envelope, then passed it around for the others to peruse. She was relieved to find that there was no perfume on the paper.

"It has to be a woman's."

For a moment there was a hint of panic in her voice. Could it be possible that some strange woman in Seattle knew something about the fate of her Sergeant Amos Flyer? Had she met him on a rest-and-recuperation junket to Singapore or Saigon? Did they have sex, or worse, did they make love? Did they laugh between the sheets? Did they make love at night and in the morning, too, the way that she and Amos had when they first met? How on earth did she get my old address in San Francisco? The envelope had been addressed to her old apartment. The manager there, an old friend, had forwarded it to Persephone's new home.

Slowly, carefully, she opened the envelope. Somehow Persephone was certain that this letter would have more to say about her husband than the first. Steeped in anticipation, her three sisters held their cups of tea in the air before their lips as she slowly tore at the seal. All they would dare taste at a time like this was hope and expectation. They all sighed in unison when they saw the number of pages contained in the letter—at least a dozen. Would the information be hidden, couched in innuendos or sequestered carefully in the code that mistresses used when they communicated with wives? Still frozen with ceramic cups filled with orange pekoe hovering in front of their faces, they waited in silence until Persephone finished the final page, then folded the letter back into its envelope.

She dropped the letter into her purse, then began to weep softly, her face in her hands. Then she lifted her head to face her impatient sisters.

"Remember when you girls would do my makeup for me?" She smiled. "Remember when you would dress me for school and comb my hair for me? You"—she pointed to her oldest sister—"helped me put on my first pair of pantyhose, and you taught me how to coordinate my outfits. I never seemed to be able to pick out my own clothing. As you can see, I can't choose outfits for myself."

She gestured toward the clothing that hung from her body.

"The next time I come home, maybe the three of you will dress me again, for old time's sake. Perhaps it'll be for my Amos's homecoming. You all remember how scared I was when I got my first period?" Persephone's voice broke as joy gave way to heartfelt sincerity. "My sisters have always been there for me, no matter what. *Je vous aime tant.*"

She rose from her chair and moved from one sister to the next, embracing them each in turn. As she hugged each one she whispered into an ear, "Finally, after all of this time, we have word from Amos."

The sisters rose from their chairs, one after the other, their teacups and saucers dropping and spilling and shattering. The tea would stain the floor for years. Not even Priapus's child bride, on her hands and knees for three full hours, would be able to scrub away the discoloration.

"My lover's words are written upon a forearm. *Mes soeurs*, we have another sister."

Clearly impatient to begin her flight to the West Coast, she clutched the precious letter to her bosom. There was a woman in this world—a stranger who would become more familiar than family—a woman who had cut Persephone's name and old address into her arm, a woman who was suffering the same sadness and love, a woman who was living in Seattle.

She glanced toward her father, who was with his friends on the other side of the house, dreaming of the scorched metal scent of artillery pieces and the soft, sizzling sound of burning white phosphorus. To her amazement, Persephone noticed a bulge in her old father's pants. Either the old fool had hidden a lance in his clothing or the septuagenarian was having an erection.

"If the old fool chooses someone who is underage," she said suspiciously, "we should think seriously about putting him in a home."

The two women did not know each other immediately. Each had imagined the face of the other in a hundred ways. So, for a time, they stood in the crowded United Airlines gate casting nervous glances in every possible direction. The force of the crowd—the hurried and the harried, the disembarking passengers and the loved ones who ran to meet them—forced the two women to within arm's length of each other. At one point their shoulder bags accidentally collided. At another point they jostled each other, back to back, the smaller woman's shoulder blades cupped in the small of Persephone's back.

Eventually they brushed past each other, their hands barely touching. Now earnest inadvertence yielded to unconscious intention. Lovely Mai, in high heels, stumbled near the edge of a carpet and found, as if by accident, Persephone's brown hand to give her balance and stability. Now a flurry of polite excuses and apologies gave way to long minutes of rapt attention as platoons of passengers swelled and faded in the background.

The first sight of the other seemed to be the confirmation of something already known deep in the heart: loneliness can recognize itself. Persephone and Mai stood staring at each other as one hundred eighty tickets were presented at the gate and given seating assignment. They stood mutely as the plane was filled and lifted noisily into the sky above their heads.

The two women, thrilled at the touch of the other, embraced shamelessly and silently at gate 79 of the United terminal. They then walked, hand in hand, without words toward Persephone's car and toward the rest of their lives together. The conversation about Amos and Trin could wait. The information was so scant. Without saying a word, they had reached an agreement, an accord.

They would discover pieces of the secret in tidbits, offhand remarks and casual slips of the tongue. Things would be blurted out, and they would share bittersweet hours of stunned, contemplative silence. Together they would learn to cook. Personal griefs and recollections would be measured, spiced, and mixed together in the course of a thousand recipes. Inexorably, the secrets would leak out over time as shattering moments of insight and regret—in soufflés that collapsed in the oven and in cassoulets that soared in taste and texture. At other times they would ooze out with the viscous perfection of poured honey.

Mai had lost a husband who could make her feel this way, a man who could do things to her—Vietnamese male things, things of smear and spittle and flying thighs. Over time she would admit that there had been another man, a man who was no one at all. Persephone had lost a man who could do these other things to her, Creole things of muscle and thrust. Both men . . . all three men could speak into their woman's legs, calling out the sweetest of beasts.

Now and again, in the remaining years that they had, each woman would demonstrate what love had once been by taking the part of the other woman's man. Each would learn to see what the male lover had seen, and far beyond. In the darkness of bedrooms in the Mission District and in Bernal Heights, each woman would become husband to the other, a pair of hands in the opaque blackness probing and sliding softly from secret place to private place, from outcropping to inlet, a craving pair of lips tasting and pecking at flesh.

"Are we lesbians, honey, if I do for you what your man did—if you imagine your young soldier on top of you when I'm doing it? Not that I can do everything he could do, but *presque tout*, almost everything. God, my man could use his tongue! I love that Creole lingo. That's it! Right there. You've got it. Now a little side to side. Oh, that feels so good. Amos, honey, why did you leave me? I can see your face, *mon cher*. Amos, you could always taste me like no man ever could. No man can inhale me like that. No man on earth. Oh God, Amos, is that you?"

The Vietnamese woman would throw open her legs and scream out Trin Adrong's name as Persephone, in the spiritual guise of a young Vietnamese soldier, knelt between her legs conjugating Mai's inner dialogue. But in the throes of utmost passion, while her husband was speaking into her crotch, she would invariably reach around her friend's shoulders to lovingly search her spine for a tattoo, for the change in texture caused by ink and needles, for the lacquered body of a sephardic fiddle. In the lowering light there would be the flutter and slap of suddenly sensitive skin, the medley of ligament and the tender intrigue of moistened knuckle and finger. In the dark, two women would sigh, tingling with hope, engorged with memory.

"Are they dead, Mai?" Persephone would whisper into the dark. "Do you feel that Trin and Amos are both dead? If they lost all of their senses, Mai, did they lose them one by one so that each power lost conferred all of its strength on the remaining ones? When their eyesight finally failed them, did their ears hear our longings? When their hearing went, in their deafness, did they ever feel us? Were they near to each other when they died? Maybe their armies met on some unknown field. They say that scent is the most powerful sense. In death, could they smell my ardor and yours? Did we rise up in their nostrils with their very last breath?"

"I think that no one is alive," Mai would answer softly. "No one is most certainly alive."

One sunny morning—a morning lost among so many—a pensive Persephone sat at the kitchen table dipping *chà giò* into a bowl of hot *pho gà*. She closed her eyes to better appreciate the broth and spice. The subtlety of the flavors of Vietnam had never ceased to amaze her. If there had never been a war, she thought to herself, I would never have tasted this. I would still have a husband and we would have our own restaurant. Slowly an idea—Amos Flyer's idea—crept across her face, illuminating her skin with growing enthusiasm.

"What do you think about opening a little restaurant?" she asked without knowing if Mai could hear her. "I saw a perfect spot for it today up on Potrero Hill. I swear it's just perfect. It's a beautiful little business location with living space in the back. We could wake up in the morning and be right there at the workplace. The back yard is fenced in, with plenty of room for a vegetable and flower garden. We could grow our own herbs, spices and vegetables. With Amos Flyer's pension money and my widow's benefits, we have enough to lease the place with some left to start renovations. But best of all, behind the house is a beautiful little hill."

Persephone was silent for a moment. Had she just acknowledged for the first time that she was, in fact, a widow?

"Until the restaurant is finished," she began again, "we could support ourselves by selling food to go. We can perfect our recipes and do some public relations at the same time."

She lifted the bowl to her lips to drain it of soup.

"I've tasted your cooking, girl, and you and I are exactly what this city needs: Vietnamese and Creole food for the soul. Yes"—she sighed—"I think we can make a big dent in this town. At least we can survive until we know what happened to our men, until the day that Amos and Trin come walking through our door." Persephone closed her eyes again and exhaled deeply.

"Until the day . . ."

12

the biscuit libretto

Like a brand new trooper, a slick sleeve, a scared-shitless FNG walking behind point for the very first time, like a grunt spooked by booby traps—punji sticks and toe-poppers—and humping through a tall stand of elephant grass, the Biscuit Boy felt his way fearfully through his newfound dreams. These were not the reveries of the past: flashy, manicured visions of a fast, new, uninsured German car, a sweaty, designer athletic suit, and a neck draped both with expensive gold chains and with the arms of a light-skinned black girl with gold lipstick and carrot-red hair.

Now he dreamed of a raucous, colorful pageant of living ebony parading and dancing in unison to a glorious cacophony of voices, brass horns, and drums. In his mind he saw a sea of swaying feathers and painted leather. He saw skirts the color of red clay soil and headdresses decorated with the manes of lions long dead. Such sounds, such movements, and such earthen and obsidian colors had never before found a place on his pillow. He dreamed a score—an entire choreography.

Suddenly the music in his dream tumbled off-key, then quickly dissolved into complete dissonance. The drumming died away to a single self-conscious beating. A hundred smiles faded from a hundred faces. Intricate, practiced dance steps ossified into stances of frightened attention. Women held imperiously aloft *en l'air* were set down to cringe and cower *à terre*. The suddenly stifled people, breathless and sweating, were then rudely herded offstage en masse and brought to a standstill in a place of cruel darkness that was hidden from the light of day and even from the prying eyes of God.

The revelers and serenaders, whose regal carriage had been so suddenly transmuted into postures of staggering bewilderment, were chained to cement anchors and then to one another. Next, each was forced to carry his or her own ballast to the center of a dry river-bed and watch as their captors abandoned them for higher ground. The captives waited fearfully, hour after hour, for the advent of some unknown thing. For a coming flood, came the whisper. There is a coming deluge, came the awful rumor.

The sound of onrushing water was heralded by the crying of the children, the moaning of the women, and the impotent muttering of the strongest men. One of the leaders raised his long-fingered black hand for complete silence. He then canted his head to listen. In the distance there was a deep thunder that grew louder and louder. Behind it came the towering wall of water.

From each mouth a thin wail of despair rose up vainly to meet it. In the next instant, children were pulled from their mothers' arms and washed away. Those mothers who held tight felt their children die. One tearful mother, a woman whose face was marked with tribal tattoos, broke her child's neck before the waters could come and suffocate him.

In mere moments, almost all the people were drowned and doomed to be forever forgotten. All were maimed and twisted by the sheer strength of the waters. But those few who managed to hold their breath and stand fast until the mighty deluge subsided did something that could only come to pass in a dream: their living, straining bodies changed the course of that onrushing tide. They had slowed it up and sent it down another path altogether.

In his bed at the city jail, a sleeping, sweating Biscuit Boy comforted himself by reaching beneath his soaked pillow for his cherished books. He, of all of the prisoners that had ever languished in the city jail, had somehow found a way to control his time machine. The cryptic operating instructions and the crowded panel of arcane instrumentations were right there, under the cover leaf and between the preface and final paragraph. Only he, of all the thousands of prisoners before him, had discovered that the secret dials and toggle switches that maneuvered the bed through time had always been there between the bindings.

He had just finished reading his eleventh novel since coming to jail and had already begun writing the book report that his lawyer demanded. The moment his probing fingers touched the spine of one of his books, the sleeping Biscuit Boy realized that his own tragic dream was coming true—that he, too, had been swept away by the waters. Somehow his new, hopeful dreams had become a living nightmare. He could not draw a breath. He must surely be drowning. There must surely be others of his own kind dying along with him. His arms were pinned to his side by shackles, and he felt a desperate, groping hand clamp down over his mouth. The sharp fingernails of the hand dug into the flesh of his cheeks. Some desperate swimmer must have found his body and mistaken it for a floating refuge.

All at once the waters swept him upward in the darkness, turning him head over heels and sweeping him downstream. Somewhere in the blackness his neck was snagged and turned sharply and he felt a dull pain coursing down the core of his vertebrae. Slowly the cold dullness spread, numbing his blinking eyes and forcing his blue tongue up and out of his throat. His lungs burned with hunger. Tasting air that he could not have, he dreamed that the floods had prevailed once more . . . and once again, there was no ark. In the distance he saw the poor, decimated hillside that had once been his home. Down below he saw his mother looking so small and sad from this height. Then he saw the face of the woman he loved.

In one final, desperate effort to swim to the surface, he kicked his feet wildly, spreading his toes for the best grip in dark water. But soon his kicks became little more than an erratic spasm, and then a mere spastic twitch at the knees. In just a few seconds his feet hung limp. As he surrendered at last to the flow, he heard one final, booming voice in the distance. It was inhumanly powerful. It seemed to fill the world. Was it the voice of God? Could it possibly be the awesome voice of God?

"They're killin' a nigger over there! Hey, you stupid muddy bastards, they're killing the nigger right over there!"

It was the voice of the supreme being screaming down the mainline to the deputies that were crouched down and hiding at both ends of the darkened hallway.

"Get the fuck down here right now or the son of a bitch is gonna die on your watch! I can see his stupid face turnin' blue!"

That brought them running, batons and metal flashlights drawn and upraised. Every light on the mainline flashed on. An electric alarm sounded and a half dozen dazed deputies advanced toward Bernard Skelley's cell from every direction. When they arrived at his cell, the supreme being's tattooed arm was extended from his cell bars in Sistine repose; the thumb and fingers hung lazily in a closing position; the index finger of his right hand was barely separate from the other digits and was pointing to the cell located directly across the mainline. Within his cell, the supreme being had draped his naked body with a sheet.

The deputies had been somewhat ready, the key to the cell was out, and the shift commander had armed himself with a pistol that was drawn and cocked. When the door opened, they looked up to see Calvin the Biscuit Boy hanging from the overhead light fixture, a makeshift rope tied around his stretching neck. Hurriedly, they cut him down and immediately began CPR in the open doorway of the cellblock.

The shift commander was shaking his head in sheer disgust; they had reacted too slowly. This was going to look bad in the morning report and even worse in the morning newspapers. They had been given advance warning and had failed to stop a murder in the jails. The boy certainly looked dead. He watched dejectedly as a deputy blew air into the lungs of the Biscuit Boy, while another pushed on his chest cavity. The angry shift commander felt his overdue promotion slipping away with each compression of the boy's chest. The breath of life had come too late.

"I don't suppose anybody saw who did this," sneered one deputy to the cell full of men, who had seemingly just been roused from a deep slumber.

"Was it a suicide?" asked a deputy who had been told to expect some kind of an incident but had not expected to see a hanging.

"Yeah, right," said another in a mocking voice. "First he made himself bloody, then he went and hung himself! It was supposed to look like a suicide, you idiot—just look at those cuts on his face. Someone tried to keep him from calling for help. Who did this?" he screamed at the supreme being.

"All I can tell you"—Bernard Skelley smiled—"is that they all had black skin. Beyond that, you know I can't tell none of them apart. Never could tell none of you dusty fuckers apart. The cell was as dark as East Oakland. All I could see was teeth and eyes, like in them old movies when them niggers see a ghost. What took you so goddamn long? If it was me, I woulda just broke his fuckin' neck, none of this phony suicide shit."

Down the long hallway the main cellblock door swung open and slammed against the wall. The loud sound woke the entire jail population. A gurney appeared, and three paramedics rushed down the hallway toward the recumbent body.

"Somebody call the man's lawyer," said Bernard, as the medics knelt beside the body. "Somebody call the man's lawyer. He's that Mestican fella that works for me. I don't even have to pay the bastard. He warned you fools about this. You know," he grinned, "tomorrow mornin' I'm walking right out of this fuckin' place. You're gonna have to open this door and let me out of here. Shit, by this time tomorrow I'll be doin' the nasty with some fine little creamy-white, Anglo-Saxon bitch, and you bastards will be right here where you belong."

Even as Bernard screamed from his cell, Richard Skelley, the brother of the supreme being, was being booked and strip-searched at the Hayward City jail. A warrant had been issued for his arrest, and two officers had dragged him away from his ring-toss booth at the carnival. He would wail and lash out during the search, as black hands probed his body cavities for contraband.

Just days before, on a cold, foggy day in San Francisco, his little daughter and her dog Hotspur had been led down to the evidence room of the Hall of Justice to see the bedstead with the huge spread-eagle carved into its grain. Margie Skelley Dixon had held her hand as the little girl broke down sobbing at the sight. Minnie had kissed her dog's face and begged over and over to know why her daddy had done those terrible things to her mouth and to her tummy and to her dreams, all of those painful, lonely hours of hurtful pretend.

"Skelley, Richard R., grab the wall and put your feet on those marks there on the floor. We drew lots this morning, and the loser is gonna search your asshole for contraband."

"The contraband ain't in his body," one black deputy in the Hayward City jail would laugh as he landed a punch to the right eye of the struggling, aggressive suspect. "His own pasty-ass body is the contraband. Wait'll the boys down on the cellblock find out that you've got short eyes, Skelley, that your white supremacist ass likes to take advantage of little girls.

"I tell you, there ain't nothing down in that west cellblock but stir-crazy, angel-dusted, bean-eatin', genuflectin' Catholic Mexicans, and them brown fuckers just worship their sweet *mamacitas* and their little, virginal sisters. It's some kinda religious shit."

"Yeah," said another deputy, "them fucked-up white-boy tattoos of yours are gonna run away and hide when they get a load of all them Virgin of Guadalupe mainline tats. *Mi vida loca*, man. *Mi vida loca*. But don't you worry none, Mr. Superman. I promise you that if one of them spics takes and shoves a knife in between your ribs, you just go ahead and pick up the white courtesy phone and one of us house niggers will come running down there lickety-split. Yowsa, boss, we sho will. I don't know about my partner here"—he winked at his shift commander—"but I'd sure as hell be more than willing to risk my life to save your white supremacist ass."

The two deputies laughed as they led the prisoner down the hallway to the Mexican end of the jail. "*El otro lado,*" as the inmates called it. *Nichos* had been drawn on every wall. Each one contained colorfully drawn votive candles and icons. There were crucifixes everywhere, and rosaries were draped over every bunk *en el otro lado*.

Dreams in this bay were a confused confluence of Olmec arche-types, Zapotec women, and auto parts. One *vato*, dreaming of a girl named "La Happy," who had huge breasts, little resistance to sug-gestion, and no moral compass whatsoever, woke to see Captain Richard Skelley of the New Aryan Army as he sat down on a bunk at the entrance to the bay. The *vato* smiled when his bleary eyes re-solved into focus and he saw the verdant spread of racist tattoos on the body of the gringo. He pushed "La Happy" from his mind and began moving from bunk to bunk, homeboy to homeboy. One by one, with a shake and a giggle, he began waking his *carnales*.

When Biscuit Boy awoke, he saw the faces of three nurses and a young doctor hovering above his own body. There was a bright light shining directly into his eyes and an oxygen mask strapped tightly over his mouth.

"You're a lucky young man," said the young doctor through his white mask. "The ceiling of your cell wasn't high enough to allow for much of a drop, and the ligature that they used was much too thick. Your neck isn't broken, but you almost suffocated to death."

"Did I drown in a flood, doctor?" asked Calvin in a hoarse, anguish-filled voice that was muffled even more by the mask. Each breath brought with it a stab of pain that ran across his chest and up the left side of his face.

"I dreamed that I was drownin'. I dreamed about a huge flood washin' my people away. Then I seen my hill from way up above."

One of the nurses, a woman of African descent, pulled down her surgical mask and moved toward the head of the operating table. Calvin recoiled when he saw her up close. There were symmetrical scars burned into her cheeks and forehead. This woman had been in his dream. This woman had killed her own baby rather than see it suffer. The nurse calmed him by placing a dark index finger on the mask. She then swabbed the young man's head with a cool cloth and smiled sweetly.

"You're gonna be all right. We just had to make a small cut to help you breathe. Your mama's out in the waiting room. She's been here all night. I think your brother's out there, too. You'll see them both in a few minutes. But first, let me tell you something. That wasn't no dream, dear boy. That was death that you were seeing, but not your death . . . not exactly."

One of the white nurses turned to glance at the other.

"It's sad for a black boy to die—real sad—but it's a tragedy if he dies when he's just opened his eyes, when he's just looked back to see who he is. Listen to me, baby, it was your dreams that were being lynched in that jail cell, and you were right there to witness it. I heard it was black boys that did this to you. May the good Lord have mercy on the dreamless."

Jesse's car pulled off of Highway 101 at the San Francisco airport exit. He parked his car at the short-term parking lot and walked with Eddy Kazuso Oasa to the coffee shop nearest his gate. It was six o'clock in the morning and neither had spoken a word during the ride. It was far too early for substantive conversation. Both men needed breakfast and a caffeine fix before even attempting to speak.

"No chorizo and eggs at this place," said Jesse as he perused the disappointing, plastic-encased menu. "*No caldo de rez* and no god-damn menudo, either."

There was nothing but Disneyland fare in both columns: pigs in a blanket and waffles with raspberry syrup and raisins.

"No Moko Loko. No Spam and eggs," moaned Eddy. "Damned haole food. Do you think he did it out of gratitude?"

"I can only hope he did," answered Jesse, pensively. "It's always the same way, isn't it, over and over again? We start out doing our jobs—sometimes hating the client, but doing our jobs. Then something happens. We stumble onto the humanity in even the worst people. Sometimes we find out that they're more than simply not guilty, they're innocent, like the supreme being."

"It wouldn't happen," answered Eddy, "if we didn't do the job. I guess you've got to believe in the principle first. Somebody's got to disbelieve the evidence. Shit, did I say that? It's too damn early."

"For me, Eddy, it still boils down to one thing: Where in the courtroom do I want to sit? I can't go sit with the prosecutor and the cops and the immense power of the state. I can't sit with the bailiff, putting dark people, people like you and me, in and out of holding cells day in and day out.

"I look around the courtroom and there's this guy sitting there that everyone hates, and everyone believes him guilty before one shred of evidence is presented. There he is, disheveled, toothless, smelly, and inarticulate. He's been accused of something horrible. Maybe he's an old-time heroin addict, or maybe he's a lost peasant from Guatemala or he's a seventeen-year-old black kid who's been stripped of his cultural memory. Next to him is an empty chair. I know where I belong.

"I've got to sit with the fools, with the grunts. There's only one chair for me to take. So I sit down and take his part, even someone like Bernard Skelley. If the prosecutor can get the evidence past me, then maybe my client did something. It's the jury that has to decide that anyway, not you, not me. Did you ask Bernard why he sent us the warning?"

"Yes," said Eddy with a smirk. "He said that if a colored boy is going to get killed, it should be a white man who does it. How can mud kill mud? he said. Then he started running off at the mouth about the war that's going to be fought here, a war to purify America. He said that white women have to be defended. He said a lot more than I wanted to hear. He always does."

"His brother Richard is certainly one staunch defender of women, isn't he? It's all bullshit." Jesse laughed. "Bernard may believe all that supremacist garbage in the daytime, but late at night he knows what is really happening. I know that he did it because he could never thank us for what we did for him. He knows that without our brown asses in his corner, he'd be doing a life stretch up in Pelican Bay. He gave us Biscuit Boy's life in repayment. That's what he did. I don't know about you, Eddy, but it's the best fee I've ever gotten."

"To the Biscuit Boy." Eddy smiled as he raised a tiny glass of expensive, transparent orange juice in tribute. Then, remembering the folded piece of paper in his jacket pocket, he reached for it and handed it to Jesse. As Jesse took it, the smile faded from Eddy's face as he realized, once again, where the plane would be taking him this morning. The ticket for Montgomery was lodged in his jacket pocket. When his plane landed, he would be picking up a rental car and driving to the prison in Huntsville.

Anvil Harp, the putative spouse of Princess Sabine Harp and the father of Little Reggie, would be waiting there for him. As the plane lifted off, Jesse would be making his way to the homeless encampment on Potrero Hill. Under constant pressure from Eddy, Mr. Homeless had reluctantly agreed to speak.

"I got a call from Princess Sabine last night," said Eddy. "Somehow she found out about my trip to Alabama. Boy, did that girl turn on the charm. She said that I was not to believe a single word that the pernicious beast Anvil Harp had to say. She pleaded with me not to go and speak with him."

"If she doesn't want us to speak with him, we must be doing the right thing," said Jesse, grimacing slightly as the food was placed on the table. It looked as plastic as the menu. He smiled at the waitress. It wasn't her fault. Then a suddenly clear recollection of Princess Sabine's home sent a chill down his spine. For the first time he realized that with the exception of Sabine and her crowded, stifling apartment, the entire world was being dragged, second by second, into the future.

"It sounds like Miss Alabama is afraid of something."

"She's terrified," retorted Eddy.

"Did you have a chance to visit Calvin last night?"

"Yeah," said Eddy, his mouth filled with a generic-tasting Spanish omelet that had the texture of cellophane. "He'll be out of the hospital just in time for the trial. He's a lucky kid. He's finished Ralph Ellison and he's reading James Baldwin now. The kid is reading a book every three days. That piece of paper is his latest book report."

Jesse unfolded the paper and began to read. With each word,

Jesse's smile grew larger and larger. Jesse read the last sentences aloud: "Me and my friends be always talking about being black and all, growin' up on the mean streets and whatever. We rap about how bein black is hard. Then I read this book, I did not never know what black mean. Now I know I ain't suffer. Other people before me suffer for me. We ain't nothin', sellin' drugs and doin' dramas. The streets is mean 'cause we be on them."

"The boy is becoming a real person. Is he following your hand signals?" asked Jesse, his face beaming with pride.

"He's getting much better at that, too. Now he responds without even thinking. The jury will never see it. You've been pushing him hard, Jesse. The kid looks tired."

"There isn't much time, Eddy. You know as well as I do that the Biscuit Boy we saw that first evening, months ago, was dead meat on the witness stand. The jury would have convicted him for stuttering. This book report on *The Invisible Man* is amazing. Did you read it?"

Eddy nodded, smiling. He had read it. There was a look of sadness in the face that surrounded his smile. Calvin Thibault had to stand accused of multiple murders in order to discover that an intelligent being lived within his body.

"The last time I saw him, I asked him to do some supposing," added Jesse. "I asked him to suppose what the world would be like today if the library at Alexandria, Egypt, hadn't burned down. I gave him a book on the subject. I wonder if he'll ever have an answer."

Anvil Harp wore trustee's clothing that was cleaned, pressed, and heavily starched. There were razor-edged creases on the sleeves and on the pant legs. He walked smartly, making severe right angles at every turn. Every shirt button lined up with the buttons on his trousers. The Marine Corps loved men like him, and Anvil was a willing lover. If the corps hadn't drummed him out years ago, he would be a master sergeant by now. He was heavyset, almost fat. His face was round, and despite his dark skin, his cheeks were red. He looked nothing like his son Reggie.

After seven years inside, Anvil had finally been given trustee status. He had the run of the kitchen and the woodshop and the prison laundry. Now he could go to the commissary anytime he wanted. There was a swagger in his walk as he entered the interview room. He explained to Eddy as he sat down on his metal stool that his new status as a trustee allowed him to get one day's credit for each day served—day for day, as the prisoners called it. It would cut his remaining time in half.

"Shit, I could be a free man in eleven years." He smiled. "But that ain't what you come all this way to talk about, now is it? You come about beautiful Miss Sabine and Reggie, ain't you? Well, let me say my piece and then you can leave me the fuck alone. Leave old Anvil to his eleven years, two months, and seventeen days. I own them years. At least they're mine, 'cause Little Reggie Harp ain't mine. That misbegotten child sure ain't no kin of mine. No sir."

There was no anger in his face, only a look of disgust. In the time it took to hang his head, then slowly raise it again, a gentler expression had settled in.

"I don't mean no disrespect to you, but I got some strong feelings about the subject of Sabine. All I do in here is think about it. All I can really say is that I loved that woman. I reckon I still love her. When it's real good, I guess love can be just like a life sentence." He laughed. "You might say that I done dedicated my whole life to her."

As abruptly as it had arrived, the smile disappeared from his face. Eddy noticed for the first time that Anvil was not aging well in prison. The background he had done on the prisoner stated that he was fifty-nine years old. He looked much older. Each look of concern brought a dark grid of wrinkles to his face.

"Seven years ago I was convicted of murder in the first degree by the state of Alabama. Premeditated, deliberate, cold-blooded murder is what the judge called it, and that's just what it was. Make no mistake about that. Ain't that something? I ain't never stole so much as a hubcap in my whole life and here I'm a convicted killer. Not just a murderer, but a murderer with—how did the judge say it?—an aggravated sentence and a malicious heart. You see, I went and killed me an old man, a real old man who already had one foot in the grave. That's what I did."

The prisoner nodded to himself, then settled back into his chair to recount the familiar tale.

"Seven years ago I got down my old M-1 carbine from the Korean War. I dusted it all off and cleaned it up to where it looked brand-new, spankin' new. Then I went down to brother Angelo Butler's gun store down on Maple Street and bought some high-test bullets. They cost me a week's pay.

"Then I went out to the shootin' range and zeroed in the sights. It felt real good to shoot—it's been a long time since Inchon. Then I looked at the targets and policed up the brass, just like the old days in boot camp. Then, when I was all locked and loaded, I commenced to go lookin' for that old bastard. That's right, Mr. Eddy, I went hunting."

He leaned forward as if to whisper, though the strength of his voice remained the same. It was a hollow gesture of secrecy.

"Now, I'm sure you know this here prison is full of innocent men. To hear them fools tell it, they was all screwed by the system, by their lawyers. But in my case, the jury went and did the right thing. You see, I'm the only guilty man in this place, because I'm the only honest man. I went out on purpose, looking for the enemy.

"Well, it didn't take long to find him. I just went to all the places that chillun and young 'uns go to. Sure as flies find shit, I found him at Mae's Gravy Boat, this little café over on the south side of Selma. They got fried fish and okra in there. Mighty tasty, too. Mostly colored folk goes there. It's a hangout. There he was in there all gussied up in a wrinkled, three-button suit and a flannel tie. He had a raggedy wig-hat on his scalp that looked like a dozen black tarantulas had landed smack dab on his head.

"And he was just soaked from head to toe with all that stinky after-shave that he be wearin'. That old fool always did smell like a whore-house. Who on earth ever heard of a real man wearin' makeup? I swear to God, he put foundation powder on his skin 'cause his face looked like a dry lake bed, like a road map of Nevada. It was Old Spice that he wore. I remember now. I hate that shit. I could always catch whiffs of it on Miss Sabine's dresses."

Sadness flashed across his wide face as he inhaled the recollection of a soft white chemise, the memory of a petticoat.

"Well, there he was, ugly as a stump—ugly as a frog, flirtin' with all the pretty young waitresses and them high school girls that comes in all the time for a pork sandwich or a slice of pecan pie and a Cherry Coke. He's carryin' on, waving a fat wad of money in front of them and tellin' them how they brings out the devil in him. Well, I walks into the Gravy Boat and called out his name.

"I remember that my man Jackie Wilson was playing on the jukebox. It was 'Lonely Teardrops.' Jackie died too soon, you know. Well, anyway, I called out the old man's name, and when he turned around I flipped off the safety and I pumped six rounds right into that sick smilin' face of his. It's a semi-automatic rifle, you see. But first, I waited one full second so that he could see what was bein' done to him and just who it was that was doin' it.

"Shit, one minute he's smilin' like Judas Iscariot, and the next minute his face looked like one of them waffle things that white folks eat, all covered with jam, strawberry or maybe even raspberry. I've never had a waffle, but I like pancakes. Anyway, one of the cops said on the witness stand that they found his false teeth in the parking lot thirty yards from the café. They'd been blown clean out the window. His hairpiece landed in the chili warmer."

Anvil Harp placed both hands on the small shelf in front of him, then rose up slowly from the stool. Eddy began to ask a question, when Anvil raised his hand sternly to silence him. Now Anvil's face was devoid of the trustee's elation. Now his dark lips quivered with emotion as he spoke, his yellowed teeth flashing in and out of view, and his eyes opened impossibly wide.

"Listen to me." He began poking himself in the chest with the index finger of his right hand. "I been knowin' Princess Sabine since the first time she ever looked in the mirror and liked what she seen. I'm the one she sent over to the grocery store to get them Kotex sanitary napkins. I been knowin' Princess Sabine since the first day that she ever washed her feet and slapped on them high heels. It was me . . . I was there closing my eyes when she tried on her first brassiere.

"I been seein' every man that ever looked at her. I bad-mouthed 'em and cursed 'em all. I was out there in the audience for every goddamn one of them beauty contests. You see, Mr. Eddy, I been lovin' her all of my growed life and—shit—I ain't never touched her . . . not once. Oh, I touched—held her hand and such—but not in that special way. You understand. . . ."

Anvil winked while Eddy winced.

"Now, mind you, I ain't one of them sissy-queers—shit, we got a million of 'em in here. A meaner bunch of bitches and pillow fluffers you ain't never seen. I sure ain't one of that bunch. I'm all man. I wanted her. I ain't never made love to her or even touch her breast, and the good Lord know that I dreamed about it every night. I damn near wore out my right hand and my dick daydreamin' about Miss Sabine. I loved her even after she became . . . unnatural."

He was silent for a long moment, the discomfort filling his face.

"She . . . got this taste for young boys."

Anvil Harp closed his eyes as he spoke the final syllables of the sentence.

"They run her out of Alabama on account of it. They finally caught her with a twelve-year-old boy and stripped her of all of her beauty titles. That twelve-year-old was my youngest brother. She shoulda chose me. It shoulda been me instead." He sobbed without tears. "I was just too old. But it weren't her fault, Mr. Eddy. It weren't her fault. She didn't have no choice in it. After what happened, well, I went and enlisted for Korea. Ain't there some kind of sayin' about love and war?"

"All's fair," said Eddy.

Anvil's right thumb was poking at his own chest. His voice dropped down until it was barely audible.

"I asked her to marry me a thousand times, but she always said no. Mr. Eddy, there been only one growed man in that woman's life, only one growed man has ever touched Princess Sabine Harp in that there special way, and I shot him dead in Mae's Gravy Boat café. I would do it again today. She was born married to him."

Anvil used the sleeve of his trustee shirt to wipe away the mist that had formed in his red eyes. The starch and the stiffness of the fabric only irritated them further.

"Was Princess Sabine sleeping with her son, Little Reggie?" asked Eddy.

The investigator had flown two thousand miles to ask that question. Angrily, Anvil pushed a button on the wall to the right and yelled to a guard seated above the interview booths. Clearly, the question had stung him.

"Billy Junior, we're through in here. No disrespect to you, Mr. Eddy, but there's only so much I can stand at one time."

He pulled out a small piece of paper, folded it, and pushed it through a slot in the security screen that separated the visitors from the prisoners.

"Give it to Miss Sabine, please. Tell her I love her as best I can. I still love her. Tell her I'm sorry for killing her father. Tell Little Reggie that I'm sorry for killing his father." His saddened eyes were fixed on Eddy's eyes. "I'm sorry for them, not for me."

Eddy unfolded the sheet of paper, then realized that he had not obtained permission to do so. When he looked up, Anvil Harp had disappeared from the interview booth and was already going through a second door. Quietly he read the seven words written there.

"Eleven years, two months, and seventeen days." Eddy then called out, "Little Reggie is dead," in a condolence-filled voice.

"Thank God," said Anvil Harp, as the door closed behind him.

Jesse penetrated the perimeter at the northwest corner, stepping around stacks of bottles and cans and between a half dozen stolen shopping carts filled with plastic and smelly piles of junk. His presence had been announced by a dozen skinny dogs of various breeds that barked and circled him as he walked. Dust rose up around him like the smoke from a flare.

There was no menace in these dogs. They had become as hungry and reclusive as their masters. Their masters' malaise had been conferred upon them in long, cold nights of shared food and shared bedding. These dogs had glimpsed Hue and Quang Tri.

Passing through the outer defenses, he checked the terrain. There were small tentlike constructions along the perimeter of the encampment. They were made out of boxes and rags. Behind them a deep slit trench had been dug. Four poles marked its corners, and a sheet had been wrapped around the poles to form a semiprivate outdoor toilet. A cloud of flies hovered above the trench.

Behind the toilet was a pathetically small shelter fashioned from pallets and dirty blankets. Jesse bent down to look inside. It was clear that only one person slept here. The lawyer had noticed that the rest of the dwellings were multiple, communal spaces. There was a plate of cold, half-eaten food on the dirt floor. On the other side of the tiny room was a strange sight: a pair of tennis shoes had been placed side by side, the laces tied together. Someone had carefully placed a small black-and-white photograph beneath the tongue of one of the shoes.

In the other shoe were five nine-millimeter bullets. Jesse picked up the photo and saw that it was a picture of Princess Sabine posing in the nude. Her body was draped seductively over the arm of the sofa in her apartment. The small shadow of the photographer could be seen on the wall behind her. No professional had taken this picture. Jesse replaced the photo and then, out of respect for the dead, backed slowly out of the hooch. It was then that he noticed that a small crucifix had been dropped into the other shoe. Even someone like Little Reggie deserved a standdown.

Near the center of the compound he spotted what he knew must be the communal kitchen, the mess hall. None of the other structures were large enough to accommodate a fire or cooking utensils, and this was the only structure that was not made of cardboard. It was a large metal half-cylinder that had been inverted to form a small Quonset. At each end were poncho liners that kept out both the bone-chilling fog and the prying eyes of the police.

Jesse pulled a poncho liner aside. He noticed that it was an olive-drab army-issue liner that was being used as a door. It was of Vietnam vintage, much lighter than Korean War issue. The lawyer stepped cautiously into the dark hooch. In the center of the dirt floor a fire was burning. At the top of the hooch was a jagged hole that allowed some of the smoke and fumes to escape. Jesse could see that the metal had been recently cut. At the far end were a dolly and some oxyacetylene tanks. Someone had brought in a cutting torch and done the job right.

The scents of marijuana, human sweat, and canned food mixed with the smoke and heat to form a cloud that hung in the still air inside. There were empty ration cans everywhere. As Jesse moved, the rancid smell of unchanged clothing and unwashed hair forced him to change direction. He pulled a handkerchief from his pocket and placed it over his nose and mouth. It smelled exactly like the underground bunkers back in Dong Ha.

He located a plastic milk carton and sat down to wait for his eyes to adjust to the darkness that filled all but the center of the room. After a few minutes he removed the kerchief from his nose. His olfactory system had reached some sort of equilibrium. In time he saw that there were three other men in the hooch with him. Two were huddled quietly at the far end, sucking on a hand-rolled marijuana cigarette, while the third sat alone at the very edge of the firelight.

One man was black, while the other two were white. All three wore clothing that had not been washed in months, if not years. The jacket of choice was a "one each" U.S. Army field jacket in olive drab. All were slick with grease and perspiration.

"You don't belong in here," said the voice near the fire. It was a firm but gentle voice. "You should be leaving." Two other voices grunted their agreement.

Ignoring the admonition, Jesse moved toward the fire. The face of the man seated there was lit by a shaft of light that poured through the vent hole above. His matted hair had once been light brown and curly. His skin beneath the filth and sunburn was smooth, even youthful. It was the man's eyes that caught Jesse's attention. They were filled with distance and dread. He had seen many such eyes in Vietnam. Life, perhaps death, had betrayed this man.

"I need to speak to you. I know that you spend your days up on the hill—somehow you have managed to gain safe passage through the guns and the gangs. I don't know how I know, but I'm sure that you know something about all of the killings up here. You know what happened to all of those boys. I think you know what happened at the Amazon Luncheonette."

"You should be leaving," repeated the voice, this time with menace.

"So that's how it is," said Jesse disdainfully, while inspecting the area around himself. Using the toe of one shoe, he casually prodded a paper bag from Klein's deli.

"You can take money right out of my pocket; you can eat my food every day, but you won't let me rest my tired feet in this splendid palace of yours."

After a moment of silence the softened voice responded, "You can stay. Though I understand the true motive for your generosity, I still want to thank you for the food."

"Don't mean nothing," answered Jesse. "Don't mean nothing."

The two men in the distance suddenly stopped moving, the glow of the cigarette hung immobile in the blackness. One of them slowly exhaled his precious lungful of smoke. The two men with the dying joint turned to stare into the intruder's face. A stranger had uttered the grunt's mantra. The man by the fire raised his head to look directly at the lawyer, to study his face.

"Who are you? Do I know you?"

"*Supongamos,*" said Jesse, while facing away from the man. "Supposing Oscar Wilde was wrong and men did not kill the things they love, amigo, what would America, west of the Mississippi, be like today? If Wilde had been allowed to love whomever he wished, what would sustain the seventy wars that are being fought somewhere in the world at this very moment?

"Or suppose this one especially: Suppose the Nicene Council, back in the fourth century, had not deleted women and their writings from the New Testament and from the church. Suppose the female apostles had been allowed to live on in the Bible. Do you suppose there would have been a Vietnam War?"

The man near the fire began to weep.

Calvin shifted nervously in his seat as the prosecutor pored over a page in his voluminous notebook. The defendant looked at his lawyer, who was making the secret sign to calm down. Calvin inhaled deeply then remembered to sit up and place one hand on each knee. His body language had occasionally been extremely defensive.

After running his finger down the page, the prosecutor stood up, then placed himself between the defendant and his lawyer. He knew that the two were communicating somehow, and he intended to block Calvin's view.

"You told the inspector, did you not, that you knew that Little Reggie had the gun?"

"I know that he almost always be carrying a gun," answered Calvin, "so, on the tape, I guessed that he had one that night. If you listen to the tape, Mr. Cling, you can hear that I was ask a trick question. I been forced into giving that answer. On that night, the night when Mai was killed, I ain't knowin' he had the gun until I saw it in his hand."

Despite the obstruction by the prosecution, the witness saw the signal to elaborate. Calvin continued his statement.

"Everyone on that hill have a gun, sir. Even the little kids have guns. They takes their guns to the playground when they ride on the swings. When they ain't got decent clothes or shoes on, they got heat. They be strapped when they go to the store to buy penny candy or a root beer."

"You also told the inspector, did you not, that you knew that he was going to kill her?"

"When he pull out that gun, knowin' him the way I did, I knew that those women be in danger."

"You're not answering my question," continued the prosecutor. "You knew that Little Reggie was going to kill those women before he actually did it, didn't you?"

Calvin turned his gaze to the jury.

"If Little Reggie Harp be here today, pointin' a gun at you, I be sure that the crazy fool would use it on one of you, maybe more. That's what I mean by that answer. If I had knowed that he was going to hurt those women, I woulda tried to stop him. All I know when I knock on the front door of the Amazon Luncheonette was that I be near . . . her."

"You wanted to be near her?" asked the prosecutor.

"I always want to be near her, near Mai. From the first time I saw her I could not stop thinkin' about her, to smell her perfume. I thinks she is . . . was the mostest beautiful woman I ever seen."

"Who was it that put Mai in the refrigerator?"

"I put her there," answered Calvin. "I thought she be safe in there. I thought Reggie be satisfy if he think she suffocate in there. I schemed to let her out as soon as he leave and it be safe but she kick the door open."

Now a shining tear began to wend its way down the ebony cheek of the defendant. Jesse sat upright in his chair, surprised by the emotion evident in his client's face. He hadn't given the sign for an emotional display.

"Until the day I die I never be forgettin' the look on her face when she run past me into the street. She hate me. That pretty face couldn't stand to look at me. I love her so much and she hate me for bein' with him. I want her to stop—not to go out there. I know what Little Reggie could maybe do to her. I never had no time to explain to her. . . ."

"There's no question before the witness," interjected the prosecutor.

"The witness is allowed to explain," answered the judge.

"I ran out behind her and scream at her to stop, but nothin' on earth could stop her. She be screamin' something and can't hear me callin' out to her. Then I hear the first shot. Miss Persephone already be down. Blood everywhere. Then I seen him shoot Mai. . . ."

Now the tears were streaming down the Biscuit Boy's face.

"God, I be lovin' her."

"You got the gun from Reggie, didn't you? He handed you the gun right after he killed those two women."

"Yeah, he done that."

"You said on direct examination that you tried to shoot Reggie right there in the street, isn't that right?"

"Yeah."

"But Reggie had removed the clip."

"Yeah, I mean yes."

"It was your job to hide the gun, wasn't it?

"Yes."

"It was your job to hide the clip, wasn't it?"

"I never seen the clip, sir."

"And you hid them both under the front porch of Princess Sabine Harp's apartment?"

"Yes, but only the gun. Reggie always keep it there."

"You killed Reggie Harp just one or two days after the murders at the Amazon Luncheonette, didn't you? You were afraid that he would spill the beans about your part in the murders. First you sent him a note saying that he was a dead man, then you killed him."

"I didn't kill him, sir. I want to kill him, I'll tell you that, for what he done to those three boys, for what he done to Mai. I try to kill him that night. He be such a sick boy. He got no place to live, did you know that? He be livin' with those homeless vets down at the bottom of the hill. That crazy mama of his won't let him in, so I be bringin' him food that my mama cook, and I kicked it with him a little bit, but not too long 'cause he be livin' near a outdoor toilet.

"That mama of his always be askin' boys to come in her house, offerin' them food and beer, and always showing those pictures of her, some with no clothes on. I never seen none of them pictures, but I heard. She be lettin' any fool boy into her house, but she didn't never let her own son to come in."

Calvin glanced toward his lawyer for some indication of how well he was doing on the stand. The lawyer seemed pleased. Calvin's English was much better than before, but not so good as to destroy all poignancy. This case needed poignancy. Jesse gave Calvin the signal to elaborate about Princess Sabine.

"Boys would come out her house swearin' that they had been to bed with her, seen her titties and everything. They say she tied them up with string. Weird stuff. Jesus, that make Reggie so mad. It drive him crazy. It turn him into a crazy killer. I know he shot those three boys. Everybody know it, even without seein' it.

"But I always know there be somethin' wrong with him. If there was a pretty new car on the block, he scratch up the paint. If someone plantin' some pretty flowers, he'd wreck 'em. I think he hate anything pretty. That's why he kill those women. He hate anything nice. If there be another bullet in that chamber, I swear he be dead that night. Good thing the gun be empty or there be another body out on the sidewalk."

"Mai Adrong, Persephone Flyer, and Reggie Harp," said the prosecutor reproachfully.

"No," said Calvin. "There be another man out there that night. He run over to the bodies of the two women. It be the homeless man that I seen on the hill, Mr. Homeless. He's all the time preaching against violence and drugs and such. He tells crazy stories about spiders and about what happens on a hill. Reggie aim right at him and pull the trigger but nothin' happened. The homeless guy never even look up. He saw Reggie, but went right back to what he doin'. It look like he be sayin' something to those women."

After almost two full days of cross-examination the prosecutor sat down at his table, leaving the crowded courtroom silent, and an exhausted Calvin anxious to leave the witness stand. Jesse was openly proud of his client and smiled at Eddy Oasa, who was seated in one of the attorneys' seats just behind the defense table. Eddy nodded his head imperceptibly. The boy had survived. He had explained himself clearly and answered every question in a manner that the jury could understand.

"Just one or two more questions, your honor," said Jesse who did not rise from his table. "What is your name on the street?"

Calvin smiled at the question.

"Biscuit Boy."

"How did you come to have that name?"

A look of calm and deep affection descended upon Calvin's face as he considered his answer to the question.

"I be stealin' pastries from the back yard of the Amazon Luncheonette. I be takin' the pastries just to taste somethin' that her hands be touchin'. I use to go up there and watch Mai all day long. I know when she wake up in the mornin' and I know when she go to sleep at night. Before the kids go to school I be watchin' her window to see the lights come on in her bedroom. Then I run up the hill to catch the sound of her mixin' machine and the smell from her oven."

Calvin closed his eyes but continued to speak.

"I be standin' across the street and just watch her movin' back and forth in her kitchen. She be the most prettiest thing I ever seen. Well, one morning I'm fixin' to steal some of the pastries that she leave on a bench in back. I seen the homeless guy takin' them, so I reckons I'd try it. But she nabbed me. I won't never forget that for as long as I live.

"I reach out for the pastries, but her hand come out and grab mine. Then I hear this laughter that sound happy and sweet like a kids' playground and I look up to see that face smilin' at me. *'Duá bé giao bánh bích quy,'* she say."

One or two of the jurors had looks of pure amazement on their faces. Could they really be hearing a black boy from the projects speaking Vietnamese? Was it possible?

"Then in good English she translate. She say, 'Biscuit Boy.' She turned my hand over and, with her other hand, put a stack of hot biscuits in my palm. I feel like she had put one of her titties—" He turned his head to look at the face of his lawyer. "—breasts on my palm."

With his eyes once again shut tight, he swooned at the thought.

"Mai teach me how to say my own name in Vietnamese, and she be usin' that name every time she catch sight of me. I learn to say my name by sound at first, but, Hong Ha, the Vietnamese interpreter who come up to the jail, wrote it out for me, with all them accent marks and stuff. I needs to know how to spell my name correct, you see. When she give me that name, my life been change forever."

"How did you feel about Mai?"

"I been waitin' a long time for this here trial by jury, Mr. Pasadoble. I passed a lot of time upstairs, in my bed in the jail, readin' and learnin' things. I wasn't livin' life before—when everythin' around me was the enemy, when every day be war. What I mean to say is I love Mai when I be a stupid boy stealin' biscuits. Now I be a man charged with killin' her, I know there ain't no words to say what my heart feel for her."

"No further questions, your honor," said Jesse Pasadoble. He smiled and gave his client a thumbs-up for all to see. It was not semaphore. The time for secrets and signals had passed. Calvin stepped down from the witness stand and walked to the defense table, where he touched his lawyer's shoulder lightly, then sat down. The Biscuit Boy sighed deeply, closing his eyes to fight the incessant desire to cry.

Without knowing it, Jesse had been sucking on his sliver of jade. He had slipped the sliver of jade into his mouth by mistake after digging into his coat pocket for a mint. Suddenly the courtroom, which had been silent for the few moments it took for Calvin to leave the witness stand and walk back to his seat, became alive with the strangest, most disconcerting sounds. Jesse glanced frantically around the courtroom to locate the source of the disturbances and saw that no mouths were moving; no one was speaking. Yet there were distinct voices—voices without timbre or tenor, bass, or baritone, voices without words, without volume.

It was long moments before he realized that he was listening to the jurors. He was hearing their hearts. He slumped in his chair. Was it possible to hear the innermost thoughts of another being? Then a question struck him like a blow to the face: Could peasant warriors in Vietnam have used these slender green stones to penetrate the U.S. Army's Signal Corps and its web of cryptography? Could the NVA have listened in on us back on the hill near Laos?

He turned his head toward the jury box. One by one, each juror had gone to the orphanage door, and after overlooking him on the first pass, they had begun to consider Calvin. They had begun to adopt the Biscuit Boy. One by one, they were shaking off their initial revulsion toward him and were coming to embrace the existence of a reasonable doubt. Their skeptical hearts had been opened to the possible presence of both genuine love and the whole truth.

Now Jesse knew its secret, why only select soldiers had been given the jade. It wasn't fear that activated the power of the green stone. Now Jesse knew what had been so different about the two burned corpses he had found at the base of that hill near Laos, two small bodies with slivers of jade set upon their tongues. Like those two soldiers, Jesse was fighting in this trial to save a life. Those dead soldiers had been unarmed. They had both been women.

Jesse carefully removed the jade from his tongue. Slowly he became aware that the judge was staring at him, and that he needed to shut out the voices in order to speak. He stood up slowly and addressed the judge.

"Your honor, at this time the defense rests."

He sat down, grabbed his stack of notepads, and began to mentally prepare for his closing argument. After the morning recess the jury would be brought back and would be forced to hear almost two hours of convoluted, confusing, and repetitive instructions. By the time the judge was finished, most of the jurors would be nodding off or half-asleep. Two experienced jurors had brought dark glasses for the occasion. After that, the two lawyers would be allowed to sum up their cases.

This jury, once hostile and closed-minded, was now open and receptive to the defense. During recess they would be eagerly waiting for the summations. Jesse had heard it in their beating hearts. Miraculously, each one of them had come to see something of themselves in the Biscuit Boy. They no longer believed that Calvin had killed the three boys that were dug up on the hillside. That had been thoroughly disproved through the compelling testimony of a single surprise witness. Now they knew for certain who it was that had strangled Little Reggie Harp.

But still, the Biscuit Boy had been there when those two bullets had insulted the flesh and spirits of Mai and Persephone. There was still the question of accomplice liability. In the eyes of the law, an aider and abettor who intends the same result that the actual perpetrator intended is just as guilty.

If he and Calvin could get past that, there would be no penalty phase, no life-without-possibility-of-parole. The miracle would have happened. For the first time, Jesse began to realize that the impossible could happen: Calvin could be acquitted of everything. He could walk from this courtroom and into a new life.

Jesse would have to tell the jurors the story behind this case—without telling them all of it. They would never believe the entire story. Who on earth would? He breathed deeply to relieve the incredible stress brought on by the mere thought of it. A pain descended from his head to his neck and shoulders. His fingers were desperately rubbing the dog tags in his pocket. This closing argument would have to be like none other. Jesse clenched his fists and felt every muscle in his upper body tightening. Risks would have to be taken.

Fate had given him possession of four tragic lives. No, he had been given possession of nine lives, including Calvin's, Little Reggie's, and those of the three boys on the hill. To do justice to this case, it would take three decades to tell their stories. He would begin at the very beginning and feel his way through. The jury could only believe so much. He knew where he should begin—with the death of a friend, a Creole sergeant, years ago and ten thousand miles away.

13

the soloist

"Ladies and gentlemen of the jury, my name is Jesse Pasadoble, and I have been given a very great privilege and honor. I have been given the opportunity to defend Calvin Thibault."

Jesse turned to face his client, his back to the jury. The lawyer and his client made eye contact. Calvin smiled.

"When I first met you in the jail upstairs, Calvin, I felt the way that each of the jurors felt when they first laid eyes on you: I felt that you were guilty. If not guilty of the crimes charged, you must certainly have been guilty of something. How could it be otherwise? How could it possibly be otherwise? You were a young black man from the Potrero Hill projects, one of the poorest places in the city. You live on a hill where the fences are topped with concertina wire, the shopkeepers are armed, and the earth is mined with failure. You were and are a boy born in a combat zone."

Jesse turned to address the jury.

"Ladies and gentlemen of the jury, I felt the same way that you did, and when he first opened his mouth and began to speak, I became even more sure of his guilt. Here was a boy who spoke in code, the secret, stilted language of the sidewalks and streets. He spoke the lingo of millimeters, Teflon rounds, and calibers. Nothing that could come from his mouth would ever be believed by me or by you . . . by anyone. You heard his taped statement right here in this courtroom. Who on earth could believe someone who speaks like that?

"But I am a defense lawyer and I couldn't afford to feel the way you did. I can't afford to confuse belief with truth. It is my job to defend the boy, to protect him from an assault of lies, to be his point man and guide him through this war of words. So I set about not to change him but to give him the tools that he would need in order to reveal himself to you—and to himself.

"I gave him books to read and I forced him to read carefully and to write about what he found on the pages. In time we broke the code of the hill. You saw and heard the results. The heart must have a lyric. It must have a grammar or it can never hear itself. The heart must articulate or it will never be heard. On this witness stand you each saw a far more eloquent young man stating honestly and clearly what is now so apparent to us all: that he is innocent."

Jesse walked to the prosecutor's table and bent down, placing the palms of both hands on the oak surface. He leaned forward, his face coming within inches of the police detective's face.

"The young man you heard from this witness stand could have easily withstood the rigors and deceptions of an interview with a veteran homicide detective who had already made up his mind about this case."

Jesse stood upright then walked back to face the jury.

"This young man could tell each of you, and did tell you with candor and precision, of his deep love for Mai Adrong. Can any of you doubt that he loved her life while despising his own as he stood by helplessly on that night in the Amazon Luncheonette? Something has changed since that tragic evening when Persephone Flyer and Mai Adrong—two vital and powerful women—were brutally murdered. I'm sure you could see from his testimony that Calvin was heartbroken by it when it happened.

"Look at him. Once his own spirit was a riddle, an unbreakable code. What has changed is Calvin's newfound ability to name the things within his own soul, to give them voice. You have to know that your life is empty before you can begin to fill it. Ladies and gentlemen, the first step is to give a name to the emptiness."

Jesse extended his arm and pointed toward his client.

"If you can recognize heartsickness, then you will see it there, in his face. Does any one of you have any doubt whatsoever that the boy you saw up on the witness stand could compose a love poem for beautiful Mai Adrong? The stupid boy that you heard on that cassette tape could never do that. That boy's voice, speaking to us from the past, could barely defend himself from a set of devious and manipulative questions, much less the cruelty and the savagery of Little Reggie Harp. What Calvin Thibault could never do, the Biscuit Boy can. Biscuit Boy has left the hill and is now engaged with the world around him. For that accomplishment alone, I am proud to be his lawyer."

Jesse walked toward his client, extended his hand, then shook hands with him. The Biscuit Boy rose from his chair and smiled, clearly moved by the gesture. In the audience the Biscuit Boy's mother beamed with pride, for a precious moment forgetting the charges against her son. Jesse left his client and walked across the courtroom to resume his place in front of the jury.

"In his past life there were no reasons to wake up in the morning and no particular reasons to go to sleep. There were no clocks in his home, no alarms to set, no calendars to mark. No one went to work in the morning and came home exhausted at night. There were no magazines in his living room, no books or newspapers. There was no Mozart in his life, no Brahms, no Modigliani. There were only boys doing battle for dominion of a squalid hillside. There were only children foraging for money and food. This building around us now is filled with prisoners of that war."

Jesse paused for a moment during his summation. He glanced at some notes, but his mind was elsewhere. The war that left two women and four boys dead on the eastern slope of Potrero Hill did not begin this year, or in this decade. It did not begin in this city. It began years ago—eleven thousand days ago, to be exact—on another hillside far from this courtroom, far away from here.

He began his summation again, weaving in and out of the law and the facts of the case, invoking the testimony of witnesses, imploring twelve citizens to take the path of most resistance: true impartiality and reason. He cajoled them into seeing the world through Biscuit Boy's eyes. He cozened them into deploring the district attorney's bitter accusations. He terrorized them with the very nature of Little Reggie's existence.

After two and a half hours on his feet, Jesse sat down dazed and weary beyond belief. He sat while the prosecutor offered his rebuttal. Jesse did not hear a word of it. He sat while the bailiff cleared the courtroom and the jury was led away to deliberate. Jesse did not realize that he was alone until Biscuit Boy was led away to the jails. As he rose to leave the courtroom, he saw a solitary figure seated in the rear of the courtroom. It was Carolina. Jesse stopped walking for a second, unconsciously placed the jade into his mouth, then continued toward the last row of seats. He sat down next to her with a weary smile on his face. Carolina would hear the story behind the story. She would believe.

His wife was walking all over his black and sweat-sheened face. The small impacts of her feet, like muscle spasms, could be seen moving across his brow and onto his cheeks. Now, full-size in his mind, she was sitting on his forehead, the weight of her brown buttocks spreading the wrinkles of his face, pulling the edges of his lips back into a deep, satisfied grin. Then there was her odor. Her skin always smelled like a newborn puppy. The aperture between her thighs had a salton scent of sweetness. There was the sensual burn of her nylons on his ears—or was it the burn of pain, his life seared by grim reality?

Above his position there was the sound of a mortar round whistling in overhead. It was close in by the sound of it. No more artillery, he thought. There was a deep *whoomp* sound as the round landed on the far side of the hill. They were too close now for the big stuff. Pretty soon it was going to be hand grenades, then slingshots. In the distance he heard the whistles and bugles that were the communications systems for the NVA. The sounds grew closer and closer with each shift of the wind. Now they were clear as a bell. Their stern, expressionless riflemen were on the move. Why were those men down there so willing to die?

The sergeant groaned as he wrapped his bleeding leg with a sleeve torn from someone else's shirt. The dead boy in the torn shirt wouldn't be needing it. Somewhere back in the world his loving parents were being plagued in their sleep by the first dark premonitions of his death. On the far side of the hill the aid station was down and wounded bandages were lying everywhere. All the defensive holes on this side of the hill were collapsed and down.

"I don't want no more of them compacts! Do you hear?" he screamed over his left shoulder toward his scattered troops. He glanced behind himself as he shouted, but what he saw did not register. His dear wife's lovely eyes were blocking his vision. There was a mass of motionless men on the east side. A few were crawling. A few more of the walking wounded were erecting small PSP shelters.

There were ammunition cases everywhere, claymore bags and empty smoke canisters. There were many more helmets than there were heads. The troops that had gathered together each night to do some supposing would never gather again. There would never again be a quorum. The sergeant wondered if Jesse Pasadoble was still alive.

"None of them contracts!" he cried out again. "*Pas encore!* I've heard you guys making them deals and I know it's some kinda sick shit!" He was repeating himself. He tied off the sleeve, then cursed and untied the bandage. He had forgotten the sulfa powder. "It ain't natural. *Ce n'est pas naturel.* It's just plain sick," he muttered.

His mind had flown back over a dozen years to a frozen field in Korea. Compacts had been made back then.

"Listen up, lieutenant, if I get shot in the nuts or if my face is gone, you've got to do me. Put your carbine next to my ear and do me. My wife likes to look into my eyes when we make love. You've got to promise me."

His friend, a young first lieutenant from Florida, had nodded his stern agreement, shook hands with the sergeant, and countered with his own contractual conditions: "If I lose my legs, sarge, or if I can't ever move them again, you have to take care of me."

The lieutenant had been a star athlete at the University of Arizona. His fiancée had absolutely adored his athletic skills. She had once been a gymnast and a head cheerleader.

Compacts were not unusual in the field, they happened when the probability of being dismembered or maimed grew imminent and it was clear that support wasn't coming. It wasn't death that gave rise to such gruesome agreements—the sight of dismemberment did. A clean, quick death was a bad thing, but a long, disfigured life was something else again. Endless death was unimaginable; a crippled, mangled life was too damned imaginable.

"Buckle up. Drop your racks and buckle up," he groaned to his boys, as he keyed the portable radio and began mumbling to someone on the other side of the hill. They had dropped their racks long ago, days ago. He scanned the channels until he heard a voice. He didn't know the date, much less the time, and he didn't bother rotating the crystals.

"Listen, man. I need to talk directly to Douglas MacArthur. . . ."

The bandage on his leg came undone. His own muscle glistened there beneath the cloth, the white of wet bone shone through. The sergeant raised himself up and began moving toward the Salon.

"None of them deals!" he cried out again.

The sergeant crawled on hands and knees toward the Salon des Refusés. As he moved, bullets pierced the earth on both sides of his body. To his left was an Indian boy from Bravo Company. He was a foolish, gregarious child who had been right there to greet a mortar round. His legs were gone forever. The legless boy sat up with a startled look in his eyes, his waistline stunned and leaking.

He was sitting, blackened and swaying, in the center of a crater. There was brass everywhere, and pieces of concertina wire had pierced his clothing. There was a rare, wood-handled Walther P-38 in his right hand. A true collector's weapon. Carefully, with his prized pistol, he took aim at another—a legless, lesser man—and killed himself.

The sergeant dragged himself to the entrance of the Salon. Using his arms, he pulled his deadened body into the operator's chair and struggled for the handset of the big radio. Below him he could see the brown-uniformed horde moving in squads up the hill toward his fragmented, diminishing troops. The killing zone had moved upward and upward, but it wouldn't matter in a minute or two; there was snake and nape in the pipeline. Soon the base and this side of the hill would be charcoal and smoke. The wrath of God was about to descend on Mount Carmel. The blasphemers would be revealed.

Inside the radio installation he located a piece of notepaper and, miraculously, a sharpened pencil. Remarkably, some signal gear was still up and running. Everything was analog now. He had shitcanned all the crypto gear hours ago. The generator behind the Salon was gunning and sputtering. All its meter readings were low, and a warning alarm was sounding. The cooling system had been riddled with bullets. He grabbed the handset and began screaming for help.

All of a sudden his wife Persephone's eyes and lips came into clear focus. Back in Louisiana, before moving to San Francisco, his wife had been a high school biology teacher. She had moved to the West Coast to be closer to her husband. They had dreamed of opening a restaurant, but until they could afford it she taught at Daniel Webster, the local grammar school on Potrero Hill.

The sergeant decided that she would be dressing for work about now. She would know that the white thing sticking out of his leg was a shattered fibula. He smiled as he thought of Persephone's musical mornings in the bathroom.

"I'm shaving my legs," she would sing out loud, while giggling uncontrollably, "because I'm not really a mammal at all. Never mind the potential for breast milk and for birthing live babies from my body. Now I'm shaving my armpits because I'm not a liberated woman, and furthermore, I have no biological need of goosebumps and hair follicles—none whatsoever."

After she left the shower stall, her song would change.

"I'm putting foundation on my face because my pores need to be clogged up, and this red stuff on my cheeks and lips is a clear but subtle echo of my perfect genitalia. But never mind those crimson-faced and purple-assed baboons and all of those silly social anthropologists, I'm still not a mammal! What mammal pours hot wax on its own crotch, then rips it off? Now I am curling my eyelashes, God knows what that means.

"I am surely one confused female nonanimal, put on this earth to please the male of the species during those interludes between tours of duty. They say that the male of the species always has the brighter feathers. Is that what all those flashy ribbons and medals are about? If so, why do women even bother with makeup?"

Sergeant Flyer laughed out loud, but the movement sent stabs of pain up his side. He glanced at a smudged meter and saw that the orientation of the antenna was completely wrong. Above his head, a mortar round had shattered the dish. He pushed a toggle switch and heard nothing. The antenna did not budge. The pneumatics were dead. He would be limited to line-of-sight radio. He groaned to his troops as he keyed the radio and began mumbling unintelligible jargon to someone far away, someone in an air-conditioned radio installation in a secured area.

"Strongarm, strongarm, this is Dodge City, over."

He then smirked unconsciously as he waited for a response. The call signs always seemed so fucking stupid, in Korea and now in the Nam.

"Strongarm, strongarm," he repeated with angry, self-conscious desperation.

There was a hash of garble and a flurry of hard syllables that caused the sergeant to slump even lower. They would be sending movers but no troops. They needed the troops just across the border in Laos. All that would be forthcoming today would be a couple of flybys, a couple of Phantoms armed with sidewinder missiles and napalm. The only rides coming down from the sky were dustoff rides for the wounded and the dead.

"You'd think the bastards could spare an Apache gunship."

He glanced down toward the base of the hill and saw the enemy coming even closer. Their fire teams had linked up: now there were two platoons in advance-and-cover formation—a frontal assault. There was little to stop them now. Without help the boys could only slow them down. Suddenly the Southern white voice of a forward air controller came on the smaller radio. That would be him circling overhead in a small Cessna. His job was to direct artillery and airstrikes, to report on the location of smoke rounds, and to adjust fire. The sergeant spoke to him briefly, then dropped the handset.

In the last minutes of his life he was able to scribble the name of his wife and her latest address on the slip of paper. He kissed the paper then folded it carefully and shoved it into the pocket of his shirt. Maybe someday someone would tell her what really happened up here. The Department of the Army would surely send her some bullshit form letter.

Down the hill the whistles of the enemy were growing even louder. Now they were shouting out that crazy battle cry of theirs. Amos Flyer knew what it meant—he had heard it once before. It meant that on this day they would all rather die than suffer defeat. The sergeant looked around for a weapon and found nothing. He slumped back and began, once again, to remember his beautiful wife. He remembered her past. In his last seconds on earth, he remembered her future. He recalled with an infallible memory that she would surely be a widow.

Down below the Salon, one of the NVA soldiers, a young man named Trin Adrong, had grabbed an armed satchel charge from a younger soldier. He had stripped himself of his pack and his shirt. His narrow, hairless chest was gleaming with sweat. He had removed his hat, then strapped the satchel charge to his chest, the detonator string held tautly in his right hand.

He had placed a copy of Mao's poems in the front of his pants. In truth, it was a Catholic Bible, hidden between crimson bindings. He had dashed ahead of the two platoons that were now positioned to give him cover fire. His Russian-made wire-rimmed glasses bobbed on his wide nose as he ran. He went at full speed toward the Salon des Refusés, his sandaled feet unmindful of the ravaged, uneven terrain that cut his ankles and shins with each step. The Chinese-made watch on his wrist had stopped working months ago. The concussion from an air strike had disabled it. Even as he ran toward his own death, Trin hated the Chinese and their cheap watches.

Twenty meters up the hill a bullet smashed his right ankle, the same one that he had broken as a boy while playing in a soccer tournament in Nha Trang. His speed dropped down to a hobble, but still he moved forward, focusing his entire being on the net and the goalie up ahead. Another bullet blew a kidney into his stomach sack before exiting just above the pelvis.

The undigested rice in his gut swelled with blood. Despite this foul recipe filling his throat, he limped onward, a trail of red rice marking his path. The sliver of jade that he had placed on his tongue earlier was cutting into his cheeks and lips. He had always carried the stone for luck and nothing more. Only women knew how to use them.

As he ran, he looked to his right to see a young, brown-skinned enemy soldier—a sergeant—taking careful aim at the satchel charge. Trin turned his body to protect the explosives. Immediately after the muzzle flash, he felt the contents of one lung filling the space in the other as black blood sprayed from his left nostril. He felt the cold wind of another exit wound. He felt himself inside out, the secret self exposed to the air and the insects.

Trin Adrong dreamed of his beautiful, barren wife as he staggered on. He dreamed of her past. He had promised her three children. He dreamed of a small restaurant on Tu Do Street in Saigon, a tiny tentable bastion of decadent capitalism that had supported four extended families and had once filled his heart with joy. In his last instant on earth, he dreamed of her future. She would be a widow. Then, somehow, he saw her in Hong Kong, opening her heart and legs to another man. Though his escaping blood boiled with envy, he wished her love and forgetfulness, then spat out the jade stone.

Down the hill from the Salon, the sapper was crossing what was once the outer perimeter. The weeping Creole sergeant at the top of the hill threw open his arms to embrace his naked wife, her stomach heaving as if in birth. For the first time ever, her soft brown skin wasn't just a bit too dark. For the first time ever, the soft rolls of flesh beneath her breasts were acceptable, perhaps even beautiful. Her careful, complicated makeup was beautiful. Her feminist, biological protest songs were suddenly lovely beyond belief.

Even her three overbearing sisters—women that only an ancient Greek playwright could love—were beautiful. The sergeant suddenly burst out laughing. Wasn't this a strange place to realize his love?

"Supposing," he said aloud to no one, "supposing there had never been slaves in America. Supposing we all spoke French. Would I have died anyway, maybe on the Maginot Line or at Dien Bien Phu? My family would have moved to Toulouse. Like all of the other African boys I would have been drafted into the army.

"Or just maybe I would have lived out my life loving Persephone on a saxophonist's pay, playing Madagascar jazz in some dingy bistro in Tripoli. We would have had children who would never have heard an English word. They could live out their lives without once saying Vietnam. God bless Le Duc Ellington et Le Comte Basie! God Bless Monsieur Jacques DeJohnette!"

He began to laugh out loud.

"Everything turns on jazz! *Toutes les choses.* Everything."

A hundred meters from the metal container box, eyes that had been frantically searching the wreckage and rubble for a target of opportunity suddenly settled on black arms upraised to caress. The stumbling sapper with his satchel charge had made the inner perimeter and had to be protected at all costs.

The eyes, peering over gun sights and down a long barrel, saw the breasts that were lifted up by the dark palms of the enemy sergeant, and for a moment thought of his own young wife in Hanoi. Her breasts were smaller than the ones that the American black man was caressing, but they were more firm and absolutely hairless and as smooth as wet stones. He smiled as he pulled the trigger. Wasn't this a strange place to think of breasts?

The AK-47 bullet that he fired was made in China and left a ring of machine grease at the point of entry: on the left heel of the Creole staff sergeant. The thin trail of Chinese grease veered sharply upward at the kneecap and followed the busy projectile to the hip bone, where it changed course again.

The woman from Louisiana smiled softly and with deep satisfaction as her husband jerked and shivered in passion, the heat in his thighs searing his eyesight. She felt his fluid love as it gushed into his pants, and she kissed him tenderly as the exiting bullet deflated his right lung and shattered his sweating, stubbled chin. She kissed the new wound as if it were a set of alluring lips.

She smiled with a woman's satisfaction as he collapsed, fully sated. As usual, the man always fell asleep right after an orgasm. Never had no staying power. Perhaps, after all these years, he has come to accept me as I am, she thought. I should have withheld sex, she mused. You might have stayed home. You might have longed for me. She reached over to gently touch his shoulder. His weight shifted under her touch. He was still awake . . . still alive, and still far away.

Just down the hill the sapper was running straight for the Salon des Refusés. He was going at full speed now, and his wounded ankle was little more than a flapping stump. His mouth was open wide and he was screaming a single stirring phrase over and over again. The phrase could barely be heard above the support fire and the volleys of return fire from the hill. His comrades heard him and his words inspired them. They would speak of his words for years to come. Then the single voice was lost in the roaring din of jet engines.

"Carolina, think about the stratifications of an open hillside, a place where earth has given way and time itself is left exposed, layer upon layer—silica, clay, diatoms, and ash. Down here at this level is the time of the swelling sea; here, the time of the desert when hot, rising air would have haunted our eyes; here is a jagged karst, a time when the world shook an abrasion into its own skin; and here are the fossil dead, here you will find love and war in the same shamble of strewn bone. Here and there, where the world has shifted and cracked open, one era will touch another. And once upon the rarest time, human hands and eyes from the distant past can seek out and find . . . search for and contact . . . hands and eyes of the present time . . . our time."

Jesse stood up from his seat next to Carolina, his eyes fixed and burning into hers.

"I know that you might be skeptical. You don't believe that such things can take place."

Carolina began to protest, but Jesse continued on. The profound fatigue that had descended upon him when he had finished his formal summation had vanished completely.

"Believe me, it happened. I am a living witness. It happened here in this city, on Potrero Hill, and on a hill near the eastern edge of Laos. I was there, at both places. Carolina, almost three decades after that enemy sapper ran up that hill in Vietnam, at the very same instant in time that his body flew toward its own doom, Persephone Flyer looked up to see two boys standing in front of the glass door of the Amazon Luncheonette.

"Persephone knew one of the boys. In fact she had just met him the week before. Somehow she had been drawn toward this frightening boy. Mai knew one of the boys, too—the one she had christened the Biscuit Boy. It was the sight of the second boy that sent a cold chill down her spine. There had always been rumors on the hill that he was insane. There were those who spoke of demonism and incest. Others told of a bad seed.

"Mai looked deeply into Reggie's face, while he stood there leering back. He had a handsome, almost pretty face, but his eyes were inhuman. A shudder ran down her back as she realized that she had seen those eyes before: in her own husband's altered face when he went off to fight a war, eyes that looked down on her love as an expendable, bourgeois luxury. Mai saw death in Reggie's eyes and knew that her husband's war had reached across time to claim her."

"Oh no, it's that fool Little Reggie and one of his little lackey friends. I'll take care of it," she said wearily as she walked to the door. Persephone opened the door and the young man with Little Reggie held up an empty pot and smiled sheepishly. The lid was in his other hand. Behind her, Mai spoke the young man's name in a strange mixture of tenderness and worry.

"*Duá bé giao bánh bích quy*. Biscuit Boy."

"I'm so sorry, boys," said Persephone, opening the door just wide enough to speak face to face, "but we're all sold out. There's not a drop of spaghetti sauce left. Come back on Saturday and we'll have seafood gumbo and salmon croquettes, too. I'll save some especially for the both of you."

As she attempted to close the door the one named Little Reggie suddenly pushed violently at the glass, shoving a stunned and frightened Persephone backward into the kitchen.

"Get out of here, boy!" she shouted. "Go on, now, get out of here before I call the cops!"

Little Reggie reached inside his jacket and pulled out his nine-millimeter pistol. Grinning weirdly, his head cocked to one side, he pointed the gun directly at Persephone's face.

"You already forgot about your future lover man, old woman?" sneered Little Reggie. "I treated you right the other night, now didn't I? I give you a little sniff of cocaine and a little roll on the kitchen floor, and I didn't charge you shit for the coke, neither. I knows about womens. I knows about bitches. For a minute back then you forgot you was a fuckin' widow, didn't you? You felt like a real woman. I figure you owe me somethin' more than a few wet kisses and a hug. I could see it in your eyes, bitch. You wanted more. You want some of what Little Reggie's got. You see, I likes older women. Never had nothin' but older women. Shit, I been gettin' laid since I was five years old. I gots experience."

He smiled proudly toward Calvin.

"No one can say that Little Reggie can't do the nasty."

Persephone looked painfully toward Mai. There was no judgment to be found in her face. The boy with the gun turned to his friend who was still standing in the doorway. "Get in here, Calvin! Get the fuck in here, goddamn it!"

Calvin stepped inside, closing the door behind him. He looked at the gun, then looked at beautiful Mai. His dark eyes were filled with apology and fear.

"I just wants a little somethin' for all my troubles," said Little Reggie with a cold, leering smile, "and I know exactly how I wants to get paid." He turned toward Calvin and pointed toward the bedroom in back.

"That's where I'm gonna screw the bitch, right back there."

"I'm sorry I ever laid eyes on you, Reggie, or whatever your name is," said Persephone in an angry, seething monotone. "Be happy with what you got, boy. You got a moment of weakness, that's all. Dear Lord, I should have never let you touch me or kiss me. But it's been so long." She looked into Mai's eyes again as her voice trailed off into mute contrition.

"Now, you got it all wrong, lady," shouted Reggie. "It was me bein' generous. It's me who's gonna give you a mercy fuck—and put you out of your widow misery."

He stepped forward and put his left hand on Persephone's breast, but she brushed it away and stepped back.

"It was me offering to give you a mercy fuck," screamed Little Reggie angrily. "I'm fixing to give you the real deal instead of one of them battery vibrators." He placed his hand over his crotch as he spoke. "The real deal beat a dyke bitch's tongue any old day." He leered at Mai as he spoke. "Take a real man to turn a lesbian around. Now give me what I want! Don't you know your husband ain't never comin' back?"

"I'm calling the police," said Persephone. She turned to walk toward the back room. At that instant Little Reggie swung the nine-millimeter Glock, slamming the metal muzzle savagely into the side of Persephone's head. As her friend fell heavily to the ground, Mai began to scream but stopped suddenly as the dark automatic pistol was leveled at her face.

"Chink bitch, get the fuck into that refrigerator!" Reggie shrieked as he motioned with the gun toward the new Sub-Zero. Sweat was pouring from Reggie's face and neck. His shirt was stained with it. It was not the sweat of exertion, but the wet, oily gleam of excitement. Calvin winced at the sheer coldness and cruelty in his friend's face and voice. He had seen it before, and the sight of it now sent waves of desperation through him. Mai opened the door and climbed in.

"Get that rope over there and tie it shut," Reggie shouted at Calvin, who did as he was told. As Calvin closed the heavy door on the refrigerator, he saw Mai making the sign of the cross and moving her lips in silence. He left the door slightly ajar so that she would have air, then he tied the door handles together using a slip knot. He hoped that Mai had seen the fear in his face. He hoped that she would stay put.

"Please don't move," he whispered desperately into the darkness of the refrigerator.

A sweating, tearful Calvin watched as Little Reggie smashed out the lights in the front room, then dragged Persephone's limp body by the arm into the small bedroom. Reggie pulled her onto the bed, then turned toward Calvin and smiled a toothy, carnivorous smile as he unzipped his pants. His other hand had snaked down the front of Persephone's dress and was wriggling within her brassiere. As he worked, the low light of a bedside lamp filled Reggie's face with haggard, ghostly shadows.

"You can have some of this when I'm done." Reggie laughed in a brutish, guttural voice. "You earned it, my man. You a virgin, ain't you? Now that I think of it, if you don't fuck her after I'm done, I'll shoot you; I'll cap your sorry ass right here."

Suddenly a thought struck Reggie, causing him to stand silently for a moment, the gun in his hand lowered.

"Is you a virgin, Calvin? You a cherry, ain't you? You ain't touched my mama? You see my mama naked, ain't you? You dead if you seen my mama."

Calvin shook his head, no. Suddenly the smile returned to Reggie's face.

"I know you dig the gook bitch. Go ahead, go get her. It's easy—just do what she don't want you to do. That's how I learned. We partners, ain't we? Sure, we be partners."

Calvin turned away angrily and walked to the front door. His face was a grid map of agony and frustration. As he did so, he heard the sound of two sharp impacts and of glass breaking and falling to the floor. Little Reggie had smashed both of the cherished framed photographs with his gun. Reggie despised photographs; his mother's home was filled with them. In the darkness, Reggie shouted out to Calvin to be on the lookout for cops.

Suddenly Calvin saw Persephone running wide-eyed through the kitchen, her panties around her right ankle. She was breathing hard and sobbing loudly. There were tears and mascara streaming down her face. Calvin watched her run through the front door and out into the street. Ten seconds later he watched as a cursing Little Reggie came hopping through the kitchen, zipping up his pants while holding a shoe in his left hand and the Glock in his right.

Persephone ran across the street in her bare feet. Her panties fell off as she ran and were blown beneath a car on the south side of Twentieth. When she reached the pay phone across the street, she lifted the receiver and began to dial 911.

Jesse placed his hand on Carolina's knee. He leaned toward her until their faces were just six inches apart. He noticed that Carolina's large eyes were even larger now. She was shivering. Jesse slowly began to realize how chilling these words could be to someone who had led a quiet and normal life. For an instant he considered stopping, but that was impossible now.

"At precisely the same instant in time, nearly thirty years before, on that ravaged hill in Vietnam, the Creole staff sergeant keyed the radio for his final call. He contacted Strongarm just as his tearful wife in San Francisco heard the dispassionate voice of the emergency operator. Back in the Amazon Luncheonette, Mai Adrong slipped out of the refrigerator, stepped past Biscuit Boy, and began to run toward her friend at the exact same time that her husband, Trin Adrong, began his run up the hill near Laos—a lifetime before. She approached Persephone just as the terrible shots rang out, both from Reggie's Glock and from the rifle of a North Vietnamese soldier providing cover fire for her husband. Hearing both shots, she began screaming in the street, her mouth a perfect resonator for her husband's last words: *'Tien Lan! Tien Lan! Tien Lan!'*

" 'Forward, comrades!' She screamed the chilling NVA battle cry. *'Tien Lan!'* When Mai reached the body of her dying friend—her dying sister—she flung herself forward to protect her with her own unmarked body. Persephone Flyer, in turn, threw her weakening arms around her friend and, sobbing and sighing, locked her lovely fingers together. In the same microsecond—in the same place—years before, the widower Trin Adrong threw himself headlong into the Salon des Refusés, into the outstretched, embracing arms of the American sergeant."

Jesse's gaze moved slowly across Carolina's lovely face. Her eyes were filled with tears.

"As with all deaths hand to hand, for an instant in time the two men embraced and could have been mistaken for lovers. Face to face, their sweat and fear mixed with the molecules of charged air between their bodies. For a slice of a second they saw each other perfectly, they saw the face of the enemy as if in a mirror.

"For the thinnest slice of a confusing, then crystalline moment, one soldier caught a sullen glimpse of Persephone and the other saw poor Mai. In the street on Potrero Hill, the women, clutching each other, envisioned the image of their own husbands in the other's dimming eyes. In the last instant before the satchel charge drove his atoms against those of the container box, the sergeant mouthed a single word into the radio handset."

Jesse's eyes rested on his own left hand. Carolina had placed her small hand upon his.

"Persephone spoke a single word into the phone before the bullet slammed savagely into her skull and cut through her brain, through her memories, through a hundred recipes.

" 'Amos,' she moaned, just as death began in her. Her lips had formed their most precious word.

" 'Persephone,' he grunted just as death began in him, just as all those nights of work performed by his parents in their marriage bed disintegrated into a fine, wet dust. He spoke her name as Trin's glasses were blown from a faceless head, as his Bible flew and burned—the scrap of paper in the Creole's jacket rising on the hot concussive wind, then settling into the Bible, somewhere in the book of Ruth."

Jesse paused, gathering himself and forming the next few sentences in his mind. Somehow they came easily, effortlessly. Carolina remained silent.

"Weeks later, a platoon of NVA would revisit the abandoned hill to reclaim their dead. A young soldier would find the glasses, the Chinese wristwatch, and the Catholic Bible in Vietnamese, and carefully close the book on an unreadable text; on a cryptogram—Persephone's name and address in San Francisco, our city.

"Sergeant Flyer uttered 'Persephone' just as the dog tag and chain around his neck passed through him as though he were entirely without substance, as though the space between his atoms had increased a billionfold."

Jesse reached into his pocket and pulled out a dog tag. He held it up for Carolina to see. She read the name of Amos Flyer.

"As he died, the chain and this dog tag pierced the metal container wall to hang undamaged on the other side—as though something, some small thing in all of the wars between humans, between men and women, must remain undamaged. In the midst of flames they each spoke the other's name, fully wedded at last."

Jesse stopped speaking for a moment. The effort to tell the story in its entirety was taking its toll.

"In the same instant that the first gunshot rang out, Mai came running from the Amazon Luncheonette, her bare feet bleeding and leaves of lemon grass streaming from her pocket. She was screaming Persephone's name and some strange words over and over again into the night air. Though Reggie could not understand them, the words frightened him. They were words of immovable purpose moving.

"Turning away from Persephone's body, Little Reggie saw Mai approaching and saw curious faces beginning to appear in the lighted windows of Twentieth Street. Shades were lifting, curtains were separating. Witnesses were watching. He didn't hide his face; for some reason he wanted to be seen. He wanted identifications to be made. Closing his left eye Little Reggie began tracking Mai with the sights of the nine-millimeter, refusing to pull the trigger until the shot was clear and certain.

"When the small woman fell onto the body of her dying friend, when the embrace was perfect, he squeezed off a single round. It would be enough. Reggie smiled to himself. Without knowing it, he began laughing out loud. This was even better than rape. This was better than love. Every witness heard the name 'Calvin' echoing through the streets and dove for cover as Little Reggie ran from window to window, pointing the gun as a grim warning.

"Suddenly he stopped, as though he had been surprised by something he saw. Slowly he lowered the gun and attempted to fire a third round toward the direction of the dying women. For an instant, Calvin thought he saw someone kneeling by the two bodies. When he looked closer, he saw only a single, dark mound of death. He could discern no distinct forms. A confused Reggie walked toward the luncheonette and gave the gun to Biscuit Boy. As always, it would be his job to clean it and hide it away.

"The Biscuit Boy, shivering with hatred, suddenly leveled the gun at Reggie, then pulled the trigger. The hammer clicked, slamming a firing pin into an empty chamber. Reggie laughed at the impotent boy with his harmless gun, then the two ran south down Missouri Street toward home."

Carolina had never been in a courtroom before. She had never heard a closing argument. She had always refused to take part in the staid and stylized combat that she considered to be Jesse's substitute for the land war in Asia that so dominated his life. Jesse smiled at her. Carolina smiled back, wondering how it could be that such sensitive arguments and passionate words could flow from such an inaccessible, seemingly unfeeling man.

Suddenly the thought struck her. Perhaps only a man who had gone dead inside could speak so easily of death. Perhaps all the words had been learned by rote, an entire vocabulary taken from some arcane dialect of grief. How did Jesse feel about words? wondered Carolina. Were metaphor and symbol just another form of ammunition? She had always hoped otherwise, but the day would be coming soon when she would give up trying to understand him . . . or to love him.

"On the cold sidewalk, two women descended degree by degree until they were the temperature of the ambient air, of the soil. But in the last few seconds of their life they had found the answer to their fondest and most dreadful question. Gone were the fears and the endless speculations that had haunted their lives. Now they knew for certain how their dear young husbands had perished. Now they knew that they had always been cursed in their knowing. They understood that two marriages, worlds apart, had resulted in two more. The two women, like their husbands, embraced in death."

Jesse pulled his eyes away from Carolina and turned them toward the now empty jury box.

"But before the final flicker of light was fully extinguished, both women heard a single voice, a single set of lips against their ears. A man ran through a haze of gun smoke, up to the women, just after the bullets found their targets. He was a man in rags and torn shoes. He wore a filthy army fatigue jacket and jungle boots. He kneeled down beside the women and spoke to them despite the hail of gunfire that sliced the air above his head.

"He blessed them even as claymore mines were being clicked off just beneath his position by squads of desperate boys. He tended his panicked flock despite the horrific moans of grief and pain around him, despite the roar of air support. He bent down unmindful of bullets at his shoulders and just above his hair. On Potrero Hill he had finally found the strength to open the body bags and bravely look upon the face of death.

"As a good field chaplain should, he absolved Persephone and Mai of their few sins, sending them from this shattered place to the placid arms of God. Then, after his final amen and shalom, he kissed Mai's face and neck, her beautiful face and neck, and began to whisper.

" *'Je suis ici, mon amour,'* " said Jesse, recalling the chaplain's words as he had spoken them to the jury.

" *'Estoy aquí. C'est moi, Vô Dahn.* Remember me? I am the one who is no one. If French were the universal tongue, my love; if only Oscar Peterson were really Oscar Fils de Pierre; if only there were Mexicans in space illegally dashing across Martian borders and Aztec soldiers in County Cork—then you would have a loving husband today, my dearest Cassandra. You would both be alive today.'

"He touched the faces of the two women, closing their eyelids with his fingers. Before speaking his final words to them, he wondered, once again, what Mai had done since he left her in that small apartment in Hong Kong. After so many years, he had found his Vietnamese lover once again. He had always longed to see her, to touch her perfect skin. He had floated around her in recent years, swimming just out of sight, living just outside the perimeter of her life, wondering who she had become and how she had met the other Amazon woman.

"He kissed her one final time before running away. But as he ran, he resolved to perform a single act of mercy, a single act of violence."

Jesse walked to the defense table and stood in front of his chair. He ended every closing argument at this spot. He turned to face Carolina.

"Like Abraham, he had heard the behest of heaven, but this time no angel would intercede. The third man, the ragged stranger, the army chaplain who testified before you, Carolina, and who so long ago abandoned his flock and his post on an anonymous hill in Vietnam, sobbed his final words to Mai before disappearing into the night: 'You can love me less, but please love me forever.'

"Calvin Thibault is no soldier. There is too much humanity in him, and it is growing stronger each day. I asked the jury to set him free, Carolina, would you?"

Carolina nodded yes as he continued to speak. She would set him free.

"The brutal warrior in this case has already been punished. He shares the grim fate of his five victims. Little Reggie Harp was a creature of desire."

Jesse walked back to Carolina and sat down even more weary than before.

"And when desire is stripped of humanity," he said as his final words, "all that remains is war."

14

a night in tunisia

On the third floor of the Hall of Justice, in a courtroom jammed with angry and saddened parents, Judge Steven Shaiken was in the process of sentencing defendant Jeremiah Bigelow, who had been convicted of thirty-four counts of child molestation.

"Quiet in the courtroom!" cried the bailiff in a vain attempt to intercept the scores of exclamations of grief, revenge, and rage that were flying across the courtroom and striking the back of the defendant's head. When silence fell there was a perfect grouping of invisible darts crowded into a cowlick bull's-eye.

"On court thirty-four," said the judge wearily, "like all of the counts that preceded it, I find no reason to sentence you to the midterm, and given your past record and your cruel and heartless behavior in this case, I certainly find no reason at all to sentence you to the mitigated term. Therefore, you shall receive the aggravated term of eight years in prison for this the thirty-forth and final count. Now, sir, I think the arithmetic here is fairly straightforward. I never took algebra in high school, Mr. Bigelow, but I've got a feeling that some good, old-fashioned multiplication is all that's needed here."

One or two nervous laughs were quickly choked off in the audience of tearful parents and tiny victims. The judge adjusted his bifocals while he scribbled his computations on a sheet of yellow paper. At his desk below the bench, the clerk mimicked His Honor's every move, including the snaking tongue that slid out of the left side of his mouth and wriggled with each phase of the computation.

Upon reaching a product, the judge retracted his tongue, sighed and drew a heavy line across the paper. Below the line was a single total. The clerk turned and whispered excitedly to the judge. The two were in agreement.

"Mr. Bigelow, the aggregate term that you must serve is two hundred and seventy-two years in state prison."

A wave of applause grew from a tentative ripple into a tsunami that washed across the jury box and the defense table and drowned all decorum. Suddenly the defendant at the defense table began to quake with emotion, his shoulders heaving and his gray fingernails digging into the oak table where he had sat stoically for thirteen weeks of trial by jury. The defendant stood bolt upright. With his chest heaving he stared at the judge.

"Mr. Bigelow, I will now read your credit for time served into the record and then I will proceed to review your parole rights."

"His parole officer's grandfather hasn't been born yet," muttered the prosecutor smugly and almost beneath his breath.

Some parents of the victimized children began to laugh at the prosecutor's remark, laughter that was a weak hybrid of relief and melancholy. The defendant had heard both the prosecutor's remark and the derisive laughter in the audience behind him, and began to scream. His face turned beet red and his eyes welled with tears.

"You punish my desires," he screamed while sobbing. "I can't do that kind of time! You punish my desires! Two hundred and seventy-two years! I just can't do that kind of time!"

Judge Shaiken's face suddenly lost its official demeanor. Now an almost fatherly tenderness settled into his eyes as he removed his bifocals and looked down from the high bench into the tear-drowned eyes of the convicted man.

"Son," he said softly, "the law of this land, in all of its wisdom, does not require that you do all of that time. Just do what you can, son. Just do what you can."

Three floors below Jeremiah Bigelow, Jesse sat alone in the House of Toast. There was a cup of cold coffee in front of him that had a shiny film of rainbow-hued oil floating on its surface. Using a toothpick, Jesse was carefully probing the liquid in an effort to save a tiny gnat that had flown into the slick. He slowly lifted the gnat from the goo and set it down softly on a paper napkin that might serve to absorb the sludge. As he bent closer to watch the life-and-death struggle of the little insect, the table began to fill with lawyers. Like true defense attorneys, each new arrival at the table looked at the gnat and wondered if it could be saved.

"Jury's out?" asked Newton, who already knew the answer to the question. "You can't do anything about it now, man. All I want to know is: do you have a shot?"

Jesse nodded without looking up. Biscuit had a shot.

"Any requests for readback?"

It was the voice of Chris Gauger. Jesse shook his head.

"Not a peep," said Jesse. "They slammed the door on that jury room and haven't made a sound for five hours. They didn't even ask to have the physical evidence."

"They know what they're gonna do," added Matt Gonzalez, who was leaning over to see what Jesse was watching so closely. "Whatever the verdict is, they ain't gonna wait three or four days to decide it. Is that some kinda mosquito?"

"No, it's a gnat," answered Jesse solemnly, "and I think he's about to succumb to this coffee."

Jesse tried to smile, but couldn't. The pressure of the verdict wouldn't let him. Calvin Thibault could die of old age in prison. It would be better than the death penalty, but not much better. Jesse looked around the table at his friends. They had come to support him, to distract him. Soon enough the stories would begin.

"I had this guy, just last week," began Newton Lam, "a young punk Sureño—you know, one of those lost kids from the gangs down on Thirteenth Street. This kid had about as much of a future as a flightless pigeon in Chinatown. Anyway, he's got this girlfriend, a cute little *chulita* named Dorothy Lopez.

"Now Dorothy goes to night school over at State and she gets this part-time job with a big architectural firm. They let her work around her class schedule and she could do her homework during her lunch hour. Our Dorothy is moving up."

A groan traversed the full diameter of the table. Too many stories began this way. No one really wanted to hear the end of this tale, yet no one would leave while it was being told.

"She rents an apartment in the Richmond District and moves our boy in. She cooks for him, does his laundry, she even irons his gang clothing. Red shirts, red socks, even the guy's underwear is red. She's going places, and for some reason she wants to take the punk with her—God knows why—but our hero wasn't going to better himself without a fight."

"Women are like that."

It was Freya, who had taken the seat next to Jesse's.

"Anyway, the fool starts to beat her. He beats her when she gets good grades; he beats her when she uses a word that he's never heard—which ends up being a whole lot of abuse. The day she finished a *New York Times* crossword puzzle, he almost killed her. He beat her for twenty minutes when she trimmed off all that long Mexicana hair and had it curled at a beauty parlor. But the last straw was a tiny leather miniskirt. When she put that little thing on to go off to work with all of those male architects, it sent *mi hombre* over the edge.

"So my man, 'Wanderer'—that was his gang name, given to him because he once walked the five or six miles to Daly City, a legendary exploit in some circles—my man Wanderer pulled a gun and ordered her to quit school and to quit work and to move back to his Rancho Grande, his bitchin' little house trailer parked behind Chewy's Casa de Menudo."

"Ah, young love," sighed Freya. "What I wouldn't give to wake up in the morning to the smell of raw tripe."

"When she steadfastly refused to quit her job and her classes," continued Newton, "the idiot shoots her twice, point-blank, in that beautiful, hopeful face."

"Oh, God," groaned Jesse, "did we really need to hear this story? It's just tragedy—plain old run-of-the-mill, depthless, heartrending tragedy; beauty slaughtered by mindless, numbing stupidity. Where is the irony? How could this story ever hope to meet our table's lofty standards of Olympic ignorance?"

Newton only smiled. The look on his face told everyone seated that there was more . . . more than just endless death for a lovely young woman and a life sentence served out in a room of frigid concrete and steel. There was more here than just the savage shattering of a promising future.

"After the defendant was sentenced for murder, I was stopped in the hallway by a small woman—a dark, very Indian-looking woman.

It was the defendant's mother. I had only seen her once, at the arraignment. She never attended a day of the trial. With four other kids, she couldn't afford to. She stopped me by pulling on my sleeve as I was leaving the courtroom. I remember that I looked directly into her eyes. They seemed so filled with compassion and grief, but that was only my imagination.

"I took her small hands into my own and was about to offer her my deepest condolences when she spread her lips and spat a huge wad of spit into my face. I swear, she must've been saving up that sputum for a whole week. It took both sides of my handkerchief and one sleeve to wipe it off. Then she sneered at me and spoke a sentence I'll never forget."

The entire table had grown silent. Every lawyer sat poised to hear the woman's words.

" 'There's no justice,' she shrieked. 'I read about this guy over in Nevada—this man in Carson City—who kills a woman by shooting her twelve times, and he got twenty-five years to life, Mr. Lawyer. My boy only shot that little bitch two times and he gets the exact, same sentence! What kind of justice is that?' "

A muffled groan made its way around the table. There was no gesture, no human sound to adequately express what they felt. The groan was more like a silent prayer, a benediction for the dignity, the delusion, and the dolor of motherhood. In her mind her son should have received one-sixth the sentence of the man in Nevada, having used that fraction of bullets to do the job.

"I had this guy . . ."

It was Chris, starting another story in order to break the spell of sadness. As expected, the mood of the table changed the moment those four magical, incantatory words were spoken.

"I had this guy who was charged with bank robbery. He and his codefendant had been cellmates in Soledad Prison and had spent their nights trying to come up with an airtight, foolproof way to rob a bank. When they were released, they came to San Francisco to report to their parole agents and to put their magnificent plan into action."

The table of lawyers settled into their chairs, enthralled by the endless possibilities that this scenario presented. There were newly filled cups of coffee on the table. Even the gnat on the napkin seemed to be listening as his wings dried. Above the insect, Jesse seemed to have forgotten about the twelve jurors that were, at that very moment, deciding the fate of his client.

"As part of their plan they bought a real junker, one of those big gas-guzzling Oldsmobiles. They bought a pistol, some ski masks, gloves, some magnets, and two sets of stolen California license plates. First they glued the license plates back to back so that all they would have to do to change plates is flip them over. They glued the magnets to the fenders, and the double-sided plates were held in place by the magnets. Pretty smart, eh?"

No one answered. If these guys were really smart, Chris would not be telling their story at this table. Everyone knew that the robbers had been caught—that was a given—but no one knew how it had happened and how the two suspects had ensured their own failure. Therein lay the tale.

"So, my boy is the wheel man. He gets in his car every day for two weeks and drives around the bank so many times that he can do it in his sleep. He knows that block: every parking space, every driveway, every rut in the road. He drives it in the daylight, he drives it at sunset. He drives around that block at two in the morning with no lights. Pretty soon he's driving it with his eyes closed, counting out the seconds, stopping at stop signs and making the turns perfectly. My man was ready! This wasn't going to be one of those amateurish, sloppy, drug-induced jobs that had landed him in prison four times.

"So now comes the big day. It's the shortest day of the year, so the bank is still open when it's dark outside. My boy had checked the calendar and chose this day for the auspicious lighting conditions. He has thought of everything. Following their master plan, he dropped his partner in front of the bank and took up his position around the block. His buddy puts on his generic, secondhand ski mask, pulls out his untraceable pistol, turns on his stolen walkie-talkie, then saunters into the bank. In a few minutes, just as planned, he screams into the walkie-talkie, 'Come and get me, man. Come and get me.'

"Just as planned, my man jams on the gas pedal and starts his triumphal tour around the block. Now my man is grinning from ear to ear. This is going to be a walk in the park. My man is so confident in this score that he closes his eyes and counts out the stops and the turns just like he practiced."

The table was buzzing. Now the key to the story had been placed in front of them. There it was: the incredible hubris of a four-time loser. The potential for irony was staggering.

"So now the gunman is running like a madman out of the bank, the alarm is ringing behind him. The wheelman is speed-shifting with his eyes shut. In his excited condition what he doesn't realize is that he is moving at twice the speed of his practice runs. He makes the first turn all right only because the parking lot at that corner is empty. He runs over a few shrubs and a tricycle and steers that Oldsmobile right down the sidewalk toward the bank."

"Oh, Christ," moaned Jesse.

"My wheel man is dreaming about what he's gonna do with all of that money. He's dreaming about drinking wine from bottles that have corks; he's dreaming about buying a whore who uses deodorant and has all of her teeth. He's even thinking about an ocean voyage over to East Oakland."

"He's thinking big," said Matt Gonzalez.

"On the seat next to him the walkie-talking is squawking, 'Come and get me, come and get me,' the bank alarm is getting louder and louder, there are sirens in the distance and frightened pedestrians on the sidewalk are diving left and right to avoid his speeding bumper.

"So my man arrives at the bank, throws open the door, and looks around but can't see his partner anywhere. He gets on the walkie-talkie but there's no response. Now he's pissed. He thinks the bastard has run off with the take. So he steps out of the car and the moment his feet hit the pavement—*boom!*, *boom!*—a bullet slams through each ankle. Screaming in pain, he falls to the ground with his arms raised in the air. 'I ain't armed,' he screams over and over before he realizes there ain't no cops on the scene, not a single cop. There's nobody around."

No one at the table dared to breathe or even swallow their coffee as they waited impatiently for the arcane denouement that must certainly follow. Chris paused a long moment to make his friends suffer, then began once again.

"Here he is, lying on the ground, his ankles are bleeding profusely, the car is running, and my man thinks his double-crossing partner has made off with the take and shot him in the feet to keep him from following. As he's lying there bleeding on the sidewalk, he begins to hear a faint whisper. He stops groaning a moment to listen and the whisper grows louder. Now he can just make out the words that are being repeated over and over again, 'You stupid motherfucker.' "

Now the table of lawyers was alive with that tension and human energy that precedes unrestrained laughter.

"My man looks carefully around himself and suddenly realizes that his partner is right there next to him . . . lying just a few feet away."

"Under the car . . ." Jesse's head fell back in amazed disbelief.

"Under the car," repeated Chris Gauger.

Now the entire table exploded with laughter.

"You mean to say," said a breathless Matt Gonzalez, "that when the gunman exited the bank he was run over by the getaway car?"

Chris nodded in the affirmative. "Smashed by a daydreaming fool who was driving with his eyes shut."

"The gunman was six feet from the door when he was hit. The car dragged him thirty feet. He was so pissed at the driver that he used his last ounce of strength to shoot him in the ankles. It seems that he had recognized the boots that they'd purchased for the robbery at a local navy surplus. There they were, lying in the street, their blood mixing to form a small lake, the ratpack of bills spewing red ink all over them. They see all of that ink and think they're bleeding to death so they're screaming like banshees. The guy under the car was still screaming, 'Stupid motherfucker' into his walkie-talkie when the police cars arrived."

The human energy burst forth in waves of laughter, filling the corridors and hallways that communicated with the House of Toast. Never a laughter of ridicule, it was rather the laughter of sympathy, of frustration at the futility of crime at the street level, at curb level. It was laughter at the perfect robbery.

"My boy went to trial in his custom, motorized wheelchair. So did the codefendant. Those two wouldn't even look at each other. They spent the entire trial trying to short out the other's battery pack. They never spoke a word during the entire proceeding."

"Where are they now?" asked Freya.

"They're both in Folsom Prison now, campaigning righteously for wheelchair access to the mess hall."

All of a sudden the smile on Jesse's lips faded. At the entrance to the House of Toast stood Manny Valenzuela, the bailiff from his trial court. The bailiff signaled to Jesse, who rose from his seat just as the little gnat lifted off from the napkin. The jury had a verdict.

Calvin "Biscuit Boy" Thibault walked jauntily down Seventh Street, the Hall of Justice disappearing in the fog behind him. He was wearing a large smile and the new, used suit that his lawyer had purchased for him. It was a three-button, single-breasted Italian suit. This very morning he had bidden adieu to his time machine; he had rolled up the mattress and blankets of his jail bed and cast one long last look at the torn cocoon from which he had emerged. The entire jail had celebrated his release.

He turned up Mississippi Street and made the long climb up to Twentieth Street. At the corner he cast a short glance to his right and caught a glimpse of what was once the Amazon Luncheonette. The street was cast in full sunlight now, the darkness of that night somewhat dispelled. Someone had converted Persephone and Mai's lovely building into a drab laundromat. His eyes did not linger there long.

Straight ahead was the hill that had once been his home. But now nothing about it was familiar to him. Now he saw with new eyes, eyes like a starlight scope, tuned to foreign spectrums. Now he saw what he had never seen before: roaming squads of fatherless boys, single mothers living on C-rations, marauding bands of tiny mercenaries proudly wearing their insignia of rank and assignment. On the side of the hill he saw the killing zone where four boys had gone down. Biscuit Boy gazed upon his own hill of birth and saw dimly what had once been his own impoverished life.

Calvin smiled to himself once more. What had his lawyer said to him so often? When desire is stripped of humanity? Now he saw the truth of it in every corner, cupboard, and crevice of Potrero Hill. Desire was there, leaking from the drainpipes and heading for the ocean untreated. Desire was leaping electrically down the wires that dangled from all the rusting antennas that clotted the rooftops. Desire was being pumped into gas tanks and rammed violently into the chambers of cheap weapons. Desire was being smoked in crack pipes and injected into the crooks of arms.

Humanity was hard to come by on this hill, but desire was everywhere. Calvin could never have suspected that naked desire was leering at him at that very moment from an apartment window on the hill. He could not have known that purest desire stripped of humanity was sizing him up, evaluating his strength, and moving into a position of strategic advantage.

High up on the hill there were old friends beckoning him back, welcoming him back to his old world. Biscuit could see their arms waving, their cell phones and guns glinting in the sun, but he turned his back to them. "Where are you goin', man," they screamed at him. "You can't make it out there, even in them new threads. Is you crazy?" they yelled. "Is you out you brain? Ain't nothin' out there but the enemy."

His little brother Angelo the Pickle was up there, too, waving him away, telling him to never come back.

Duá bé giao bánh bích quy. Biscuit Boy considered kickin' back with the fellas, firing up a pipe full of crack cocaine, and tellin' all the boys about his murder trial—about how he had walked scot-free. He glanced up toward the apartment of Princess Sabine. He knew she was at home. She was always home. A mental image of her naked body made him grin. She had shown her photos to every boy on the hill. He hesitated for a moment while Sabine's face slowly dissolved into the face of beautiful Mai. Biscuit Boy raised his voice as he turned and walked away from it all.

"If that there library over in Alexandria, Egypt, was still around here today, there sure as shit could be plenty of homeboys on the moon," he called out to his old friends as he walked down Missouri toward Eighteenth Street. "Brothers on the moon." He imagined a golden BMW cruising the lunar surface, the woofers of a boom box flailing vainly in a vacuum.

Biscuit Boy never heard the bullet that sent him to the coroner's office.

When the padre heard the gunshot, it was broad daylight. The sound of a high-velocity round snapped him out of his meditations. He immediately laced up his steel-arched jungle boots and bolted from his hooch. The ancient book that had been on his lap tumbled to the ground. Triangulating echoes, he ran as hard as he could toward the source of the sound.

He ran up Mississippi Street to Twentieth, and when he saw what waited for him there he let loose a cold howl of fathomless grief that could be heard by all on the hill. Every living human being on Potrero Hill was chilled to the marrow by the depth of sadness in the scream. Bones decomposing on the hill near Laos shivered in their root-bound graves when the cry reached them. Upon hearing the voice of a long lost son, the Mekong sloshed and swelled its recognition. Bodies buried in her silt trembled and rose surface-bound, as if anxious to hear the howl.

Lieutenant Calvert, Padre Carvajal, Mr. Homeless, Vô Dahn found the Biscuit Boy shivering spasmodically and spurting blood on the sidewalk, his arms still clutching the large manila envelope of personal items that all released prisoners are given. Just this morning the padre had witnessed the exaltation at Biscuit Boy's acquittal on all charges. There had been joyous volleys of gunfire all over Potrero Hill. There had even been a celebration at the homeless encampment. Now, this afternoon, happiness had suddenly transformed into mourning. There was blood on the boy's new secondhand suit. His face was filled with the look of helpless disbelief that the army chaplain had seen so often.

Strewn in a wide circle about Calvin's body were paperback books and dog-eared pieces of notepaper. The paragraphs that he had written at his lawyer's direction were bloodstained now, fluttering and tumbling off to join all the other windborne litter that was destined to embrace the gutter and curb. Calvin was bleeding profusely, breathing sporadically, and coughing up lumps of black bile onto the cement beneath his head.

The bullet had entered at his neck below the jaw and had exited just beneath the right ear. The sidewalk behind him had been splattered with cartilage and hair.

The chaplain knelt by Biscuit's side. He had knelt just this way for the two beautiful women. He held Biscuit's hand and bent down to brush his left ear with his lips.

"*Ta là loì nói. Ta là dao.* I am the Word. I am the Way."

He had begun to pray when he chanced to look up and see his own violent death coming for him. But the chaplain refused to budge— he refused to bend to terror or turn away from his flock as he had done so long ago. On this day he would stand fast and properly send the boy to meet the Father. As death advanced, he spoke aloud for all the hill to hear.

"God damn every deskbound colonel in Da Nang."

The first round missed his head by inches as he made the sign of the cross on the boy's forehead. The second round, just seconds later, entered at Vô Dahn's back, entering near the bridge of a Sephardic violin.

Months before, on this same street, the padre had run from the bodies of Persephone and Mai, the fingers of his hands still wet with their blood, his face wrenched and distorted with agony. He had staggered down to the homeless encampment and crawled into his hooch, where he had sat davening and shivering for hours, bathed in yellow candlelight and clutching an ancient, earth-stained bag made of oiled lambskins. Just a few years ago he had returned to his ancestral home—the collapsing house on the pockmarked hill in Mexico—and unearthed his written inheritance. In recent months his songs in Ladino and Yiddish had brought tears to the eyes of his homeless comrades.

Sometime near dawn, after the police, the ambulance, and the medical examiners had left the scene at the Amazon Luncheonette, carrying with them the bodies of Persephone and Mai, the cantor had emerged from his hovel and walked quietly across the compound to the poorest of the hooches. In his right hand was the tallis he had removed from his ancient copy of the Torah.

The thick woven cloth had been pressed between those scrolls for ten generations. Kneeling down beside a sleeping Little Reggie Harp, he had wound the ends of the tallis around his palms and stretched it between his hands. Then after a short Southern Baptist prayer and a request for forgiveness in Yiddish, he had strangled the life from a yellow-eyed boy who had chosen not to struggle.

After Reggie's shoes were removed from his feet, a black homeless veteran—a Marine corporal with enormous dreadlocks—had sung "Day Is Done" in a perfect tenor. The padre had thought fondly of skinny Cornelius as he listened while preparing a small monument to the dead boy. He had placed a metal crucifix in the left shoe. It had been removed from the body of one of Reggie's victims just as the poor dying boy had breathed his last. The padre himself had pulled it from the boy's neck.

The photograph of naked Sabine had been taken from the body of a second boy. The photo had been taped to a string and worn around the kid's neck like a dog tag.

In a few months the padre would testify to all of this. He would say to the members of the jury that he had witnessed the executions of all of those poor boys and that Reggie Harp had been the murderer.

"Why didn't you save them? Why didn't you intercede?"

"I am a chaplain, sir, a noncombatant. Only force would have stopped him. I spoke to Reggie, pleaded with him, but he wouldn't listen."

In response to Jesse's questions, and despite his Fifth Amendment rights, he would confess to the jury that he had twisted the tallis until the boy's breath was gone.

"There are mercy killings during wartime," the padre would quietly explain, "when there's no choice, no way out, when someone is wounded beyond hope. Reggie struggled for air, but he did not really resist. There was a strange look of irony in Little Reggie's eyes as he experienced the very death by strangulation that he had arranged for Calvin in the jail."

The padre's voice broke as he related from the witness stand that on Reggie's purple face there had appeared an unmistakable expression of gratitude.

"He seemed curious about death."

After a decent enough burial, the padre had called in a phony bomb threat in hopes that the authorities would find the shallow graves. It was he who had informed Sabine of her son's crimes and of the exact location of his grave. It was he who had witnessed her cackling and dancing wildly on the dust above her dead son's body. It was the padre who had heard her sickening confession in the moonlight, and he had sworn by his sacred calling to keep it a secret. He had been forced to change his mind, to break his vow of silence, when Biscuit Boy was charged with the crimes. Despite these admissions, the prosecutor would never file charges against him.

The chaplain would explain to the jury that it was Reggie who had killed his friends out of jealousy, shooting as they walked from Sabine's apartment. It was he who had murdered the Amazon women. He had slaughtered them for their beauty and for their pure and resolute hearts. He had dishonored their eyes because they would never have given him a second glance; he had dishonored their bodies because they never would have lured young boys into their home and used them the way Princess Sabine had. He had despoiled Persephone and Mai because destruction is the only power left to men who cannot love.

Vô Dahn would tell the absolute truth, that the killer behind the killer was still out there. The true fiend was even more devious, more dangerous than Little Reggie, and that person was living free and unchecked on the hill. Even while he was testifying before the jury, Vô Dahn knew that his own days on this earth were numbered.

Jesse drove to Glen Park, parked on Surrey Street, and bounded up the stairs to Carolina's small house. The porch light came on and the front door opened. She stood silently, wearing a T-shirt and tan shorts. Jesse was surprised to see that she was wearing lipstick. Carolina never wore makeup. It was obvious to Jesse that she hadn't put in her contact lenses because she had to lean forward and narrow her eyes to mere slits in order to see who was standing three feet in front of her.

"Topolina," said Jesse. She looked like a pretty mole when she squinted like that. Carolina grimaced. She didn't really like the name.

"Are all of your closing arguments like that one?" she asked. Greetings could wait. The question had plagued her from the moment she had left the courtroom. "Are there always two summations, one for the jury and one for an empty courtroom? Are they always so passionate?"

"It wasn't empty," answered Jesse, still standing out on the porch. "You were there. But you're right. I always talk to the empty jury seats after the occupants have gone to deliberate. I tell them what the Evidence Code won't let me. As for the passion, it must have been the jade," he said with a look of calm amazement in his face.

"Come in," Carolina said with a confused smile. Jesse hadn't been on her front porch in weeks and he had never before mentioned anything about jade.

"Are you hungry? Are you happy about the verdict?"

"Why wouldn't I be happy?" asked Jesse as he entered the front room and followed her toward the kitchen. "It was a complete acquittal on all counts. What have you got to eat?"

"I asked the question because I know you, Jesse Pasadoble," said Carolina without turning around. "Only you could find the negative in a victory, focus on it, and embrace it with open arms. You've lived your whole life that way. That's what you've done to us," she said almost beneath her breath.

After a moment of private reflection she shrugged the moment away and said in a jaunty, playful voice, "I have tofu and broccoli marinated in organic soy sauce."

"I don't know why, but I think that's about to change," said Jesse quietly as he put his arms around Topolina's waist and pulled the back of her body toward his chest. "And I'm not talking about the tofu. I'm so damned tired of seeing the death in things."

Despite the deep tenor of weariness in his voice, he raised his hands to cup her breasts.

"Besides," he said with a growing smile, "you know very well that you can't feed tofu and broccoli to a Mexican." He kissed her neck softly. "That would be a blasphemy, an abomination in the eyes of God!" he exclaimed. "Organic soy sauce is even more poisonous to La Gente than strychnine or arsenic. Only spirulina is more virulent to La Raza. In fact, hundreds of Mexicans died in Ciudad Juarez in the great spirulina outbreak of 1892."

Carolina laughed, then turned around slowly. She looked into Jesse's eyes and saw a man whose face and demeanor she knew well, yet his inner being, his soul, had always remained a stranger. The man she had heard in the courtroom was no one that she had ever known. And now that unknown man seemed to be evolving, changing into something else, someone else.

Somehow she sensed, with both trepidation and eagerness, that a new being was forming beneath his brown skin. The man with his arms around her was not the Jesse Pasadoble that had walked out on her. Perhaps the dead thing inside of him was gone, finally put to rest. Carolina shivered with uncertainty. She closed her eyes for a moment to regain her composure. The man she loved, someone she didn't know, was becoming another person altogether. Perhaps she was about to discover that she didn't love him. Or perhaps this night would reveal why she always would.

"I have a can of menudo that you left here the last time you stayed over." She pulled away from his embrace and walked toward the cupboard. "Actually, you left six of them, but I couldn't throw all of them away. I guess I'm just a sentimental fool. I can heat that up and throw in some chopped onions and oregano and half a bottle of chili sauce." She shuddered as she recited the recipe for his favorite concoction. "I have some whole-wheat tortillas in the freezer."

"No tortillas de harina?" said Jesse dejectedly.

"Don't tell me," said Carolina with a sigh of resignation, "there was an outbreak of whole-wheat plague down in Quintana Roo in 1928?"

"Nineteen twenty-seven," said Jesse in a professorial voice. "And don't laugh. It decimated whole towns. Thousands of Mexicans rioted in Chetumal, killing anyone who sold rose hips or alfalfa sprouts. Did you know that Mexican Customs at Tijuana has dogs that sniff out herbal teas and ginseng? The *federales* no longer allow psychological self-help books into the country from California."

"I do have one package of frozen flour tortillas." Carolina sighed patiently. "Just let me open the windows so the smell of tripe and lard doesn't settle into my curtains and the upholstery."

"Now you're talking." Jesse smiled. He pulled Carolina's lips to his own and kissed her deeply for two beats and a measure. Their bodies began a slow, swaying dance near the stove.

She opened her eyes during the kiss and saw to her astonishment that his were closed. She had never known him to do that, never. Jesse could never give in to the moment. He could never lose control. She had always wanted to dance with him, just a two-step, but he wouldn't allow it. When their lips parted, she noticed that Jesses's lower lip and chin were dark red. Carolina blushed when she saw it. Somehow the lipstick made her feel naked. He then kissed one of her eyelids and the other, then bent down to kiss the two rising points on her shirt where her breasts were sequestered.

Now she knew for certain that something was different—some basic, alchemical change must have taken place. They joined lips again just as the phone began to ring. Carolina hesitated at first, unwilling to give up this unprecedented and precious moment of intimacy, but reluctantly answered it on the fifth ring. Business had been very slow of late, and it just might be a client needing a photographer.

Slowly the look of joy on her face turned to one of regret and confusion. She handed the phone to Jesse, explaining nervously that it was Eddy on the line and that something was dreadfully wrong. Eddy sounded terrible. She could barely understand what he was saying. Jesse took the phone from her. As he listened to Eddy Oasa the glow of the morning's victory in court dissipated into nothingness. The romance that had filled the kitchen just moments before evaporated like steam. After five minutes without speaking, Jesse laid the phone gently in its cradle, then slumped down into a couch.

"What's wrong?" asked Carolina. "What's wrong?"

For the first time since infancy Jesse cried. He sat on the couch and sobbed endless, unstoppable tears; a long, belated deluge for the children on the hill, *pour les enfants dans l'enfanterie*, for the infants who had always made up the infantry. At long last, after twenty-eight dry years, he shed his salt tears for skinny Cornelius, Indian Jim-Earl, the sergeant, and all those boys in both uniforms that had littered that hill so long ago.

He wept for the prisoner of war, Hong Trac; for Hollis and lonely Evie and her tamale pies; for Trin Adrong and Amos Flyer, locked in their widowers' embrace, for Persephone and Mai, who wished with all their being to know how their husbands had died. Their fervent wish had been granted: they had been forced by fate to reenact it, every moment of it.

"The Biscuit Boy is dead," he sobbed through clenched teeth. "It was a head shot. The padre was shot, too. They're both dead. I just know it. They're both dead."

At that moment the body of Vô Dahn lay face-down on a table in the emergency room of San Francisco General Hospital. A young nurse examined his back with some curiosity. Just then a harried surgeon flashed into the room and began to scrub up at a nearby sink.

"Fill me in," he said without removing his mask.

"Doctor, the patient is stabilized," said the young nurse. "His vitals look good. There was substantial loss of blood. He sure looked dead when he got here. I thought he was gone until he started feeling my kneecap," smiled the nurse. The doctor glanced downward at the nurse's kneecap.

"There is a large tattoo on the upper-right quadrant of the patient's back," she added. "You should look at it carefully, Dr. Beckelman. It looks like a large brown spider with a scarlet violin on its abdomen. I've never seen anything like it. The entry wound is right on the bridge of the violin. The police officer out in the lobby said that it was a nine-millimeter bullet."

"It's a fiddle spider," said the doctor as he began to probe the wound with his gloved finger. "It's also known as a Mexican brown recluse. There is an exit wound ten centimeters from the midline."

The nurse made notations as the doctor spoke.

"He's a lucky man. The bullet was deflected by something that should not be where it is. He has a broken rib, a very old injury that was never treated. That twisted piece of bone kept the bullet from hitting the heart."

The doctor moved his bloody index finger from one hole to the other.

"The projectile left a jagged circular wound and an abrasion in the center of the Star of David tattoo. He's one of us." The nurse and the doctor shared a moment of mirth.

"Must be Sephardic," answered the nurse. "Only Sephardim allow tattuage of the skin. I think it's beautiful," she said almost wistfully. There was a clear note of envy in her voice.

"Haven't had too many Jews in here," said the doctor with an obvious note of pride in his voice.

"What do you suppose America would be like if there had never been Jews on its shores?" said a third voice. "None of them are here because they're all over in geriatric." The startled doctor and the nurse looked at each other in bewilderment, then back down toward the patient. The man should be unconscious. It was that damned anesthesiologist again. He had done his usual shoddy work, then dashed off to intensive care to flirt with the nurses.

"I'm not very good at this, but I think there would be no humor in America," continued the dazed, groggy voice of the padre. "No vaudeville, no Henny Youngman, no one-liners, no knock-knock jokes—just the polite, lace-ridden twittering and giggle of British naughtiness. All the Jews would've ended up in Honduras. ¿Quién sabía?" The wounded man on the table managed a shrug. "Who knew?"

"You know, Dr. Beckelman," said the nurse, suddenly aware that the doctor was not unattractive, "he just might be right."

"You can call me Eliot," answered the doctor.

The assistant medical examiner smiled to himself as he turned on the recording equipment. The body that lay languishing in the autopsy room would be the last that he would ever cut open. He was getting out of the business of death before it killed him and his young marriage, before it destroyed his ability to embrace romance. He wanted to adore his wife's smooth skin without seeing it sliced and pulled back. He wanted to buy skin creams for her, sweet lotions and oils.

"The body is that of a young African-American male, eighteen years

of age. There is remote scarring about the neck, possibly the effects
of a ligature. But for a wound to the neck and lower jaw, the body is
unremarkable. . . ."

"Princess Sabine shot them both," cried Jesse. "It's her sick revenge for the death of her son, for the death of Little Reggie, her
second husband. She's holed up in her apartment right now,
shooting it out with the cops. They've secured the hill and set up a
perimeter around her home."

Carolina moved toward him and touched his shoulder. To her
surprise, he did not pull away.

"Eddy said that there were reports that she was firing Reggie's nine-
millimeter like an Olympic sharpshooter. She's already wounded three
police officers."

Jesse's shoulders slumped. He lifted one arm and wiped away the
tears with a cuff of his herringbone jacket. He hadn't changed his
clothes since leaving court that morning. Carolina, who had sat
down beside him, got up from the couch and kneeled down in front
of him. She needed to see his face.

"She lured those three naive boys—maybe there were others—
into her house and forced them to satisfy her special cravings. Then,
to protect her—or out of jealousy—Little Reggie killed each of her
child lovers, one by one, and buried them on the hill. Maybe Calvin
helped with the burials. Nobody wins, Carolina." Jesse sighed. "Nobody wins. Boys die to secure a hill, and as soon as they're airlifted
away, the hill goes back to the North Vietnamese. As soon as the
NVA have it, they leave it for the jungle and for the Montagnards.
And the padre—*pobrecito*—when he walked away from that war, he
walked right into another one."

As he wept Jesse remembered the day that he had first gone to the
homeless encampment to speak to a possible witness. In a blinding
flash of recognition he had found an old friend, a man who had
walked away from a war. Somehow Jesse had recognized the face in
the dark, not from any of its features—there were none to be seen—
but from a faint aura that hovered beneath the eye sockets, a small
warpage of space around the stubbled chin and chapped lips.

This man, Mr. Homeless, had a mouth and a voice box that had
recited far too much, had spoken even more than the eyes had taken
in or the spirit and mind could process. There could be no doubt

that the homeless man in the dark was a military chaplain. No one else on earth could have so much finality, so many last words littering his voice box and cluttering his tongue.

"Do you despise me?" asked the man in the filthy fatigue jacket. "Do you despise me because I deserted my flock? For so long I've desired to ask you that question. Even after all of these years, Jesse, I can still feel your eyes staring at the back of my head."

"No one despised you, padre," said Jesse quietly. "You know how we were back then. We were confused and dying and hardening in that condition. Our bodies were pinned down while our hearts were stampeding. When you left, we were all wounded by it. We . . . I felt alone. We knew that one of us . . . you had to remain human. You were our template. We could look to you and see our former selves. We could see what we might once again become.

"I guess that leaving was the only human thing to do. But what is one sane act in a sea of insanity? Sometimes I feel like I'm still standing there, padre, with the war at my back and you in front of me mumbling and screaming and walking through the dead toward the river. You shitcanned that war in a few minutes; the rest of us have taken years. I still haven't gotten there."

The padre sighed; it had taken so much longer than a few minutes. The chaplain moved toward the narrow shaft of light that shot through the hole overhead. For the first time Jesse could see the face of the other man. Tears, like rivulets, had washed away the layers of black dirt beneath his eyes. The other two homeless men had taken their leave and were rustling around in the compound, playing with the dogs.

"It's that speedometer of yours, isn't it? Too fast for this world? You're out of step . . . can't dance . . . can't touch a living thing because it's always dying in your eyes . . . can't love." The padre rambled into silence. ". . . can't love."

"Where did you go, padre? What have you been doing all these years? How did you get here?"

The padre shook his head in disbelief. The voice that issued from Jesse's mouth was the voice of the eighteen-year-old soldier, not the voice of the lawyer.

"First, tell me where you've gone, Jesse. What do you do? Until a few moments ago, when you asked about Oscar Wilde, I thought I would never hear supposings again."

"I go into the jails and do triage," said Jesse. "I try to keep the state from compounding the crimes of this world. I haven't gone far."

"I see," whispered the chaplain. A smile may have appeared on his face. "This time you're the guerrilla. Me, I followed my flock and I followed the only woman I have ever loved. I knew where she would be because she had written it on her arm."

For an hour Jesse stood near the fire as the padre told his bizarre tale of three hills: one in Laos, one in Chihuahua, and one in San Francisco. As he spoke the padre slipped almost absentmindedly from English to Spanish and occasionally into Cantonese, Ladino, and even Yiddish. When the two men were finally about to part, the lawyer touched the chaplain's shoulder softly, then handed him a subpoena.

"Was Wilde right? Do we kill the things we love?"

"*Alleh bridder*," said the chaplain. He rose from his seat and threw his arms around the shoulders of the Chicano sergeant. "Aren't we all brothers? Don't things die around us because we can't love them? That's the same as killing."

"I know that you saw it all," said Jesse as he pulled away from the padre's embrace and shoved aside one of the ponchos that hung at the entrance.

"I know you saw what happened to those two women on the hill."

"The women on which hill?" asked the padre. There was no answer forthcoming.

"You're speaking of Mai and Persephone, aren't you?" said the padre. His mind had flown from the two Mexican Painted Ladies in Chihuahua to the burned female bodies on the hill near Laos before settling on the Amazon Luncheonette.

"Don't you know what's wrong with heaven, Jesse?"

The voice in the dark seemed very far away. Jesse shook his head as he stepped outside.

"There are children in it," whispered the chaplain.

Jesse let the poncho fall and began to traverse the compound toward his car. In the distance he could just make out the army hooches of Dong Ha. Beyond was the road to Quang Tri.

"After all this time I am only certain of one thing," cried out the padre. "I am certain that a man can truly make love to a woman only when he has amnesia."

The assistant medical examiner turned off the tape machine and extinguished the overhead lights. Only a shaft of sunlight from the outer hallway allowed him to see anything at all. After cleaning up, he ran the fingers of both ungloved hands through his hair, then rubbed his aching neck. It was gesture of both fatigue and sorrow.

His friend the chief medical examiner would go on seeing the dead every day until his retirement, and then he would dream of them. He would go on describing his halcyon days, his formative months in the morgue at Da Nang, as a coroner's paradise. He would go on fearing that this wife was waiting up for him, sitting quietly in the dark, inhaling oxygen, and exhaling affection and loneliness into the stale air of their living room.

The assistant sighed wearily though his skin was still quivering with excitement. He breathed deeply, then laughed spasmodically, involuntarily. He wanted to call his wife and tell her that one of the rarest events in the field of forensic medicine had occurred on this day, in this very room. Then the assistant was suddenly stricken by a horrible thought. Had that been a look if disappointment in the chief's face this afternoon? Disappointment at a miracle?

"... *a tactile exploration of the musculature of the lower appendages reveals ... no rigor. There is no rigor at all. There is no lividity whatsoever.*" *The voice of the assistant medical examiner began to rise in pitch as he spoke into the microphone.*

"*In fact, there are pockets of warmth in the groin area and beneath the arms! Despite being refrigerated for an hour or so, the body is maintaining heat.*"

The assistant began to quake with excitement. He ran to the telephone and called the chief.

"*I think he's alive! It's a miracle! It's a miracle!*"

The old man had taken his time walking down the hallway and through the double doors. When he finally arrived, he saw what he had seen once or twice back in Da Nang, "dead" boys who had managed to snap open their own body bags, "dead" skin that had recoiled at the touch of the scalpel.

"*Call an ambulance,*" *said the chief medical examiner in a monotone. He stood in the doorway but did not enter the room. "Start warming him up." His voice trailed off as he walked back into the hallway.*

"You're a doctor, you know what to do. By the way, there are no miracles. If you think it's a miracle, you're certainly not cut out for this work."

After the boy had been whisked away to the hospital, the assistant had stood silent and motionless in the autopsy room for almost half an hour. He was certainly not cut out for this job. This was his last day of work in this building, and the thought of cutting open another deceased human body made him ill. The feel of life beneath his gloved fingers today had been exhilarating, overwhelming. Like a newborn baby, Calvin Thibault had coughed and cried before filling his lungs with life-giving air.

The assistant medical examiner took off his white lab coat for the last time and threw it onto the table. He smiled to himself. This had been a monumental day. Today he and a young black boy had both risen from the dead. He tossed a ring of keys onto a stainless-steel counter and walked out of the building toward his car and toward his lovely wife. As he walked, the carbon dioxide in his nose transformed into expectation. At this very moment she would be naked. She always showered before dinner. Her wet skin was always so provocative.

When he unlocked his car, he realized that he had not written the autopsy summation. He considered returning to the building but instead extended the middle finger of his right hand and pointed it defiantly toward the gray edifice that loomed above him. Then he jumped into his car and drove away. Anyone could write a cause of death. Who on earth could write a cause of life?

Carolina took Jesse's hand and pulled him up from the couch. She led him through the main hallway of her home and into the bedroom. The bed had been unused since he last left, so long ago, so she removed the dusty bedspread and turned back the sheets and blanket underneath. She undressed him, then herself, then pulled him onto the bed. As they kissed he sobbed a full stratification of tears; a wrenching, rippled core sample of himself: There was belated proof of a sentient childhood, then a silvery stratum of innocence; a green layer of budding sexuality veined by lines of nascent romance; a deep cobalt layer formed by the pressurized brutality of the infamous blue ballet; then a coal-black layer, denser and deeper than all the rest combined, for all the dark years that followed—years of life without loving.

"Poor Calvin." Carolina sighed. "Found innocent and found dead on the same day."

"Not innocent," whispered Jesse grimly, "just not guilty. Only God knows who's innocent, and I'm not so sure He cares. Even I don't know what really happened on that hill. I know that someone called out Calvin's name," said Jesse with growing intensity. He reached out and held Carolina's face, forcing her to look into his eyes.

"Someone called his name. Witnesses heard it. No one could say if it was a male's voice or a female's. Maybe it was poor Mai using her last breath to call out the name of her killer."

Jesse's voice sounded detached and feverish. His eyes were red and glazed with distance. Carolina had heard this voice and had seen this face before. Her heart sank. Her hopes that Jesse had changed began to fade away.

"Calvin could have reached out for her as she ran from the refrigerator," said Jesse almost robotically. "She might have pushed him away or she might have told him how much hatred and disgust she felt for what he and Reggie were doing. Maybe Calvin was telling the truth on the witness stand when he said that he had taken the gun, leveled it, and pulled the trigger. Only it wasn't Reggie that he wanted to kill. He aimed it at Mai and shot her in the back."

Carolina began to cry. Nothing had changed after all. This was the same unknowable Jesse Pasadoble, the waking narcoleptic whose heart fell asleep whenever love or comfort came near.

"Maybe the padre's confession to me at the homeless encampment was nothing but a pack of lies. Maybe that whole story about *arañas* in Mexico was a big pile of bullshit to explain away his cowardice in Vietnam. And I bought it. Maybe he was a coward. One or two of the troopers thought so. Could I have been wrong when I began to think that he was the only sane man in Southeast Asia? Maybe he was mad. Shit, he still is . . . or was."

Now Jesse's whole body was shaking with confusion and anger. Carolina reached for him but he pushed her hands away. The old Jesse was back.

"Maybe that hillside near Laos—that huddle of scared boys who gathered to suppose another world—never existed at all. Cornelius,

Jim-Earl, and Roosky. It's just a dream, Carolina, just a fucking dream. Maybe Sergeant Flyer napalmed his own location out of evil and nothing more. I thought, way back then when I had that jade in my mouth, that it was love that made him do it. I could see so clearly that it was crippled love, so strong that it almost burned me. To avoid the fire, I crawled into a hole just in time. I guess I've never crawled out."

Jesse closed his eyes, then covered his face with both hands. Behind his fingers and palms a radio installation had just evaporated, turning two husbands into cinders. Above everyone's head the roar of jet engines signaled the inferno to come. All the cryptographers and all of the NVA whistle blowers had failed. Nothing at all had been communicated to anyone. Carolina touched his shoulder but he pulled away violently.

"You didn't die on that hill, Jesse," said Carolina softly. "Your life went on. I can feel you. I can touch you. You're here with me. The heart just needs some lyrics," she said, recalling Jesse's own words. "It needs to articulate. You can't keep hiding among the living; you can't keep forcing your soul to mumble in code. No one can ever answer you. Not me, not anyone.

"I know that I can't really comprehend what you've been through, but I know enough to understand that you have a choice to make and you have to make it now, tonight. Supposing you choose life, Jesse? Suppose you choose life just this once?"

Jesse reached down to the floor and found his pants. He probed a pocket for the sliver of jade, then placed in on his tongue. After a moment of immobile silence he went limp, as though the skin and features of his outer body had suddenly been deprived of its skeletal framework. His eyes squeezed shut and his lungs collapsed as something within him took leave.

A moment later he was coughing and heaving huge breaths like a drowning man who had been pulled from a deep, cold river. Calm now, and with open eyes, Jesse saw Carolina dimly, and with leaden, unresponsive hands reached out for her. He strained with all his might to touch Evie's arm as she lay soaking in the hot bathtub.

"Thank you so much for the lemonade and the tamale pies," he said as he seized Carolina. Then he eased her downward in soft commands, unspoken orders, kissing her eyes, her thighs. Surrendering to her breasts, he adored the fall of hair on her shoulders. All at once their pounding hearts were pressed against their ribs like quarter-notes on a treble staff.

Probing here, retreating there, Jesse, in full light, in coequal rapture and dance without strength moves, in choreography without dominion, relented finally to his own human desire, and suffered the impact—the painless penetrations—the living heat of friendliest fire.

"Biscuit Boy loved Mai with all his heart," he whispered lovingly into the shell of her lovely ear. "In the end, Sergeant Flyer loved us all with that airstrike. He loved us all."

Suddenly the phone rang again. Carolina let it ring thirty times before answering it. This time when she walked back into the bedroom her face was beaming. She handed the phone to Jesse.

"Biscuit Boy is alive," Eddy said, his voice almost loud enough to be heard without benefit of a telephone. "He's come back from the dead!"

As Eddy spoke, Jesse thought of a day so many years ago when a body bag at the edge of a landing zone had moved ever so slightly. It could have been just prop wash or a trick of the wind, but something made Jesse walk over and unsnap the bag. Somewhere in all those awful injuries there had been a pulse. Jesse always wondered where that boy was today. Were his darkest dreams encased in green plastic?

"I just talked to him at the hospital!" cried Eddy. "He says he's never going back to the hill. Never! The homeless guy, the padre is alive, too. It's unbelievable! The police have captured Princess Sabine. I was there when it happened. She was wearing a magenta swimsuit with matching baton and high heels.

"It was amazing! She was firing Little Reggie's gun like a sharpshooter. I was afraid the cops were going to kill her, so I gave Inspector Normandie a small suggestion. He got on the bullhorn and announced that Princess Sabine Harp had been named Miss San Francisco County Jail. A committee of impartial judges had agreed unanimously. When she heard that, she dropped her gun and demanded to be escorted to her dressing room by only the handsomest of policemen."

After he hung up the phone, Jesse Pasadoble buried his face in a pillow and laughed harder than he had ever laughed in his life. Biscuit was alive! Padre was alive! There were survivors on the hill.

There were boys who had pulled through. Neither of them would ever go back to the hill.

At that moment, high above their bed, an Afro-Mexican deep-space probe, launched from a newly supposed world and fitted with sensitive recording devices, was searching the next star system for soundless scat and alien rhythms. One unusual section, built by Nigerian scientists, was specially designed to respond to fourth-stream music and permutations of bop, to alien melismatics and to embouchure without humanoid lips. If such were ever detected, the entire craft would pivot and go seek out the source.

Guidance rockets would roar to life at the sound of subtly dissonant bars and semi-quavers, a trumpet slurring upward to somewhere far beyond high e-flat. The sensors and gauges aboard the ship would dance at the faintest presence of countermelodies and descant lines and barely measurable traces of the Ellington effect.

Back on earth, the sliver of jade slipped from Jesse's smiling mouth into Carolina's. She instantly stopped moving as she saw it all. She saw the restless dead on every hill, the hellish rolling orange fire of gelatinous petroleum as it engulfed whole platoons of young men. For a timeless moment she squinted over the sights of a rifle and squeezed the trigger as Trin Adrong staggered by.

She heard the last confession of a young Chicano soldier. She witnessed battalions of Mexican and Irish infantry and cavalry invading Spain, delivering independence to the Basques of Euskady, and finally bringing a decent cuisine to the dinner tables of Madrid and Granada. Finally she heard the faint signals from an Afro-Mexican space probe.

Then she turned away from Jesse and spat the jade stone onto the hardwood floor where it shattered into a dozen pieces. Slowly the look of pained intensity that had filled her face for a dozen measures began to fade away in favor of laughter. In her ear the faint echoes of harsh commands slowly transformed into improvisations of brass and percussion; the sharp staccato of gun fire was syncopated, diminished in favor of the beat of her swelling heart.

"I just heard such wonderful things!" sighed Carolina, " 'All the Things You Are' and Rachmaninoff at the same time!"

"You heard Mingus," said Jesse, his voice filling with fatigue, "the African bass player who would have been born in Tunis. He would have brought Arabic jazz to Sicily. Did you hear him, grunting like a

platoon sergeant and feeding lines to his boys, commanding them to
be free, to go where the trumpet and drum kit have never gone?"

"There was a second song," sang Carolina, "melodic and ethereal."

" 'Reincarnation of a Lovebird,' " mumbled Jesse, now barely
awake. "Sicily would be the cultural center of the world."

"People will dance to that new music of their own free will," Carolina said while kissing his face and neck. "*Ecoutez-moi, mon amour,*"
she said without realizing that she was speaking in an unfamiliar
tongue. "The dead can sit out eight bars while the living love. Let
them rest," she said softly. "Let them rest."

Jesse, beneath her, smiled as the weight of the world slipped from
his shoulders. He tried to say something but forgot what it was. Just
moments later he could barely remember his own name, but he
knew that for the first time in decades he would sleep a dreamless
sleep.

Up on Potrero Hill, at the homeless encampment, a dozen dusty
veterans would gather to greet Vô Dahn, who was covered in bandages and still high from the medication and the botched anesthetic.
Despite orders from Dr. Beckelman, the padre had put on his filthy
clothing, then slipped out of the hospital through a service entrance.

Once at the homeless encampment, he hugged each soldier and
bade him farewell. He then began the long walk down the hill. The
homeless vets followed him as he walked down Twentieth Street and
crossed Third Street, and they formed a platoon and moved closer to
him as he walked toward the bay. One soldier even had enough
courage to go with him as he crossed the boatyard and walked out to
the end of a small, rotting pier.

"Where are you going, padre," the soldier had asked. "Where are
you going?"

All the vets would watch as Vô Dahn slipped quietly into the dark
waters and, face up, began to float away. The waters would surely
heal his wound. Years ago he had found Cassandra . . . Mai . . . in just
this way. Now he would find her again. As they had before, the waters would take him to her. They would dance together as they had
in that bedroom in Hong Kong, the room on a hill where Cassandra
had loved no one so very much. Cloaked in forgetful remembrance,
they would love again. Thirty yards from the pier, the padre raised
an arm and pointed to the dark sky overhead. A family of spider
monkeys turned to listen.

"Look up," he cried. "All of the electronics—all of the mechanics and hydraulics aboard that Mexican starship way up there . . . *tournent sur le jazz!*" he cried out.

Homeless veterans on both sides of the bay heard him as he floated away. Some looked to the sea and saw him disappear in the swells of an outbound current. Some looked to the sky to see the lonely, rhythm-hungry spacecraft spinning by.

"Everything turns on jazz."